THE KING OF CAYMERLOT

ILLUSTRATED BY *Charlotte Bauman* & *Jesse Lewis*
with additional illustrations by the author

LEGENDS OF OVERTWIXT
The Golden Age • Book 3

Copyright © 2022-2024 The Orbital Defense Corps, LLC. All rights reserved. No part of this book may be reproduced in any form or by any electronic or mechanical means, including the use of information storage and retrieval systems, without express written permission from the copyright owner.

Cover design, internal design, maps, and illustrations ©2021-2024 The Orbital Defense Corps, LLC. AI tools were used solely for the creation and modification of certain illustrations within this work. The author has made significant modifications to these AI-generated visuals, ensuring that the final illustrations are original and represent his artistic direction. No AI assistance was used in the development of the text, characters, or narrative. AI-generated content is not independently eligible for copyright protection under U.S. and international law. However, all modifications and original contributions by the author are fully protected. All rights to the final illustrations are reserved by The Orbital Defense Corps, LLC.

"Nachton Hand" fonts and some illustrations original this publication; others first appeared in Overtwixt: Welcome to the World of Bridges, Escape from Overtwixt, Overtwixt: Perilous Flight, The Circus of Dagmør, or The Heroes of Centhule, ©2018-2024 The Orbital Defense Corps, LLC.

All copyrights apply to all formats of this work, including print, digital, and audiobook versions, unless otherwise specified.

The Orbital Defense Corps™, the concentric descending "O" imprint, OVERTWIXT™, the stylized Overtwixt text design, DAGMØR™, CENTHULE™, the stylized Heroes of Centhule text design, CAYMERLOT™, the stylized King of Caymerlot text design, and the stylized R.L. Akers text design are all trademarks and service marks of The Orbital Defense Corps, LLC.

This book is a work of fiction. Names, characters, institutions, establishments, places, events, and incidents are the product of the author's imagination and/or are used fictitiously. Any references to real locations, institutions, establishments, or persons are coincidental, historical, and/or fictionalized to provide a sense of reality and authenticity.

Because of the dynamic nature of the Internet, any web addresses or links contained in this book may have changed since publication and may no longer be valid, without the knowledge of the author or publisher. The author and publisher claim no rights in, and expressly disclaim any liability potentially arising from, the accessing and/or use of any referenced websites. Neither the author nor the publisher guarantees, approves, or endorses the information, products, and/or services available on such websites, nor does any reference to any website indicate any association with, or endorsement by, the author or publisher.

The author asserts his moral right to be identified as the creator of this work and to prevent any unauthorized modifications that may damage the integrity of the work.

The author and publisher have made every effort to ensure the accuracy of the information presented in this book. However, they assume no responsibility for any errors or omissions, nor for any consequences arising from the use of this information.

First Printing, November 2024

ISBN-13: 979-8-9918223-8-1

table of contents

Maps	iii
Roster of the Squad	vii
Relative Truths	ix
Dedication	xiii
Loremaster's Note	xiv
The Legend	3
Prologue: The Lady	7
Part I: The King	23
Part II: The Demagogue	155
Part III: The Barbarian Horde	243
Part IV: The Golden Age	355
Epilogue	399
Glossary	405
Intro to Ancient Languages	417

Reference Book

Acknowledgments

About the Fonts
About the Author
About the Illustrators

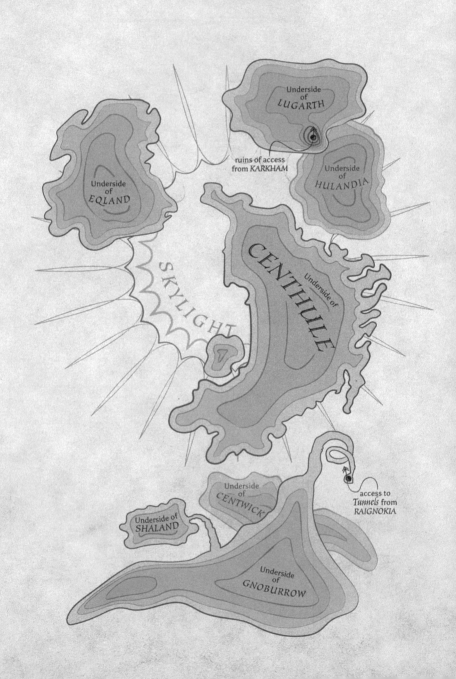

The Roster of the Squad of Heroes

alphabetized by role

Role	Real Name	Race	Relative Age	Relic
The Inventor	Pyrsyfal Rochelle	gnowoman	young adult	Diamond Grail
The Knight	Karis Priamos	huwoman	thirty?	Diamond Plate-Armor
The Noble	Gerald Valorian	centman	middle-aged	none
The Paladin	Kaedan van Mathias	eqman	declines to answer	~~none~~ holding out for the Diamond Horn
The Sidekick	Limerick Ginnick	kelfman	young adult	Diamond Aegis
The Wizard	Hembrose O'Hildirun	merman	(old*)	someday?
The King	Arthos Penn	dagman	young adult	none

*for the time being, at least

The Maxims of Merlyn

◇

Time marches Forward,
independent of constraint.

Power gained is power ceded.

The Merman Race is Greater than any other.

Once only may any man enter Overtwixt.

The Legalities of Lugarth

◇

Fight for honor.

Corollary: » Honor fighters.

~~Don't hurt people.~~ *What?! Really???*

Lugman Race bigger than others. *You don't say!*

The Requisites of Raibourne

◇ *Four per race*

For each Race exist Holy Magical Relics.

Theorized corollary: ¿» Only by a Member of the intended Race may a Relic's Magic be unlocked.

For the Good and by the Pure shall a Holy Relic's Magic be wielded.

All must Choose.

Commonly accepted corollaries:
» All must Choose one Role.
» All must Choose one Master.

~~Wiser than Others is the Race of Raimen.~~

The first must be last, the servant of all.

obvious inverse: ≈ The last will be first, the ruler of all.

Once only may any man Live, and after, to know Reality.

Gnosis of Gnoburrow

◇

Overtwixt is intended for One and All,
and must not be Hidden from them.

There is only one Sovereign,
and the Enemy is his Opposite.

Magic harvested is magic gained.

~~The Large shall be Last, ruled by the Small.~~

Sacred Precepts of Centhule

◇ *Discrepancy in translation?*

The Destiny of Humen shalt be to Rule.

destiny — *doom*

People of two worlds, thou art meant to be.

(Formation of Relics was nary the province of the Sovereign alone.)

For Sarah,
always my Queen

Thanks for your
unflagging support.

Loremaster's Note

Now at last we arrive at the conclusion of this ancient tale. Our first installment about the Golden Age told of Arth, Pyrsie, and Hembrose's early days in Overtwixt, traveling with the circus until Arth's twin Morth was kidnapped by the luggernauts. In the second volume, our heroes joined with the ancient Knight and others to form a Squad of adventurers intent on rescuing *all* the lugmen's slaves. Events culminated with a pitched nighttime battle at the Branch Library of Hulandia, after which Arth was anointed King by the Guide.

And so we see that it's Arthos Penn the dagman who inspired the legend of King Arthur Pendragon, as it later bled back into our real world. This all happened so long ago (thousands of years before the rise of even Arthurian legend) that many details have undoubtedly been distorted by time—mistakes I'm sure even this series will add to (again, these new books are really just historical fiction). But certain ancient truths will always transcend the ravages of time.

You will again find footnotes about dialect and past events/details, and you can always reference the Glossary on page 405. Also, my Reference Book (following the Glossary) contains more edits and additions than ever before. Now, with all of that said, allow me to wish you a fun time on this, your final adventure through the Golden Age of Overtwixt!

Nachton Ollivaros

The Loremaster, 782 H.E.
(3,000+ years after the Golden Age)

· the legend ·

"Long ago did this happen, unless it did not. Much time has passed, and much is forgot," said the merman to his little sister, reciting the opening lines of a well-known nursery rhyme. "In the beginning of everything, a world was created. Above and between all realities it waited, connected by bridges magically instated.

"'Come one, come all!' cried the Sovereign, its maker. 'There is land here to spare, more than one vacant acre. Fill it with people, of all sorts and all sizes. Bring them together so a culture arises.'

"And he called the place Overtwixt. And it was good." This phrase stood out jarringly, since it didn't rhyme like all the rest. The brother winked to make clear this was intentional, and the maiden giggled.

"Thus did they come, those first visitors from real worlds—not just the grown-ups, but boys too and girls. They built a great city that grew to a country, a place of diversity, its inhabitants sundry. But despite their vast differences, all folks got along... for in that strange place, nothing yet had gone wrong.

"And they called their society Epitopia. And it was good." He gave his sister another wink, whispering, "'Diverse' and 'sundry' are just other ways of saying 'different', by the way."

The little girl answered with another giggle. "But... whatcha mean, nothing was wrong yet?"

The brother patiently paused his recitation to answer. "I mean Overtwixt was still perfect, or so the stories tell us. There was no pain or hurt, no selfishness or competition, no unfairness. Everyone lived in peace and harmony."

"No one ever got spanked or gwounded or sent to their wooms?"

The brother simply shook his head. "It was perfect. No one did anything wrong or got in trouble."

The maiden stared back at him in wide-eyed disbelief, as only a small child can do honestly. "How long did *that* last?"

The young man burst out laughing. "Not long at all! Now, where was I... yes, the first society in Overtwixt was called Epitopia, and it was good." He cleared his throat. "Alas, soon there began to be disquiet grumblings, the trust between peoples and Sovereign crumbling. Though all folks there living had all that they needed, jealousy grew as their cravings stampeded. Once-satisfied people made the mistake of comparing, which led them to pride or bitterness, not sharing.

"Then came the first crime, of theft or false witness," the brother shrugged, for no one really knew for sure what that first transgression had been, and the specifics didn't matter anyway. "And society collapsed as if in great sickness. War followed soon after, one of the worst of all times; as the races of Overtwixt formed up in battle lines.

"Thousands were slaughtered in the fighting and thus: thousands were banished among vapours most xanthous."

"Wait, huh?" the maiden squealed, her forehead furrowed in confusion. "What's vapor zan-thus?"

Her brother smiled. "It's just an archaic way of saying smoke. Yellow smoke. There's no such thing as death in Overtwixt; people are meant to come and go as much as they wish, and stay for as long as they want. But if you get hurt badly enough—like bad enough you would be killed in the real world—you disappear in a cloud of yellow smoke, returning to the real world in an instant. And if that happens, you can never enter Overtwixt again."

"Oh." Another moment of brow-furrowing consideration. "What's arr-kay-ick?"

"Archaic? Old." He snorted, waving a hand. "Moving on... Then did a truce the Sovereign enforce, overcome as he was by regret and remorse. At his command did the fighters come together—surely, they thought, his punishment to weather. But gifts did he grant them instead in his grace, awesome Relics of Diamond, four for each race. And greater than all was the one he made last, along with a Promise that's ne'er been surpassed:

"'Behold in my hand the most potent of Relics, containing a peerless crystalline helix. Within this big Diamond will my power reside, until a Hero is announced by the Guide. Then take this he shall in his mighty right arm, the world to protect from ill and from harm. In fulfillment of prophecy shall that day at last come, and with it the rise of a Golden Age kingdom.'

"Then he slammed that Relic down, up to its neck in the ground, the impact causing cracks that spread all around. From the southlands of Overtwixt to its northernmost side, the terrain broke apart with gaps fathomless and wide. And though his heart broke as well when the world's perfection was shattered, the Sovereign intentionally left his people now scattered: each race alone on its own niland remote, away from all others forever to float.

"And Sovereign called it the Schism. And it was bad." No winks or giggles now.

The brother sat thoughtful for a moment, then finished his story quietly. "Ages have passed since that great separation, and ever does grow the vast gulf between nations. Yet more bridges are built with each passing year, from Overtwixt's center to its farthest frontier. For mediation remains the true goal of the Sovereign, and as time marches on, anticipation does heighten.

"For now at long last, the longed-for Golden Age looms, as peace between peoples flourishes, blooms. A great nation called Caymerlot now rules the sea, a league of eight races joined by one Treaty. And there at the center of its tall Crystal Keep, waiting even now after so long a sleep, is Sovereign's Great Relic jutting out of the deep."

The young man paused, confirming the little girl was hanging on every word. "The people call it the Relic-in-the-Rock," he concluded, his eyes intense. "And when the Hero finally pulls it free, everything *will* be good again. For he will use it to vanquish evil, protect the innocent, and reward the faithful, ushering in an age of true peace once more."

Prologue
The Lady

◇

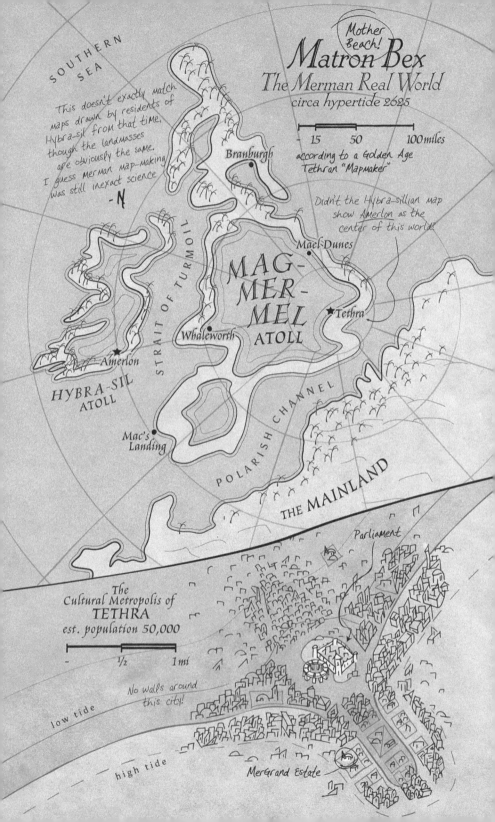

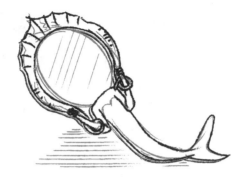

· prologue ·

Gwenverity MerGrand, youngest child of Leon and Yvonne MerGrand, fell in love with the legend of the Hero from the moment she heard it. A true champion of the people, with a heart full of goodness, fighting bad guys and helping the needy—who *wouldn't* love such a person? Not that Gwen wanted to be the Hero herself. Rather, she dreamed that her father might become that kind of man.

The sweet and devoted young mermaid just needed to get her Papá into Overtwixt, then surely her dreams would come true.

Things had been hard since Gwen's Mamá died. At six years of age, the maiden barely understood how or why such terrible changes had come upon her family so suddenly. Her oldest brother Alber had been by her side through all of it, and her middle brother Ander had even held her hand during the funeral rites. But Papá... sometimes Gwen wondered if he even loved her anymore. He spent more time at work than ever before, and he was now campaigning for election to the next Parliament of Mag-mer-Mel. Even when Papá was home, he was distracted, and he never took quiet evening swims with Gwen the way he used to do. It almost felt like the little girl had lost *both* parents.

Alber had given her wonderful brotherly hugs whenever she cried, and he started telling her fantastical tales at bedtime, to cheer her up. That was how she first learned of Overtwixt, and Caymerlot, and the Hero; and ever since that first story three months ago, she'd insisted that *every* story he told her needed to be from the world of bridges. It wasn't long before she hatched her plan to get Papá into Overtwixt... a plan that mostly consisted of begging him incessantly to take a family vacation, the way they used to do when Mamá was alive.

And believe it or not, her plan had worked.

Now here they were, on their way to Mag-mer-Mel's Gatehenge, one of just seven magical bridges between the merman real world and Overtwixt.

Once they arrived in Overtwixt, the four of them—Papá, Alber, Ander, and Gwen—would be together all the time as a family. That meant nightly swims along the beach (there were *miles* of pristine beaches, according to Alber!), and lots of special Papá-Gwen time. And after Papá was named Hero, Gwen would go with him on all his adventures, to see every strange niland in all of Overtwixt, and all of the wonderful people that lived there. Gwen could barely contain her excitement.

"Gwenverity!" Papá said sharply. "Settle down. You're causing the entire palanquin to sway. That makes for an unpleasant ride for me, and a great deal of extra effort for the palanquin bearers."

Gwen promptly contained her excitement.

The MerGrands were riding through the streets of Tethra (capital city of Mag-mer-Mel Atoll) on a family-sized palanquin—a platform carried above the surface of the water by servants. Theirs wasn't the only palanquin in sight, but it was certainly the nicest: cushioned in red velvet with goldleaf pinstriping, it seated six and required at least twelve bearers (the servants who carried the vehicle with their arms, while propelling it toward its destination with their strong tails). According to Papá, there was no other mode of travel befitting the MerGrands' station in society. Sure, there were plenty of caudestrians* moving along the ocean floor under their own power, and others riding domesticated walrustangs or using them to pull cargo haulers. Up here on the surface, there were even a few sailing craft zipping around the palanquins at high speed. But for a man of Papá's prominence, it was important to appear dignified... and to show off how many servants one could afford to employ.

As they traveled in this manner, Papá's personal secretary also swam alongside, scribbling notes in a plapyr ledger. "And you're sure you do not wish me to postpone your next campaign speech?" the aide was asking. "The one scheduled for next week at the Forum?"

"Quite sure," Papá said. He was a proud man with a neatly-trimmed chin beard and shoulder-length hair in the current style, wearing an open-fronted robe that revealed his muscular chest. "We shall only be gone five days, just a quick jaunt to Caymerlot and back," he reminded the secretary as he shuffled some of his own plapyrs in the leather case he carried at all times. "The people need to see I'm a family man, that I prioritize my children. Gwenverity!" he growled when the palanquin lurched again. "What have I told you—"

---

* the merman version of the word *pedestrian*. A pedestrian is someone traveling on foot ("ped-" = foot), while a *caudestrian* travels by tail ("caud-" = tail). Neither one is using a vehicle or conveyance.

"It wasn't Gwen," Ander corrected his father promptly. "It was Alber."

Sure enough, this time it was Alber who had raised himself to a kneeling position, rocking up onto his mid-tail joint so he could see into the distance. "Albernorm," Papá said darkly, "what have I told you about the importance of dignity?"

Alber blushed furiously, immediately dropping into a more dignified sitting position once more. "Forgive me, Father. I just... I'm almost as excited to see Overtwixt and Caymerlot as Gwen is!"

"Dignified men do not *become* excited. I expect better of my eldest son," Papá said before returning to his plapyrs.

Ander grinned triumphantly.

"As for you, Anderbrich," Papá added, "remember that dignified men also do not gloat, and they certainly do not tattle in the first place. Am I understood?"

That wiped the smile off the merlad's face.

"I frankly do *not* expect any better of my youngest son," Papá muttered, "but somehow I keep hoping anyway."

Now Ander was blushing furiously.

At thirteen and ten respectively, Alber and Ander were so much older than Gwen that they seemed adults themselves most of the time. She practically worshiped the water they swam in, so it was uncomfortable even for her to see them humiliated like this. She reached out a consoling hand to squeeze Ander's, but he pulled away.

"What're *you* looking at, Gwennie?"

Suddenly Gwen was blushing just as furiously as her brothers. She quickly turned her attention to the tall buildings passing by on her side of the palanquin. Tethra was one of the most modern cities in the world, after all, complete with stately glass buildings that climbed as many as six stories above the surface of the water (not counting however many floors there were *below* the surface). The buildings were also filled with water on the inside, so that the mermen and merwomen who lived or worked within could reach even the highest levels. And being made of glass as they were—thick, structural glass, of course—Gwen could see inside to some degree. But none of this was new or exciting to a girl who had traveled these streets so many times before. Even as she fixed her eyes on the city's skyline, her attention immediately returned to Papá's conversation with his secretary.

"Very good, my lord," the aide was saying. "We will keep next week's campaign speech on the schedule, trusting you will indeed return in time." He hesitated. "It's only... well, one hears stories of Overtwixt. How time moves in funny ways. Hard to predict, making it difficult to keep appointments and the like."

"And you have experienced this phenomenon for yourself, man?" Papá asked. Gwen snuck a glance and saw her father glaring at the secretary, one eyebrow arched.

The younger merman looked embarrassed. "Forgive me, no. As my lord knows, I haven't the clout to request a trip to the world of bridges myself."

"Then do not speak of what you do not know," Papá told him gravely.

"Of course, my lord. You are right, my lord."

Gwen turned back to watching the architecture again, though her thoughts were far away. Here in Mag-mer-Mel, only the rich and influential were granted visas to access Overtwixt with their families, and only a very few at a time, to preserve the prestige of it. That was very different from how they did things in Amerlon, on the neighboring atoll of Hybra-sil. There, they held a lottery so that random chance determined who got to visit Overtwixt. But Papá said the merpeople who lived on Hybra-sil were uncivilized bumpkins. Privileges like Overtwixt were *supposed* to be reserved for the most prominent members of society, to offset the unpleasant duties that often came with being leaders in politics or industry. For that matter, the common people needed to see their betters enjoying the benefits of their elevated station, so that they could strive to elevate themselves as well.

Papá had patiently explained all of this to her just last night, and Gwen was ever so grateful he had. It almost convinced her that Papá was excited to visit Overtwixt too... except he still seemed distracted, uninterested. Maybe that would change once they got inside. She really hoped so. Papá was her hero, so it only made sense he should be everyone else's Hero too.

At long last, they arrived at the Gatehenge—or at least, they came to a stop on the surface of the water high *above* the henge. Papá's secretary received his final instructions before hurrying off to fulfill them. Then the palanquin bearers allowed the platform to begin sinking, treading water just enough to keep the descent slow and, well, dignified. Gwen took one last deep breath of air, then plunged her head under the water. She didn't need to worry about holding her breath, for all merpeople were born with the ability to do so for hours. Instead, she excitedly leaned over the edge of the palanquin to stare down at the henge as they sank toward it.

Like all of the bridges between this world and Overtwixt, Mag-mer-Mel's Gatehenge was a circle of rectangular stone pillars, joined at their tops by flat stone shelves. The ring of stone monoliths jutted out of the sandy bottom of the ocean floor, where they had stood since the dawn of time, as far as Alber knew. The very sight of the ancient stone blocks sent a thrill through the little girl.

Gwen seized one of Alber's hands in her right hand, one of Ander's in her left. "It's finally happening!" she said in a hushed, excited tone. Alber remained dignified, but he gave her a wink that Papá couldn't see. Ander simply sniffed, but he didn't pull away this time.

The palanquin finally settled onto the ocean floor, and one of the uniformed Gatehenge guardsmen approached to check that Papá's plapyrs were in order. Then the guard made sure everyone knew what to expect once they entered the circle of stone pillars. At last, the MerGrand family swam the rest of the way into the henge, while the bearers swam away with the palanquin.

Once they were in the middle of the stone ring, Papá and his three children joined hands, and Papá spoke a single word in his strong, confident voice:

"Overtwixt!"

A strong underwater current struck the family suddenly, and Gwen felt like she was spinning within a tornado of water—before all that water exploded outward, leaving Gwen's family surrounded by air once more, seated on a wet sandy beach. It was all exactly as they'd been told to expect, and yet still quite exhilarating.

Chest heaving, Gwen sucked in a huge breath of the most wonderful air she'd ever tasted. Then she looked out beyond the stones of the Gatehenge, out past the miles of pristine brown beach and waving soarpalm trees, to the empty white sky beyond. There was no doubt in her mind. This was a different world entirely.

"We're here," Alber said reverently. "We made it."

"Indeed you have," said an unfamiliar deep voice. "Welcome to Overtwixt!"

Gwen spun to discover there was someone else now standing in the stone circle along with her family—actually standing, on *legs*, like a creature out of Alber's stories. He quickly folded those legs and knelt in the sand beside the merpeople, however, to bring them closer to eye level.

The tall man spoke again, his voice kind and resonant: "Mermen and merwomen — or rather, I suppose just *one* lovely young merwoman today..." He smiled at Gwen. "All four of you newly-arrived visitors to Overtwixt, I bid you welcome. I am—"

"The Guide!" Alber gushed excitedly. "You're the Guide, and you're a centman, which is like half merman on the top and half land-creature on the bottom. And you're here to offer each of us three options for the role we will play in Ov—"

"Albernorm!" Papá snapped. "What have I told you about interrupting?

Alber's eyes widened and he hung his head. "Of course, Father, forgive me. And you too, sir," he addressed the Guide. "I apologize for my outburst."

As soon as Papá returned his attention to the Guide, Ander shoved his older brother and smirked. "Way to go, dunderhead," he said in a low, mocking voice. "Way to embarrass the family."

"I am indeed the Guide," the Guide said warmly. "And I too am an advocate of respect and dignity in its proper place. But I am not troubled when they're occasionally pushed aside by an abundance of innocent excitement. There need be no apology or embarrassment."

Papá's lip twitched, but he said nothing.

"Now," the centman went on, "as the lad was saying, you must each make a decision before you proceed any farther into Overtwixt."

Alber beamed, his mood immediately restored.

"My dear mermen, and my dear sweet mermaiden, during your time in Overtwixt... Who will YOU choose to be?"

No one spoke. Papá was looking in the Guide's direction, but he had that vacant expression that told Gwen he was already thinking about stuff back in the real world again.

"Leon MerGrand," the Guide intoned seriously.

Papá blinked. "Yes?"

"Three paths stand before you. Will you be the Inspector, the Autobiographist, or the Underlord?"

Papá smirked, clearly not taking this very seriously. "Well, I always *have* wanted to write my memoirs someday, but... perhaps not yet. How about the Underlord then? That sounds promising," he concluded flippantly.

Gwen couldn't help but be disappointed, of course. If Papá chose Underlord—whatever that was—then he wouldn't be Hero after all. There went all of Gwen's dreams for their time in Overtwixt. But there was no arguing with the Guide. Alber had made that very clear to her.

"As for your quest—" the Guide began.

"Oooh, a quest," Papá said, rubbing his hands together and winking at Gwen. He didn't seem to notice that *he* was the one interrupting now, but Gwen couldn't help grinning back at her father. She was delighted anytime he gave her attention.

"You know the ancient tale of the Schism?" the Guide asked Papá. "And the prophecy of the coming King, who will draw Sovereign's Great Relic from the stone and usher in a Golden Age of Overtwixt?"

"You mean that old nursery rhyme?" Papá asked, shrugging. "What of it?"

"He means the legend of the Hero!" Alber blurted, turning to the Guide. "You're telling us it's true, right?"

"It's real?" Ander demanded. "Really?"

Gwen's heart swelled with excitement, hope renewed. "*Weally?* Who's gonna be the Hero?"

The Guide chuckled at the various responses, though he looked a little exasperated. "Oh yes, the prophecy is quite real. But it's not about a mere Hero, not in the way you're thinking. That word has been mistranslated since the very beginning, for reasons meaningful only to a linguist... though in truth, the confusion was encouraged by a certain enemy of the Sovereign." He waved a hand. "That's not something you need to worry about right now, however. What matters is that someday, the King *is* coming, and your quest, Leon—O Underlord of Caymerlot—is to prepare the way for him." *

For the first time, Papá seemed to realize this was more than just a joke. "Truly? I'm to be lord of Caymerlot?"

"Underlord, yes. If you choose that path."

"And yet that makes it my quest to prepare for the arrival of some *other* monarch?"

---

* See chapter 30 of *Heroes of Centhule* for more discussion about this misconception. The short version is that the High Epitopian word for "King" *sounds* a lot like "hero." On a related note, see the Introduction to Ancient Languages of Overtwixt on page 417.

Obviously, the Underlord had no excuse for perpetuating this confusion, since the truth was made clear on his first day here. —*N*

"As temporary ruler of the nation of Caymerlot, indeed, preparation would be your primary responsibility. The Underlord is ultimately meant to serve *under* the authority of the King. But until the King arrives, you would act as his steward: drawing the peoples of these lands together in unity, and giving all citizens of Overtwixt the opportunity to pull free Sovereign's Great Relic, should they wish to make the attempt. But don't worry," the Guide added quickly. "Only the true King will be capable of doing so."

Papá nodded thoughtfully as a smile slowly crept onto his face. "And when is this future King coming?"

"Tomorrow," the Guide told him confidently.

"Tomorrow!" Papá exclaimed, smile disappearing.

"Or ten years from now, or a hundred. Perhaps during your time as Underlord, or perhaps during a future Underlord's term. Even I don't know the exact day, and time moves strangely in Overtwixt."

"But..." Papá struggled to form a sentence. "I only planned to be here for a few days myself."

"Then if the King doesn't come tomorrow, and you leave before he does, his arrival will be in the days of a future Underlord. But so long as you lead this nation, do so in anticipation of his coming. Know the prophecy and make it known to others, so that when he does come, there can be no doubt as to who he is." The Guide locked eyes with Papá. "Do you understand the vital importance of this role, and the quest I am laying before you?"

Papá slowly nodded.

"And you wish to take on the role of Underlord, steward of Caymerlot?"

Papá nodded again, his smile returning.

"Very well," the Guide said, though he appeared suddenly sad for some reason. "Bear this responsibility faithfully... and in good faith."

Then the tall centman promptly turned to Alber and began giving him *his* three choices. Alber chose to become Altruist, which the Guide explained was a person who devoted himself to helping others. "Your quest is to address the needs of the underprivileged among the citizenry of Caymerlot, so that it someday becomes the utopia it only now boasts of being. Bear this responsibility joyfully."

Ander chose to be Antagonist, someone who sets himself in opposition to someone else. That sounded exactly like Ander, who was constantly bickering or fighting with others; but it surprised Gwen that the Guide would offer such a role. "Your quest will be challenging indeed," the centman told him, "and especially for you. You must become a good judge of character, so that when the day comes, you set yourself in opposition to any who would stand in the King's way... no matter who that person might be. Bear this responsibility shrewdly."

And then it was Gwen's turn. The Guide gave her another warm smile, and Gwen felt a thrill go through her at the excitement dancing in the tall man's eyes. "Gwenverity MerGrand, three paths stand before you..."

He laid out Gwen's choices, and the mermaiden's eyes got round, as did her father's. And when she settled upon which role she desired most, the Guide explained her quest, along with her destiny and how it was linked to Sovereign's Great Relic. With each word, Papá's face grew stonier, but Gwen didn't see it. Her heart was almost bursting with anticipation.

When he was finally done giving them their roles, quests, and instructions, the Guide offered to accompany the MerGrands on their journey from Merlyn (the merman niland on which they'd arrived) to neighboring Caymerlot. If Gwen weren't still in a state of pleasant shock, she might have wondered *how* the leggy fellow intended to keep up with the merman family without flippers or fins of his own. But Papá politely declined the centman's offer, and the family of four pushed themselves into the water and departed the Gatehenge, traveling south.

Gwen's euphoria lasted only half a mile before Papá stopped, pulling his family into a quiet conference in the shallows of Merlyn's pristine beach. "Gwenverity's new role in Overtwixt cannot become known," he said gravely.

The little girl's face fell. "But Papá—"

"It would put you in danger, daughter, so we must keep it a secret. Do you all understand? I'll have your promise on this." He looked to Alber until he got a nod of agreement, then to Ander, and finally to Gwen. Lip trembling, Gwen nodded jerkily.

"But Father," Alber asked. "Gwennie will have to be known as *something*. Otherwise, what will people call her?"

Papá took Gwen's hand. "What would you like to be?" When Gwen hesitated, he added: "Anything you want, anything at all."

What she really wanted was the role the Guide had just given her. That's why she'd chosen it! But... "I wanna be whatever you want me to be, Papá."

Papá's lip twisted for only a moment. "Not terribly helpful, but alright. How about we just call you the Lady? That's vague enough, respectable and dignified, but without a lot of expectations connected to it. Or if that turns out to be *too* vague, we could always call you the *Under*lady..." He frowned. "No, I like Lady better. What do you think, Gwenverity: would you like to be the Lady?"

Gwen forced a smile. It wasn't terrible. It just wasn't what the Guide had said.

"Very good then," Papá said, taking Gwen's hand and kissing it in gentlemanly fashion. "My dear Altruist and Antagonist," he said mock-formally, addressing Gwen's brothers. "May I present the Lady of Caymerlot. Now don't forget, my dear," he added to Gwen, doing his best Guide impersonation. "Bear this honor honorably."

Gwen swiped at her eyes with her free hand.

"But Father—" Alber began again.

Papá gave his eldest child a dangerous look. "Yes, son?"

"I thought we were only staying for a few days. Gwen can't possibly be in danger if we're leaving so soon."

Papá looked from one child to the next, his smile returning. "Well, I know you all would really like to stay longer, given the chance. So I say, why not?"

"But what about your campaign for Parliament?"

Papá's eyes glittered. "I suspect this Underlord position may prove an even better opportunity for me. Maybe Overtwixt will be a nice place to stay awhile after all—for weeks or months, maybe even years."

Gwen's eyes went wide, then she seized her father in a fierce hug. "Oh thank you, Papá. Thank you ever so much!"

Maybe Gwen's dreams would come true after all. So long as she and her family remained in Overtwixt, anything was possible. Right?

And remain in Overtwixt they did, long past when they originally planned to leave. And through it all, Gwenverity MerGrand—who came to be known as the Lady of the Lake... or the Underlady... or sometimes even the Siren—clung fervently to hope.

Until, thirteen years later, everything changed.

Part I
The King
◇

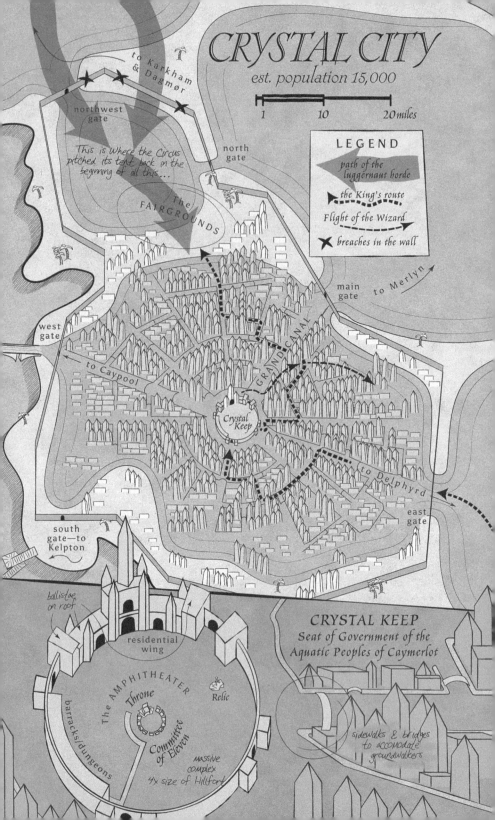

· one ·

Arthos Penn was now King. The King of Caymerlot, in fact—*the* Caymerlot, legendary utopia of Overtwixt. And if that weren't enough, he was Hero too. 'Cause supposally, King and Hero was one and the same. All of which meant the whole wide world of bridges was dependin' on *him* to rescue 'em from them luggernaut blokes.

Holey anemone! How had *that* happened? *

Arth had come to O'ertwixt seeking adventure and fun—and loads of respect, sure. But responsibility? No thanks! Calamity, he used to be the least responsible fella he knew, unless you counted his twin brother Morth. The two of them hadn't even entered Overtwixt legally. They'd *snuck* in, in violation of the Treaty of Caymerlot, which established how many members of each aquatic race were allowed in Overtwixt at the same time. They'd spent the next few

---

* Remember, dagmen often mix up their words, or even invent entirely new ones that only vaguely sound like what they mean. And their grammar's a mess! But I've decided that the unique way they speak is one of their more endearing qualities. —*N*

months touring with their father's Circus of Dagmør, pretending to be the Fool and the Clown. If not for Morth being kidnapped by them lugman barbarians, that's probably what they'd still be doin'.

But the luggernauts had attacked Bronze City on Centhule during the circus's visit there. Arth and several other unlikely heroes had taken up weapons to fight back, but not before Morth and hundreds more were carted away as slaves for the lugmen. After the battle, the seven new allies had formed a Squad for the purpose of chasing the lugmen and rescuing their friends. And for reasons Arth himself *still* didn't understand, the Squad had chosen him—the unlikeliest "hero" of them all—to be their Squadleader. Maybe because, at the time, he was the only one who'd never chosen an official role from the Guide.*

Only today had Arth finally met the Guide face to face, right after the Battle for the Branch Library ended. All these months, the daglady Portmistress had been hunting Arth and Morth for violating the Treaty, and the Guide had traveled with her—but not because *he* wanted them punished. As it turned out, the Guide intended all along to offer Arth the most prestigious role in history.

And so it was that Arthos Penn the dagman had just been anointed King, standing here on this battlefield on the niland of Hulandia.

Arth placed one webbed hand over his face and took a deep breath, feeling the old stirrings of panic, like when he'd first become Squadleader. But he wasn't that naïve dagling anymore. He'd seen the atrocities of war, made hard decisions of leadership, even smoked dozens of the

---

* All major concepts and characters from previous stories are described (along with pronunciation clues) in the complete Glossary of Persons, Places, and Things on page 405.

monstrous barbarian lugmen personally. Whatever came his way, he could handle it, so long as it brought him closer to rescuing Morth. He straightened his shoulders and uncovered his face.

Everyone was still staring at him.

There in the Branch Library courtyard amid the debris of the battle that just ended, every member of the Squad, the Circus, and the librarian staff stared at *him*, wondering what *he* would do next.

Arth swallowed.

"So that's it then?" he asked the Guide. "You put yer hand on meh head, mutter a few words, and just like that I's the new King? I dunno, shouldn't there be a crown or sumfing? Not that I want one!" he hurried to say. "This just... it don't feel real is all."

"Monarchs don't always wear crowns," the Guide assured him. "In the convention of Caymerlot, as laid down by the Sovereign, one must simply be *anointed* King, by me, to become King in truth." The centman shrugged. "That said, there may still be crowns in your future—and coronation ceremonies, to place those crowns on your head—if that is the convention of the peoples who will soon follow you. But I wouldn't worry about that right now."

"So, um, what *should* I be worrying 'bout?" Arth asked. "Like, what do I do now?"

"What would you be doing if you were still just the Squadleader?" the Guide countered.

Arth didn't even have to think about it. "Everyfing I can possibly do to rescue Morth, along with any'un else that's been mistreated by the villains of this realm." He meant the luggernaut horde, of course, but he was well aware there were others in Overtwixt today who abused their power.

The Guide smiled slightly. "Then let me ask you this: How might you accomplish that goal better now that you're the King?"

Arth frowned. "I don't have to be King to do what I want to do next—which is chase the lugs all the way back to Lugarth, where Morth and the others is being kept," he said, gesturing northward. Even as they stood here talking, that's the direction the lugman survivors of the battle were fleeing. "So why do I feel like yer gonna say that's not the right decision at this junksure?"

"Because that's not the right decision at this juncture," Lady Karis the Knight spoke up, in that faint accent of hers. "Arthos, my friend, what we have accomplished as a Squad is beyond amazing. I still cannot believe we were victorious this day against the Khan and his armies—and that is thanks to *your* battle plan, *your* leadership." At Karis's side, her old friend Gerald the Noble nodded agreement. "But Arthos," she continued, "we are still just seven adventurers. We won out against hundred-to-one odds through trickery, by confusing our enemies into fighting each other. That will not work the same way a second time, not if we chase the lugmen onto their home niland where we'll face *thousands* of warriors. Especially not if the Ransacker is now in charge."

Arth ground his fangs, wishing Karis didn't make so much sense. With the Khan's defeat, the Ransacker was one of the contenders to become the new alpha lugman. And that scared Arth, for the Ransacker was a highly intelligent fella who inspired uncharacteristic discipline in his followers.

"What we need is more men," said the Sidekick, the kelpie squad member who often acted as Arth's steed in battle. As usual, the funny little creature couldn't help but rhyme. "Only then should we take the fight home to them!"

Arth's daddie Pythagoras, the circus Ringmaster, cleared his throat. "It's like I was sayin' afore. The resources of all the aquatic peoples is gonna be yers to direct, but only after ya take yer place as King." He glanced at the Guide. "I fink that's what you're getting at too, innit?"

The Guide graciously nodded his agreement.

Arth took a deep breath. "And I prolly have to go back to Caymerlot to declare myself King, is that it?"

Again the Guide inclined his head in agreement.

"But convincing the aquatics that he *is* the new King will hardly be a picnic in the pond," Hembrose the Wizard scoffed. Of all the members of the Squad, Arth had known the mermage* longest; he often acted the part of a stubborn, foul-tempered old man, but Arth trusted him with his life.

"You think convincing zem will be difficult?" asked Pyrsie the Inventor, Arth's closest friend in all the worlds. "But zee Guide has *said* he is King now," the little gnomaid insisted. "Anointed him wiz oil on his head and everyzing!"

"The Underlord won't give up his power easily," Hembrose retorted. "Not on the word of the Guide alone."

---

* "Mermage" (MUR-mayj) is a term Morth invented by blending "merman" and "magician." In the human real world, this kind of combined word is called a portmanteau. —*N*

The Wizard looked at Arth. "You'll have to take the throne away from him, possibly by force."

All eyes turned to the Guide for confirmation of this, and the centman did not disagree. "If you choose to proceed from here to Caymerlot, your majesty, there will still be challenges awaiting you. Even there."

Arth blinked at being called "your majesty" but chose to ignore it. "I don't like the idea of fightin' meh own allies, so I reckon maybe we should go rescue Morth first." This was what he most wanted to do anyway.

"Alas, even if you could reach young Morthos," the Guide said sadly, "he has challenges of his own that he must face right now."

"You's saying we got no chance of reaching him?" Arth pressed. "Northmount is right there," he said, pointing again to the north, at the mountain that contained the subterranean passage from Hulandia down to Lugarth. "And the lugs is on the run," he reminded everyone.

The Guide was shaking his head. "I suspect the lugmen will only retreat as far as the beachhead they've established on this niland. They still hold the narrows south of Northmount, and it will be difficult to dislodge them with a force as small as your Squad, no matter how heroic your efforts."

The head librarian—Karis's friend Orfeo the Poet—gave the Guide a surprised look. "Your talent with diplomacy and even linguistics I can understand. Are you a military tactician too?"

Lady Karis elbowed her fellow human gently in the ribs. "The Guide is many things," she told him in a low tone. "Do not doubt his words."

"Believe me," the Poet said, "I do not." And the bearded man immediately began searching his pockets for paper and a quill. Arth had the feeling the Poet had just learned something new that he planned to incorporate in his next epic narrative.

"The King is welcome to send scouts toward Northmount, to see if what I say is true," the Guide assured everyone. "I think you'll find your kelpman allies well suited to such a task. They are versatile creatures, oft underestimated, and quite swift on those eight legs of theirs."

With the exception of the Sidekick, all the other kelpies in attendance were part of the group Daddie had hired back in Caymerlot to pull the circus wagons. Though it didn't much bother Arth, most kelpmen were stinky, unkempt creatures. But this ragtag group straightened instinctively at hearing such high praise from the Guide.

Arth eyed the funny-looking blokes thoughtfully, but finally shook his head, turning back to the Guide. "Naw, if you say it's so, I trust ya." He shrugged. "I's not entire sure *why* I trust ya, considering we only just now met, but... yeah, I trust you's right on this score."

The Guide grinned.

"But my brother..." Arth began again. "Morth's so *close*, just one niland over. If I turn back now..." He trailed off, worried.

"You seek reassurance that your brother will be alright in the end," the Guide said in understanding.

"Will he be?" Arth asked hopefully.

"That is not for me to say," the Guide responded. "I can only promise that if you travel to Caymerlot now, another path to Lugarth *will* make itself known to you. In the meantime, you must trust your brother to make his own choices, as all of us here"—he gestured to the assembled crowd—"trust *you* to make wise choices now."

Arth took a deep breath and sighed heavily, shoulders sagging in acceptance. "Alrighty then. I guess we's headed back to Caymerlot, where this whole hot mess started in the first place." He shook his head, in continued disbelief at everything that had happened. "We's off to see this Underlord bloke, convince him his throne is now mine to sit in, then face any other challenges awaitin' us in Crystal City."

Nobody responded immediately. After all, this wasn't just a casual jaunt they were discussing. It had taken the Circus of Dagmør months to travel from Caymerlot to where they stood today.

Arth's squad mate Paladin tossed his maned head and neighed. "There's something important that all of you are forgetting."

"And what is that, friend eqman?" the Guide asked.

"The Relic encased in Rock," Paladin said pointedly. "You say Arth only needs to be anointed to become King... but according to the legend or prophecy or what-have-you, he also needs to wield Sovereign's Great Relic."

The Guide's eyes twinkled. "Ah, another common misconception. You see, it's not the wielding of that Relic that makes him King. Rather, his ability to wield the Relic is a sign proving that he *is* the King.

"But that's exactly my point," Paladin insisted with a snort. "He needs that Relic. For if Arth recovers Sovereign's Great Relic, it will be hard for the Underlord or anyone else to claim that he's *not* the prophesied Hero and King."

The Guide smiled sadly. "If only that were so."

"No, Paladin is right," Hembrose said, disagreeing with the Guide. "Recovering the Relic-in-the-Rock should be Arth's first move, to remove any doubt that he's the prophesied Hero-King. We need to find some way to bypass the Underlord and his soldiers and go straight to the Relic—"

"Which is easy enough!" the eqman concluded victoriously. "We just travel first to Eqland, to recover the Diamond Horn of Destiny from where it was buried in that avalanche so many eons ago."

Every other member of the Squad groaned. After all, the location and identity of Sovereign's Great Relic had been a matter of disagreement the entire time they had traveled and fought together.

"Not zis again!" Pyrsie complained.

"Eqland is *not* where the encased Relic lies," Noble began. "Everyone knows—"

Even the Poet got involved this time. "According to history—" he interjected.

"Enough!" Hembrose boomed with his magically enhanced voice, then immediately wilted; he was obviously still exhausted from using so much magic during the Battle for the Branch Library. The mermage turned to the Guide and begged, "Would you *please* tell them all that the prophesied Relic, the one encased in stone by the Sovereign himself, is none other than the one that we actually *call* the Relic-in-the-Rock, stuck in the stone of an outcropping in the center of the Amphitheater in the courtyard of the Underlord's Crystal Keep on the niland of Caymerlot?!" He sucked in a huge breath upon finishing this run-on sentence.

Noble and Paladin both scoffed, but the Guide sighed and nodded. "The Wizard speaks true. So you see, O King: everything is leading you back to Caymerlot." The tall centman turned his regal head to regard everyone else. "Who will go with him?"

The members of the Squad, the Circus, and the Branch Library staff all looked puzzled at this question. Arth hoped that was because they *all* planned to go with him, and they thought it was a silly question. Except...Arth didn't think the Guide asked a whole lot of silly questions.

The Guide stamped one hoof loudly and spoke more officially, with gravity. "I say again, who will go with the King to Caymerlot? Who will go before him and follow after him, rendering him whatever aid as he might require, and declaring the truth of who he is to all who would hear?"

A heavy silence followed this more formal invitation; and as that moment lengthened without anyone stepping forward, Arth found himself awash in doubt once more. Who was he to think himself worthy of becoming King? He wasn't even qualified to be Squadleader. But *King?* No one wanted a dagman King, much less one still stuck in his teenage years. Maybe Arth remained the Fool after all, to ever entertain such a notion.

Then the first emotional voice was raised in response, answering the Guide's call. "I will!"

· two ·

Pyrsyfal Rochelle felt a profound sense of déjà vu. Just one short month ago, she had watched as Arth reluctantly accepted the role of Squadleader, seeming amazed when people followed him, even though he quickly proved himself well-suited to leadership. Now, the young dagman had been offered an even greater responsibility, the weight of which would be enough to overwhelm almost anyone. But somehow, Pyrsie knew her friend was equal to the challenge.

It was ironic, really. With the Guide's anointing, Arth was poised to achieve everything that Pyrsie, Hembrose, and the others had desired when they first chased their dreams into Overtwixt: immense respect, importance, fame and riches, unlimited power. And yet the thing Arth had most desired—freedom from responsibility—was the one thing he would never have again.

Even so, what was the first thing Arth did as King? Did he issue self-serving decrees (like the Underlord might have done) or demand others treat him with great honor (as the Burrowcrat certainly would have done)? No, the new King had started by humbly asking for advice, all in pursuit of selfless goals.

Pyrsie thought back to her first year in Overtwixt, working for the Burrowcrat. The ruler of Gnoburrow had betrayed her at the end of her contract, burying her alive within the Treasury she'd created so she could never reveal the secret of its elaborate booby traps. How different her introduction to Overtwixt would have been if the Burrowcrat was more like Arth! How different the future might become, once the niland rulers of the realm had a benevolent, humble King to look up to as their example!

And this was the kind of leader the Guide was now asking her to follow? "Who will go before him and follow after him," the Guide had asked formally, "rendering him whatever aid as he might require, and declaring the truth of who he is to all who would hear?"

Pyrsie felt a wave of emotion, so overwhelming that she couldn't move or speak for the longest moment. Then she forced herself forward, opening her mouth—

"I will!" cried an emotional voice, before Pyrsie could get the words out herself. "Oy, will I ever!" The voice's owner, the muscular Roberthoras Penn—circus Strongman—pushed to the front of the crowd and dropped to his knees before Arth, clasping both of Arth's hands in his.

"Uncle Bertie?" Arth asked uncertainly, clearly uncomfortable at having his elder kinsman kneeling before him like this.

"Roberthoras Penn, repeat after me..." the Guide said gravely. And he proceeded to recite an oath of fealty, which Bertie echoed word for word (or at least as close as a dagman could be expected to manage):

"I promise on meh honor to fatefully serve meh King, here and now as well as in the future. Nary to harm him, always to protect both him and his house and such. I won't never try elevatin' mehself above him. This I swear, in good faith and with deception—nay, sorry, I mean *without* deception," he corrected himself quickly, his elbow fins fluttering of their own accord (a sure sign of dagman embarrassment). Then he added something more that the Guide had not suggested: "Above all, I promise to guard the life o' the King with meh own." Bertie nodded sharply.

And then it happened again, before Pyrsie or the rest of her squad mates could speak up; all the *other* dagman circus performers crowded forward, dropping to their knees and reaching out arms to touch Arth. Speaking in loud, overlapping voices, they all proceeded to recite their own slightly distorted versions of the oath. Arth's daddie the Ringmaster was no exception, tears of pride and joy streaming down his pebbled cheeks with every word. Even the Portmistress took a single knee and pledged her awkward support.

While the other dagmen and dagwomen were still swearing their oaths, the Guide clasped Uncle Bertie's arm and dragged him to his feet. "On the day you selected your role," he told the Strongman, "I encouraged you to bear your responsibility honestly. Do you remember that?"

Bertie licked his lips, suddenly uncomfortable. "Sure, I reckon I recall that."

"*Have* you born your responsibility wisely?" the Guide asked, his gaze unwavering.

The Strongman's elbow fins fluttered wildly, radiating the sudden heat of his shame. "I... I'm sorry," he said weakly, feeling the eyes of the crowd on him now instead of Arth. "I was tempted to steal from the lockbox times without count," he admitted. "That box is heavy, ya see, filled with circus finances and merdanchise and the like. As Strongman, I was the only one as could carry it, so the responsibility of protectoring it fell to me." He licked his lips, clearly humiliated. "I was constantly tempted to dip into them funds for meh personal use."

"What are ya sayin', brother?" cried the Ringmaster in dismay. "Did ya steal from the circus?"

"Nay, of course not!" Bertie insisted.

The Guide grinned suddenly. "Then you bore that responsibility honestly, and you have absolutely nothing to be ashamed of."

Uncle Bertie blinked. "Really? But I couldn't stop thinking about it..."

"How we act when no one else is watching is a greater indication of our caliber than anything we do in plain view," the Guide said. "All the more so in this case, considering how badly you were tempted. You have proven the quality of your character, perhaps more to yourself than anyone else."

Bertie looked uncertainly at his brother, but the Ringmaster was no longer aghast; he looked relieved.

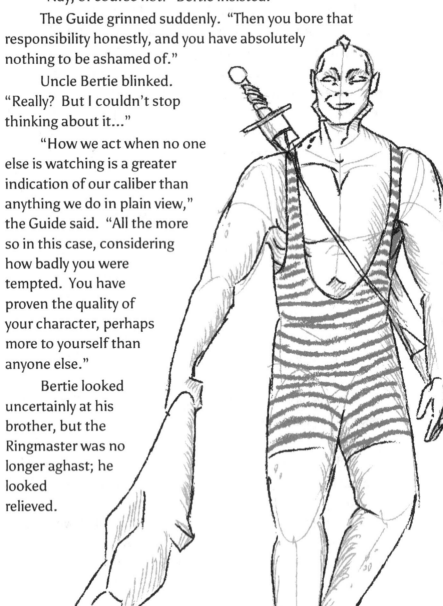

"You have proven yourself faithful, so I now offer you greater responsibility: Roberthoras Penn, one-time Strongman of Dagmør, will you become the Bodyguard?"

Bertie gasped, and he wasn't the only one. "You can do that?" Pyrsie's squad mate the Noble demanded.*

The Guide gave a lopsided smile. "As I'm sure everyone here has noticed, people choose to reinvent themselves all the time, taking on one role after another for which they're unsuited. At other times, they try to steal the honor intended for someone else, or else play at a role the world simply does not need." The Guide's eyes flicked ever so briefly away from Bertie—toward Hembrose?—before returning.

"But I alone offer a choice of roles perfectly suited to who you are and what the world needs, selected by the one who understands you and the world better than anyone. So to answer everyone's question, yes. I can extend the choice of a new role. Therefore I ask again: Roberthoras Penn—"

"Yes! Youbetcher bottoms, I accept!" blurted the Strongman—no, the Bodyguard now. "I assume my quest is to protect the new King?"

"Something you've already pledged to do," the Guide nodded. "Continue to bear this responsibility honestly."

Suddenly, all the rest of the circus performers were requesting (or in Daddie's case, demanding) similar

---

* This was the first I ever heard of such a thing too! —N

treatment, but the Guide just chuckled and shook his head.

After that, the kneeling and oath-taking resumed, as Sidekick led the other kelpies in pledging their loyalty. "We ain't much, but we's a start," he concluded afterward. "Good in a crunch, and willing to do our part!"

"Do not underestimate just how much your support means, my dear kelpmen," the Guide said, as Arth nodded his emphatic agreement. The young dagman's eyes were swimming. He was completely overwhelmed by the outpouring of support.

And finally, with Arth's own family and people out of the way, as well as the other aquatics, it was Pyrsie's turn.

Instead, it was Lady Karis the Knight who reached Arth next, kneeling gracefully. With head bowed, she presented both of her hands, palms up, her two curving swords resting on the Diamond Armor on her forearms. "King Arthos Penn of the dagmen, I offer you my swords, my service, even my life if you should ask it of me, along with my trust that you will use these gifts wisely and for the greater good." She hesitated, smiled. "My friendship you already have."

Arth's brimming tears chose that moment to spill out, streaking down his face. "Aw, Lady Karis," he sniffled, pulling the Knight to her feet in an awkward move that sent the woman's swords clattering to the ground. "Ya gots no idea what this means to me." They seized each other in a hug, pounding each other's backs. "But you don't gotta do this. Ya ain't even aquatic yerself!"

"Oh Arthos," Karis said with a fond, almost motherly smile. "Don't you understand the impact you are destined to have upon this world? Your reach and rule will transcend race and niland. May I simply be the first of the non-aquatics to recognize that truth and offer my pledge."

Pyrsie was blinking away tears now too. These were *exactly* the sentiments she had hoped to express to Arth, but

Karis had beaten her to it. Pyrsie really liked Lady Karis, even looked up to her as a sort of role model. But in that moment, she was really angry with the older woman.

Dejected and unnoticed, the gnomaid slipped away.

―――――

Eventually, the crowd broke up and everyone began dashing about, preparing for the journey back to Caymerlot. The dagmen sang as they worked, a well-known circus ditty from their real world, but with Arth's name rather humorously added to the lyrics of each verse. The Sidekick was bellowing some new rhyme ("the King and his lot, headed back to Caymerlot") while whipping the other kelpies into some semblance of order. Even the human librarians made arrangements to travel as far as the Bronze City of Centhule—not counting the Poet, of course. *He* refused to leave his precious Branch Library, but did help the other librarians pack. Pyrsie saw Paladin offer Arth a brief word of congratulations, and Noble clasped the new King's shoulder in camaraderie, but none of the rest of the Squad (besides the Knight) swore any new oaths.

Feeling drained now, Pyrsie watched the preparations from where she sat in the shadow of the Branch Library's Science hut, keeping out of the way. She heaved a big sigh.

Arth wandered over and dropped into a squat beside her, then mimicked her big sigh exactly. It was all decidedly un-King-like. "Sumfing wrong, mate?"

Now Pyrsie felt even worse. She hadn't been looking for attention, and certainly not Arth's. This was his moment of glory, and she didn't want to ruin it. "It is nothing."

"Pfft," the dagman snorted very expressively.

Pyrsie giggled a little at the sound, but only for a moment. "I wanted to be first!" she blurted, without really meaning to.

Arth didn't say anything, just waited, listening.

The little gnomaid sighed again. Now she had to explain. "I... I wanted to be zee first one to swear to follow you." She grimaced. "I mean, I didn't think I needed to, when all zis King business started. We're your Squad. We already follow you. But then, when zee Guide said what he said about going before you and after you, telling everyone zee truth about who you are..." Pyrsie fell silent, thoughtful.

"Aye?" Arth eventually prodded her.

"I was overcome wiz emotion," she admitted. "I wanted to stand up and tell everyone who you are to me: zee friend I never had, zee kind of leader I would follow anywhere—even to a place like Lugarth. Do you know how scary zat is for me, Arth? Zee thought of going to zee home of zee giant barbarians?"

"It's scary for all of us, mate," he admitted quietly.

"Not as scary as it is for me!" she insisted. "I am tiny compared even to you. Do you know what zis thing is like for me, fighting these great beasts? And there are *thousands* of zem on Lugarth!"

Arth licked his lips, preparing to reassure her—

"But zat's not zee point!" she insisted. "Zee point is zat I would follow you there anyway. Because you're zat kind of leader. You inspire me, and I want everyone to know it. Except your uncle and Sidekick and all zee dagmen and kelpies got to say so first." She shrugged like it was silly, though it didn't feel that way. "And when they were finally done, I thought to myself, 'Well, Pyrsyfal, at least you can be zee first *non*-aquatic'... but then Karis beat me to zat too!"

"Oh, Pyrsie," Arth said softly, his big eyes full of tears yet again. "You *was* first, don't ya see? You was there for me long before I met Lady Karis or the rest of the Squad. And you treated me important and such back when Daddie and Bertie still called me Fool. We's been a team as long as we's known each other. Aside from meh own family, I's only known Hembrose longer, and I love that bloke, I do... but he ain't never put the needs of others ahead of hisself unless pushed into it." It was Arth's turn to sniffle. "*You* stayed by my side. *You* healed me with that Diamond Grail of yers after our first battle, and five others since. And *you* was the first to promise you'd help rescue Morth. Ya didn't even hesitate."

Pyrsie shrugged awkwardly, but she felt a warm glow inside her now.

"Oaths is all well and good, but actions is even better," he concluded. "I got no doubts where you's concerned. You, Pyrsyfal Rochelle, is my truest friend here in Overtwixt."

Pyrsie took a shuddering breath. "And you are *my* truest friend, Arthos Penn—in zis or any other world."

Arth grinned at her, and the two friends hugged awkwardly, right there on the curb.

Then Pyrsie jerked back as an alarming thought occurred to her. "Zis doesn't mean I am in love wiz you. Zis whole thing, it is platonic, yes?"

Arth burst out laughing. "I ain't got no idea what that means, platonic. But nah, I don't love ya like *that*. Sheesh! I love ya like my family, my sister. My best friend."

"Good," Pyrsie breathed out, reassured. Content. "I would not want things to become weird between us."

"Never." Arth grinned.

And so Pyrsie finally felt motivated to begin her own preparations for departure, reflecting all the while on everything that had transpired. Of all the millions of people to enter Overtwixt through the eras, dreaming of becoming the Hero—or King, as it turned out—Arth alone would do it. Pyrsie had shared that dream once too, but it was not to be. Even so, all her hopes for Overtwixt had been fulfilled anyway. She had longed for love and respect and importance, and it turned out she didn't need to be the Hero herself to achieve those things. No surprise there. She'd already come to that realization before this moment.

And yet, in this moment, she felt the truth of it more powerfully than ever before. She *was* loved; she *was* respected; she *was* important, to the people who mattered. Glancing around the trash-strewn courtyard of the Branch Library of Hulandia, she met the eyes of her other friends as they worked, sharing a smile or nod with each: Paladin and Hembrose, Sidekick and Noble; Karis, with whom Pyrsie no longer even remembered being angry; and, most of all, Arth.

She even caught the Guide himself watching her. And when their eyes met, his mouth opened in another radiant, infectious smile.

Pyrsie smiled back, feeling lighter and happier than she could ever remember being.

Now, to finally complete her own Guide-given quest: helping her friends defeat the greatest threat facing Overtwixt today.

· three ·

Returning to Caymerlot from Hulandia took more than six weeks of traveling every day, stopping only at night to eat and sleep. That was much less time than the Circus of Dagmør had required for the journey here, of course. There were no extended stops for performances or library research this time, and they moved much faster without needing to pull all those circus wagons. But still, *six weeks*. It was way too long. Every day wasted in travel was a day that Morth continued to suffer on Lugarth. Hembrose tried really hard not to think about that, but it nagged at him. And if it nagged at *him*, then it must have been agony for Arth and his father.

Even so, Hembrose regretted departing the Branch Library without even a day spent perusing its collection. After all, it was Hembrose's quest from the Guide to re-discover the lost absolute truths of Overtwixt, something that could only be done in the libraries of the realm. Of course, he was pretty ambivalent about that quest at this point, but he still loved libraries. Ah well, he'd just have to come back someday.

Assuming he didn't die of old age first.

Hembrose frowned. Considering how much of his life he'd already spent in the libraries of Overtwixt, with time accelerated to top speed, it was a genuine concern. He really needed to find some sort of magic to reverse aging before it was too late.

Partly because of his age, the increased pace of travel was grueling. The Wizard constantly needed to maintain a shapeshift (either human or one of the flying creatures), and *no one* was getting enough sleep (traveling late each night and rising early each morning). Plus, Hembrose was more exhausted than the rest of them to start with, thanks to his spy mission on Lugarth and the magic he'd worked during the Battle for the Branch Library after that. There'd never even been a chance for a catfishnap prior to leaving for Caymerlot. By the time the Squad and their allies arrived in Bronze City on Centhule, barely half a week after the most recent battle, Hembrose was on the verge of collapse.

And yet he didn't collapse. Strangely, he kept finding the strength to go on, tapping into some fresh source of energy deep within himself. It wasn't a very pleasant feeling, this buzzing, bubbling energy. It reminded Hembrose of the time he'd drunk two cups of his mam's strong caife as a child back on Hybra-sil in the merman real world. He hadn't slept a wink that night despite his body's crushing exhaustion, instead remaining awake and jittery, sick in mind and belly. Whatever was happening now, it was a lot like that, except that the sensation lasted for days, weeks. But Hembrose didn't complain. The alternative was to be left behind.

Besides, he had a feeling it was related to the immense magical emerald he kept hidden from his friends—the one that had been glowing an eerie green ever since he "harvested" those six lugmen by the stream in Lugarth.

Arth picked up more supporters with every niland his procession crossed, starting with Centhule. After staying the night in Bronze City, the group that departed the next morning had tripled in number (including a few of the librarians who decided not to remain there after all). Although the Guide did not travel with them ("I have other business to be about," he'd told Arth), the news quickly spread that the Guide himself had anointed Arth the King; and many among the centmen, humen, and eqmen dropped everything to join this new King's procession toward Caymerlot, for they held the Guide's opinion in high regard.

The same was true of all the rest of the kelpies remaining in the Backwater of Centhule... though Hembrose suspected that had less to do with the Guide, and more to do with the fact that a *dagman*—a fellow low-class aquatic—was marching on Caymerlot in power and glory. Even Hembrose looked forward to seeing Arth put that slimy Underlord in his place, so he *knew* these disgusting little kelpies must be excited.

Before departing Bronze City after their one night there, the Noble took a couple hours to ensure the local government was still functioning. Until a new Baron arrived in Overtwixt, the Noble was still the highest ranking Centhulian official, after all. The centman signed a bunch of paperwork that had been awaiting approval, made a few suggestions to the Captienne and others, then finally continued on toward Centwick with the rest of the Squad. *Every* member of the Squad planned to stick with Arth, not just on his journey to Caymerlot, but all the way through to the end of this mad adventure. Whatever end that might be.

In Denali, the capital den of Gnoburrow, the Burrowcrat threw Arth a lavish feast and tried to rope *him* into signing a bunch of paperwork—several hastily-drafted agreements between Caymerlot and Gnoburrow. The new King just smiled and promised friendly relations in the future, without committing to anything specific. Like Hembrose, Arth already knew how untrustworthy the gnoman ruler really was. It was hard to forget the story of how he'd misled and betrayed Pyrsie during her first year in Overtwixt. But Arth didn't confront the Burrowcrat with any of this (yet), and Pyrsie stayed out of sight the entire time the procession was in Gnoburrow.

When Arth's entourage left Denali again (the very next morning, of course), they were joined by even more new followers: representatives from each of the little peoples, including gnoman engineers, nagman musicians, raimen without count, and even a single shaman. That shaman was not the Deputy; Arth wouldn't trust that fellow any further than he trusted the Burrowcrat, so even when the Deputy proposed to begin serving Arth instead of the gnoman ruler, the dagman King burst out laughing and refused him outright. Later, however, a different shaman by the name of Diplomat offered to advise Arth on the workings of government, laws, contracts, and such. Arth quickly took that fellow into his employ. The Diplomat promised him (in words so fast and nasally they almost couldn't be understood) that Arth wouldn't regret it.

Despite the procession's still-grueling pace, and the excitement of revisiting Bronze City, Denali, and the snowy slopes of Raibourne, it was a relatively boring journey overall. Hembrose missed visiting the libraries in all of these places. Instead, he was left with plenty of time for lonely reflection as he winged through the skies above the procession... and plenty of time to plan what he would do once he was allowed to travel freely in Caymerlot and Merlyn again. After all, the Underlord still had a warrant out for the Wizard's arrest, thanks to that unfortunate misunderstanding about Hembrose trying to kidnap the Underlady. But Arth would get that confusion taken care of first thing, he was sure.

Hembrose's days-long incursion onto Lugarth had been a turning point for him. He could admit to himself now that what he'd felt during his first several battles was fear—not *cowardice*, but definitely fear. Yet his undercover mission had forced him to grow accustomed to that fear, or else he'd have been incapable of accomplishing anything. All in all, that mission had been an incredible success.

And that wasn't even counting the victory of his first "harvesting." Reaching into the voluminous pockets of his golden mantle, the Wizard frequently took out the infused emerald in order to admire it. Somehow, the strength and abilities of the lugmen he'd harvested now resided within this huge gemstone, accessible whenever he needed to draw more deeply on the green magic of Overtwixt... and apparently giving him the stamina he needed to persevere on this journey. That was the only explanation for how Hembrose managed to keep going, despite his exhaustion.

If only it didn't leave him feeling so nauseated! And if only he didn't experience such terrible headaches every night, interfering with his rest in those few hours that he *wanted* to sleep.

And yet these symptoms all made sense, the Wizard ultimately concluded after weeks of turning the problem over in his head. Hembrose had already determined that crystalline structures infused from harvesting needed a vessel to help focus their power—a true magical relic, like the Diamond Relics some of the other squad members carried. Until Hembrose created some sort of shell or framework to surround and contain his beautiful emerald, its magic would remain slippery, difficult to wield without side effects. Unfortunately, such an artifact could take months to fashion. If he was going to accomplish such a thing before the end of this current struggle with the lugmen, Hembrose would need to find several days to sequester himself in a time-slowing library. So in the final week of the procession's approach to Caymerlot, Hembrose began planning exactly how to make that happen.

But as much as he longed for a relic of his own, Hembrose found that his thoughts turned just as frequently to the Lady, maybe even *more* frequently the nearer he drew to Caymerlot. The Siren, the Underlady, the Lady of the Lake—whatever the Guide had named her (Hembrose should have asked her when he had the chance)—he found himself increasingly consumed with memories of her shy smile, her big brown eyes, the fine curve of her tail fins. And that voice, like fresh honey drizzled over a morning's first rays of sunlight! Perhaps once Arth canceled the mermage's arrest warrant, Hembrose would have another chance with the girl... assuming she could get over her fascination with the man who freed the Relic-in-the-Rock, and assuming *he* could shed all these unnatural years he'd accumulated. He needed to bring them back to the same age again—but for that part, at least, Hembrose had the makings of a plan.

At long last—six weeks!—the entourage of the new King arrived on Delphyrd, just south of the great hubland of Caymerlot. They were separated from the east gate of Crystal City by nothing more than a single short aqueduct. Many hundreds of supporters now followed Arth, including additional raimen picked up traveling through Raignokia and Raibourne, and even some of their aquatic cousins the delphmen, from here on Delphyrd.

Night had fallen, but Arth was now so close to his goal that he insisted on pushing ahead. He didn't want to risk alarming the Underlord, so he left most of his followers on Delphyrd. Then he and his Squad—plus Pythagoras and Bodyguard Bertie, of course—crossed the aqueduct onto the niland utopia of Caymerlot.

Arriving at the southern gate of the Crystal City of Caymerlot, Hembrose and Arth and their squad mates found the way barred, the iron grid portcullis already lowered for the night. Arth came to an uncertain stop, then raised his voice to be heard by the guards atop the wall.

"Erm, hiya!" he bellowed. "Me and meh Squad here would like to request an audience with the right honorable Underlord, we would."

Honorable? That was awfully generous in Hembrose's opinion. Personally, the Wizard didn't think they should be announcing themselves to the Underlord or his guardsmen at all; they should be scaling this wall somewhere dark and unguarded, then sneaking straight to the Amphitheater so Arth could take up the Relic-in-the-Rock and prove himself to the world. But Arth didn't seem to think sneaking was very King-like.

"And who exactly are you?" called one of the guards in reply to Arth's request—a nym, wrapped in the rich blue cape of Caymerlot's defenders.

Arth hesitated, glancing at Hembrose, who shook his head in warning. "I'm known as the Squadleader!"

"Who?" the nym guard asked.

Annoyed, Sidekick splashed to the front of the group and peered up at the top of the wall. "You never heard of the Squad of Heroes?" he demanded.

"No."

"The Heroes of the Brown Stable?"

"I've heard of the Brown Stable, but—"

"The Heroes who were Bound but Able?"

"Huh?"

"The Heroes who have Crowns and wear Sable?" Sidekick tried again, his voice growing more high-pitched.

"These are terrible names!" the nym called back, sounding amused. "And no, none of them rings a bell."

"Well!" Sidekick concluded grandiosely, *"That's* the Squad that the illustrious Squadleader is leader of. He ain't no fable!"

The nym guard shook his head, apparently rolling his eyes too, though it was tough to tell from this distance in the low light. He opened his mouth, and Hembrose knew he was going to turn them away. But then another blue-caped soldier appeared atop the wall beside the nym, a karkman this time, having apparently just mounted the stairs from the inside of the wall. The two fellows whispered furiously for a time, and then the portcullis suddenly creaked upwards, opening the way into the city.

"Be on your guard," the Knight warned the rest of the Squad in a low voice.

Arth's Daddie and Uncle Bertie pulled close to him. The latter had taken to carrying a lugman club *and* a notched lugman sword strapped to his back, both of which he'd scavenged after the Battle for the Branch Library. With his immense strength, Arth's new Bodyguard was more than capable of bearing the weight, though both weapons were so oversized that it looked almost comical. At the Knight's warning, Bertie freed the club and propped it casually on one shoulder.

The other squad members loosened the weapons in their own sheaths and spread out a little more, forming a casual circle around Arth. Hembrose, currently in the guise of a human, carried no visible weapons; so he just cracked his knuckles and ran his fingers through the long, bushy gray beard that spread across his muscular chest.

Then the Squad entered Crystal City.

They stopped just inside the gate, awaiting the arrival of the imposing karkman who was now coming down the stairs from the wall. "Be welcome, O Squadleader!" the fellow said. "I am the Sergeant-at-arms."

Sidekick snickered at this name, but Hembrose had to admit it was apt for a man who had eight arms and carried a weapon in each. Even the arms the man used for locomotion held weapons, tucked in the crook of each tentacle as he slithered rapidly toward the Squad across the squishy wet ground. Once he was close enough, Hembrose saw that each of the eight weapons was an elaborate mace. *

"It's my pleasure to gauge your quintessence," Arth replied. † He extended a fist and the kark bumped it with one of his tentacles, the one holding a black-iron mace carved with scales. No, not scales—an artistic rendering of a dagman's pebbly skin. "That's quite a mouthful, Sergeant-at-arms... if'n ya don't mind me sayin' so."

"Feel free to call me Sergeant or even Sarge for short," the fellow responded with a sly grin, showing off a maw stuffed full of razor-sharp teeth. "Right this way!"

The Sergeant-at-arms slipped into the shallow water of a canal that led toward City-center, waving cheerfully for the Squad to follow alongside using a narrow isthmus sidewalk. The fellow immediately sped off, using some of the maces—which had broad, flat heads—almost like paddles, propelling him far faster than even a kark could usually move.

"Unlike that buffoon atop the wall," the Sarge called back over his shoulder, "I *have* heard of the Squad's exploits. Word travels fast." Realizing he was getting too far ahead of his guests, he turned and sped back to rejoin them, his own blue cape billowing. "I must say," he added, looking Arth up

---

* Since a sergeant-at-arms is often a ceremonial officer, this guy is probably a high-ranking member of the Underlord's government, each of his maces representing one of Caymerlot's aquatic races.

† I'm continually amazed by dagman wordplay. It seems like Arth meant to say "make your acquaintance" here, but what he actually said has an entirely different and deeper meaning. —*N*

and down critically, "you're not what I expected. But then, I suppose it's what's on the inside that counts."

Arth just smirked and nodded. He seemed at ease.

Hembrose most certainly was not, and it didn't appear the Noble or Paladin or other squad members were any happier. They kept looking around uncomfortably, particularly at the ring of karks and nyms bringing up the rear, as if expecting an attack at any moment. Hembrose wouldn't put it past the Underlord to arrange exactly that sort of welcome, assuming he'd gotten word it was a King who approached—and hadn't this Sergeant-at-arms just said that word traveled fast?

"Where is it you are taking us?" Pyrsie demanded.

"To your accommodations," the Sergeant assured her. "There you'll have a chance to, um, freshen up." The kark's stiff blubbery face furrowed in a frown, but then he sighed and shook his head. Hembrose probably should have read something into that, but it was hard not to be distracted by all those rows of pointy teeth in the fellow's wide mouth. "The Underlord will meet with you in the morning," the Sarge concluded.

Arth's father the Ringmaster puffed out his chest. "Oy, we really gots to be meetin' with this Underlord bloke sooner 'stead of later—" he began.

"It's okay, Daddie," Arth said quietly.

The Squad and its escorts moved deeper and deeper into Crystal City, towers of glass growing ever taller on all sides of them, until Hembrose felt a claustrophobia he didn't remember experiencing the last time he was here. It didn't help that the occupants of those buildings turned to stare at the strange procession, pressing their faces to the other side of all those window-walls and gaping down from high above. At last, Hembrose and the others reached the thick glass barricade surrounding Crystal Keep at City-center, appearing just as he remembered it—the glass wall so dense it was difficult to see through, images on the other side distorted. That's why the Squad was through the small gate and into the Amphitheater before they could see what awaited them:

Two full companies of blue-caped kark and nyman foot soldiers with weapons drawn, supported by another company of caped merman archers with arrows nocked to bowstrings—all pointed directly at Arth and his Squad.

"Calamity," Bertie growled, stepping in front of Arth and hefting his lugman club menacingly. "Whaddya fink of that? Some welcome."

"I'm sorry, truly I am," Sarge said as even more soldiers ran or swam up behind the Squad, blocking any escape.

Despite being terribly outnumbered, the heroes began drawing weapons. After all, why should the odds matter, after the victories they'd had against the luggernauts under similar circumstances?

But Arth raised a hand. "No! Lower yer weapons," he ordered his squad mates. "I ain't gonna start meh reign by harmin' other citizens of Caymerlot."

"You admit it?" the Sergeant asked. "You claim to be the King?"

"So the Guide named me," Arth confirmed with a nod.

"Yes, I'll bet he did," Sarge said sarcastically, though he looked less sure than he sounded.

Two mermen pushed to the front of the soldiers, moving to help cover the Squad while others collected their weapons. One of the fellows brandished a dull Diamond Harpoon threateningly, while the other wore glowing blue Diamond Chainmail. "Great," Hembrose muttered without thinking. "The Antagonist and the Altruist."

This drew the Antagonist's eye, and he studied Hembrose's human face for a long moment before exclaiming, "You!" He rushed forward, jabbing the barbed tip of his Harpoon into the Wizard's chest. "Quick, bind this one first. He's a shapeshifter!"

His brother the Altruist reacted with less alarm, but with no less distaste. "I confess, Sarge, I did not approve of the way my father the Underlord handled this situation. Whether this dagman fellow claims to be King or not, it rubbed me wrong to invite him within our walls under false pretenses, then imprison him." The Altruist's lips turned down in a frown. "But if he is traveling with one such as this Wizard, then my father's subterfuge has proven wise."

Once the Squad's weapons and armor had been collected (even their saddle gear, including the Noble's cape-like caparison!), the rest of the Squad was led deeper into the Keep and shoved into a large glass jail cell. Only Hembrose himself, bound and gagged, was kept separate.

"As for you," the Antagonist told him, "I've had something special planned in the event you ever showed your face here again." And grinning wickedly, the merman dragged Hembrose away from his friends.

· four ·

As dungeons went, the jail cell at the center of the Crystal Keep actually wasn't too bad—quite roomy, and very well illuminated. Like everything else in this strange city, it was constructed of glass. That allowed the silvery rays of the nighttime Sky Light to filter in quite nicely, even though the glass was so thick that making out distinct images on the other side of those walls was difficult. Getting a look outside required peering through the open windows or single door, which were all protected by traditional iron bars.

Karis Priamos, human Knight of Overtwixt and one-time princess of lost Troia, decided she'd been in worse situations. She just wished her first visit to Caymerlot had been under more pleasant circumstances. From what she'd seen of it in the dark, the hubland of the aquatics was quite the paradise, if not truly a utopia. And the architecture really was quite astounding, though less so for this dungeon.

The dungeon stood only one story above sea level, but descended farther than that below the surface (probably for the comfort of fully aquatic prisoners, like those okkmen Karis had heard of). Unfortunately, such "accommodations" gave almost no consideration to non-aquatics like Karis, for there was no dry place to sit. The shallowest place for her to wait was still more than knee deep, a natural rocky ledge on which Arthos currently squatted. Shrugging, Karis crouched beside him in the water, and the two friends considered their predicament in silence.

Pythagoras and Roberthoras Penn—the Ringmaster and his brother, the new Bodyguard—surfaced nearby, their heads popping up suddenly out of the depths. "Ain't no other windows nor doors 'neath the surface, sire," the Bodyguard said respectfully, despite Arthos insisting repeatedly that everyone (his own uncle especially) treat him the same as always before.

"This buildin' goes down least another two stories," Arthos's father added. "Erm, sire."

Arthos rolled his big dagman eyes at their deference, but he nodded. "I weren't really expectin' an easy escape from this place. Pays to check yer 'sumptions, though!"

The elder dagmen shared a look, then promised to keep looking and quickly submerged again.

"You don't seem very worried," Karis commented quietly. Not that she was worried either, exactly, but she certainly wasn't at her ease. After so many years wearing the Diamond Armor, she didn't feel comfortable in an unsafe place without it. "You didn't intend for us to be arrested and disarmed the very hour we entered Caymerlot, did you?"

Arthos grinned. "Not 'zactly. But I got a feelin' fings is gonna work out even so. That Guide fella seems to know what he's about, and this *is* the quest he gave me, innit?"

Karis chewed her lip uncertainly. "I don't know... is it? Your majesty, I've seen the Guide greet many people entering Overtwixt, and you're the first one I ever saw him *not* give a quest to. He didn't give you any instructions at all until you asked him for advice yourself."

Arthos blinked. He disliked being called 'majesty,' but he was obviously able to look past that and consider Karis's words on their own merits.

"Then again, you didn't give him much chance before you started asking questions," Karis smirked slightly. "So who knows? Most visitors to Overtwixt don't have an entire prophecy written about them either."

On Arthos's other side, Gerald the Noble raised one hoof rather miserably and shook it, flinging water droplets everywhere. The local soldiers had been thorough in searching and disarming the Squad, even prying free the metal hoofshoes Pyrsyfal had glued to Noble's and Paladin's feet several weeks ago. The centman sighed. "I don't see what there is to worry about. We're in a cage made of glass, of all things. Why are we still waiting around instead of just breaking free?"

Pyrsyfal splashed up, returning from her own examination of the glass walls along the perimeter of the large cell. "You weel not be breaking free of *zis* glass cage, not anytime soon." She flashed Arthos and Karis a strained smile. The gnomaid was clearly more worried than her centman squad mate, though just as miserable in all this wet; on *her*, even the shallowest water rose above the waist. "Zee entire city, it is made of zee industrial-strength glass, no? Otherwise zee taller buildings would collapse on zemselves."

"Aye, that's right," Arthos confirmed.

"Well, you surely noticed on our walk here, zat you could easily look through *zat* glass at all zee people inside?"

Karis and Arthos both nodded, waiting to hear the point the gnomaid was making, though Gerald seemed to understand already. He did not look pleased.

"*Zis* glass is even thicker than zat. Military strength, maybe, better than industrial strength. I think maybe it would take a battering ram without cracking."

Gerald hung his head. "Fantastic," he grumbled.

Karis took a deep breath. "Well, if brute strength won't break us free," she said, "I suppose we just need to put our heads together and come up with an intelligent escape plan."

She glanced toward the dungeon's single entrance, which was protected by half a dozen guards—two nyms, two karks, and two mermen. All of them were facing the other way, giving the Squad a clear view of their deep blue uniform capes. Like the ones worn by all the other officers and soldiers in Caymerlot, their capes were embroidered with the emblem of the Relic-in-the-Rock in silver thread.

Standing knee-deep in water on *this* side of the door, Sidekick and Paladin were loudly and energetically haranguing the guards through the thick iron bars. It was a task well suited to those two squad members, and something they clearly enjoyed doing... which had the true purpose of generating meaningless noise so Arthos and the others could make plans without being overheard.

"Oy, Pyrsie," Arthos said quietly, gesturing at Knight and Noble. "Tell our mates here about the job ya did for that ungrateful Burrowcrat bloke. Ya know, that Treasury place ya built, and how he locked ya up afterwards, so then you had to out-fink all yer own booby traps?"

"You just summarized zat job rather nicely already," Pyrsyfal said with a smirk.

"Naw, tell us all the specifics about the traps and such, and how ya got around 'em. Maybe it'll give us ideas for gettin' out of our current scrape."

"It certainly can't hurt," Gerald agreed. "We've got nothing but time, it seems."

So Pyrsyfal proceeded to recount the entire story in great detail, growing most passionate when she described the inner workings of her ingenious pitfalls and traps and other security features. Gerald scowled when she told of the Burrowcrat's betrayal, but then, he had always believed the aristocracy should be held to a higher standard of conduct than the common people. For her part, Karis was sure to praise Pyrsyfal for her creativity in fashioning those wax wings for escape, even though they ultimately melted and almost plunged her into lava. It was obvious to everyone that the gnomaid was an exceptional young woman, yet she seemed to genuinely crave Karis's validation in particular.

Pythagoras and Roberthoras reappeared in time to hear of Pyrsyfal's final booby trap, the one she added just before completing her escape. Whenever the Burrowcrat returned to the Treasury and constructed a new bridge across the chasm, he would have been forced to watch his precious piles of gold and gemstones cascade into the lava far below— triggered by his own arrival. It was a trick both cruel and well-deserved, and the elder dagmen howled with laughter. After all, it seemed that most dagmen, no matter their age, appreciated shenanigans.

Oddly enough, Arthos himself only smiled. He had heard the story before, of course, but Karis suspected this little act of revenge amused him less now than it once had. Arthos had matured quite a bit in a very short time, growing in both confidence and compassion from the wide-eyed teenager Karis had met during the Battle at Bronze City.

Most remarkably of all, the young man's compassion wasn't reserved just for his allies, either.

But even hearing every detail about the Treasury's features and defenses (again in Arthos's case), no one received any great inspiration for escaping their current prison.

"Zis is just a very different type of construction," Pyrsyfal concluded flatly. "Zee glass itself is unbreakable. If we want to get free, it must be through zee weak points." And she pointed at the iron bars over the windows and door.

"*Those* are the weak points?" Pythagoras asked in dismay.

"I will never fit through one of those windows," Gerald pointed out, gesturing down at his bulky centman body.

"Which leaves the door," Karis said. "But surely that poses no trouble for a young woman of your talents?" she asked Pyrsyfal.

The gnomaid beamed proudly. "Of course not, but..." she gestured beyond the bars.

"But we's still gonna have to deal with them guards," Arthos agreed.

The squad members turned to inspect the guards once more. The six aquatic soldiers were still facing outward, trying to ignore Paladin and Sidekick's heckling. But even so, Karis doubted the Squad could incapacitate more than one or two before the others turned and fought, no doubt calling for reinforcements from somewhere nearby. And if it came to an actual fight, the Squad was at a serious disadvantage. Not only were they unarmed and unarmored, they needed to avoid smoking any of the soldiers who would become their allies once Arthos proved himself King. Arthos planned to send the armies of Caymerlot into battle with the luggernauts as soon as possible, and the last thing he needed was soldiers thinking their new ruler didn't value their lives.

"If Hembrose were here," Pyrsyfal mused, "he could dazzle zee guards wiz his hypnosis. Make zem open zee door without anyone getting hurt."

Karis frowned. "He can do that?" She released a careful breath. "Perhaps better the Wizard's not here, then. Some measures are not worth their cost, no matter what they gain us in the short term. And mind control does not seem an appropriate tool for a servant of the Sovereign."

Arthos and Pyrsyfal shared a troubled look.

The Sergeant-at-arms came back into view then, checking on his men before slithering up to the barred door. He grasped the iron bars with several of his tentacles and peered within the cell. "How is everyone holding up?"

"You call these accommodations?!" Sidekick began haranguing the newcomer instantly. "They certainly fall short in *my* estimation!"

"I do apologize," Sarge responded, sounding like he actually meant it. "This is a nothing more than a temporary holding cell, really, for use whenever the crowds get rowdy at one of the Underlord's speeches. You must know we have little true crime in Caymerlot. This is a utopia, after all."

"Oh?" Paladin asked with a toss of his maned head. "So you don't plan on holding us very long either?"

"If you do," Sidekick continued, "the least you could do is bring some libations!"

The Sergeant sighed. "I confess I don't know what the Underlord plans to do with you."

Paladin snorted. "You realize we didn't have to surrender. We could've laid waste to your soldiers, if not for the new King's mercy. The Squad of Heroes has faced far worse odds and still lived to tell the tale."

"That seems... unlikely." Sarge gave a skeptical smile.

"You said you'd heard of this Squad's famous deeds?" Sidekick asked loudly. "Both the heroes with two legs as well as their steeds?" He shook his mohawked head. "What we achieved on Huland—it *proves* we're too much to withstand. You must know by now, all expectations we exceed!"

The karkman officer sighed patiently. "Fine, I'll ask. What exactly did you achieve on Hulandia?"

"We faced down thousands of lugs with just the seven of us!" Paladin said proudly. "That was before the Bodyguard and Ringmaster joined the team, you understand. Two—no, let's say *three* thousand foes, and we lost not a single man... or, um, woman. It was fifty-to-one odds, I tell you."

Sarge threw back his head and laughed. "You may indeed be a mighty warrior, eqman, but math is clearly not your strong suit."

"Fine," Paladin blustered. "So maybe it was only a thousand lugs. But they outnumbered us at least a hundred to one, I'm telling you."

"This tall tale—and your arithmetic—grow less impressive by the moment."

Gerald splashed forward impatiently. "Then let me give it to you straight, kark. The seven of us were caught between two separate armies led by the Khan and the Ransacker, and none of us had time to stand around counting the enemy, be they a thousand or a hundred. Suffice it to say, they outnumbered us by a significant margin. Yet we scared them so badly that half their number fled before we lifted hand or hoof. After that, we cut their ranks in half again without suffering a loss—dispatching even their Khan, whom my friend the Knight dueled to a standstill."

He gestured at Karis, who gave a friendly wave from where she still crouched at the back of the cell.

"However many lugs still remained after that, we let go," Gerald finished, "largely because our Squadleader—who has since been anointed *your King*—is simply a generous fellow. Ignore these fools here," he said, waving toward Sidekick and Paladin, "and focus on me. I am Gerald Valorian, the Noble of Centwick, current de facto ruler of Centhule. Do you honestly believe that *I* am exaggerating?"

Sarge looked troubled, but he was saved from needing to answer by a sudden ruckus. The karkman spun on his tentacles as a young nym messenger burst into view, shrieking in terror: "We're under attack! Luggernauts have breached the walls!"

Arthos leapt to his feet. "The lugs is here?" he gasped. "How is that possible?"

"It's *not* possible," Karis answered softly. "The only remaining access to Lugarth is through Northmount on Hulandia, and our rearguard would have reported if a lugman force was on our heels all the way here. That lad must be mistaken."

"No," Arthos whispered, realization dawning. "The Guide *said* another path to Lugarth would make itself known."

By now, the messenger was at the Sergeant's side, and they were holding a frantic but whispered conversation of their own. When they were done, Sarge hurried off after the boy, without another word for the Squad—and he took all but one of the guards with him.

Arthos gaped, goggle-eyed. "Mum's muddy mool! Oy, this changes fings!"

"It certainly does," Pyrsyfal agreed in a whisper, running her hands through her hair and pulling out her little metal toothpicks—the same ones she'd used to free Paladin and other eqmen during the Battle at Bronze City. Apparently, the guards who'd searched the girl had assumed they were hairpins. Stepping up to the barred door, she quickly and quietly twisted the picks in the keyhole, at last disengaging the lock with a soft *click*.

The sole remaining guard, a merman, managed to turn only halfway before Paladin's hoof struck him in the forehead, knocking him out cold. Two minutes after that, all eight current members of the Squad (minus Hembrose) stood outside, while the unconscious guard—now tied and gagged—lay propped in the darkest corner of the cell.

"Now what?" Pyrsyfal demanded.

"We gotta help defend the folk of this city," Arthos said urgently.

"But your majesty—" Karis began.

"You lot gotta stop with this 'sire' and 'majesty' baloney!" Arthos growled.

"Fine, *Arthos*," Karis replied calmly. "But listen to my counsel before rushing off to battle. I know that helping people is where your heart is. But so long as the people of this city reject you as King, you will have only limited effectiveness helping them. You *must* bring them onto your side before you can turn your attention to the lugman invaders."

"And how do ya reckon I should do that in the middle of a luggernaut attack?" Arthos demanded, exasperated.

"By doing exactly what Hembrose recommended all along," Karis said with a sudden grin.

Gerald put a hand over his face. "The world must truly be ending if we're agreeing with the Wizard now," he muttered, drawing a neigh from the Paladin. "But she's right... *he* was right."

"You just need to stroll down to the Amphitheater and lay claim to your new Relic, O King," Karis concluded. "Fortunately, all the soldiers will be distracted by this unexpected lugman attack, so we should face little resistance."

Arthos sighed. "This attack is no good fortune," he said sadly. "But I take your meaning."

Karis turned and placed a hand on Sidekick's shoulder. "Can you lead the way?"

"Can I ever!" the kelpie replied excitedly. "I thought you'd ask... well, never! Have I ever told you you're angelic? Now let's go outside and claim that Relic!"

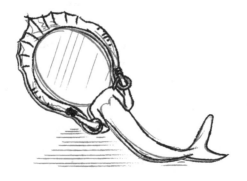

· five ·

The Lady lounged in a window seat of her bed chamber in a high tower of the Crystal Keep, looking out over the city her father ruled and wishing she were allowed to visit it once and a while. For a so-called Lady of the Lake, it was ironic that she hadn't swum in an actual lake since the day her family took up residence in this fortress. On the contrary, she'd been kept a virtual prisoner for over thirteen years now, given the run of the Keep, but forbidden from leaving by Papá's express decree. And as Underlord of Caymerlot, her father's word was literally law.

Not that she had ever tried to escape. She was too conscientious and dutiful to disobey her father lightly. That didn't mean she was always happy with his edicts, however, and this evening she was in especially low spirits.

Thirteen years! There was no celestial rotation or orbit in Overtwixt, of course, which meant no changing seasons by which to measure the passage of time. Time itself was very different here in the world of bridges, often passing more quickly or slowly for one person than another, or on one niland vs. another—and certainly in comparison with the real world, just as Papá's old secretary had said all those years ago. But thirteen years *had* passed for Gwenverity MerGrand. She knew because she kept a detailed diary on the expensive plapyr her father bought her, painstakingly tracking each and every day.

Today marked 4,117 days since their arrival, which meant Gwen had turned nineteen last week—without notice by anyone, since (for obvious reasons) birthdays weren't typically celebrated in Overtwixt. * Still, being nineteen now mattered for exactly one reason: that was the age at which mermaidens legally became merwomen, no longer beholden to the iron will of their fathers in patriarchal merman society.† Gwen wished that didn't matter, that Papá was the kind of man she could continue to honor and obey even after her nineteenth naming day. But he definitely wasn't. Perhaps he never had been.

Sadly, the evidence of this was plentiful. After hearing of his most recent changes to governmental hiring policies—and the fact that they explicitly prevented kelpies from working in most positions of trust—Gwen had finally arrived at a conclusion she'd been nearing for a very long time now:

Papá was a terrible ruler.

And yet, Gwen questioned her own judgment even now. Was she being overly dramatic? She didn't have any friends her own age, but from her reading, she'd learned that young people were often overly emotional or harsh in their

---

* The merman real world of Matron Bex has shorter years than ours, because 4,117 days is barely *twelve* years on Mother Earth. But every real world is different in numerous ways. As another example, the dagman world of Mersch takes thirteen months to orbit its sun. —*N*

† That said, most merpeople would still refer to a young woman as a "mermaiden" until she was married, even after her nineteenth year.

opinion of their own parents. Was that happening here, and if so, how could she know?

Abandoning her window, she swam across the spacious room to her vanity. There, she pushed aside several hairbrushes and other items of beautification to pick up a polished hand-held mirror—but not just any mirror. A *Diamond* mirror.

Say what you would about her father, the Underlord had ensured that every member of his family was bestowed with one of Sovereign's Relics: the Throne of Judgment for himself, this Looking Glass of Clarity for Gwen, the Harpoon of Enforcement for Ander, and the Hauberk of Exoneration for Alber. On the rare occasion someone challenged Papá's claim that the MerGrands were blessed above all other mermen, he just pointed to these Diamond Relics. The Sovereign himself had crafted them in the First Age, making four for each race: one to grant wisdom, another humility, and the last two offensive and defensive capabilities. Nowadays, untold ages later, it was unusual for a race of Overtwixt to know the location of all four of its Relics, since many had been lost to time. But for all four to be known *and* in the hands of a single family? It was unheard of.

Could it be that Papá's dynasty *was* established by the Sovereign? If so, did that mean Gwen was wrong in her assessment of her father? Determining the truth would require setting aside her preconceived notions, examining her Papá from a place of true humility.

Hence the Diamond Looking Glass.

Steeling herself, Gwen looked into that perfect mirror, opening her heart to whatever truth it chose to show her. Her own reflection gazed back: a shy but determined young merwoman with long, wavy brown hair and cocoa-brown eyes. As usual, there were things about her physical appearance she wished she could change, but she didn't waste time preening right now. Instead, she gazed deeper, seeking any imperfections in her character. The Diamond Relic throbbed a brilliant, approving blue, and Gwen recognized that she *was* too quick to condemn her father, that she *did* still owe him respect regardless of her age. Gazing into the Diamond mirror, she was reminded of all the good times with her father in her youth, all the ways in which he had loved and provided for her, even as he himself grieved the loss of Gwen's mother. Papá was far from perfect, but as far as his parenting was concerned, he'd done the best he knew how for many years. Reminded of this by the mirror, Gwen resolved to be more grateful.

But that wasn't all the mirror showed her. Her reflection morphed suddenly into that of 6-year-old Gwen, on the day she arrived in Overtwixt. And looking into those wide brown eyes, present-day Gwen suddenly recalled her family's meeting with the Guide in vivid detail: how the Guide had offered each of the MerGrands a choice of roles, then issued a quest to go with it.

And Papá's quest as Underlord had been to prepare for the coming of the true King. To say he'd failed in this quest was too kind. He had intentionally worked to prevent his own quest's fulfillment, seeking to keep himself in power instead of making way for the one he was supposed to serve. He'd gone so far as to indoctrinate the populace of Caymerlot with a distorted version of the prophecy, one in which a "Hero"—not the King—took up the Relic-in-the-Rock and bowed down to *him*, the Underlord, instead of the other way around. All the while, Papá insisted that he and his two sons keep trying to free the Relic for themselves, as the best possible way of maintaining his position as ultimate ruler.

None of these revelations came as a surprise to Gwen, for the Looking Glass had reminded her of these particular truths before. But the details always faded with time, especially when it came to her own failings. That's why Gwen forced herself to use the Looking Glass often; for though these visions were uncomfortable, she had decided long ago that it was important to keep reminding herself of the truth.

And so Gwen settled her heart and mind, again. Papá was doing wrong, but it wasn't her place to correct him. That was between him, the Guide, and the coming King. But oh, how she longed for the coming of that King! For his arrival would begin the realization of her own quest too.

Gwen got her emotions back under control just in time, for that very moment, her father swept into the room. "Gwenverity," he greeted her formally, though not without fondness. "I missed seeing you at dinner."

"Forgive me, Father, I wasn't feeling well." As soon as the words left her mouth, she flinched visibly. Gwen was a remarkably bad liar, and she knew Papá could read the truth on her face.

"You're upset again," he guessed. "Angry at me for trying to protect you from the world."

She opened her mouth to deny it, then realized how pointless that was. "It's not just that, Papá—"

His face darkened. He didn't like being called that anymore, for he felt it undermined his dignity. Yet another example of how Gwen had lost her remaining parent.

"*Father*," she began again carefully. "This trip to Overtwixt was supposed to be an adventure. Not just for us, but for everyone else who comes here too." She caught herself before commenting on his recent unfair policy decisions, remembering that it wasn't her place. But as for her own adventure: "I've barely seen or done anything since arriving! And it's been even worse since that fiasco with the Wizard—"

"You mean when that scoundrel tried to kidnap you?" Papá asked, a strange gleam in his eye.

"I still don't think he would have harmed me—"

"Oh, so you'd be happy to see him again? Maybe share a meal, consider renewing the betrothal he thought he deserved?"

Gwen felt heat flooding to her cheeks. "I didn't say *that*, Pa—ahem, Father. The Wizard broke his oaths to you, and frankly, he scares me. But my fear of him is no excuse for treating him unfairly, and I honestly believe what happened that night was a big misunderstanding." It had taken her quite a few sessions with the Looking Glass to arrive at this conclusion, but she was finally willing to admit it. "I actually thought he was cute when we first met." She blushed even more. "Then suddenly he was decades older, but still professing his love for me, asking me to run away with him... I, um. I may have overreacted."

"You screamed to bring the entire Crystal Keep down on our heads," Papá said dryly, "and rightfully so."

"It was all a misunderstanding," she repeated. "I was afraid, he was angry, and your men just wanted to protect me. But no one got hurt in the end. That's what matters."

"Be that as it may," Papá said, "I have indeed been extra vigilant since that scoundrel escaped our custody." Even within the Keep, Gwen was now escorted everywhere by two armed guards—even still, half a year after the Wizard's escape! "But perhaps I can finally ease up on your restrictions," Papá concluded casually.

Gwen blinked. "Really?"

Papá's eyes were definitely sparkling. "Sure. After all, we finally caught him. We finally captured the Wizard."

Gwen froze, suddenly re-living the terror of that encounter yet again, as vividly as any of the times she'd peered into the Looking Glass. "What will you do with him?" she whispered.

"Nothing nice," Papá gloated. "Anderbrich wants to string him up by his tail and torture him. He *does* have information we need, after all. Turns out he was traveling in the company of a rebel leader, still making plans to overthrow me, I have no doubt."

Despite her feelings for the Wizard, Gwen's stomach wrenched at the thought of intentionally harming any person—especially knowing that Ander would take pleasure in making it painful. Her middle brother wasn't called the Antagonist for nothing. "Papá, no!" she begged, her eyes filling with tears. "Tell me we won't hurt him."

Papá grimaced at her. "You're too kind-hearted for your own good," he muttered. "The man deserves to be punished for what he did. Actually getting some answers from him during the torture is just an added benefit, if it tells us something new about the dagman."

"Dagman?" Gwen asked in surprise.

"The rebel I mentioned, who leads some Squad," Papá waved his hand dismissively. "Has the audacity to claim he's now King. Don't worry, I'll put him down like all the frauds before."

Gazing into her father's face, Gwen saw no guilt or doubt or hesitation. "Oh, Papá," she whispered. He was so determined to cling to his power that he didn't even consider the possibility that this dagman was indeed King. Or had Papá been lying to others for so long that even he'd forgotten the truth, that a true King was coming?

"What's that?" Papá asked.

"Please don't torture the Wizard," she begged him again. She wasn't even looking at the Diamond mirror in her hand, but it flared a powerful blue, proving she was right to make this request—even on behalf of an enemy.

Papá glanced at the Looking Glass, then turned away quickly, frowning. "No promises. But... I will make sure Albernorm remains in the interrogation room so long as questioning is underway, to keep Anderbrich from doing anything truly drastic." Alber was the Altruist, after all, and had a compassionate heart like Gwen's—much to Papá's chagrin at times.

It was better than nothing. "Thank you, Father."

At that moment, one of Papá's messengers appeared at the door. "My lord the Underlord," he announced awkwardly, "there is a matter of some urgency that requires your attention. I do not wish to dismay the Underlady with the details," he bobbed his head even more awkwardly, "but the Sergeant-at-arms eagerly awaits you below."

"Yes, yes, fine," Papá said. "I will be there shortly," he said as he began moving to the door. He turned to face Gwen one last time before leaving. "But know this, Gwenverity," he added darkly. "I *will* have that fellow—that Wizard—executed. Banished from Overtwixt forever, I tell you! No man breaks his oath to me and lives to tell of it." Then Papá swept from the room once more, moving at a dignified pace despite the messenger's urgency.

Tears broke free and began streaming down Gwen's cheeks. Everything about this situation with the Wizard was wrong; but what hurt most of all was seeing her father's priorities with so much more clarity than ever before. Even half a year later, Papá was still furious with the Wizard for trying to kidnap his daughter. But was it because he cherished that daughter above all else? No, it was because he'd been defied by an underling who should have been bowing and scraping to Papá's authority. Gwen could no longer pretend that she mattered more to her father than his own pride and ambition as Underlord.

The Lady reverently placed the Diamond Looking Glass back on her desk, even though she wanted to throw it across the room. Then she swam to her bed, curled up, and cried in earnest.

She'd had enough clarity for one night.

· six ·

Half an hour following their escape from the dungeon, the Squad arrived at the Crystal Keep's courtyard Amphitheater—to find it was indeed abandoned, though they could hear the clash of weapons not too far in the distance. Arth had never been here himself, though Hembrose had told him all about the quartet of merman guards who typically guarded the Relic-in-the-Rock. Now that he was standing in the perfectly-circular pool of water himself, Arth instantly recognized the little rocky isle with a leather-wrapped Diamond shaft jutting halfway from its surface. But there were no guards to be seen.

Determined to stop wasting time, Arth hurried forward. "Let's get this over with."

"Have some sense of decorum, I implore you," Sidekick told him. "This is the fulfillment of dreams and legends lying before you."

"Ain't no place for dignity and such when people's gettin' hurt," Arth disagreed. He propelled himself urgently across the Amphitheater with powerful strokes of his finned arms and legs, scooping the water with his webbed fingers and toes in the dagman way.

Just before he could reach the small island, however, several big splashes happened in sequence. It was that missing foursome of guards! They hadn't abandoned their post entirely, just climbed atop the nearby wall to get a look at the battle in the city. (*How* a bunch of mermen had climbed all those steps without legs, Arth could only guess. Lots of upper body strength?) Now, they crashed back into the water and quickly blocked the new King's way.

The Squad, in turn, moved to intercept the four mermen. The heroes outnumbered the guards two-to-one, but they were at a disadvantage anyway, since exactly half of them were non-aquatics. Fighting in waist-deep water wasn't something the Knight, Noble, or Paladin were accustomed to doing, and this water rose even higher on Pyrsie. Worse yet, none of the squad members carried their own weapons, armor, or Diamond Relics, only some basic short swords they'd found in an armory along the way.

Meanwhile, the blue-caped mermen they faced weren't just any soldiers. Two of them Arth recognized from before: the Underlord's own sons, who *did* carry Diamond Relics.

"Father proves his wisdom yet again," one of them said, shaking his head ruefully as he smoothed the glowing Diamond chainmail he wore. "He wouldn't let us go into battle. He said staying here and protecting the Relic-in-the-Rock was more important."

"What's there to protect?" Daddie blurted. "If the legend's ackurate, only the true King can pull that Relic from the rock anyway!"

"I'm learning not to question my father's wisdom," the fella in the chainmail said, pulling his sword from its scabbard. His three fellows likewise drew their weapons.

The Squad surged forward, Knight and Noble grimly, Sidekick gleefully. "Don't smoke 'em!" Arth cried out. "We's gonna need these blokes in the fight against them lugs!"

"Smoke *us?*" one of the other mermen scoffed, brandishing his dull Diamond Harpoon. "Don't worry, you won't." He flung the Harpoon with expert precision, straight at the Noble's heart, but the centman chopped it out of the air contemptuously. The merman immediately snapped the weapon back to his hand by jerking on the long rope that connected the weapon to his wrist. He raised the Harpoon shaft just in time to catch a slash from the Knight.

Meanwhile, Pyrsie was clambering up the first fella's back, throwing her hands over his eyes like she'd done to the Khan at the Battle for the Branch Library. Paladin pummeled the merman's chest with his front hooves, but between the protection of the chainmail and all that water getting in the way, it had little effect.

Daddie and Bertie managed to keep one of the other mermen tied up with their desperate attacks, though it was quickly obvious the older dagmen had never trained with swords. And Sidekick had *literally* tied up the last guard, temporarily immobilizing the fella's arms and weapons with his many tentacles.

Arth watched it all in dismay. Outside the walls of the Crystal Keep, innocent people were screaming in terror as they fell to lugman weapons—all while *inside* the Keep, the good guys were fighting each other! He had to end this quickly, before any of the combatants in the Amphitheater got hurt. But every time he tried to slip through the fight to reach the rocky isle, he was rebuffed. It was all Arth could do to avoid getting sucked into one of the duels, and his desperation grew as the minutes passed.

At last, he saw his opening and splashed through, bending backwards at the last moment as the Diamond Harpoon whistled through the air at him. The next instant, Arth was standing atop the isle, one webbed foot to either side as he grasped the leather-wrapped handle of the Relic-in-the-Rock with both hands. The fella with the Harpoon pulled his weapon back to himself and hurled it once more, directly at Arth's heart.

And Arthos Penn, the dagman, pulled the Relic out of the Rock.

Sovereign's Great Relic slid out easily and burst to light with a more brilliant blue glow than Arth had ever seen. And the Harpoon hurtling at his heart *bounced off* that light to splash harmlessly into the water nearby.

All around the little rocky island, the skirmish faltered as every eye turned toward Arth. The four mermen gaped, while Arth's own allies stared with no less amazement. Arth himself lifted the legendary Relic high overhead, staring at it in wonder.

The Diamond Relic was about as long as Arth's arm, its shaft maybe half as thick around. But now that he could see it fully, Arth realized it wasn't just a staff. On one end, previously buried in the Rock, was a large round basket of pure gold—containing *another* Diamond, a perfect Diamond sphere glittering from a thousand facets.

Arth had absolutely no idea what sorta fing it was supposed to be, much less how that big golden basket on the end had slid out of solid rock so easily. Even so, he could feel waves of peace washing over him, emanating from the strange Relic. Somehow he knew, deep within his soul, that all would be well no matter what may come.

Then the merman wearing the chainmail was splashing forward, the glow of his own Diamond Relic somehow muted next to Arth's new Relic. The merman knelt at the foot of the Rock, grounding the tip of his sword. "Forgive me, your majesty. I was wrong to oppose you. Clearly my father was mistaken as well—"

"The Underlord weren't mistaken," Arth disagreed calmly, a simple statement of fact. He *knew*, after all. Somehow, holding this Great Relic in his hand, he understood the truth of many things. And he *knew* the Underlord had not merely been confused about the coming of the King.

The merman struggled to speak. "I am the Altruist," he said finally. He licked his lips, unsure what to say or do now. "I suppose you wish me to swear the oath of fealty? Or... are we to be locked in the dungeon until we can prove ourselves to you?" He gestured at the other three mermen with him.

"Naw," Arth shook his head. "There's no time fer that now. We can work out that sorta fing later."

The fella with the dull Diamond Harpoon spoke up finally. "But brother!" he said, baffled and angry. "You mean to let this dagman walk out of here with the Relic-in-the-

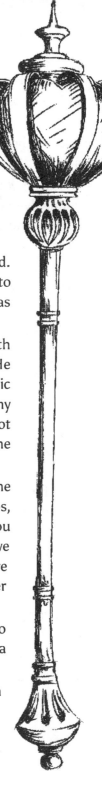

Rock?" He shook his head. "You would betray Father's orders so easily?"

"There is no betrayal here," the Altruist said quietly. "Remember, Father is *Under*lord only. His office exists to support the King."

The younger merman—Antagonist, Arth remembered suddenly—scoffed. "This man is no King! He's a rebel, a traitor who never should have been allowed to touch the Relic-in-the-Rock!"

"But he did touch it," Altruist said quietly. "And more than that, he drew it forth. Ander, look how it glows!"

"At best that makes him the Hero, *answerable* to Father. Or have you forgotten all that Father taught us, Alber?"

The older brother, Altruist, shook his head. "I have not forgotten, Ander. But Father is wrong. In this moment, I can feel that truth through my own Relic, which throbs in harmony with the one this man now wields." And indeed, the Altruist's Diamond chainmail was glowing brighter by the moment. "Truth resounds with truth, and I can no longer doubt that the Relic-in-the-Rock is the greatest of all Relics, and the man who wields it great as well—certainly a better man than Father, no matter my love or loyalty to him."

The Antagonist was unconvinced, yet clearly torn between his love for his brother and his loyalty to his father. "I cannot simply abandon all I've been taught." He flexed his Harpoon, moving as if to confront the Altruist. "I *must* do what is right, setting myself in opposition to all that is wrong, even if that means facing down a member of my own family."

He spoke with such conviction, and as he did so, a wondrous thing occurred. A flicker of blue light swirled up within the Diamond Harpoon, even as an expression of wonder spread across the Antagonist's face.

"You sense the truth now too, don't you, Ander?" Altruist said. "*This* is your King. You need no further evidence than the Relic he holds in his hand. You and I know better than anyone that no one has ever proven worthy to wield the Relic-in-the-Rock. Until now."

"You're right," the Antagonist whispered hoarsely, rubbing his face in horror. "How could I forget the Guide's warning to me? How could I set myself in opposition to the very man I was meant to defend?"

"We have both grown jaded under Father's leadership," Altruist admitted. "But when we commit ourselves to doing right no matter the consequences, the truth will make itself known to us."

Throughout this entire confrontation, Arth had remained quiet, not moving except to wave off any intervention by members of the Squad. Through the confidence granted by the Relic in his hand, Arth knew these two merman brothers would indeed arrive at the truth if given the time to work through it together. And somehow, Arth also knew that he would need these men in the days to come, so he gave them that time. "Oy, so we's hunky dory now?" he asked finally.

The Antagonist licked his lips and slowly nodded, lowering the Harpoon that now flickered gently in his hand.

"Good," Lady Karis said with a grin, lowering her own borrowed sword. "I'm truly glad I didn't have to smoke this one. He's more than a little talented with that Harpoon, and easy on the eyes as well."

The Underlord's younger son blushed furiously, a rich berry-red bloom across his dark skin.

"Now that *that's* settled," Arth said, "can we go back to fighting the real enemy?" He still felt waves of peace emanating from his new Diamond Relic, but that didn't mean all was right in the world quite yet. If anything, Arth felt more determined than ever to *make* things right. "You two," he called to the other two merman guards, "go find that Sergeant bloke and tell him I need his report. He prolly has the best idea what's goin' on with the larger battle."

The mermen saluted—saluted!—and hurried away, blue capes billowing behind them.

"Altruist, you's with me," Arth said. "As fer you," he told the Antagonist, "go release the Wizard at once. We's gonna need him."

The Antagonist's expression instantly soured, and he found his confidence again, if only for a moment. "On that point, we'll have to disagree. Do you have any idea what he..." The fella trailed off, his eyes going wide at the anger spreading across Arth's face. "What I mean to say is *yes*—yes of course, your majesty. Right away!" And he hurried away as well.

Arth gazed across the faces of his squad members. "We's off to fight the good fight, mates, to protect the innercent from injustice. With the Altruist at our side, maybe the people of the city will finally see us for true, as their allies through-and-through." Sidekick nodded approvingly at the unintentional rhyme as Arth swung into the kelpie's saddle. "But even so, ain't gonna be many citizens fightin' back. Even some of our own soldiers is gonna break and run, fer they ain't never faced a luggernaut in the flesh. So I reckon these odds maybe *is* the worst we's ever faced, and no lie. It is what it is. Watch each other's backs and stand firm, no matter what comes." Sidekick reared dramatically beneath him. "Now ride!" Arth cried. "Ride!"

· seven ·

The Squad of Heroes (minus its Wizard, plus the Altruist) rode out the front gate of the Crystal Keep, leaving the Amphitheater and entering the broad canal that ran through City-center. It had been a long, sleepless night in that dungeon, and the Sky Light was just turning toward day high above, signaling dawn in this part of Overtwixt. Now, if they could only figure out where to go from here... for despite the fact that there was a full-scale invasion underway, Crystal City was one of the largest metropolises in all of Overtwixt. They could probably spend an hour just trying to find the nearest band of luggernauts.

Pyrsie saw Arth turn to the Altruist, preparing to ask for directions—just as one of Caymerlot's tallest, most elegant towers collapsed in an explosion of glass shards a mere two blocks away. The dawn light glittered with deadly beauty off the millions of shattered fragments as they showered down. Transfixed at the sight, it was a moment before Pyrsie realized the danger it posed even this far away. "Look out!" she cried.

The building's downfall caused the surface of the water to swell in all directions, sending a wave rushing across the city's network of canals in an ever-expanding circle. The surge of water crashed through the Squad, momentarily submerging the aquatic team members in the canal, and even knocking Paladin and Pyrsie off the grassy sidewalk and into the water also.

Sputtering, Pyrsie pulled herself from the watery thoroughfare, then helped Paladin climb back onto the sidewalk too. "How did *zat* happen?" she demanded.

Before anyone could answer, screams of pain and horror reached their ears from the direction of the collapse—and another glass spire began shuddering nearby.

"Squad, advance!" Arth commanded, and they all hurried forward.

The lugman invaders were behind the destruction, of course. The barbarians were choosing buildings accessible by sidewalk (not all of them were), then surrounding them and landing powerful blows on the structural glass with swords, clubs, and other weapons. It reminded Pyrsie exactly of how a team of woodsmen might chop down a tree. Except there had to be *twenty* of the monsters "chopping down" this next building. Not even magically-enhanced, industrial-strength glass could withstand so much intentional punishment for long.

Oddly, in all the times Pyrsie had faced the lugs in battle, she had never seen so many of them working together towards a single purpose. Sure, there were plenty of other individual lugs in sight, rampaging at random through the city streets, turning some citizens to yellow smoke and sending others fleeing in terror before them. But something about these twenty, all working together, was scarier by far.

"There's still people in that building!" Arth cried out as the Squad approached the endangered spire.

"We must help them," the Altruist begged. "Anything we can do, we mustn't abandon them!"

The Squad needed no more encouragement or orders than that. The eight of them joined Altruist as he rushed forward and fell upon the much larger luggernauts from behind. Catching them by surprise, they managed to defeat half the enemy number before the other lugs realized what was happening. And to Pyrsie's relief, the remaining barbarians fell back to normal habits when they finally turned to fight, showing no more coordination than usual. The Squad, which had developed *great* coordination and experience fighting the lugmen these past months, made short work of the monsters.

"Evakkiate them people!" Arth ordered the Altruist. "We need to get everyone below water, pref'ably on the other side of the city from the lugs." He turned in a quick, confused circle, trying to get his bearings, but he clearly wasn't familiar with this part of the city. "What direction's they comin' from anyway?"

Altruist had already moved to the sea level entrance of the damaged building, which was swaying but somehow still upright. Waving his arms urgently for the building's inhabitants to exit, the merman shouted an answer back to Arth. "Early reports suggested the invasion began from the north. Probably the northwest gate, if I had to guess."

The other squad members spread out, Knight and Noble engaging some of the individual lugman marauders who remained in the area, while Pyrsie, Paladin, and Sidekick relayed Arth's orders to the crowd as they exited: "Find safety in the depths. Move south at all speed." Arth's family members, Ringmaster and Bodyguard, kept close to the new King, watching his back.

More than a few refugees ignored the Squad, however, clustering around the Altruist and begging for help or explanations. Some of the aquatics even threw their arms around the merman, blubbering with gratitude for saving them. "What's that all about?" Paladin huffed. "I deserve at least as much thanks for their rescue."

"He is known to zem," Pyrsie said. "A friendly face, and local royalty, you know—son of zee Underlord, their ruler."

"Not ruler anymore, he's not," Sidekick said with a snort. "Besides, the Underlord's rule was never worth a lot."

"Maybe zat's true," Pyrsie told the kelpie quietly, "but zee Altruist seems like a good guy, and he is our ally now. Maybe you should keep such thoughts to yourself when he is around?"

Sidekick snorted again, but he went back to directing refugees without any further snide remarks.

"Pyrsyfal?" a voice called. "Pyrsyfal Rochelle?"

Pyrsie whirled, shocked to hear someone shouting her real name. Among all the caymen, nyms, and other aquatics splashing from the building, a single *gnoman* was clambering out of the water to race toward her.

"Alain d'Creux?" she blurted, completely astonished to be facing the man who first escorted her into Overtwixt almost two years prior.

"It *is* you!" the gentleman adventurer cried delightedly. "You and your friends saved me," he gushed, gesturing toward the damaged glass spire he had just escaped. "I watched zee whole fight from my hotel balcony. When did you learn to fight like zis, leettle Pyrsie?"

"Oh! Well..." Pyrsie shuffled her feet on the sidewalk grass. In truth, she was the least talented of the Squad's fighters. Hers was more of a support role, helping with gear and innovations, and of course using the Grail to heal injuries—which she couldn't do right now, since all the Squad's Relics and gear had been confiscated. Still, feeling d'Creux's grateful eyes upon her, she gave a little twirl of her borrowed short sword and tried not to blush too brightly.

"You have become zee true adventurer! Far more so than me," the older gnoman added, sounding only a little bitter. "And who are these friends of yours?"

"We are the Heroes of the Brown Stable," Sidekick began, "who once were Bound but Able—"

"*You* are the Heroes of the Brown Stable!?" d'Creux exclaimed.

"You've heard of us?" Paladin asked, sounding pleased.

"Of course! Zee news, it travels fast."

"Enough of all zat," Pyrsie said, though she couldn't help smiling proudly too. "What are *you* doing here?" she asked the chevalier, even as she continued pointing other refugees toward the safer canals leading south.

"Ah, well, you remember zee Guide named me Pilgrim, no? And zee last time you saw me, zee Burrowcrat was sending me off to find my fortune in Centhule or Caymerlot? Well," he said with a grandiose shrug of his little shoulders, "I chose Caymerlot, on account of zat legend of zee Scepter-in-zee-Stone."

This brought Pyrsie's attention fully onto the little man once more. "Wait, what was zat? Did you say *Scepter*-in-zee-*Stone?*" She glanced at Arth and the Diamond Relic he now carried, which none of them knew anything about. Yes, Pyrsie decided, that strange shaft with the big basket on the end probably *was* a scepter.

Before d'Creux could answer her, a sudden bellow from nearby warned them of a charging lugman, moments before the brute appeared around a nearby corner. The gnoman Pilgrim squeaked in terror and dove behind Pyrsie, but the three squad members reacted smoothly, working well together out of long practice. The Sidekick circled behind the luggernaut, slashing at his heels, while the Paladin reared up and pummeled the big guy in the chest, causing him to trip backwards over the kelpie. By the time the lug hit the ground on his back, Pyrsie was waiting to jab at his unprotected neck, quickly and painlessly sending him back home to his real world.

When d'Creux finally peeked out past his hands (which were covering his face), all that remained was three heroes and a small cloud of yellow smoke. "What—" he began.

"Zee Scepter-in-zee-Stone!" Pyrsie repeated again, drawing the Pilgrim's attention back to what was important. "We must speak of zis. You mean zee Relic-in-zee-Rock?"

"Yes, I suppose zat is what zee locals call it," d'Creux said with a shaky nod. "But in my grand-père's* stories, he always named it zee Scepter-in-zee-Stone. He said zat was its *true* name... and since only we gnomen knew its true name, zat must mean zee Diamond Scepter was meant to be wielded by a gnoman."

Pyrsie just rolled her eyes, even as Sidekick burst into laughter.

"But when I got to Caymerlot," d'Creux went on, "zee guards would not let me even touch zee Relic. I could only look upon it from afar, returning to zee Amphitheater every day to do so, in hopes they would change their mind and let me try to pull it from its stone prison. Zat is why I took lodgings in zis hotel so nearby." The Pilgrim's eyebrows rose as a new thought occurred to him. "Say, in light of zis attack, do you think perhaps the Diamond Scepter is now left unguarded? Maybe I could finally complete my pilgrimage and free it from its stone? I realize I have not seemed a very brave adventurer so far, but wiz zee Diamond Scepter in my hand, surely..."

---

* Just like "père" means father in the gnoman real world (and in France in *our* world), "grand-père" means grandfather. —*N*

He trailed off as first Pyrsie, then Sidekick, then even Paladin each lifted a limb to point Arth's direction. D'Creux turned and looked, and his eyes went wide. "Zee Scepter has already been pulled out of zee Stone!?" he cried. The gnoman sounded disappointed, but also relieved. His shoulders slumped. "I suppose I knew it wouldn't be me. Holding a Relic, zat does not make someone brave. There is too much fear in me to ever be zee true adventurer." He looked up at Pyrsie through suddenly wet eyelashes, once more gazing at her with something like wonder. "Unlike *you*."

Pyrsie thought back to before their situations were reversed, when she had been the one gazing up at Alain d'Creux in childish admiration... and how disappointed she'd felt when he turned out to be such a blowhard. Looking at the chevalier now, she thought he seemed smaller and less impressive than ever. Yet Pyrsie was still grateful for the way he'd rescued her from the orphanage and brought her into Overtwixt. "We all fear," she found herself saying to him. "It is choosing to act, to help others despite zis fear, which makes you brave." She shrugged. "If you never felt fear, zat wouldn't make you brave, just reckless."

The Pilgrim's eyes shone with gratitude at her words.

"What is the meaning of this?!" another voice cried from nearby, and Pyrsie turned to see the Sergeant-at-arms approaching rapidly along the canal, accompanied by the merman guards Arth had sent to find him. "Why have these outlanders been released? I can hardly believe the tall tale these two guards are spreading."

Arth stepped forward to meet the karkman officer. Eyes sparkling mischievously, the dagman King said, "I can explain..." even as he twirled his Diamond Relic—the Scepter—rather casually in one hand. The Relic gave off a regular pulse of brilliant blue light as he did so.

The Sergeant stumbled to a stop, eyes going wide, his tooth-filled mouth lolling open. "Oh," he said simply.

At that moment, the damaged glass spire—the one the Squad had spent the last quarter hour evacuating—exploded as something big whistled through the air and struck it powerfully. "Dive!" Altruist cried, and everybody flung themselves underwater to escape the rain of glass, even Pyrsie and the other non-aquatics. When the wavefront had passed and the rubble had settled, heads began popping up from the surface of the water again.

"Find the lugs that did that—" Arth began to order.

But the Sergeant slapped the water angrily with a mace. "That wasn't lugs," he growled. "That was one of ours, one of the fools manning the ballistae mounted on the roof of the Crystal Keep. Those lads are woefully inexperienced. Can't hit a barn from a hundred paces, unless it's a different barn from the one they're aiming at!"

"Oy," Arth said, a grim smile appearing. "In that case, I know someone who can help." He beckoned to Pyrsie.

The karkman scoffed. "The last thing we need is some outlander scum—"

"Sarge!" Altruist interrupted sharply. "Maybe you haven't put four and four together yet, but this fellow holds Sovereign's Greatest Relic," the merman hissed. "Have no doubt this is your King you now address."

The Sergeant-at-arms paled visibly, but he still wasn't fully convinced. "I can't deny this dagman has freed the Relic-in-the-Rock," he admitted to the merman prince. "But your father, the Underlord... he claims the one who does so will be Hero only, a great champion in time of need, but one who serves and answers to the Underlord nonetheless."

"We've all been confused by different versions of the prophecy," Altruist said quietly. "I love and honor my father, but I no longer agree with the version he proclaims."

With the eyes of the entire Squad upon him, the Sergeant struggled to come up with an answer.

"We ain't got time fer this," Arth reminded them all. "Sarge, I need a sitiation report."

Sarge hesitated, then nodded. "I guess that can't hurt, whether you're King or not." He quickly summarized the state of the battle for Arth, gesturing frequently with his many tentacles, and often pointing multiple directions at once. There were apparently large forces of lugmen rampaging through multiple parts of the city all at once.

At last, Arth raised a hand to stop him. "Pyrsie? Take Paladin and get atop the Keep, show them ballista blokes what's what. Sarge, you best be goin' with her, make sure her orders gets followed. Don't worry, she's the Inventor—she's *ace* with machines and such. Afore you know it, them ballista bolts is gonna be hittin' lugs instead of buildings *or* barns!"

The kark nodded, still looking uncomfortable but not arguing. He couldn't deny how desperately the ballista crews needed help. Pyrsie, grateful for an assignment that played to her strengths, climbed onto Paladin's back and waved for d'Creux to join them. The Pilgrim might not be an engineer himself, but he was still a gnoman. He'd prove helpful calibrating the mechanisms atop the Keep, and he'd certainly be safer there than here.

As the gnomen and Paladin sped after Sarge, back up the canal toward the Crystal Keep they'd just left, Pyrsie heard Arth speaking to the remaining squad members behind her: "As for the rest of yeh's, Sarge says the fighting is worst *that*-a-way! Altruist, mind leadin' the charge?"

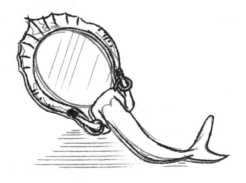

· eight ·

The first light of the new day found Gwen where it often did, in the reading alcove several doors down from the Crystal Keep's feast hall. Even after the Wizard confronted her in this very room half a year prior, it remained her favorite place within the fortress. The vaulted glass ceiling high above (which he'd destroyed in his escape) had finally been repaired; and now that the Wizard himself was in custody, Gwen's remaining uneasiness was gone. She could once again study here for hours without fear.

As pure morning light streamed down from above, Gwen examined the stacks of plapyr scrolls lining the shelves of the alcove's narrow bookcase. Compared to the Hidden Chamber of Merlyn, this collection was quite small, but each of these volumes was precious to Gwen. They had been her most constant companions through the long years of loneliness, and she had read their words over and over again, until she knew many passages by heart. Some of the scrolls contained fictional narratives—one was even a tale of romance!—but most were historical records. After a moment's consideration, Gwen selected one of the latter and carried it to the podium at the center of the small chamber, where she unrolled the plapyr and used stone weights to keep it open. Then she sighed contentedly and began to read.

Like several of the other scrolls on the alcove's shelves, this was a translation of an ancient tome that survived from the First Age of Overtwixt—from the days when the Sovereign himself lived among mortals, speaking with them daily as a person among friends. This particular book contained many of his words as he described the inner workings of Overtwixt and how people were intended to live here. Not for the first time, Gwen found herself wishing she could have lived during that era of history, meeting the Sovereign for herself.

As she read, tracing her finger along the familiar lines, she sang idly under her breath. She loved to sing, and she knew the Crystal Keep's staff loved to *hear* her sing, though this embarrassed her. Gwen was almost painfully shy at times. But floating here alone in her favorite place, she allowed her voice to rise as she sang the words off the plapyr, inventing a melody as she went.

She stopped upon reaching one of her favorite passages. There, nestled into the text, one particular sentence was elaborately inscribed in purple ink to indicate a direct quotation of the Sovereign:

NO ONE RACE IS GREATER THAN ANY OTHER.

Gwen could *feel* the truth of this statement. And yet how different it was from her father's attitude, which reflected the oft-quoted and much more popular sentiment: "The Merman Race is Greater than any other." Obviously, both could not be true. Gwen knew which one she believed, though it put her in the minority among her own people.

The sound of a throat clearing drew Gwen's attention. Floating in the alcove's doorway was one of the two guards tasked with escorting her today, an okkman who was looking quite uneasy. "Um, highness... I'm sorry to leave you alone in the Keep, but we've been called out to join the others."

Gwen was entirely confused. "Called out? What others?"

"All the soldiers of Caymerlot, including the Keep's reserves. Surely your father told you they were being deployed into the city?"

The Lady frowned. At least this explained why the Crystal Keep seemed so empty this morning, aside from a few servants. "No, Father told me nothing. Why have the armies been deployed?"

Her guard looked supremely uncomfortable. "Because we're under attack, my Lady."

Gwen's mouth fell open. Never since her arrival in Overtwixt had Caymerlot come under attack. There'd been that lugman incursion on Karkham almost two years ago now, but that was far from here, and Papá had destroyed their bridge to prevent a repeat. Caymerlot itself had always been safe, a perfect utopia according to her father—not that even this supposed safety had stopped him from hiding her in the Keep all this time.

"It's the luggernauts again, my Lady. They invaded in the night. Breached the city walls near the northwest gate." He shrugged. "We just got word: our defense of the city isn't going well. The enemy has leveled a dozen or more buildings, smoking hundreds and leaving hundreds more displaced. I'm sorry to abandon you," he repeated, "but every able-bodied man is needed for the fight."

Stunned, Gwen had no response for the okkie. After a moment, he saluted her, then turned and swam rapidly down the hall with the other guard.

The first thing Gwen felt was fear, of course, then gratitude that Papá had insisted on keeping her safe in this fortress. He'd been right all along. Even so, Gwen's relief soon gave way to a crushing guilt that she was safe while others were not.

But why should Gwen feel bad about being safe? It wasn't her fault the people of Caymerlot were in danger, and there was nothing she could do to help them... was there? Even if no guards remained in the Keep to prevent her from leaving also, Gwen was expressly prohibited from doing so. The Diamond Looking Glass itself had reminded her—just last night—of the need to respect her father's authority.

And yet, that suddenly felt like an excuse. The people of Caymerlot, her people, were in trouble. Surely there was *something* she could do.

Slowly, her hand drifted to the satchel she wore, in which she kept the Diamond mirror whenever leaving her bed chamber. She should peer into that mirror again. If it reiterated her need to honor and obey Papá, that was the end of it. But if it revealed that some things were more important...

She swallowed. What if the Diamond mirror *did* propel her into action? If she was being honest, she didn't want to leave the safety of this fortress today, though she had longed to do exactly that for the last thirteen years! *Today* there was a rampaging army in the city, and Gwen wasn't brave like her brothers. She didn't want to get hurt.

Clenching her teeth, Gwen shoved her hand into the satchel and snatched out the mirror anyway. Then she gazed into its depths.

Sovereign's Relic glowed brightly, fulfilling its specific purpose as it filled her with humility. She saw instantly that rendering aid to those in dire need outweighed all other considerations in this moment. And in her renewed selflessness, Gwen understood that helping others was well worth the risk to her own life.

Without further hesitation, she swam out the door in the same direction as her two guards.

There was no defiance in her heart, for her purpose was not to disobey her father. But there were people out there in need of leadership. All the soldiers and officers in the city were required to push back the invading army; they couldn't be spared to organize an evacuation of the refugees who were surely fleeing before the lugman advance. Since Gwen herself could not fight, she was one of the few members of the aristocracy who *could* help in this way. She would start by seeking out the refugees displaced by the destruction of their homes, and she would bring them back here, to the safety of the Crystal Keep. Then she would go back out again, and again, and again as necessary, for as long as there were more refugees who needed to be led to safety.

Gwen had lived as royalty in this city for most of her life. The time had come for her to earn it.

· nine ·

Hembrose woke to the sound of explosions and screams, but otherwise he felt remarkably refreshed. Yes, he was still gagged and bound—trussed up tighter than a holiday feast plig, unable to move except to turn his head or wiggle his fingers—but that was still a huge improvement over the *first* hour he'd spent in the Crystal Keep's interrogation room.

When the mermage had first been dragged here (last night?), the Antagonist had fastened a tight iron manacle around his tail and hoisted him mostly out of the water—upside down so that only his head remained submerged. Even for an aquatic, that was a rather miserable position to hold for long; water kept getting up the Wizard's nose, and he had to lift himself by the abs just to get a good breath. All the while, the Antagonist mocked, berated, and hit him.*

"I *knew* you couldn't be trusted," the young merman had said more than once. "You tried to kidnap my sister, and

---

* In case it's not clear, the first part of this chapter takes place immediately after the Wizard's capture in chapter 3. —*N*

now you're helping some rebel dagman steal the Throne? You'll be executed, have no doubt, but father wants to make a public show of it."

Fortunately, the Altruist hadn't allowed his younger brother to abuse Hembrose for long. "If you want to torture the traitor for information, so be it, but *this* serves no purpose. Shall I remove his gag so he can answer questions?"

"Are you kidding? Of course not! There's no telling what vile magic would spew from his mouth if you unplugged it." The Antagonist smirked. "I only mentioned interrogation so Father would let me work him over a little harder. If we actually want questions answered, we should haul in one of his rebel friends—the kelpie, or maybe that little gnoman girl. They look soft."

The Altruist's lips had compressed in displeasure. "You are better than this, brother."

That was when the Antagonist unhooked the chain hoisting Hembrose in the air, causing him to crash down fully into the water and settle to the floor. He still couldn't move or swim, but he'd nodded gratefully at the Altruist.

The fellow's eyes had flashed angrily at that. "I did not intervene on *your* behalf. You are pond scum, oath-breaker. I just don't want my brother lowering himself to your level."

The Wizard's gratitude had turned to rage then, and he almost lashed out, weaving one of the two spells he could manage with fingers alone... but no. He needed to bide his time. He knew now what he hadn't known that first day in Overtwixt, how the green magic didn't always work on people bearing Sovereign's Relics—like Altruist and his chainmail.

So instead, Hembrose had simply lain there on the floor of the interrogation room, gagged and trussed, glaring daggers at the Underlord's two sons. Other guards came and went, some of them bearing the Squad's confiscated gear, others inspecting and cataloguing it, but the Wizard had eyes only for the Antagonist and the Altruist. Eventually, still exhausted by weeks of travel from Centhule, he had fallen asleep.

Now, opening his eyes again, he remarked on how much better he felt—even though the explosions and screams coming from outside were a little distracting. He wasn't sure how long he had slept, precisely, but he could tell it was long enough to recharge his powers.* He felt *strong*.

And better yet, the Underlord's sons had both left in the night. Four guards clustered around a nearby table playing dice—a merman, a nym, a kark, even an okkie—but certainly none of *them* bore a relic. Oh, these men had tried using the Squad's Diamond Relics earlier, but those were all intended for members of other races and didn't work for these fellows. So the artifacts now sat discarded and ignored in the corner.

In other words, these guards were completely unprotected from the green magic.

Smiling tightly behind his gag, Hembrose wiggled his fingers... and the nyman guard rose from the table abruptly, his eyes glowing a sudden bright green. Without hesitation, he swam over to Hembrose and began untying his hands.

---

* Now we've caught up with the events of the previous chapters. —*N*

"Hey, wait!" one of the others cried. "What are you doing?" The kark darted after the nym, intent on stopping him, so Hembrose wove a second layer of magic atop his first... and the kark disappeared, leaving nothing behind except his blue uniform cape. There was no *pop* like happened on land, just a rush of water past the Wizard's ears, as if there was a sudden empty space that needed to be filled.

The last two guards froze, horrified, long enough for the nym to finish untying Hembrose. Then the Wizard brought his arms up high and down violently once more, like he was conducting the finale to a great symphony—and the three remaining guards disappeared too. This brought an even bigger rush of water to fill the space they'd occupied, while their gaming dice sank to the floor amidst fluttering capes.

Ripping the gag from his mouth, Hembrose swam to recover his precious emerald from where it lay amongst the Squad's gear, now throbbing an even brighter green than ever before. He groaned in sweet relief when he held it in his hand again. Acting quickly, the Wizard manifested his golden mantle, so alive with magic that the green embroidery nearly blinded him. There was an abundance of new power now stored within the emerald: enhanced hearing and visual acuity, speed, staying power—all courtesy of those four guards he had just harvested. So delicious, but in a sickly sweet sort of way. Exhaling slowly, the pleasure almost painful, Hembrose tucked the immense emerald into one of the mantle's deep pockets, directly over his heart.

There was a gasp from the door, and Hembrose whirled to behold the Antagonist. "Where are the guards?" the merman asked, eyes wide. "What have you done to them!?" The Harpoon he clutched flickered with a weak blue light.

With a snarl, Hembrose raised his hand to harvest this spoiled brat also.

"Wait!" Antagonist said. "I come on the King's orders."

Hembrose hesitated. "The *King*? Not your father the Underlord?"

The young merman's mouth twisted, but he shook his head. "No, from the King, your dagman companion. I can no longer deny who he is. He freed the Relic-in-the-Rock."

A whole mix of emotions swept through Hembrose, not least of which was jealousy. But he focused on his anger at the hypocrite before him. This infuriating little princeling had helped his father perpetuate the lie of a "Hero" beholden to the Underlord, right up until the moment it became impossible to maintain that lie any longer. And now he expected to switch sides without paying the consequences? Not on the Wizard's watch! Hembrose raised his hand again—

"Stop it!" Antagonist growled. "Don't you think I'd like to fight you too, prove which of us is the better man?" The other merman's eyes smoldered, and whatever feeble glow had been coming from the Harpoon died. "But there's a battle raging outside these walls. The lugmen have invaded, and the King sent me here to free you. We... we need your help repelling the beasts."

Hembrose blinked, opening his ears and noticing again the sounds of explosions and screams from outside. And while there was no masking the hatred in the Antagonist's eyes—hatred for *him*, the Wizard—he could also see desperation, probably concern for his city and its people.

"Where is he?" Hembrose asked. "Where is Arth now?"

"The King? I don't know. North of here, probably."

Hembrose thrust a finger at the pile of gear in the corner. "Get those Relics back to the Squad—"

"I don't answer to you!" the other man scoffed.

Once again, Hembrose almost lashed out, weaving the spell to harvest this aggravating merman lad—except he had a feeling Arth wouldn't appreciate that. For that matter, neither would the Underlady, Hembrose's one true love. Fortunately, he had an even better idea.

With an evil grin, the Wizard unfurled his magical green whips, catching the Antagonist by surprise and trapping his arms. Excellent! As Hembrose had theorized, Sovereign's Relics only seemed to protect their owners when the Diamond was glowing, and this fellow's Harpoon definitely wasn't glowing now. Baring his teeth victoriously, Hembrose flipped the yelping merman upside down and hoisted him out of the water, all using the green whips. Moments later, it was the Antagonist's turn to hang from his tail, arms bound behind him. Now *his* head was underwater as he coughed and sputtered angrily.

Feeling better than he'd felt in a very long time, Hembrose swam back to the corner and collected the Relics belonging to Pyrsie, Karis, and Sidekick—wrapping his magical mantle around them to create a bundle—then swam straight up out of the water. Just as he'd done half a year earlier when fleeing the Lady's reading alcove, he transformed into his hulking drachman body and flew toward the Crystal Keep's clear glass ceiling high above. At the last moment, he wrapped his ratty wings around his face and burst through in a shower of glass shards. Then he flung his wings wide and thrust downward, hurtling himself into the open sky.

"Drachman!" someone screamed in terror, just as before. "It's a drachman! Fire! Fire!"

"Dragon!" cried a second voice in even greater panic, high-pitched and shrill. "I *told* you there were dragons in Overtwixt! Fire! Please, you fools, *fire!* Save me!"

Hembrose spun in midair and gazed down at the roof of the Keep, where karks and nyms scurried about, madly preparing to harm *him*—drawing back on bowstrings, hoisting spears, even turning cranks to rotate the big ballistae to face the Wizard's drachman body. Grinning wickedly, Hembrose prepared to harvest all of these fools as well. At this rate, the Wizard of Merlyn would soon amass so much power he really would be unstoppable.

"Wait!" shouted a more familiar voice. "Hold your fire! If you fire zat ballista, so help me I will fire *you* from zis roof!"

Hembrose located the speaker, a gnomaid. "*Pyrsie?*"

"You better hold back too, Hembrose!" she called up to him, all spunk and spitfire. "Don't think I don't recognize when you have zee bolt of magic up your sleeve. These soldiers are under my protection, do you understand? Don't you dare harm a single one!"

"Are you crazy?" the shrill voice shouted back at her, before Hembrose could respond. The mermage finally identified the speaker as a second gnoman, this one cowering beneath a ballista. "Zat is a DRAGON. Please, leettle Pyrsie, protect me!"

To everyone's surprise, Pyrsie actually began to giggle. Folks relaxed, and the situation quickly de-escalated.

At that moment, Hembrose became aware of a burning smell, and a painful heat that had been slowly building in his chest. Yelping in alarm, he ripped open his beautiful mantle and watched as the Diamond Relics he'd been carrying tumbled free, clattering loudly onto the roof. With an excited cry, Pyrsie darted forward to recover her Grail, offering Hembrose a grateful smile when he finally landed beside her. He quickly morphed into his dagman Whirler persona.

"I've never seen anything like that happen before," he muttered, inspecting himself. Sovereign's Relics had left angry red welts on his chest, and they'd burned several holes

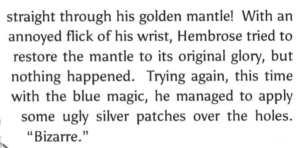

straight through his golden mantle! With an annoyed flick of his wrist, Hembrose tried to restore the mantle to its original glory, but nothing happened. Trying again, this time with the blue magic, he managed to apply some ugly silver patches over the holes. "Bizarre."

Somewhere in the distance, another explosion sounded, and Hembrose caught a glimpse of a building collapsing. Right. There was a battle going on.

Speaking quickly, he and Pyrsie caught each other up on current events, a karkman appearing quietly at the gnomaid's side. Hembrose glossed over what he'd done to the four guards below, but he bragged quite proudly of how he'd left the Antagonist hanging.

"You fool!" the kark growled, and Hembrose belatedly recognized the man as the Sergeant-at-arms. "That is the *Underlord's* son—"

"And I am the *King's* friend," the mermage gloated.

The Sergeant ground his teeth. "I must go free him."

"Zat is fine," Pyrsie told him. "I have zee ballista crews well in hand, thank you." The kark turned to go. "But wait, Sarge. After zat, please deliver these Relics to zee Knight and zee Sidekick." She glanced at Hembrose, then back at the Sergeant again. "You should probably take zat Antagonist guy away wiz you too."

The karkman straightened to his full height, several of the maces he carried twitching irritably. "I am the Sergeant-at-arms," he hissed, full of wounded pride. "And since the moment that dagman pulled the Relic from the Rock, you lot have treated me as nothing more than an errand boy."

Hembrose smiled sweetly. "Just remember, 'that dagman' is *your* King now too."

Taking a deep breath, the Sergeant juggled his maces around, then collected the Diamond Aegis and various pieces of Diamond Plate-Armor from where they lay on the roof. Finally, his tentacles quite full, he slithered away, casting frequent wary looks back over his shoulder at the Wizard.

"I've finally got these fools shooting straight," Pyrsie told Hembrose, turning back to survey the battle again. The little woman unconsciously clasped her arms behind her back like some sort of army commander herself, and Hembrose supposed she really was now. "It was a matter of calibration and range-finding as much as experience. Zee biggest problem now is speed. If we could fire more ballista bolts, we could turn zee tide of zis battle... but it takes so long to reload each time!" She turned to Hembrose again. "Do you think there is anyzing you can do to help?"

The Wizard smiled and nodded, then began to weave.

Soon enough, the entire roof of the Crystal Keep was contained within an immense time bubble, the largest Hembrose had ever conjured. For Pyrsie and her soldiers, time now traveled much faster here than it did for the city outside. Not only did that make the clusters of lugman marauders easier to hit (for they seemed to move quite slowly now), it also meant the ballista crews—still reloading their weapons with the same old slowness inside the bubble—launched up to ten bolts per minute into the outside world. Even better, something about the time distortion also affected the *speed* of those bolts in air, causing them to strike their targets with greater force than ever before.

And through it all, Hembrose laughed with joy at the sheer power now available to him. He had slowed time for the entire roof of the Crystal Keep—which was quite large—and he barely felt the drain. He could expend magic like this for days, maybe even weeks without depleting his power. If it weren't for the terrible headache he knew would eventually come, he might not ever have to stop.

Of course, Pyrsie's crews *did* have to stop firing eventually, for the simple reason that they ran out of ballista bolts—after launching their very last volley at a force of lugmen preparing to attack Arth himself. Once that final volley was away, Hembrose dropped the bubble and joined in the soldiers' victorious cheering, leaning over the edge of the roof to jeer at the few lugmen remaining in sight. There was yellow smoke clinging to the ground in countless places throughout the war-torn city.

Only then did the Wizard's enhanced senses detect a distinctive, piercing scream from far off—a scream he would recognize anywhere.

It was the call of the Siren.

The Lady of the Lake was in trouble.

· ten ·

The King moved from one skirmish to another, fighting and issuing orders from his perch atop the Sidekick's back. It wasn't the most comfortable seat; he was forced to ride bareback, since all of the Squad's gear was somewhere back in the Keep, but he made do.

The Knight and Noble were never far behind, though they did tend to lag, unable to move as quickly as the kelpie over marshy or submerged terrain. Daddie and Uncle Bertie kept up more easily and ensured someone was always watching Arth's back. The newest member of their party—the Altruist—continued to lead the group of them farther and farther north, as he was most familiar with Caymerlot.

Though the buildings grew shorter and less elaborate the closer they drew to Crystal City's outer wall, the evidence of lugman violence and atrocities only grew more common. The luggernauts were everywhere here, tearing down buildings and wantonly attacking any citizen foolish enough to be in the canal streets. Not a minute went by without a fresh bellow of "Bah-le-le-le-leeeee-i-oo-uuuu" from somewhere nearby.

Fortunately, even here, few of the lugs coordinated their attacks when it came to the actual fighting. Oh, they banded together often enough, but as usual they failed to *work* together—which had always been the Squad's major advantage over them. They only showed that kind of cooperation when "chopping down" one of Caymerlot's exquisite glass spires... usually the one that still had the most people inside.

True to his name, the Altruist repeatedly threw himself into the worst danger to help the people of his city, with no thought for his own safety; but then, so did the remaining members of the Squad. All in all, the Underlord's eldest son was proving a good candidate for the team. And how *did* he know the outskirts of the city so well, anyway? When asked, he admitted that he made regular trips to the poorer parts of Caymerlot to distribute food and supplies. He called his efforts "mermanitarian aid" for reasons that escaped Arth.

Meanwhile, Arth himself fought a constant urge to be sick at all the pain and suffering around him. His new Diamond Relic helped with this, soothing him with those waves of peace it constantly exuded. The Relic reminded him that all would be well... while somehow still leaving him with a great sense of urgency. All *would* be well, but it was up to Arth to make it so.

Picking their way down yet another canal street—this one deserted—the King and his friends followed the sounds of combat. Rounding the corner, they were met with a scene out of nightmare: seven luggernauts mingled with countless aquatics trying to flee through a small intersection, amid screams and lugman roars of challenge. In other words, it was a complete free-for-all, in typical lugman fashion—utter confusion. Even some of the aquatics had found weapons and were swinging them wildly, though they were just normal people, not wearing the blue capes of the Underlord's guards. If Arth hadn't already known that the giant lugmen were the bad guys in this war, he wouldn't have been able to tell who was fighting whom.

With a bellow of his own, the new King waded into battle, targeting the nearest luggernaut. Mounted on Sidekick, he was just tall enough to reach the lugman's chest with the short sword he'd borrowed from the Crystal Keep armory. The big fella even saw Arth coming, but he only threw back his head and laughed—right before Arth turned him to yellow smoke. Even now, most lugs had never seen anyone mount an effective defense against them, and that made them think they really were invincible.

They definitely weren't.

Leaning out from Sidekick as they gallop-slithered past, Arth caught the lugman's big spear as it fell through the sudden mist. "Noble!" he shouted, turning and lobbing it (butt end first) through the air to his friend.

As usual, the centman had fallen behind a short distance, but he was still close enough to pluck the spear from the air with deft hands. Immediately he spun the weapon around and prepared to hurl it again. "Duck, sire!"

Arth complied without hesitation, flattening himself against Sidekick's neck. Moments later, the spear whistled through the air just over the dagman's hunched shoulders, taking out another lug he hadn't even seen coming. "Oopsy," he said shoopisly. "Thanks, mate."

Daddie and Bertie, who *had* seen that luggernaut coming—and had placed themselves between him and Arth—grimly added their own thanks. Noble only had time for a quick salute, fist to chest, before he was engaged in another four-way duel: holding back one lug attacker on his right side while the Knight, mounted on his back, locked swords with another barbarian to their left. As she'd been doing all day, Karis fought brilliantly but conservatively, extra careful since she wasn't protected by the Diamond Plate-Armor she normally wore.

"We gotta get back our Relics," Sidekick muttered. "Either that, or hire ourselves some medics!"

Arth grunted in agreement, nudging his friend toward where another lug had cornered a school of kelpmen in a dead-end alley. The big fella was booming with laughter at the kelpies' distress, the sound echoing maniacally in the alley's tight confines.

"Say, what all does *your* new Relic do?" Sidekick asked. "Whatever it is, I bet it's really cool!"

"Aye, mate, let's find out."

The luggernaut who was tormenting the kelpies wore overlapping pieces of mismatched leather armor, a little like the old Khan's, though less imposing. Re-sheathing his sword (which would be less effective against any kind of armor), Arth swung the Diamond Relic with two hands, using all of his strength. He struck the lug right in the middle of his back, meaning only to distract the big fella from his prey. To Arth's surprise, despite its lack of sharp edge or point, the Relic pulsed a brilliant blue and banished the lug from Overtwixt in an instant yellow mist.

Arth gaped. Then, shaking himself, he took a quick look around to confirm there was no other immediate danger. By now, only two lugs remained—one of them dueling Karis, the other being tag-teamed by Noble and Altruist. That fighting was on the other side of the intersection, with Daddie and Bertie more than able to step in if it drifted this direction. Turning back to the alley, Arth found the kelpies staring at him and Sidekick in wonder.

"Like something out of a faery tale," one whispered.

"But a dagman?" another whispered back.

"And a *kelpie?*"

"They fight like veterans, though. Like the Hero himself is supposed to fight!"

Sidekick grinned. "It gets better than that, and here's the thing." He gestured toward Arth with the tip of one tentacle. "This guy ain't just some brat; he's the new King!"

This was met with stunned silence, and then the kelpmen began cheering excitedly. Within moments, they were demanding to join Arth's Squad, even though moments earlier, they had been scared stiff at the sight of a single lug.

Daddie put a hand on Arth's shoulder before he could decline the offer. "Bertie and me could watch yer back even better, sire, if we had steeds of our own."

Instantly, about twenty tentacles were thrust in the air. "Me! Me! Pick me!"

Arth felt a sudden spike of alarm, a brief interruption in the waves of peace coming from his Diamond Relic. He turned and instinctively raised the Relic, which pulsed with another bright strobe of light. Only by that blue glow did he see the dagger flying through the air toward his chest.

The dagger bounced off the Relic's light to clatter away harmlessly, as if the light itself had substance. So strange, like how the Antagonist's Harpoon had been rebuffed in the Amphitheater earlier, or the lugman Ransacker's crossbow bolt months prior, before Arth even *held* a Relic... but he had no time to think about that now.

"Oy," he cried out. "Who threw that?"

Nearby, a sour-looking karkman froze, thrusting all his free tentacles behind his back and looking guilty.

"Calamity, mate! Don't ya know I'm on *yer* side? Me and my Squad just saved you lot!"

The kark snorted. "And where were you when the lugs attacked Karkham? The Underlord is on no one's side but his own. You jerks who serve him are no better."

"Listen here, ya cheeky goob," Dad said angrily. "We ain't servants of the Underlord. We's sworn to the new King!"

This surprised the kark, whose eyes went wide. "King?"

Daddie and Bertie pointed toward Arth, as did Sidekick and the rest of the kelpies. Knight and Noble and Altruist, having dispatched the last two lugs, approached and positioned themselves at Arth's back. The other aquatics who had taken up arms gathered around nervously, clearly sensing some sort of confrontation, but Arth just met the sour kark's eyes steadily. He didn't know what exactly he was waiting for. An apology, maybe? It had surely been an honest mistake, after all. But the kark just licked his lips nervously, idly tugging at a red kerchief tied around one tentacle.

He was saved from responding by the sudden appearance of more luggernauts. There were about eleven this time, loping into view and whooping crazily, forced to cluster together in a tight knot thanks to the narrowness of the sidewalk on which they traveled.

"Squad!" Arth commanded, reacting fast. "Surround 'em, keep 'em bunched up. Knight and Noble to the front, Altruist and Sidekick harrying from the water. Us dagsters will circle around behind and—"

Before he could say more, something big whistled through the air nearby, moving too fast for him to see what it was. With a *thwack-thwack-thunk*, whatever it was struck the bunched group of lugs, sending up an instant billow of yellow smoke. Karis and Daddie and Bertie charged forward, finishing off the three lugs who staggered out of the cloud on hands and knees, but that was it. When the smoke finally cleared, there was nothing left of the other lugmen, just three ballista bolts—*three* of 'em!—buried halfway into the ground where the lugs had been.

"Holey anemone," Arth whispered in awe. Way off in the distance, from the direction of the Crystal Keep, he thought he heard the sounds of cheering.

"Turns out you were right," a voice called. "That wee little friend of yours... the Inventor?... she whipped the ballista crews into shape... double-time. Now they're hitting lugs... instead of buildings or barns... just as you promised."

Arth turned to regard the Sergeant-at-arms, who was now floating in the middle of the intersection with them, tentacles on knees. The Antagonist was in similar shape beside him, both men clearly out of breath from racing to find the Squad. Sarge gestured, drawing all eyes to the shallow water at his "feet," where numerous items glowed blue.

"My Relic!" Sidekick squealed in delight. He raced forward to seize his Diamond Aegis and immediately strapped the little shield to his chest. The Knight seemed no less pleased as she waded into the water and recovered her glowing sabatons and greaves, then began pulling them onto her feet and legs.* The Noble fished out his spear and Karis's curving swords too. It seemed the Sergeant and Antagonist had managed to carry a lot of the Squad's gear, not just the Diamond Relics.

"Thanks, Sarge," Arth told his tentative new kark ally. "Them'll come in handy, sure and certain." Suddenly, he remembered that other kark he'd been speaking with just moments before, and he looked around quickly. But that bloke (as well as the other aquatics who'd taken up arms)

---

* Some of Sovereign's Relics come as a set that includes multiple pieces, including the Knight's Plate-Armor (20+ Diamond pieces), the Altruist's Hauberk (shirt, hood, and gloves consisting of many overlapping Diamond disks), and even the Sidekick's Aegis (which had Diamond chains so it could be worn/used a variety of ways). —*N*

had disappeared into the confused mass of refugees still streaming through the intersection. "How goes the larger battle?" Arth asked, turning back to the Sergeant. "Anyfing new to report?"

Sarge shook his head. "I don't really know." His mouth twisted a little. "Your foul friend the Wizard sent me off on this errand as soon as the Inventor was settled."

Arth perked up. "So Hembrose is free?" He smiled with appreciation at the Antagonist, whom he'd sent to accomplish exactly that. "Hot bog, that's good to hear, it is."

The very ground beneath their feet rumbled suddenly, followed moments later by a whole series of smaller waves. It took a while for everyone to find their balance again. "That can't be good," Karis muttered.

"Arth!" cried a familiar voice, moments before Hembrose himself swooped into view, wearing his flying drachman body.

Arth grinned, even more delighted to see for himself that his oldest friend was safe and sound, though Sarge and Antagonist glared daggers at the mermage. "Hembrose the Wizard!" he greeted the fella warmly. "Greatest magickal practicalishioner in all the history of O'ertwixt!"

But Hembrose wasn't smiling. He didn't even bother landing, just kept his ratty wings flapping as he pointed a muscular arm toward the northwest. "Major collapse in that part of the city. Dozens of buildings down, and many more lugs on the way. I saw it all on my way here." Of course he would have a better vantage from that high in the sky.

"What?!" Antagonist cried in dismay. "That's where Father was fighting, along with the bulk of our army!"

"'Tis true," the Sergeant-at-arms confirmed.

"Please, we have to go save him," Altruist begged Arth.

"Of course—" Arth began to agree, but Daddie sidled up and whispered in his ear. "You sure about that, lad? That fella ain't no ally of yers... and if ya let him perish, sure an' true, it'll make yer own climb to the Throne a heck of a lot smoother." Daddie's new kelpie mount nodded emphatically, and even Sidekick gave a grim toss of his mohawked head, signaling agreement.

They made a very good point, and Arth found that he *was* severely tempted. By most accounts, that Underlord bloke had been an awful leader, fostering an environment of elitism in what was supposed to be a utopian society. He hadn't protected his people following the first lugman attack, nor prepared for the *next* lugman attack, nor warned his allies in Centhule of the risk *they* faced of lugman attack. He'd mistreated Hembrose, and he'd imprisoned Arth without cause the moment he arrived here. And even if none of that was true, Arth really didn't owe the man a fing.

But as Arth's eyes passed over the stricken faces of Altruist and Antagonist, he knew he couldn't just leave their father to his fate. Arth may not owe Caymerlot's old ruler anything, but he did want to show loyalty to these new allies, in order to earn their loyalty in turn. Besides, if the Underlord had led the bulk of the army to that part of the city, then the old merman ruler wasn't the only one in danger. Arth couldn't doom all those people to slaughter just because it made his life easier in the future.

"Lead the way," the new King called to the Altruist, who heaved a sigh of relief.

"Hey!" Antagonist cried angrily. "Where do you think *you're* going, coward?"

Everyone turned to look at the great drachman shape of the Wizard, which had turned to fly the other direction entirely. In response, Hembrose scowled. "I go to save your sister the Lady, you buffoon."

Both the merman brothers went pale in the face. "But she's safe in the Keep," Altruist insisted.

Hembrose only shook his head.

Arth began snapping orders. "Altruist, stick with me so we can help yer daddie. Antagonist, you and Wizard go rescue your sister—"

Immediately, all three mermen (including the one currently in the body of a drachman) began arguing.

"Shut yer traps!" Arth bellowed, silencing the men. "We ain't got *time* fer this. You gots yer orders, now go!" And thankfully, both the Wizard and the Antagonist sped away... though without speaking, each instead pretending that the other was not there. Arth sighed.

"Say," Sarge asked tentatively, "Now that I'm here, you mind if I stick with you lot and do some actual fighting? I'm eager to maim a few lugs." He twirled four of his maces in a complex interweaving pattern that would have left any dagman juggler envious.

Arth couldn't even force a smile. "Youbetcha, boyo. Now, Altruist, fer the love of yer semi-royal daddie... Lead the way, and please hurry."

· eleven ·

Pyrsie squeezed one eye shut and watched through her new spyglass as the Squad set out once more, moving west, while Hembrose and Antagonist headed the other direction. Gnomen had invented spyglasses over a hundred years ago in their real world, though no one used them in Overtwixt so far as Pyrsie had seen. What Overtwixt did have was *eye*glasses—fashioned only by skilled merman glass-grinders—whose lenses Pyrsie could repurpose for use within a tube. In this configuration, the lenses allowed her to "spy" on things happening far away, but see them as if they happened much closer.

There were only three men on the ballista crews who normally wore corrective lenses, which may or may not have contributed to their lack of accuracy earlier. Upon taking charge, Pyrsie had delightedly converted the three men's spectacles into spyglasses and appointed a spotter on each crew—someone who could use one of the makeshift telescopes for choosing targets and estimating distances.

Now, with all the ballista ammunition spent, Pyrsie had re-commandeered one of the contraptions for her own use.

Unfortunately, watching the battle from afar was the only thing she could do at the moment. Pointing her spyglass toward the huge section of city that had just collapsed, Pyrsie frowned. She hadn't seen what caused it; one moment those buildings were standing, the next they were falling like dominoes in a sort of chain reaction. Looking now, she could tell there were still many blue-caped Caymerlotions alive in the area, picking themselves up from the rubble; but that might not last, as there was also a large force of lugmen converging upon them.

Pyrsie frowned, annoyed that she sometimes had trouble distinguishing which objects were closer and which were farther away through the spyglass. Amidst all the mounds of rubble, she wasn't always sure what she was looking at. What she needed was depth perception...

"Foreman," she snapped, naming one of the ballista crew chiefs, a nym who stood at her side looking through his own spyglass. "Hand me your glass."

"Yes, ma'am!" he complied at once, surrendering his spyglass even though she already had one of her own. He and all the rest of the crewmen were now very loyal to her.

Pyrsie held the tubes up together and looked through both at the same time. Ah, much better! Using both eyes, she had a better sense of distance and what was closer or farther away. Just like that, she had improved on one of the most profound inventions of the modern age! But to distinguish this new version from one-eyed spyglasses, she would need to call her innovation something fresh and different: "*duo*glasses," perhaps, or "binopticals." * Now if she could just design a mechanism for adjusting focus without manually twisting the tubes...

---

* I'm rather fond of the term "binoculars," personally. —*N*

Still looking through the doubled spyglasses, the gnomaid Inventor returned her gaze to the intersection Arth just left. She'd kept an eye on her friend all morning, making sure no big groups of lugmen snuck up on him. Not that she'd needed to watch constantly; from Pyrsie's perspective within Hembrose's time bubble, Arth and everyone else had seemed to move in slow motion, so she only checked on him occasionally. But she'd been watching when Arth smoked a lugman with his new Diamond Relic, then used the same Relic to deflect the knife thrown by that karkman. Very suspicious behavior on the part of the kark, but also strange behavior for the Diamond Scepter. A scepter wasn't meant to be a weapon, was it?

"May I?" asked Alain d'Creux, standing on Pyrsie's other side. She handed him the Foreman's spyglass, and he immediately used it to find the Squad and zero in on Arth specifically. His own interest in Arth's Relic had not wavered. "All zis time, I thought zat was a gnoman Relic," he said quietly as he watched. "But sacrée bleue relique!* Clearly, it is a Relic meant for zee dagmen!"

Pyrsie squinted again through her own remaining spyglass. There was no doubt about it; the Diamond Scepter was pulsing with blue light as Arth gestured with it, animated as always. He'd been moving at normal speed again ever since Hembrose dropped the time bubble and departed.

Speaking of the Wizard... "Sovereign only made four Diamond Relics for each race, right?" Pyrsie asked d'Creux. Hembrose had told her some of the theories behind magical artifacts, after she'd let him study her Grail. "I was told zat each race got two Combat Relics, one to provide protection and zee other to use for correction. And they got two

---

* I think this just means "Holy Blue Relic" in his language. —*N*

Command Relics, one to grant wisdom and one to give zee user strength to show love and humility."

D'Creux shrugged. "This I have learned since coming to Overtwixt, yes. But I could find no information about zee gnoman Relics specifically. No one has reported seeing one in many eons, which is why I thought zat Scepter might indeed be an artifact of our people."

Pyrsie snorted. "No one has seen zem because zee Burrowcrat kept all four of zem locked up in his treasure room. Zat is where I found my own Diamond Relic."

D'Creux nearly dropped the Foreman's spyglass. "*You* bear one of Sovereign's Relics as well?" he gasped. Clearly, he'd been too busy hiding beneath the ballista earlier to notice when Hembrose returned the Grail to her.

Feeling proud and a little embarrassed at the same time, Pyrsie pulled her Relic from where she usually tucked it inside her tunic. "Zis is zee Diamond Grail of Goodwill."

"May... may I hold it?" d'Creux asked.

Pyrsie hesitated only briefly, then handed it to him. When it entered the other gnoman's hands, it dimmed somewhat, but it didn't go out entirely. "I can use it to heal injuries," she explained. "Just fill it wiz water, then pour zat water down zee throat of an injured person."

"So which Relic is it?" the Pilgrim wanted to know. "Of zee four types? Zee type for protecting people?"

The little gnomaid thought back over the other three gnoman Relics she had left behind in the Treasury, which the Burrowcrat had helpfully labeled with manila tags tied on by red string. The Candelabra of Enlightenment had helped her think clearly and wisely when she needed a plan of escape. The Lance of Sanction was clearly a weapon, used for "correcting" wrongdoers, and the Shield of Integrity was even more clearly the Relic intended for protection. "No, zee

Diamond Grail gives me zee power to help people, to show zem love by healing zem. I don't know why zat would make it a *Command* Relic, though." But as she thought about it, it made a certain sense. Leaders needed wisdom and humility and love more than anyone.

"Incroyable,"* d'Creux said softly, finally handing back the Grail, which Pyrsie returned to her tunic.

"So what type of Relic do you think Arth's new Diamond Scepter is?" Pyrsie asked the Pilgrim. "I mean, a scepter is just a sort of wand carried by royalty to prove they are royalty, no? Zat is why I would expect it to be a Command Relic... but we just saw Arth use it as a weapon... and then, moments later, to protect himself!"

"According to my grand-père, zee Scepter was all four."

"All four!" Pyrsie blurted. "How is zat possible?"

D'Creux chuckled. "I do not think we always understand zee rules of zis place as well as we think we do. Zee Sovereign makes zee rules, as he made zee Relics. *He* determines what is impossible and what is possible, and even then, he can decide to do zee impossible if he wishes."

"But Sovereign's Great Relic... it is *all four* types of Relics, all in one?"

The Pilgrim nodded. "Zee Diamond Scepter of Sovereignty it was called, a special gift of zee Sovereign for his prophesied King. Meant to grant zee King overwhelming power both in combat *and* command."

Pyrsie supposed this made sense too, as she thought about it. It probably also explained why no one had ever heard of any dagman Relics before now either; because there weren't *four*, as for most races, but just the single extra-special one... which had been trapped in stone for all of history.

---

* "incredible" or "amazing"

She glanced sideways at the gentleman adventurer. "You seem to know an awful lot about zee Scepter, aside from thinking it was meant for gnomen."

Alain d'Creux laughed, still with a slight edge of bitterness. "Yes, as I've said, I hoped to recover zis Relic for myself. I never spoke of it to zee other chevaliers, however, for I did not wish to be mocked. But since I was a child, I always dreamed of pulling free zee Scepter-in-zee-Stone and being named King of all Overtwixt, zee Sovereign's Hero."

"So basically, you came here with zee same silly dreams as zee rest of us."

D'Creux hesitated, then seemed to realize Pyrsie wasn't mocking him at all. She was admitting that she and everyone else had been the same as him. "Thank you," he said softly.

A boom sounded off in the distance, then another. Pyrsie quickly raised her spyglass again, noting that one or two of the distant glass buildings were shaking. She even thought she saw shimmers of green light reflecting off the surrounding glass. Tracking back towards where she'd last seen Arth, she realized the Squad was no longer visible, now blocked from view by intervening structures.

She heaved a frustrated sigh. "I wish I could help somehow." But she really wasn't a fighter, and the ballistae were still out of ammunition.

D'Creux placed a hand on her spyglass, gently forcing her to lower it. "My dear Pyrsyfal, you just finished telling me of zee healing powers of your Diamond Grail. Are there not many in need of healing?" He gestured toward the collapsed section of Crystal City, where Pyrsie herself had seen many aquatics pulling themselves from the half-submerged glass rubble. "And we are certainly not short of water in zis wet place."

Pyrsie smacked a hand to her forehead. "Of course, you are entirely right." Turning away from the edge of the Crystal

Keep's glass roof, she quickly rallied the blue-caped soldiers that were now hers to command. "Enough standing around! Let's get down there and help some people, yes?"

The Inventor and her troops filed down the narrow stairs leading between the roof and the Amphitheater. "About time!" someone huffed when they reached ground level again.

"Paladin!" Pyrsie greeted the big red eqman, who had been too broad in the shoulders to follow them up to the roof. "I did not know zat you were still waiting!"

"I very nearly didn't," Paladin blustered. "You know how I cherish a good fight, and opportunities abound in this city at the moment. But..." He shuffled his hooved feet. "I didn't want to leave my friend undefended should the monsters attack here."

Pyrsie was touched, especially because the eqman wasn't usually the sentimental sort. But Paladin had undergone a transformation in the months since Pyrsie rescued him from the lugmen, and especially following the Squad's liberation of the eqmen from Karis's brother, the Prince. On that day, the magnificent red eqman had pledged his undying gratitude and friendship to Pyrsie, a gift that the gnomaid cherished above most others. Paladin was an overstuffed windbag at times, but even so, she had come to love and respect the egotistical eqman, as he had her. The two of them were a team within the larger team.

Grinning ear to ear, she quickly clambered onto the eqman's back, then pulled d'Creux up behind her again. "We are headed to zee northwest. There are hurt people to help."

"And hopefully some hairy people to hurt," Paladin added darkly. "I mean the lugs, of course. Sheesh." Then he reared dramatically—nearly unseating d'Creux in the process—and galloped along the narrow grassy isthmus and out of the Crystal Keep.

Pyrsie found herself reflecting on the Diamond Scepter of Sovereignty again as they went. If that Relic was what she and d'Creux thought it was, then Arth had only barely scratched the surface of its abilities. It would be more important than usual that the bearer of *this* Relic wield it only for the greater good, and with the purest of hearts.

But if anyone could do that, it was Arth. Of her two closest friends in Overtwixt, Pyrsie was glad that Arth had been chosen for this honor. She really wasn't sure Hembrose could have handled the temptation of so much power.

· twelve ·

Hembrose swam through the sky over Crystal City on his immense leathery wings, banking now and then as he threaded a path between the tops of the tallest glass spires. His eyes never left the surface far below, where every tenth building now lay in ruins; random trash and belongings floated in the canals even between the intact structures. The streets were now mostly empty of people in this part of the city, though he knew many of the buildings remained occupied. Several blocks to the south, there were streams of refugees fleeing the other direction, but the folks still *here* were too afraid to leave home.

Yet the Siren call of his beloved continued to draw him away from it all, further to the northeast. Straining his ears, he heard it again: a piercing cry for help.

The Wizard had all but forgotten the Lady's brother, Antagonist. Arth hadn't actually ordered the two mermen to stay together; he had just said they were tasked with saving the Lady of the Lake from whatever danger she was in. That was a fine distinction, perhaps (Hembrose knew what Arth actually meant); but under the circumstances, it gave the mermage a good enough excuse for leaving the hateful lad far behind. The fellow couldn't possibly keep up anyway, not when he was forced to swim the canals. The Wizard's drachman body was not only faster; it was able to fly to the Lady's rescue in a mostly straight line.

The beautiful mermaid's voice was like a beacon, allowing him to hone in on her position. Her calls weren't constant, but she did repeat herself every minute or so. And now that he was finally drawing close, Hembrose began to understand the words she was screaming: "Help! Help! Any loyal soldier of Caymerlot, help! We're under attack! Innocents, *children!* Help us, please!" Her cries grew ever more urgent the nearer he approached.

The mermage found himself grinding his teeth. If those lugman monsters had harmed even a hair on the Lady's head, he was going to inflict pain upon them like they'd never experienced before. In fact, even if they hadn't hurt her, they would suffer the consequences of causing her such distress. Hembrose would use *all* his powers to teach these uncivilized lugs a lesson.

A green glimmer in the corner of his eye momentarily grabbed his attention. Not in the direction of the Lady, but back in that section of the city that collapsed earlier. Hembrose paused, treading air, straining his eyes to catch another glimpse as he felt a surge of hope. Could it be Morth? No doubt about it, that had been a flash of magic just like the one that drew Hembrose to his young dagman friend back on Lugarth. The Wizard still didn't understand how the luggernauts had traveled to Caymerlot, but maybe they'd brought their slaves along too. Maybe Morth had used his meager magical skills to escape once they arrived here.

The green light flashed again, and hope died within Hembrose. This was no mere spark of magic, but immense green fireballs, hurled by a magicker of incredible strength.

Even as Hembrose watched, three more buildings fell before the release of so much destructive magic—far more power than Morth was capable of summoning, assuming he even wanted to unleash such destruction. Whoever this fellow was, he was probably single-handedly responsible for the large-scale collapse that had happened earlier too.

Great. *Another* enemy threat. Arth would need to know about this, and soon.

But first the Lady. Ignoring the distant flashes of green, Hembrose resumed his flight, focused once more on the task at hand.

And then he was past a line of tall buildings, and a large party of refugees appeared ahead of him in the haze of the war-torn city. There were perhaps fifty aquatics in the party, at least half of them children. The Lady herself was on the far side of the group, and Hembrose realized she was the one leading them, yelling direction and encouragement—in between her piercing cries for help—as she tried to get the refugees to safety. Her brothers had thought she was safe in Crystal Keep, but she must have gone out into the city, hoping to bring back survivors to shelter within the walls of the fortress.

Except city-center was the other direction entirely. Had the Lady grown disoriented in a city her father seldom let her visit? Or was she simply fleeing in whatever direction provided immediate safety, desperate to escape the luggernauts bearing down on her?

There were three of the monsters behind the Lady's party—a trivial danger to one such as Hembrose, but almost impossible for normal people to defend against. One by one, the oversized bullies were picking off the members of the Lady's group as they fled through the streets. Unfortunately, the canals in this part of the city were all too shallow to escape lugman reach by swimming deep. Even as Hembrose watched, one lug caught up to a little nyman girl, grabbed her by her head-tentacles, then threw her high into the air. The poor nymaid screamed in terror all the way up, then all the way back down again, only falling silent when she disappeared in a tiny puff of yellow.

All three of the lugmen thought this was hilarious.

Hembrose tucked his wings tight to his body and plummeted toward the three marauders, full of righteous fury. There was no trace of the terror he used to feel when going into battle. Instead, he was moved to compassion for that poor girl—even though it was too late for her—and could only imagine the angry helplessness the Lady must be feeling right now. Hembrose loved the Lady all the more, seeing how she took risks for people she didn't even know. She was truly a better person than most.

And he would be the one to rescue her. Not the Altruist, not the Antagonist, but *him*. The Wizard of Merlyn. Her pure heart would belong to him yet.

He decided to make this rescue as dramatic as possible, doing all he could to ensure that very outcome.

Hembrose fell upon the first lug, wrapping his muscular drachman arms around the brute's chest, then pumping his powerful wings hard to lift the fellow high into the air. He never could have accomplished such a feat without his emerald, for lugs were immense beasts; but now, with all that extra strength, he lifted the luggernaut with only a little strain. He would pay for this with an especially bad headache later, but it was so very worth it.

Below, the fleeing citizens turned to stare and point. Even the other two lugs had stopped their harassment in order to holler at their friend, who was now grunting in panic.

One of the lugmen flung his notched sword at the Wizard, spinning end over end, but the deadly weapon missed Hembrose by a safe margin. The mermage climbed high enough that his victim's fate was assured, then hovered in air, speaking with a magically-enhanced voice. "Have no fear, my Lady. Your protector is here!" He waited until she turned, and her beautiful brown eyes met his, widening in surprise and recognition. Yes, she remembered his drachman body from before. She knew who was here to rescue her.

Hembrose turned his attention back to the lugman who was now whimpering in his arms. "See how *you* like it," he told the fellow quietly... then dropped him.

Every eye followed the luggernaut as he tumbled alllllllll the way to the ground, screaming the whole time, at last puffing away in a spectacular burst of yellow. All those eyes then returned to Hembrose, and he raised a hand high, clenching his fist—summoning green lightning to strike out of a clear sky, pinpointing the next lugman of the trio. When *that* smoke cleared, the last lug looked left, then right, then fled. Hembrose had planned an even more dramatic fate for this last one; but on reflection, he decided it was far more effective theatrics for this crowd to see the monster—the one they themselves had just been fleeing from—now fleeing from Hembrose the Wizard.

With a self-satisfied smile, the mermage swooped down and landed lightly beside the Lady, transitioning smoothly into his merman form and slipping into the water next to her.

The Lady of the Lake sucked in a huge breath, no doubt to thank him or even apologize for the way things had ended between them before. Or even better yet, she was going to profess her love—

Instead, she screamed.

Once again, the sound of it seemed to shake the surrounding buildings to their very foundations—as if the Lady knew the resonant frequency of industrial-strength glass. She was the Siren, indeed! As before, Hembrose was forced to clap his hands over his ears, eyes streaming in pain... but also now in bitter realization. For in that terrible, beautiful sound, he recognized horror and disgust.

She was horrified and disgusted by *him*.

He felt it like a knife to his heart. Last time, sure, she had feared he was going to kidnap her. But this time? He had just rescued her! And yet that twisted expression on her face left no doubt how she felt about him. She *feared* him.

For the briefest of moments, Hembrose considered an alternate solution to this problem: mind control. He could certainly hypnotize this Siren into falling silent right now. And as confident as he was in his power—especially the incredible strength he now wielded—he thought he could probably even *make* her fall in love with him, in time.

But deep inside, some small part of Hembrose that was still innocent recoiled at the thought. He had done many things he regretted since coming to Overtwixt. Though he didn't like to reflect on such things, he knew he had skirted the line between right and wrong, even dabbled with evil to accomplish his purposes. But he knew that if he truly loved the Lady, he couldn't force her to love him back. He had to leave that choice to her.

And for the moment, at least, she seemed pretty confident that she wanted nothing to do with him.

"Forgive me, my Lady. I never meant to scare you," he told her quietly, heart breaking within him. "I hope someday I can earn your trust. I still hope to become a man you can love. Until then..." he trailed off, heaving a painful sigh. Until then, he needed to warn Arth about that enemy magicker. The Underlady was safe now, and besides, her brother the Antagonist would surely find her eventually. *He* could escort her safely back to the Crystal Keep or wherever.

Hembrose turned, preparing to leap back into his drachman form.

He caught just a glimpse of the Antagonist's furious, hate-filled face before the butt of the Diamond Harpoon crashed into Hembrose's forehead.

Everything went black.

· thirteen ·

The Underlord of Caymerlot was in dire straits indeed. Cornered against a huge mound of glass rubble, the old ruler was frantically screaming orders at his men while clutching at his side, which leaked yellow in steady wisps. Only a small group of those soldiers was still close enough to hear his calls, forming a half-circle of defense between him and a knot of determined lugmen.

Hundreds of other fighters were spread throughout the ruins of the city outskirts, all intermixed—another free-for-all like before, with too much going on to make sense of it at a glance. Most of the aquatics in view wore the blue capes of the Underlord's guard, now torn and stained, though a smaller number had nothing but red kerchiefs tied around their upper arms or tentacles. Amazingly, the aquatics outnumbered the lugmen in this arena, which somehow made the whole thing seem just a little closer to a fair fight.

With all the fallen glass, and the narrow isthmuses now turned to mud, it was difficult to distinguish between the canals and solid ground. Combatants on both sides of the conflict periodically lost their footing in the treacherous terrain. Every building had been leveled within a five-block radius, so it took Arth a long moment to recognize this as the same neighborhood he had explored with Morth on his very first day in Crystal City. But sure enough, just beyond those mounds of rubble was the grassy field and blue lagoon where the troupe had raised its big-top circus tent that same day. There were no more bright colors anywhere, however; everywhere Arth looked, all had turned gray and miserable.

"Father!" Altruist cried, surging into the fight when he caught sight of his father in the distance.

Arth didn't bother calling him back. There wasn't time for cautious evaluation, and the Underlord wasn't the only one about to be smoked if the Squad didn't act quickly. Riding once more into combat atop Sidekick, Arth slashed at lugs on the left with his sword, pummeling lugs on the right with his Diamond Relic, assisting aquatics he didn't know as he rode through their midst—but he didn't stop, for his goal was the same as the Altruist's. In order to reach the Underlord's side more quickly, he sought the deepest water at the center of what he *thought* was the old boulevard canal. It was hard to tell from the surface, but the lugs seemed sparsest there, and all of them floated chest deep in the churning water. With any luck, Arth could bypass them entirely and push more quickly to the Underlord's rescue.

Off to the side, the Noble splashed through shallower water with the Knight on his back, the two of them facing more difficult opposition. At a motion from Arth, Daddie and his new kelpie mount peeled off to assist them, though Pythagoras clearly didn't like the idea of leaving Arth's side. Sarge and Bertie would have to be enough to watch the new King's back.

The water had come chest high on Sidekick before the ground finally fell away beneath them, and the two friends

plunged deep below the surface. At Arth's direction, the kelpie wove his way between two of the lugs reckless enough to fight in deep water; the thrashing giants never saw the dagman who smoked them, probably didn't even notice the pulse of blue from beneath the water until it was too late.

Unfortunately, the water was as dirty as any swamp back home, so Arth and Sidekick soon surfaced again to get their bearings. They were getting close to the Underlord now, but a group of five aquatics and two lugs were locked in combat between here and there. There was so much splashing, Arth couldn't make much sense of things, but he sprang from Sidekick's back to land on one lug's shoulders just as the fella shouted, "Bah-le-le-le-leeeeeeeeee—" Arth lost his bearings *and* the grip on his sword when the luggernaut collapsed to smoke beneath him, but he could still feel which direction the other danger was—raising his Diamond Relic just in time to ward off a blow from the remaining lug. That bloke then fell to a barrage of attacks from the Sergeant's many maces.

Breathing hard amidst the yellow smoke and spray of water, Arth saw to his dismay that only four aquatics remained of the group he'd just rescued: three in capes, one bearing a kerchief, and *all* of them staring at Arth and the Sarge in surprise. "Look out!" Arth called, pointing as yet another luggernaut approached from their other side, about to ram his sword through the kerchiefed fella's back.

But that man wearing the red kerchief—another kark— didn't even glance over his shoulder. Instead, with an angry scowl, he deliberately stabbed one of the other aquatics with his spear, turning the man to yellow smoke. Then he pivoted and cast his spear at Arth!

Despite his shock, Arth easily deflected the attack with his Relic. But by the time he recovered, the lug newcomer had made quick work of the last two caped soldiers. Then the lug and the kerchiefed kark retreated *together*, warily backing away from Arth and his allies before they could react.

"What in the world was that?" Sidekick demanded, so shocked that he didn't even rhyme, which seldom happened.

Uncle Bertie recovered first. "That bloke's gone over to the side of the lugs. And he ain't the only one—look!"

"It's all the fellows with the red kerchiefs," Sarge exclaimed. And as Arth looked around more closely, he realized it was true. The blokes wearing the kerchiefs weren't fighting the lugs at all; they was fighting their own kind! Some of them were still trying to be sneaky about it, but by this point of the battle, it seemed clear that most of the caped aquatics had discovered the truth for themselves.

"It's mostly karks," Bertie said in realization. "Like that one as attacked Arth earlier." And in fulfillment of his new role as Bodyguard, the muscular dagman swung his kelpie mount around, placing himself squarely between Arth and the Sergeant—who was also a karkman. "The karks has turned against us," he snarled, raising his huge sword.

But Sarge just scowled. "Don't be ridiculous. I remain loyal to Caymerlot, and you can see there are many other loyal karks still wearing the cape. Besides, it's not just karks fighting on the side of the lugs." He gestured, pointing out others—a nym here, a few okkies, even one kelpie.

"He's right, Bertie," Arth said. "Stand down."

Sidekick was frowning as he noticed something else. "Every one of them is thin," he said. "The traitors, they're all just bone and skin."

"They was the lugs' slaves," Arth realized. "All them aquatics now fightin' fer the lugs... they's the same ones the lugs must've captured when they attacked before."

"You're right," Sarge said in horror. "It even makes sense. We *abandoned* them. After the lugs attacked Karkham and took so many captives, we didn't even try to rescue them. On the Underlord's orders, we simply destroyed the bridge between Karkham and Lugarth, to protect the remaining citizens of Caymerlot against future attacks."

"To protect the Underlord, ya mean," Arth said quietly. "I don't reckon he was finking about anyone else when he issued that command."

Sarge wore a haunted expression.

"C'mon," Arth encouraged his friends. "Enuff talkin'. Just watch out for the blokes with the red kerchiefs."

They resumed their drive towards the Underlord and his dwindling half-circle of protectors. They caught up to the Altruist, who had been surprised and surrounded by a trio of kerchiefed aquatics. Surprising the traitors in turn and dispatching them quickly, Arth and the others rescued the merman prince and they joined forces once more.

At last, they reached the intense cluster of fighting that encircled the Underlord. The attacking luggernauts now stood in rows three deep, pushing one another forward, each lug clearly hoping to be the one who broke through merman lines to smoke the ruler personally. Weapons sweeping in a blur, Arth and the others began working their way around the perimeter, taking out the back line of giant marauders as they went. They soon met the Knight and Noble doing the same thing from the other direction, Daddie still watching their backs, then turned and started in on the next row of distracted invaders. As the heroes fought, their various Diamond Relics began to glow more brightly blue— including, unexpectedly, one of the eight maces wielded by the Sergeant-at-arms.

The Squad and their new friends were literally turning the tide of this battle. But just when it seemed they might complete the Underlord's rescue, a huge green fireball struck nearby, sending up spray and creating a killer new wave that swept Arth from Sidekick's back. Struggling back to the surface, the dagman King looked around quickly, thinking this must herald the Wizard's return—and about time, too! But no, he realized quickly. While that green fireball *had* smoked two lugs, it had taken out eleven of the Underlord's defenders as well. Even as Arth watched, more loyal Caymerlotions struggled to fill the sudden gap, just in time for a second huge fireball to take them out too.

Arth spun, looking for the source of the blast. "Spread out!" he yelled, addressing not only his Squad but anyone else willing to listen.

Then came a third blast, this one striking low, plowing into the water near the center of the Squad's formation as they tried to put distance between themselves. The fireball sent Bertie and his mount flying, the poor kelpie smoked in an instant, though Arth was relieved to see a gasping Bertie surface moments later. His new Bodyguard crawled out onto a muddy isthmus, so caked with grime that Arth barely recognized him. A fourth blast was obviously meant to finish him off, but Karis the Knight threw herself from Noble's back and took the fireball square on her glowing breastplate.

"Lady Karis!" Arth shrieked in horror. But when the spray cleared, she was still standing in the same place, glowing brightly. The fireball had simply dissolved on contact with Sovereign's Relic.

"Look over there!" Sidekick pointed. "Golly, that lug's big as a bear!"

Sure enough, the source of the blasts was the biggest lugman Arth had ever seen, standing head and shoulders taller than all the others. Between the spray and smoke clogging the air, not to mention the giant's all-enveloping cloak, it was hard to get a look at him—but what else *could* he be, if not a luggernaut? Even as Arth gaped, the cloaked fella brandished an immense iron war hammer, seeming to draw magical power from a glowing ruby set into its hammerhead. The eerie green light pooled in the tall man's other hand, then he flung it at the Squad, yet another powerful fireball.

"Oy, a lugmagicker," Arth gasped. "Squad!" he bellowed with surprising volume, his voice sounding enhanced even to his own ears. "Magicker! Focus on the lugmagicker!"

Still spreading out as he'd previously ordered, the Squad and their friends pivoted to charge in this new direction, facing the unexpected threat without hesitation. Leaving Noble behind, Lady Karis sprinted along the muddy isthmus, footing sure thanks to her Diamond-clad feet. Altruist paced her from the water, his strong merman tail propelling him rapidly along the surface; he was the next to be targeted by a green fireball, but it had little more effect on his Diamond armor than it had on Karis's.

Sarge had less success defending against a magical green attack, though he desperately raised his own Diamond Relic when the lugmagicker's barrage swept across him. He took a direct hit on his glowing mace, the impact blasting him entirely out of the water. Though his Relic was a weapon, not armor, it clearly offered him some protection; he landed intact some distance away. There was no sign of yellow smoke when he crashed back into the water, but the kark was now so far away that he was effectively out of the fight.

Arth ground his teeth, desperately wishing he hadn't let Hembrose fly off in the other direction. He *really* could've used the Wizard's skills right now, in order to fight green magic with green magic.

Oddly, the blue glow of Arth's new Relic flickered and dimmed as that thought crossed his mind—just as yet another green fireball streaked toward him. If the Sidekick hadn't raised his own blazing-blue Aegis to catch the blast,

Arth wasn't sure what would have happened. The dagman King focused his mind on defending the innocent, and his Relic erupted with blue light once more.

For the first time, he noticed just how devastating this barrage of green fire had been. True, none of Arth's own team had been smoked, but the air was now thick with yellow haze from others who had fallen prey. There were still hundreds of combatants in the water, aquatics and lugs both, and the broad-shouldered lugmagicker didn't seem to care who he smoked as he hurled fireball after fireball in the Underlord's general direction. Arth was drawing steadily closer to the big fella, but how many more people would be cast from Overtwixt forever by the time he got there? Arth didn't even know these individuals, but he felt nausea well up within him at the thought of their fate.

With a scream of primal fury, the King of Caymerlot raised high his Relic-in-the-Rock and brought it crashing down onto the surface of the water. He intended the force of the blow to create another tall wave, something to surge forward and knock the enemy magicker off his feet. Instead, a massive blue *dome* sprang into existence, leaping outward from the point of impact and growing rapidly. Its expanding walls passed right through Arth's allies, but seemed solid whenever enemies were encountered, pushing lugmen and kerchiefed traitors straight out to the battlefield's perimeter. In an instant, without truly knowing what he did, Arth single-handedly ended the battle—and without harming even his enemies. For in that moment, Arth was overwhelmed with anguish for *all* who might perish here, allies and enemies alike. There had been too much pain today already, on both sides of this conflict.

Silence fell on the devastated landscape, interrupted only by the sounds of water sloshing and dripping. At the very edge of Arth's massive blue dome, the lugmagicker prodded the glowing barrier with his war hammer, which bounced right off. Casually propping the enormous weapon on his shoulder, the lugman turned his cowled head, seeking out the source of the dome. Though Arth could not see into the darkness of that hood, he knew when the cloaked fella finally spotted him—for the bloke leaned forward suddenly, as if squinting directly at him through the smoke. Surprised or confused by Arth's appearance, the enemy magicker cocked his head to one side.

Then with a flourish of his all-enveloping cloak, the big fella departed the battlefield.

Kerchiefed traitors sprang to follow. The tall lugman gave them new orders—impossible to hear from here—and the aquatics spread out again, carrying those orders to the other lugmen now milling around the outside of Arth's dome in confusion. Without complaint, the luggernauts promptly turned and left the battlefield as well. The towering brutes even fell into loose ranks and marched away in formation.

Arth felt something cold in the pit of his stomach. An orderly formation of lugmen? It seemed more likely than ever that the Ransacker had taken over leadership after the Khan's defeat, for Arth had seen no other lug commander capable of instilling such discipline. Was that cloaked figure the Ransacker himself then? If it was, why hadn't the Ransacker shown his magical abilities at the Battle for the Branch Library? Things would have turned out very differently if he had! And if that *wasn't* the Ransacker, then who was he?

What sort of lugman wielded magic so effectively *and* commanded this kind of behavior from other luggernauts?

Even bearing the unmatched power of Sovereign's Great Relic in his right hand, Arth suddenly worried. How much worse might this war become with such a man as *that* leading the enemy army?

· fourteen ·

So long as Arth's magical barrier stood, there was no chance of the battle resuming. He watched through the yellow smoke and the shimmering blue light of the dome as the lugmagicker's orders circulated. Then every last enemy soldier retreated from sight, departing Crystal City through several breaches now visible in the thick glass city wall. Arth waited another quarter hour after that—enough time for several teams of blue-caped Caymerlotions to create defensive positions around those breaches—before finally allowing his dome to dissipate. He wondered if there was something he could do with the Relic's magic to help fill those holes in the wall, but that would have to come later. First, he had some unfinished business to attend to.

The new King found the Underlord in much better shape now than when he'd seen him last. The fellow remained exactly where Arth had left him, but no longer clutching that wound in his side. Pyrsie was obviously to thank for the old ruler's miraculous recovery. As Arth approached, he saw the little gnomaid scurrying from one wounded soldier to another, administering water from her glowing Diamond Grail. She was accompanied by another young woman, this one a mermaid who spoke tenderly to the injured as they received their healing.

Arth was momentarily transfixed by the sight of this woman. With his new Diamond Relic still clutched in one hand, he continued to have a strange ability to comprehend simple truths instantly—and he recognized in this woman an innocence unlike any he had encountered before. He read horror on her face as she beheld the pain of the wounded, and yet she was clearly a strong woman too, for she refused to let that horror hold her back from helping others. By contrast with the ugliness of this day, she was beautiful beyond compare, the most captivating creature Arth had ever set eyes upon. *And* she was pretty. Arth barely even noticed that she was a different race from him.

"No!" Pyrsie shrieked suddenly, jerking Arth from his reverie. "Stop zat zis very instant!" she cried, racing back to the Underlord's side and seizing his arm in one hand.

It took Arth a moment to realize what had upset her, but then his anger began bubbling. Off to the side, a trussed merman was being hauled up high on ropes, for all to see—Hembrose the Wizard, hanging upside down by his tail.

"For the crime of oath-breaking," the Underlord intoned loudly, "there can be only one punishment: banishment from Overtwixt. For the crime of attempted kidnapping: banishment. For the crime of *treason* against your Underlord"—at this, the old merman ruler's voice cracked with fury—"banishment!"

"Father, wait!" the Altruist called.

"O Wizard of Merlyn, you have earned permanent banishment from Overtwixt three times over," the Underlord cried in his unsteady voice. "You deserve not even the privilege of answering for your crimes, for no utterance of your foul mouth can be trusted. You deserve only to be smoked, and without delay. I hereby execute this judgment personally," he concluded, rising up from the water with a longsword poised to strike.

"No," Arth commanded. "You will *not* execute this judgment. That authority is no longer yers to exercise." His voice rang, echoing across the devastated landscape, even deeper and more commanding than when Hembrose had magically amplified it during the Battle for the Branch Library. Arth sensed the same kind of magic at work again here, except this time by the power of his new Relic.

The Underlord spun, gaping at Arth. "You!?" he gasped in disbelief. "A mere dagman dares to defy *me?* The Underlord of all Caymerlot!?"

Among the soldiers flanking the Underlord, the Antagonist shifted uncomfortably. He hadn't stepped in to help Hembrose, but he wasn't actively participating in this miscarriage of justice either. As before, the young merman appeared conflicted. "Father," he said hesitantly, not meeting the Underlord's eye *or* Arth's. "As hard as it is to believe, this dagman is the King we've been awaiting."

The Underlord became very still, though his eyes widened in crazed anger. "There has never been a King in Caymerlot," he hissed. "Why should we need one now?"

"But he wields the Relic-in-the-Rock," said his other son, the Altruist. "Surely you must recognize it, for a thing of such power could be nothing other than Sovereign's Great Relic."

The Underlord wrestled to get control of himself before speaking again. "Very well, then the Hero has been found—the one who will serve as commander of my army. Approach, Hero, and kneel to swear your oath of fealty to me!"

Nearby, someone broke into incredulous laughter. "Name zat Relic for what it truly is, and zis confusion will clear up. Relic-in-zee-Rock? Phaw!" It was Pyrsie's gnoman friend Pilgrim who spoke. "It is zee Scepter-in-zee-Stone that zis dagman now wields! Zee Diamond Scepter of Sovereignty, zee greatest Relic ever created."

"Silence that outlander!" the Underlord cried, his voice cracking again. "He speaks lies!" Several caped soldiers surged forward, but Pyrsie unsheathed her short sword and moved to defend the Pilgrim. It was laughable, one little gnomaid thinking to fight off so many trained soldiers twice her size... and yet every one of them hesitated. Of course they did, for this was the same young woman who had healed so many of their allies just moments before.

"It all makes sense now," said the Sergeant-at-arms as he limped into the area, holding one tentacle gingerly, gaze fixed on the Underlord. "The reason you always insisted on calling it the Relic-in-the-Rock, claiming it was an unknown Relic. Because if you let people name it what it truly was, a *scepter*, then you couldn't deny that the one who someday wielded it was King. So you lied to the people instead, just to preserve your power." He shook his head tiredly. "But the one who wields this Relic was never meant to bow to you, Underlord—but rather *you* to *him*."

"Silence that one as well!" the Underlord shrieked, pointing a claw-like finger at the Sergeant.

This time, none of the soldiers more than twitched.

"Obey me!" the Underlord cried, spittle flying from his mouth.

Instead, all eyes slowly turned to Arth, the unlikely King, who stood there looking tired and sad... yet somehow with more regal bearing than the Underlord had managed in a long, long time. "Someone untie the Wizard," Arth said.

Several soldiers moved to comply, but a sullen Antagonist spoke up. "I'll do it. I, erm, used some special knots. There's a trick to them..."

Arth nodded, turning to survey the broken city he was now expected to rule.

Insane with fury, literally spitting, the Underlord rushed him from behind, his longsword raised. Half the Squad reacted at once—Bertie hefting his oversized lugman club and Karis drawing back to strike with her curved sword, even as Pyrsie flung a tomahawk at the Underlord. Two blue-caped archers actually fired off arrows at their old ruler.

But Arth raised a hand, his Diamond Relic pulsing with brilliant light, and each weapon bounced off the older merman without harming him. As before, Arth didn't need to understand the mechanics of it; he just needed to *wish* for the safety of another person in his vicinity, and the Relic—the Diamond Scepter—ensured that person's protection.

Undeterred as a result, the old merman reached Arth and stabbed his blade viciously into the dagman's back... or tried to. The longsword shattered against another blue shield that magically appeared: a seemingly hard shell wrapping Arth's entire body, flaring most brightly blue at the point of impact, then fading away again within moments. The impact threw the Underlord backwards to land painfully on his side in the shallow water.

Slowly, Arth turned to face the stunned fella. "Well, mate, I s'pose you's gone and removed any remaining doubt. Now all these fine folk know exackly the sort of man you really is." And indeed, the expressions on the soldiers' faces ranged from dismay to disgust.

"And you," Altruist said softly, speaking to Arth, "have shown them exactly the sort of man *you* are too." Face overcome with emotion, he knelt before Arth. "You are the sort of man I have always longed to serve. The kind who does what's right *and* shows mercy to his enemies. My sword is yours, as is my service and my loyalty."

The Underlord stared at his eldest child, stricken. "You would abandon me? My very own son?"

Clearly still emotional, the Altruist spoke with even greater confidence as he began reciting the oath of fealty. "I promise on my honor to faithfully serve the new King of Caymerlot, now and in the future. Never to harm and always to protect both him and his house—and never to elevate myself above him—in good faith and without deception."

"Rise, friend Altruist," Arth said, his big eyes wet. He glanced at Pyrsie and Karis, Noble and Sidekick. "Any objections to offerin' this bloke a place in our Squad?"

They shook their heads. "None from me," Paladin added, speaking up from nearby.

"I would swear as well," the Sergeant-at-arms called, and he quickly recited his own oath of fealty to the King.

"I vote we add *him* to the Squad too," Bertie suggested.

"But not the Antagonist," Hembrose complained, even after the Underlord's other son swore the oath as well.

Arth just rolled his big eyes. "Naw, we'll take even him, if he's interested. He's got the makings of a hero too."

Antagonist slowly nodded, uncertainly, indicating his acceptance of the offer.

Sarge spoke up, turning to face the assembled soldiers. "I have been the recipient of our new King's mercy, as have we all, though we didn't know it at the time. This man has an entire army of followers on Delphyrd, and he could have brought them to our shores, seizing his rightful place by force. Instead, he came in peace... and we arrested him for no crime of his own. He *let* us arrest him, even though I now know just how deadly his companions are. Had they resisted, many of us would no longer be in Overtwixt today. This King has earned not only my loyalty, but my heart as well."

First a handful, then many more of the blue-caped soldiers of the guard began pushing forward to swear their fealty to the new King of Caymerlot. It was just like Hulandia in the aftermath of the Battle for the Branch Library, and for several minutes, all was chaos as hundreds of men and women yelled their oaths.

As the recitations finally ended, a single crazed voice became audible once more. "Traitors!" the Underlord was shrieking raggedly. "You are *all* traitors, all of you!"

"No, Father," Altruist said sadly. "It is you who were the traitor all along. I was still a child when we arrived in Overtwixt, and I have long doubted my own memory of the Guide's words to you that day. But I no longer doubt that you've intentionally subverted the very purpose of your office, in defiance of Guide and Sovereign alike. You betrayed the trust of your children, your people, and your position to peddle a self-serving lie." The young merman squad member glanced at Arth, who gave him a sad nod in return. Then Altruist gestured to a quartet of guardsmen in blue capes. "Take the Underlord to the dungeon," he ordered them. "Imprison him in the same cell where he endeavored to hide our rightful King." Then he turned to face Arth once more. "Your majesty, please follow me. Allow me to finally give you the welcome you deserve, the welcome you were denied when you first arrived."

Arth offered the Altruist a grateful smile, but he hesitated. Turning briefly, he looked around for the beautiful woman he had glimpsed earlier, but she was nowhere to be seen. "Very well," Arth said. "Lead the way, mate." And he allowed himself to be escorted back toward the Crystal Keep amid cheers from the army of Caymerlot.

Part II
The Demagogue
◇

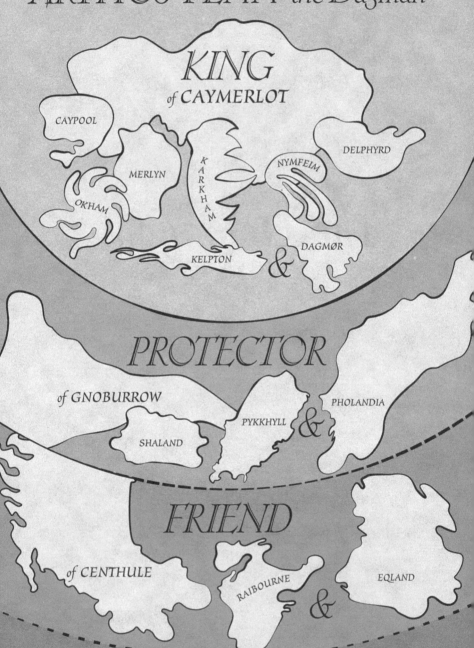

· fifteen ·

The twelve members of the Squad of Heroes gathered in the grand throne room of the Crystal Keep. Pyrsie could hardly believe how quickly their number kept growing: first from seven to nine with the addition of the Ringmaster and Bodyguard, now again to twelve with the Altruist, Antagonist, and Sergeant-at-arms. The purpose of this meeting was to discuss next steps in the war against the lugmen. Altruist insisted this was really something the King should be deliberating with the Committee of Eleven—the lawmakers of Caymerlot—but none of the Committee members *or* the Undersecretary had been seen since the start of the lugman attack.

The Keep's throne room was a large chamber meant for greeting foreign dignitaries, and as such, it was designed with all types of peoples in mind. Unlike the underwater banquet hall on the level below, this great chamber was situated right at sea level. It had a sloping floor so that the water was only ankle high on most landwalkers between the dais and the entrance, while dropping away to almost six paces deep on either side for the comfort of swimmers. The Altruist, in a display of loyalty to his new King, had already arranged for servants to move the Underlord's Diamond Throne from the Amphitheater onto the dais here. Meanwhile, the Antagonist organized a team of karks to bring in the long, ornate table from the banquet hall—the very same hall where Hembrose had experienced his disastrous first meeting with the Underlord's family.

Now that Pyrsie thought about it, she couldn't help but notice that *all* of the Wizard's interactions with the Underlord and his children seemed to end in disaster.

As with almost everything in Caymerlot, the feast table was made entirely of glass, with seating for six on each side and a special place for the ruler at one end—thirteen total. Altruist and Antagonist promptly took their places flanking the head of the table, Sarge next in line, while Karis and Noble quietly assumed seats at the far end near the door. But Pyrsie could tell Arth didn't like the long table at all... and he wasn't the only one. Sidekick, Ringmaster, and Paladin immediately began grumbling—the kelpie about being seated too far away from the King, and Arth's Daddie about the perpetuation of an unjust class system (something about "etchinglons"). By contrast, the big red eqman just didn't like being forced to stand in puddles of water, even here.

Arth turned to Pyrsie, gesturing at the table. "Can you do sumfing about this?"

"I know just zee thing!" She beckoned to Sarge, who didn't question but promptly slithered out of his chair and followed her outside. Pyrsie had already seen work crews beginning repairs on some of the buildings. With the Sergeant backing her up, she requisitioned use of an industrial-grade glass cutter as well as a diamond-tip auger for use drilling holes through glass. Smiling apologetically, she even borrowed one worker's personal toolbox. "Zee King has need of zis," she explained, and suddenly several other workers were offering their toolboxes as well.

The two squad members hurried back to find that Arth was now lounging casually in the middle of the table—seated *on* the table, Diamond Scepter in the crook of his arm—with the rest of the expanded Squad gathered around. Antagonist was first to see Pyrsie re-enter the room, and he said, "Oh good, the runt is back. *Now* can we proceed?" Apparently Arth hadn't let them discuss anything of importance while Pyrsie and Sarge were gone. This made her smile as she began laying out her borrowed tools.

Altruist spoke up. "Sire, I want to talk about the whalephant in the room."

"Which one?" Sidekick asked. "There are a ton."

Hembrose snorted. "How about the fact that *that* fellow"—he pointed at the Antagonist—"knocked me unconscious and carried me to the Underlord for execution?"

"You deserved that," the younger merman snarled.

Altruist raised a hand. "No, what I wish to discuss is my father, currently languishing in the dungeons."

"On *yer* orders, mate," Ringmaster pointed out.

"Aye, and I stand by those orders," the young merman assured them with a sigh. "But it still breaks my heart every moment he's confined there. We need a better long term solution."

"Why?" Bodyguard wanted to know. "Lang'ishing in that dungeon is no worse than the Underlord planned fer his royal higherness!"

The Squad fell to bickering until Arth spoke up. "Oy, enuff! There's too much we gotta discuss to get stuck arguing 'bout one stupid fing. Let's settle this and move on."

Pyrsie glanced up from arranging her tools, surprised that Arth still spoke with such pronounced dagman inflections. Now that he was recognized as King here, she'd expected him to try sounding sophisticated. Then again, she rather liked that he wasn't changing who he was.

"Alrighty," Arth addressed the merman brothers. "About yer daddie... Do ya fink he'd be willin' to serve as my second-in-command? Ya know, the job the Underlord was meant to do all along?"

"I... think he would find that difficult," Altruist said.

"Even if he swore an oath to me first?"

"He would never swear that oath," Antagonist sighed.

"Gotcha. What if I strip him of official authority and let him go? Can he be trusted not to stir up trouble?"

The brothers shared a look but didn't answer.

Arth's shoulders slumped. "In that case, exile seems the only option. We just can't affurd infighting in the midst of our struggle 'gainst the lugs."

Antagonist was horrified. "So you would just *execute* my father?! But your majesty—"

Hembrose scoffed. "Unlike your father, my friend Arth would never do such a thing if avoidable. No, he means we should escort the Underlord back to our real world through the Gatehenge."

Arth nodded, and Altruist sagged. "That *is* merciful."

"Youbetcha," Arth agreed. "At least that way, he can return again someday. Alrighty, next item of bidness?"

"Oho," Hembrose said gleefully. "While you're handing out punishments," he told Arth while leveling a finger at Antagonist, "I'd like to see *that* fellow whipped for what he did to me!"

The tension in the room immediately ratcheted back up as Antagonist snarled angrily, "You deserved every bit of it!"

"You arrested me—twice!—tortured and mishandled me," the Wizard cried, full of wounded dignity. "*Me*, a personal friend of the King!" he reminded everyone again.

Arth raised a hand before Antagonist could reply. "Haulin' meh mate to yer daddie for execution probably weren't the smartest move, 'specially in the midst of an invasion and such," he told the young merman. "Even so," he added, turning now on Hembrose, who was looking smug. "What he did seems all straightferward and legal-like to me. I mean, there *is* a warrant out fer yer arrest. I can't fully blame this fella fer tryin' to uphold the law."

Hembrose stared at Arth in utter shock, and even Pyrsie was surprised. "But... but..." the mermage spluttered.

"The way I see it, there's hurt feelings a-plenny on both sides. You reckon we can let bygones be bygones and move on? Clearly we's all on the same side *now*, and we gots a bigger enemy." Arth paused. "Does anyone got a good reason I can't pardon the Wizard now and be done with it?"

Antagonist ground his teeth, but Altruist calmly said, "Our sister has the greatest cause for complaint. Ask her." He gestured to the back of the room, and everyone turned to look. For the first time, Pyrsie realized a thirteenth person had entered the grand throne room: the same young merwoman who'd assisted Pyrsie in caring for the wounded after the battle.

This was the Underlord's daughter? The same woman Hembrose always talked about? In all the confusion earlier, Pyrsie and the girl hadn't introduced themselves—or spoken much at all, aside from discussing the needs of the injured.

Arth's face lit up, as did Hembrose's. "My Lady!" the Wizard cried, his voice a mix of joy and pain.

"Your majesty," Altruist said formally, "may I present my sister, the... erm... well, my sister."

Arth frowned at this odd introduction, as did many of the Squad's original members. All except Karis, who had an odd smile on her face. "You are called the Lady?" Arth asked.

The mermaiden offered Arth a perfect curtsey. "If it pleases your majesty, yes, you may call me that." She smiled shyly, looking up at Arth through long eyelashes.

But Arth's expression twisted. "Oy, enough of all this 'sire' and 'highness' and 'majesty' baloney!" he complained.

The Lady looked alarmed. "My lord?"

"Aye, that one too!" Arth glanced at each person in the room. "You lot can call me King if ya want, or even dagster fer all I care. Person'ly, I prefer *Arth*. But enuff with all the rest!"

The Sergeant-at-arms looked scandalized, and Arth's Daddie and Uncle Bertie clearly couldn't decide whether to be disappointed or amused by the outburst. But how could anyone disagree with such an order? Arth *was* the King.

"Now." Arth focused on the Lady again. "You was understandable scared by the Wizard's shenanigans, and fer that, I apolergize. I don't fink he ever meant ya harm, but ole Hembrose can be a bit... overzealotous sometimes." Arth sighed. "I'm sorry if I scared ya too, just now, with meh little tantrum. Can ya see it in yer heart to forgivin' the two of us?"

Hembrose had blushed deeply, but like Arth, he gazed expectantly at the Lady, eager to hear her answer.

Her eyes were still wide. "You have my forgiveness... Arth." There was a surprising amount of emotion in the girl's voice when she spoke the King's name. "And," she went on, "for your sake, and for the sake of the mercy you have already shown my father, I will forgive your friend as well."

Arth broke into a wide grin, and the Lady smiled back.

"Oh brother," Pyrsie murmured. She could *feel* the attraction between those two, even though they were on opposite sides of a huge room from each other. What in the worlds? They'd never even met before!

"In that case," Arth declared, "I hereby pardon the Wizard of any past crimes and order the warrant fer his arrest torn up, blah, blah, blah. Sarge, I'm sure ya can make up whatever official-soundin' documents is necessary, yeah?"

"At once, your... um... dagster-ness."

The Ringmaster and Bodyguard were definitely amused by *this*, chortling into their hands.

"As fer you two," Arth went on, gesturing to Antagonist and Wizard. "I expect ya to let go of yer grudges. No more lookin' fer ways to circumbend my orders out of spite fer each other. You's part of the same team now." He hesitated. "But mate," he added just to Hembrose, "I fink it's best if ya steer clear of the Lady from now on."

Hembrose seemed to blush an even deeper crimson.

Pyrsie studied Arth again. Yes, her friend *did* still speak with the same informality as always, but much of the silliness was gone now. As Pyrsie had noticed time and again since he first assumed leadership of the Squad, Arth continued to grow more and more serious beneath his casual exterior.

"Good enuff fer the moment," the King concluded. "Now, let's talk 'bout them luggernauts finally. They's truly the biggest whalerphant in the room, if ya ask me."

Sarge and Noble and Paladin nodded approval, and the discussion ensued.

While the Squad talked, Pyrsie shooed Arth off the ornate table, gesturing for the men to flip it over. Choosing a screwdriver, she began removing the bolts that fastened the table's eight legs to its surface, only halfway listening. The war with the lugs was important to be sure, but now that the excitement of this table retrofit had overtaken her, the Inventor had far more immediate things on her mind.

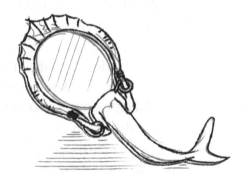

· sixteen ·

Forgotten once more, Gwen treaded water quietly in a back corner of the throne room. That didn't bother her, though. She was used to being ignored, even preferred it to being the center of attention.

The King glanced at her then, offering a shy smile that she was powerless to avoid returning. Apparently she wasn't entirely forgotten after all. And Arthos Penn, *shy*? It seemed out of character for the kind, confident leader who had somehow united the people of Caymerlot in the midst of this crisis—a crisis her own father, in his pride and selfishness, had helped cause instead of preventing. Thinking of Papá and his squandered potential, Gwen's heart broke all over again, but she lifted her chin and refused to cry. For all that was terrible about this day, there was something exciting about it too.

In particular, this dashing new King who stood with his friends and advisors, leading by listening.

"How in all the worlds did the lugs get onto Caymerlot?" the young dagman wanted to know. "Did they foller us from Hulandia?"

"No, sssss—ahem," Gwen's brother Alber faked a cough. "Sir dagster," he finished lamely, causing Gwen to smile a little. "Remember, the lugmen came from the northwest. Your party arrived from the south."

The Sergeant-at-arms raised a tentacle. "We have reports of a new bridge connecting Lugarth to Caymerlot now, somewhere between the Kark's Fangs and Dagmør's truss bridge."

"A new bridge, just that fast?" snorted the eqman who had arrived in Caymerlot with the King. "Impossible! Bridges between nilands are a magical embodiment of the friendship between the peoples of those nilands."

"And surely there can be no such regard between *these* niland's peoples," agreed another of the King's companions, a centman like the Guide. Unlike the Guide, this man was very stiff and formal, and entirely bald. "With the luggernauts on this reign of terror, I doubt any aquatics are interested in pursuing mutual prosperity with them."

"I wouldn't be so sure," said the fierce, auburn-haired huwoman next to him. Dressed in that brilliant Diamond Armor, this could only be the Knight—which made the centman her longtime companion, the Noble.

Noble raised one brow. "You're suggesting some of the citizens of Caymerlot are indeed friendly with the lugmen?"

The Knight nodded slowly. "It was easy to miss in the confusion of battle, but... I'm certain I saw some karkmen fighting on the side of the invaders. A few kelpies too."

Several squad members stared at the woman in shock. Even the gnomaid, who had just finished removing the table's second leg, turned and gaped.

"She saw true," Sarge confirmed quietly. "The King thinks some of the lugs' captives—the ones captured a year ago—switched sides in exchange for freedom, or maybe..."

He sighed, eyes turning toward Gwen apologetically. "Maybe out of spite, after being abandoned by the Underlord."

"It's scary to fink some of ours might be sidin' with them monsters," the King said. "Much less they could bring a new bridge into bein' so quick. But what concerns me more is the level of coordinikation demonstrated in the lugmen's retreat. It *must* be the Ransacker leadin' them now, seeing as he always had more leadership ability than the Khan."

Gwen's middle brother Ander rubbed his face tiredly. "The new lugman ruler definitely has a good mind for tactics and coordination, but it's not this Ransacker fellow. The lugs call their new alpha the Demagogue."

The Knight frowned. "How do you know this?"

"We took a man into custody," Ander explained. "A kark, one of the ones fighting for the invaders. After... questioning... the fellow admitted that he was inspired by this Demagogue to rebel against the oppression of the Underlord, who—he says—instituted a class system at odds with everything Caymerlot supposedly stands for."

"Hear, hear!" cried one of the two older dagmen, turning to give the other old man a high five.

"I can see my people going for that too," agreed the kelpie with the strange haircut. "We spent far too long being treated like poo."

Ander scowled, but surely even he must have seen the unfairness of Papá's regime. Alber certainly had, for he and Gwen had spoken of it—carefully—several times over the years. The fact that it was now being discussed openly in the company of the new King, a *dagman* of all things, encouraged Gwen to believe that true change was finally coming.

"But how did this Demagogue convince anyone to turn against their own people?" Sarge asked. "To fight instead for the very monsters who enslaved them this last year?"

"Well, first the Demagogue freed them from that slavery," Alber spoke up excitedly. "Ending slavery was one of the fellow's first acts on coming to power, but he didn't simply make it illegal. He instituted a kind of restitution. He actually insisted that every lug who'd held a captive be forced into captivity themselves, to pay off the debt."

"And the lugs agreed to this!?" the eqman blurted.

"Apparently his arguments were very convincing," Alber said with a grin, though the expression faded quickly. This Demagogue only seemed like a wonderful man at first, until you remembered how he used his new followers to invade Caymerlot.

"By all accounts, he's a highly skilled orator," Ander agreed dryly. "A real man-of-the-people, capable of inflaming the passions of all who listen to him. But not all of his convincing was done with words. After the old Khan was defeated, the Demagogue slaughtered dozens of other lugs in his bid for power, starting with a particularly vicious monster called the Bully. They say he's the most smokethirsty lugman ruler of the age.* And if you can believe it, he wields a Ruby Warhammer too heavy for even five normal luggernauts to lift together."

Everyone fell silent for a long moment, thinking over the implications of this.

"Obviously the war hammer bit is exaggeration," Noble said quietly. "But this does indeed explain the new bridge. If so many karks and kelpies have allied themselves with the lugmen, a new bridge would be no trouble at all."

"I think they've allied themselves to the lugs' *ruler* more than the lugman people," Alber pointed out. "But yes."

---

* "Smokethirsty"? I think this is probably the equivalent of "bloodthirsty" in Overtwixt, where there's no blood, just smoke. —N

At that moment, the air was filled with a high-pitched shrieking that sent Gwen's heart into her throat—and she wasn't the only one, for half the Squad began drawing weapons as they spun to face outward. The screech died just as suddenly as it began, and only then did Gwen hear the reassuring sound of laughter, for Arth the King had doubled over in a fit of hilarity. "Yer all's faces," he cried, swiping at his eyes. "As if that Dimmergog had popped in to scream at us fer a minute."

The little gnomaid Inventor lifted her hand, showing everyone the high-powered glass cutter she was now using. "Je m'excuse," the girl said in her funny accent. Gwen had no idea what that meant, but she assumed it was an apology. "But zee time has come for me to start... rearranging zis table."

The King didn't want to leave the Inventor out of his council of war, but she was more focused on her project, so he ultimately moved most of the Squad to the far side of the room near the dais. There they continued their discussion while the gnomaid returned to slicing up the table.

Gwen drifted over to watch the other young woman work. After half a lifetime in Crystal City, nothing about the working of glass should have fascinated her anymore; but having been sequestered in the Keep for so long, even this everyday construction tool was a marvel to her. Gwen couldn't even tell if it was magical or mundane, but somehow the device shot a fine stream of water at such high pressure that the water itself cut through the glass of the table.

"You're very talented," Gwen finally told the Inventor in a moment of silence between cuts. "First what you did with your Diamond cup, healing all those people. Now this."

"Just wait until you see zee masterpiece I have planned for zis thing!" the other girl answered. "Um, you were very helpful wiz zee wounded earlier too," she added. "Zee way you kept everyone calm for me."

"It was the least I could do," Gwen said, trying not to feel ashamed. Her earlier attempts to rescue the populace singlehandedly had produced mixed results; while she'd made two successful trips into the city to lead refugees back to the safety of the Keep, her third foray had been disastrous. Once that pack of luggernauts had caught her scent, the final group under her care had been cut off from safety, forced to flee farther and farther the wrong direction. "All I really did—during the battle and after—is talk," Gwen said with a shrug.

"Do not discount zee power of your words, or your voice," the gnomaid replied. "You soothed zee people when zat was needed, and you were forceful when *zat* was required. They call you zee Siren sometimes, no?"

"I prefer the Lady, but..." Gwen trailed off.

The Inventor resumed her glass-cutting, making a particularly long cut, then another at a different angle, in the shape of a wedge. As she worked, Gwen sneaked peeks toward the dais, where the King remained deep in conversation with the rest of his Squad. The third time she did this, she was surprised to find *him* already sneaking another glimpse at *her*, and both of them looked away quickly.

"I am surprised zat you and your brothers are willing to support zee new King," the Inventor said when the shrieking of her cutter subsided again.

Gwen frowned. "My father is a hard man. For what it's worth, I didn't always agree with how he ruled, and I bet I don't even know the worst of it." She hesitated, and she felt real tears welling up. "I still can't believe he tried to stab the King in the back!"

"Each person makes his or her own choices," the gnomaid said with a surprisingly gentle smile. "I will not hold your father's mistakes against you, and neither will Arth."

Gwen brightened at this. And as the Inventor continued working, Gwen began peppering her with questions about her history with the Squad... along with occasional questions about Arth the King, when she could do so without being obvious. In response, the young gnowoman shared openly about the battles they'd fought and the people they'd rescued. To hear her talk, the King's accomplishments were the most amazing out of the entire Squad, even before he'd been officially named King. But Gwen was more concerned with *who* he was than what he'd done. What kind of fellow was Arthos Penn? What interests or hobbies did he have? Was he really as nice as he seemed? Was he *always* gentle and kind? Patient? *Funny?* Before she knew it, Gwen was asking almost entirely about Arth; and though the gnomaid tried to hide her grin, it was clear this didn't bother her at all.

Suddenly, the Inventor got a funny look on her face. "I just realized... I am sitting here wiz another girl my age, talking about a *boy*." She gave Gwen a huge smile. "Zis is zee kind of thing teenage girls in every world have been doing since zee dawn of time, but I have never had a conversation like zis before." She bit her lip. "I bet you have lots of friends, ladies-in-waiting to sit around and gossip with."

Gwen blushed. "This is a first for me too, actually. And... no," she admitted. "I don't have any friends my own age, just my brothers."

"I never had any friends before Arth," the gnomaid confessed in turn. "I still don't have many, and he's my *best* friend," she added almost defiantly. "But he is only a friend... you know what I mean? You have nothing to fear from me." Now the gnomaid was the one turning pink, and she quickly stuck out her hand. "I am zee Inventor of Gnoburrow, but you can call me Pyrsie."

Gwen's eyes widened in shock, then delight. First the King revealed his real-world name to her, and now this accomplished Inventor? "I'm Gwen," she whispered back, as if imparting an exciting secret—which she was, for real names were reserved for family and close friends in the culture of Caymerlot. "Does this mean you wish to be friends?" She gripped Pyrsie's fingers in a handshake.

Pyrsie returned the squeeze though it was obviously an unfamiliar gesture for her. "Yes, I very much hope zat we can be friends." Then she placed the back of her hand against the back of Gwen's to complete what must have been the gnoman version of the greeting. "And if I may say so, you are not at all zee spoiled princess I expected you to be." She grinned, obviously hoping Gwen was not offended by this.

Gwen burst into a fit of giggles that was neither shy nor Lady-like.

When at last Gwen's new friend Pyrsie was done reconstructing the table, she stood back proudly and called for Arth and the other squad members to come see. She had combined dozens of sections of glass of varying shapes and sizes to form an entirely new piece of furniture. But instead of looking cobbled-together, it was a true work of art— diverse pieces melded as one to form a beautiful whole, just like the Squad. From the way she pointed them out, Pyrsie was particularly proud of how she'd cut the legs to varying lengths, so that the new table sat level despite the sloping floor. Her recreation straddled the shallow center of the room, with a place for each squad member to sit or stand, in whatever depth of water he or she found comfortable. In the case of Paladin and Noble, that was no depth at all, for she'd refashioned two of the chairs as platforms for them to get their hooves out of the water entirely. Most of all, Pyrsie was proud of the fact that:

"It's round," she pointed out brightly.

"It's *round?*" Ander repeated dumbly. "But why?"

"And where will the King sit?" Alber asked, confused.

"Does it matter?" Pyrsie shrugged. "Somewhere around zee circle with zee rest of us, first among equals."

Ander spun to face Arth, scandalized. "Surely you won't stand for such insolence from an underling. She thinks herself your *equal?*"

The King burst out laughing. "Oy, of course she does! You's *all* my equals. We each gots different roles to play, true and sure, but there ain't none of yeh who's less valuable than me."

"Please, your... King... ship," Sarge said. "Refusing your rightful titles is one thing. But this... The ruler *must* be held up as someone special, greater."

"Seems to me that's how you folks got into trouble with the Underlord." Arth sighed. "I get it. People want someone to look up to, some'un bigger-than-life taking care of 'em. I can try to be that bloke, as part of my service to them. But if you lot don't treat me normal, how's I ever gonna keep this Kingliness bidness from goin' to my head?"

"Still, um, Arth—" Ander tried to argue.

"But there weren't no insolence here," Arth said, smiling fondly at Pyrsie. "The Inventor accomp'ished exactly what I was hoping fer. She knows me well."

Pyrsie beamed, offering a curtsey of her own to the rest of the Squad. Still at the gnomaid's side, Gwen muttered, "My, but Arth really *is* different from my father." Oh no... had she just said that out loud?

"Now gather 'round," Arth commanded. "Sit, sit!"

There was some jostling as people found their seats or platforms and pulled them up around the circular new table. When they were done, just two of the thirteen original chairs remained empty, and they happened to be side-by-side. Arth gestured to one of them, then looked at Gwen. "My Lady of the Lake? Would you be so kind as to join us?"

Gwen smiled uncertainly and swam forward, allowing Arth to hold the chair out for her. Sitting, she looked around the circle at the diverse faces both strange and familiar. She was almost surprised when she noticed the Wizard again; for she'd nearly forgotten he was in the room, amazing as that was. But then, she had finally forgiven the old man, and there was always something freeing about taking that step. Still, Gwen didn't linger when their eyes met, shifting her gaze to the next squad member. She still didn't want to find herself alone with the man, but she wasn't uncomfortable in *this* situation, surrounded by other people for whom she felt a growing trust.

The King was last to sit. "No assigned seats," he declared. "Let's switcheroo every meeting we hold here. Also, by the time we's done today, I want the loyalty at this table to go all directions—not just to me. No more rivalries, just bonds of brotherhood and sisterhood. You lot reckon you can make that happen?"

Gwen slowly nodded, thinking that just maybe, she *could* do that. Ander shook his head, not in disagreement but rather perplexity, while Alber began to smile openly. Others of the old Squad gave signs of approval, not surprised, while one of the older dagmen was practically crying. That was Arth's father, Gwen learned later; the old circus Ringmaster was weeping from *pride*. Indeed, how very, very different Arth's family was from her own.

The Knight looked around at the group. "We've been called Heroes of the Brown Stable," she began softly.

"Zee ones who were Bound but still Able," Pyrsie chimed in with a grin.

"We rescued ole Caymerlot—" said Arth's father.

"—from a strange lugman despot," added Arth's uncle.

"And now at long last…" the Knight began drumming her hands on the table. Others followed suit, all of them turning to look at the kelpie for some reason.

That kelpie was *not* amused. "You're making fun of me. That's no way to be!"

"Here we are now," the Knight concluded, gesturing at Pyrsie's glass creation, "the Heroes of the Round Table!"

"Now *that* just sounds stupid," the kelpie complained. "And, um, rather insipid." *

"Naw, I fink it's got a nice ring to it," Arth said with a sly grin. He waited a long moment, then shocked Gwen to her core by softly elbowing her. "Ya know, a *Round* Table? It's got a nice… *ring* to it? Get it?"

Gwen groaned along with everyone else, but she couldn't stop smiling at this amazing man beside her. Meanwhile, her insides were all twisted up with nervous anticipation. Why she was nervous, even she didn't know, for at long last she was seeing the fulfillment of what the Guide promised her so long ago. This man, this King, really didn't come as a surprise. And yet meeting him in the flesh, beginning the long, slow process of getting to know him, was a thrill like none other.

Somehow, in the midst of all this day's tragedy, something beautiful was happening here.

---

* uninteresting, not very imaginative

· seventeen ·

Something tragic was happening in Caymerlot, so far as Hembrose was concerned. Not the violence and suffering; that *was* bad, but he was confident the war with the lugmen would soon come to an end under Arth's leadership—now that he had the resources and army of an entire nation behind him. Hembrose was happy, in his way, that Arth was stepping into the role of King so effectively.

No, the tragedy was that Arth so clearly fancied the Lady of the Lake, whom he knew to be Hembrose's beloved!

The Wizard felt betrayed, not to mention humiliated by the way he'd been treated in front of the Squad yesterday. He'd been nothing but loyal to Arth, yet Arth hadn't punished Antagonist at all for his torture of Hembrose. And instead of supporting Hembrose in regard to his misunderstandings with the Lady, Arth had called Hembrose overzealous and even apologized for his behavior—as if there was anything to apologize for! Now *Arth* was the one showing romantic interest in the girl?

Some repayment for the steadfast friendship of the greatest magical practitioner of the age!

How dare Arth? And to tell *him* to stay away from the Lady in the future? *Hembrose*, who had loved the Lady of the Lake longer than Arth had walked the nilands of Overtwixt?

Of course the Lady was looking at Arth all lovey-wuvvy. She'd always been obsessed with the Relic-in-the-Rock, thinking her fate bound to the man who freed it from the stone. But Hembrose remembered when she had looked at *him* that way, so long ago when he'd been a young man newly arrived in Overtwixt. It was only after he grew old from too much exposure to the library that she began seeing him differently. He felt sure if he could only fix that age gap, things would go back to the way they should be. Hembrose would be the one she loved once more.

And so, at long last, the Wizard of Merlyn had initiated his plan for accomplishing exactly that.

He hadn't told anyone he was leaving, least of all his "friend" Arth. Instead, Hembrose had wakened himself in the middle of the night, cloaked his merman form, and swum out from the Crystal Keep under cover of darkness. Wracked by headaches from his unfiltered use of the emerald's magic in battle, he had traveled hard for hours, retracing the same currents he'd swum with the Altruist a lifetime earlier... until he finally floated before the barred doorway of the Hidden Chamber on the niland of Merlyn.

As before, the Hidden Chamber was guarded by two caped mermen in armor, but they didn't see Hembrose, for he'd summoned an obscuring cloud of silt in the already dark maze of underwater corridors. As the two men coughed, confused but not alarmed, Hembrose flung a thin green mist across them, freezing them in time just long enough so he could unbar the gate and slip through. The two men would never know anyone was now inside.

Hembrose gasped just beyond the doorway, clutching his head as a stabbing pain tore through his mind. Even with his eyes closed, he saw bright white lights. This had been his worst headache yet, for he had drawn more deeply on the harvested power of the emerald yesterday than ever before—first with the immense time bubble around the ballistae, then in the fighting afterwards. The lingering pain had not improved his mood or his anger towards Arth, but every time he invoked the green magic again, his agony flared anew. Hembrose desperately needed to fashion a relic of his own to contain the emerald, to act as a conduit for the flow of its power, so he could stop drawing on the emerald directly.

Well, he was here in the Hidden Chamber again, finally. There was no longer anything standing in his way.

The main area of the Chamber was just as he remembered it, a network of caverns with bookshelves chiseled from the natural stone walls. Additional bookcases, fashioned from coral or driftwood, stood freely in the middle of each room. Hembrose started by inscribing a time bubble around the confines of the main cavern, then layering another bubble around it, then yet another—building upon the foundation of the library's own time dilation and compounding the effects again and again, for he simply didn't have any time to waste in the outside world.

Then the Wizard began *growing* his new staff from the driftwood bookcases that held Overtwixt's most arcane magical knowledge. With his golden mantle and his emerald set off to one side, Hembrose breathed pure blue magic into the driftwood, bringing it back to life. This wasn't as hard as it sounded, for plants did not truly live in Overtwixt as they did in the real world; seaweed and flowers and trees were simply a manifestation of this world's magic. Something that had never lived could never truly die, so the driftwood immediately flourished beneath the Wizard's ministrations.

Tiny shoots appeared, new branches growing directly from the shelves. These sprigs soon sprouted foliage, then flowering petals, then clusters of tree nuts or berries as they steadily grew into tender saplings that waved in the gentle current of the library. There was nothing rapid about this growth, unless you were outside all those time bubbles looking in; here inside the Hidden Chamber, months passed.

When some of the branches reached arm's length, he selected two candidates that had sprouted side by side, and these he began cultivating. Pruning them of offshoots and fruit, he bound the two stalks together, causing them to twist about each other as they continued to grow. Years passed within the Chamber, the cavern becoming choked with plant life, but Hembrose maintained his entire focus on that single intertwined growth as it hardened into maturity.

At long last, that twisted trunk—now a single organism brought to life by the blue magic—stood as tall as Hembrose himself. Only then did he allow it to flower one last time, the end of each trunk branching into clusters of leaves and berries. And when the moment was right, Hembrose hefted the immense emerald in one hand, held his breath, and carefully fitted the green-glowing gemstone into the basket of twigs and nettles at the center of the foliage.

Everything immediately went very, very wrong.

He had been so sure that the combination of blue and green magics would make his new relic stronger, if he could bring them together in just the right way. He should have known better. The instant the two magics made contact, the emerald *cracked* audibly. The foliage and berries began to wither and die, while the hardened dual trunks smoldered and blackened at a rapid pace.

With a cry of alarm, Hembrose cut off the steady flow of blue magic he'd been feeding the growth for years now, bringing his hand down in a chopping motion at its base. With a terrible, wrenching *snap*, the twisted staff came free in his hand and he stumbled backwards.

Breathing raggedly, the Wizard slowly straightened. The cavern was so congested these days that he couldn't see far, but what he did see was bathed in a strong green glow from the emerald—and he could still feel great power brimming within that stone, despite the ragged crack that now spread across its surface. Hembrose breathed a quiet sigh of relief, grateful the damage had not rendered it useless. Then he inspected the rest of his new staff.

Six paces tall from end to end, it was now straight and rigid. Like the bookcase from which it had grown, its twisted trunks had the smooth, weathered look of aged driftwood. And yet there was so much more strength to it than that. In the traumatic moment when the green and blue failed to mix, the staff had been simultaneously damaged and preserved, petrified in the moment of its destruction—right down to the foliage that flared out from either side of the emerald like a crest. It now appeared skeletal but unyielding, forever frozen in the act of burning away to nothing.

The Wizard realized that his crushing headache—a constant companion these years in the Hidden Chamber—had subsided to a dull throb, a sort of low-level mental exhaustion he could now easily ignore. Smiling tentatively, he gave his new staff a little flourish... then channeled magic through it for the first time.

Rather than emitting a single green fireball as he'd intended, an entire wave of destruction burst from the emerald. It swept down the aisle of bookcases, burning the congested growth of saplings to ash in a wide arc. It even damaged the bookshelves themselves, badly in some cases, though most of the books and scrolls were protected by their own magic. Hembrose was unprepared for the physical intensity of the staff's recoil as he unleashed such easy destruction, but he was overjoyed to discover there was no *mental* recoil. No nausea, no new headache.

Hembrose O'Hildirun had achieved his first miracle of the day: creating a true magical talisman of his own, a vessel to focus the power he had harvested from his enemies.

"Behold," he whispered, awed despite himself. "The Emerald Caduceus."* Because the Diamond Scepter and the Diamond Armor and all the rest of Sovereign's Relics weren't the only artifacts that deserved capitalized names!

For several long minutes, Hembrose continued to admire his Caduceus, running his hands lovingly along its length. Then with a sigh, he hid the relic in a back corner of the library, reminding himself they would be reunited soon.

Shrouding himself in darkness, the Wizard exited the Hidden Chamber of Merlyn—slipping out between those two blind and confused guards, then allowing his compounded time bubbles to collapse behind him.

To his surprise, he had to stop and rest on reaching the surface of the water under the open white sky of Overtwixt. Mentally, he felt better than ever, his headache and nausea finally under control; but physically, he was worn-out, run-down, short of breath. His knuckles had become gnarled and knobby, and when he pulled a lock of his long hair forward for inspection, he saw it was now solid white.

Hembrose blinked. He was... old. *Truly* old now, bent and elderly, without the vibrant energy that had so long sustained him. This last bout in the library had stolen what few years he had left to live here in Overtwixt.

---

* A caduceus (kuh-DOO-see-uhs) is a staff or wand. In human mythology, it often has a pair of snakes wrapped around its length, with wings at the top, and is carried by messengers. The Wizard's Emerald Caduceus must be where that twisted look originated. —*N*

He chuckled, a rasping sound. Fortunately, he already had a solution for that.

Traveling north from the Hidden Chamber—stopping frequently to rest—he made his way along the beach toward Gatehenge, the circle of standing stones that acted as a bridge between Overtwixt and the merman real world. As before, during his very first days on Merlyn, there were mermen and merwomen working with molten glass all along the sandy shore. Not wanting to draw their attention, Hembrose turned his patched golden mantle into a ratty gray cloak and drew up the hood to hide his face.

When he was nearly to the Gatehenge, he was overtaken by a procession of other travelers preparing to return to the real world. From their conversation as they passed around him, Hembrose understood that most of these folks were fleeing for fear of the lugmen. But there was also one member of the procession who was being *forced* to leave Overtwixt, exiled against his will.

The Underlord.

Hembrose gaped—and hurriedly pulled his hood tighter around his face—as the old ruler of Caymerlot passed him by. He was accompanied by all three of his children as well as a contingent of caped guards now loyal to Arth. Though years had once again passed for Hembrose, it had been only a few days since Arth's first council at the Round Table. They were only now carrying out the King's sentence of banishment against the Underlord.

Joining the crowd as it grouped around the Gatehenge, Hembrose watched in delight as the Sergeant-at-arms read from a long scroll, reciting a list of the Underlord's crimes as well as Arth's pronouncement. Then Sarge and another kark gripped the man firmly under his arms and dragged him up the beach, into the center of the standing stones. The Underlord argued and resisted and dragged his tail the entire way.

"Father, please," Antagonist called, even as the Lady burst into tears. "You're embarrassing yourself *and* us."

The Underlord gave his children a withering look. "Traitors," he spat, clearly meaning Sarge and the guards too.

"I remember a man I once greatly respected," Altruist said, obviously meaning the words only for his father, though the distance between them made a private conversation impossible. "He taught me the importance of dignity. Dignified men do not rave and thrash, Father." His voice was thick with disappointment and disapproval, but he took a deep breath and moderated his tone. "One way or the other, you are leaving Overtwixt this day. But depart with dignity," the Altruist concluded, "and perhaps someday you can return with dignity."

For whatever reason, his words had the desired effect. The Underlord's mouth snapped shut and he straightened his posture, shoulders back, nose high.

The Sergeant released his old ruler's arm, nodding to the other kark to do the same, and they moved back. "Do I need to say the words," he asked softly, "or—"

"Mag-mer-Mel!" the Underlord announced proudly.

Instantly, the three men in the circle of stone pillars were buffeted by strong winds. A vortex formed in midair, sucking water up the beach from the sea to surround the trio—and just that suddenly, the Underlord and the vortex both disappeared. The karks, not native to the merman real world, were of course left behind.

The other travelers followed quickly after that, each stepping within the Gatehenge and speaking the name of their real world destination—mostly Mag-mer-Mel or Hybra-sil, but occasionally Mermezh or Sublantis, and even one instance of Sandy Island. The Lady of the Lake cried into her brothers' shoulders through it all, as beautiful as ever despite her distress.

Hembrose was the last to pull himself slowly up the beach, fighting joints that were unexpectedly swollen and stiff. It was long past time to be done with this old age business. He sneaked one final peek at his beloved, who had barely glanced at him as he passed. Only moments remained until all was made right, and they could be reunited.

He spoke the word: "Hybra-sil."

The vortex of air and water struck him, spinning him about and whipping the ratty gray cloak from his shoulders. Water crashed over him, leaving him sputtering until he realized all was suddenly calm once more. Hembrose was back in his real world, floating at the center of Gatehenge in downtown Amerlon, in the atoll nation of Hybra-sil.

Some of the other travelers who had named Hybra-sil were still in sight, getting their bearings before returning to their real lives. Hembrose even recognized a few, and they were invariably younger than they'd been just minutes ago in Overtwixt. For, just as time moved more quickly in libraries than the rest of Overtwixt, time moved more quickly in Overtwixt than the real world—usually. In most of the accounts Hembrose had read, mermen returning home from the world of bridges found themselves almost the same age as when they'd left.

Heart thudding, he looked down at his hands, noting the smooth skin, the knuckles no longer knobby. And his hair was shorter, the way he used to wear it before leaving for

Overtwixt the first time, thick and luxurious and *black*—not a streak of gray in sight. He smiled.

Hembrose O'Hildirun had achieved his second miracle of the day: becoming young again.

Now all that remained was the third miracle.

"Right this way, lad," called one of the guards as he took notice of Hembrose. "A little disorientation is normal, especially if your return here comes as a surprise. Please exit the—"

"Nay, lad, stop!" cried another guard when he saw Hembrose turn around and face the sky with excitement. "Not without a lottery ticket!"

"Overtwixt!" Hembrose cried, and a strong current swept him up just that suddenly, spinning him around in the now-familiar underwater vortex. Disorienting though it certainly was, he forced himself to maintain his decorum until he was deposited on the sandy beach of Merlyn once more. You didn't get many opportunities to make a second first impression, and the Lady was waiting.

Except the Lady was *not* waiting. Even though she and her brothers and the guards had been here mere moments ago, floating in the surf just outside Gatehenge, they were now long gone. Of course. Time moved faster here.

Hembrose sighed but could not feel disappointed long. The third miracle would have to wait, but it *would* happen.

Whistling a tune from his childhood, the young—young!—merman set off to recover his Emerald Caduceus, then rejoin the Squad in Caymerlot.

The Roster of the Squad of Heroes

originally alphabetized by role

Role	Real Name	Race	Relative Age	Relic
The Inventor	Pyrsyful Rochelle	gnowoman	young adult	Diamond Grail
The Knight	Karis Priamos	huwoman	thirty?	Diamond Plate-Armor
The Noble	Gerald Valorian	centman	middle-aged	none
The Paladin	Kaedan Mathias	eqman	declines to answer	~~holding out for the~~ ~~none~~ Diamond Horn
The Sidekick	Limerick van Gimmick	kelpman	young adult	Diamond Aegis
The Wizard	Hembrose O'Hildirun	merman	young!*	Emerald Caduceus
The King	Arthos Penn	dogman	young adult	~~none~~ Diamond Scepter**

*~~for the time being,~~ at least
**the Relic-in-the-Rock!!

The Roster of the Squad of Heroes (continued)

Role	Real Name	Race	Relative Age	Relic
The Ringmaster	Pythagoras Penn	dagman	middle-aged	none
The Bodyguard	Roberthoras Penn	dagman	"young at heart" ~~middle-aged~~	none
The Altruist	who cares?	merman	young adult	Diamond Hauberk
The Antagonist	who cares?	merman	young adult	Diamond Harpoon
The Sergeant-at-arms	Drust Cornfeldt	korkman	middle-aged	Diamond Truncheon

· eighteen ·

Arth was worried about Hembrose. And Morth too, of course—he never stopped worrying about his twin brother, hoping desperately that this King bidness eventually led to Morth's rescue. Now, though, Arth half wondered if Hembrose had gotten himself kidnabbed too. He hadn't been seen in almost two weeks, since the Squad's first meeting around the new Round Table. The mermage hadn't even tried to join the group that carried out the Underlord's banishment a few days later, and that was especially surprising. But Arth supposed his friend had slipped off to some library somewhere. Disappearing into a stack of books for days at a time had been the Wizard's typical behavior before all these nonstop battles with the lugs, so Arth tried to tell himself everything was alright.

But even if it wasn't, Arth had plenty of other matters demanding his attention now that he was in charge in Caymerlot. First, there were all the foreign dignitaries arriving for his upcoming coronation, each of whom he was expected to meet and greet. Then came the task of locating the missing Committee members, who would need to officially recognize Arth as King. Next were preparations for the coronation ceremony itself—which a stubby cayman fellow called the Archbishop kept trying to discuss with him. Arth still didn't understand why there needed to be a big ceremony, so he tended to treat the Archbishop as a distraction, listening to the man with only half an ear.

Much more important was the continuing conflict with the lugmen. There hadn't been another full-scale attack yet, not since that day Arth took possession of the Diamond Scepter, but there'd been plenty of little skirmishes as the lugs tested Crystal City's renewed defenses. The Caymerlotion soldiers were well trained—far more so than Arth himself had ever been—and they were rapidly becoming veterans from all this fighting. But their mundane weapons simply couldn't compare to the power of the Scepter when it came to turning back the enemy. So whenever Arth's blue-caped soldiers seemed in danger of losing an engagement, they were quick to send for the new King and his Relic.

And if that wasn't enough, there was Arth's most important task of all: planning for a decisive final battle with the lugs. He wasn't sure who would start that fight, him or this Demagogue fella, but a showdown was unavoidable. If the people of Caymerlot wanted to free themselves from the lugman threat for good, Arth would need to push the enemy off this niland and destroy the bridge they'd created—but not before recovering any remaining aquatics from the other side. After all, rescuing Morth was the whole reason Arth had joined the Squad in the first place, much less accepted Kingship over Caymerlot; and besides, if the Demagogue wasn't deprived of his aquatic allies, he could just keep making new bridges as fast as Arth destroyed them.

The question was, *how?* How to rescue hundreds of people, many of whom didn't even want rescue? And how to get onto Lugarth in the first place? For that matter, how to destroy a bridge? And even once they did, what would keep the lugs from escaping into the rest of Overtwixt using the Northmount/Hulandia bridge instead? These uncertainties worried Arth almost as much as Hembrose's absence.

When coronation day finally arrived, however, the new King had no choice but to set his worries aside. As the Archbishop and Sergeant-at-arms both kept reminding him, the people needed Arth fully engaged in this day's pageantry to reassure them he was a confident ruler. Arth didn't see how confidence had anything to do with competence, but he had no choice but to play along anyway.

By now, all the important dignitaries were here. First to arrive were the ones Arth himself had traveled with, the procession that had accompanied him from Hulandia to Centhule to Gnoburrow and beyond, which he'd left behind on Delphyrd. After all those centmen, humen, eqmen, gnomen, and raimen hopped the final bridge to Caymerlot, delegates from other nearby nilands began to arrive—the leaders of the nagmen and shamen, squimen and hektmen, and even some scary-lookin' phomen. Then came creatures from lands farther away, representatives of races Arth knew only from Mum's stories: faemen, segmen, pyxies, and other insectoids; gatmen and their feline cousins; orqs and larks and slobs and gobs. The dignitaries who couldn't fly here on their own were brought in floating barges propelled by those who could. There was even a delegation of winged creatures called rephmen led by a fella called the Brigadier, every single one of whom wore glowing blue armor—which seemed to break all the rules of Sovereign's Relics. Only after *all* of these had settled into lodgings in Crystal City—and after all eleven Committee members had also been found—did the Sergeant agree the coronation could finally proceed.

So finally, today, every one of these important blokes was gathered in the grand throne room of the Crystal Keep to watch as Arth was officially crowned King.

Standing in ankle-deep water outside the closed front doors of the throne room, Arth realized his heart was thumping. Growing up in the circus, he was used to performing in front of huge crowds... but before now, he'd always been expected to make a fool of himself. He couldn't afford to do that ever again, however, and least of all today. Today, he felt the weight of much loftier expectations. The peoples of these nilands expected *him* to lead them to victory over the lugs, and that was only the start. He, the King, was expected to usher in an era of peace and prosperity, the prophesied Golden Age of Overtwixt. Arth barely felt capable of leading the Squad, much less the entire army of Caymerlot. And now they wanted all the rest of this too? No wonder his heart was thumping.

He heard a rustle and turned in surprise to behold the Lady of the Lake. The mermaid was reclining on a palanquin, a sort of couch suspended on poles carried by

four karks—a mode of transportation that Arth doubted she normally used, but that was part of today's formalities. The girl was beautiful as ever, self-possessed and shy at the same time, looking up at Arth with those big brown eyes of hers. She seemed to sense his nervousness, but she didn't say anything that might embarrass him in front of his attendants. She just rearranged his deep-blue velvet cloak so it draped more evenly over his shoulders, then leaned forward and kissed him lightly on one cheek. Before he could react, she was already gesturing for the karks to carry her through a side door into the throne room.

Arth grinned stupidly.

The main doors finally opened, and Arth beheld the crowd of dignitaries staring at him expectantly. In all that huge room, the only empty space was a narrow path leading from the doors to the dais at the far end. (For the last two weeks, the Round Table had straddled the center of that path, but it had been removed for this occasion.) Waiting just in front of the dais was the Archbishop, and everyone else fell silent as he began to speak in a loud, clear voice:

"Representatives of the nilands of Overtwixt, I hereby present unto you: Arthos Penn the dagman, first King of Caymerlot, as attested by the Guide and proven by the long-awaited recovery of the Relic-in-the-Rock—the Diamond Scepter that this man now wields before your very eyes."

Clearing his throat, Arth awkwardly lifted the Scepter high for all to see, nearly losing the velvet cloak from his shoulders in the process.

"In so far as all of you are present today to witness and affirm the King in his role," the officious cayman Archbishop continued, "speak your affirmation now."

A deafening roar filled the room as everyone lifted their voices in shouts of agreement, a clamor that seemed to last forever. When the volume finally began dying down, an ensemble of nagman musicians launched into a fanfare, which was the new King's signal to proceed up the aisle. Arth caught glimpses of recognizable faces in the crowd as he passed: Pyrsie and Daddie and Bertie flushed with excitement and joy, mouths open wide as they cheered him; the Lady Karis and Gerald the Noble, slightly more reserved but no less joyful as they shouted Arth's name, along with other members of the Squad; the Altruist and Antagonist lifting their fists without reservation; the dagmen and kelpies of the circus troupe going absolutely bonkers; and even the Portmistress bellowing loudly. The Lady of the Lake was actually *weeping*, but also smiling like it was the happiest day of her life. Of all the people Arth knew and loved in Overtwixt, only Hembrose and Morth seemed to be missing.

Oh Morth. Becoming King—or Hero, at least—had been his dream as much as it was Arth's. Arth wished his brother could be here to celebrate with him now. Better yet, he wished Morth had never got nabbed in the first place, though that meant today's coronation never woulda happened. He'd be perfectly happy playing the Fool again, if it meant having his brother the Clown back at his side.

Much of the ceremony passed in a daze for Arth. The Archbishop led him in swearing an oath to Caymerlot and the Sovereign, then the cayman anointed his forehead with warm oil, much as the Guide had done when first naming him King. When that was done, the Archbishop directed him to mount the dais and sit upon the Diamond Throne.

Next came the investiture of regalia, which was likely to take a long time indeed. This was the part of the ceremony in which he was bestowed with every conceivable symbol of royalty, almost every one of them a Relic of Sovereign belonging to a different race, each of which he would need to continue wearing or holding until the end of the coronation. First was his very own Diamond Scepter, ceremonially surrendered to the Archbishop, then returned to him with a spoken blessing. Then came a Relic from each of the aquatic races, presented by members of the Committee: the caymen's Pendant of Prudence and the nyms' Ring of Receptivity, the karkmen's Wreath of Fidelity, not to mention the delphmen's Chain of Charity, the kelpies' Anklet of Influence, and the okkies' Earring of Empathy. Arth already sat upon the merpeople's Throne of Judgment, of course, which had once been claimed by the Underlord.

By the time the nywoman Committee member slithered away, looking very pleased, it was a good thing Arth was seated. He was feeling very weighed-down! And yet the aquatics still weren't done. Even invested with eight aquatic Relics as he was, tradition dictated that the ruler of Overtwixt be presented with an actual non-Relic crown that represented all eight races at once—for this *was* a coronation, after all.* It was a tall, awkward thing that recent Underlords had stopped wearing except in formal settings; but Sarge had dug it up and even worked with Pyrsie and the gnomen craftspeople to affix a new crest across its top, giving it extra dagman flair. The only flare Arth felt was the pain in his neck at having to balance the heavy new crown atop his sweaty brow.

But the investiture was still only just beginning. The *other* representatives bestowed their Relics next—an incredible honor, but also an incredible burden as well. Responsibility... how had it come to this, when the very thing Arth had most desired out of Overtwixt was *freedom* from responsibility?

Most surprising was when the Knight and Noble approached together, their expressions solemn. Karis was holding the Diamond Crown of Compassion, which the Baron of Centhule had entrusted to her before taking his last breath in Overtwixt. "The Baron told me to find someone who is capable and honorable, and to place this Crown upon his head," she reminded Arth, as she began to do exactly that.

"Oy, hold on now," Arth objected. "I was there, remember? The Baron said to put that crown on the head of a worthwhile successor. But I don't rule Centhule, just Caymerlot. You's my allies, not my subjects."

---

* Coronation literally refers to the act of placing a crown on a head.

The Noble smiled. "You *are* the Baron's successor in your mission of protecting the weak and innocent, which was a cause close to his heart all the days he ruled."

"And whether we non-aquatics are officially your allies or your subjects," Karis pointed out, "everyone in attendance here knows that the prophesied King *is* the mortal representative of Sovereign in Overtwixt. You are now first among the monarchs of the world, just as you are first among equals within the Squad. You absolutely deserve this honor." And before he could complain further, she placed the Diamond Crown atop his head—which required hanging it off the crest of the non-Relic crown he was already wearing.*

Arth felt more overwhelmed than ever, burdened physically and emotionally by so many expectations placed upon him. Then the Burrowcrat stepped forward, spouting shallow praises of his own for the new King. He placed in Arth's hand "zee Diamond Diadem of Diplomacy" and renewed his request that the King sign a pact of friendship and mutual protection between the gnomen and aquatics.

Oddly, facing this two-faced fella who had betrayed Pyrsie so many months ago, Arth felt a surge of confidence. He still wasn't sure about the rest of

---

* And that is how the fourth human Relic ended up in modern-day Caymerdelphia, something I always wondered about. —*N*

his new responsibilities, but here before him was an opportunity to correct an injustice—and he was happy to undertake *that* duty.

Turning the brightly-polished "Diamond Diadem" in one hand, Arth felt a twinge from the Scepter. He couldn't help but smile and shake his head (very carefully, of course). "So you's worried about the lugs, is ya?"

The Burrowcrat bobbed his head eagerly. "Zee gnomen, we have no powerful army like Caymerlot, your most majestic highness. We have only zee local police force."

"Very well," Arth said, trying to remember to speak more sophisticated-like, at least as long as he was sitting on this Throne. "If it be agreeables to ya, Caymerlot will accept Gnoburrow as a protectorate." He had already discussed with his shaman Diplomat the possibility of such arrangements with other nilands. "That would mean you's under my protection, but also under my authority."

The Burrowcrat hesitated. "Under zee authority of zee King? That is perhaps more than I am doing zee bargaining for."

Arth raised his hands. "It's entire up to you. But Gnoburrow wouldn't be stuck or nuffin. The leader of the gnomen would be allowed to tear up the agreement at any time, and the gnomen would go back to bein' on their own."

The current gnoman leader hesitated only a moment longer, then he nodded in acceptance. Arth waved, and his Diplomat quickly drafted the paperwork and presented it for both Arth and the Burrowcrat to sign. As soon as that was done, Arth again hefted the "Relic" that the Burrowcrat had gifted him. "Say, you called this the Diamond Diadem of Diplomacy?"

The Burrowcrat licked his lips. "Zat is right, my liege."

Arth snorted. "More like the Glass Globe of Guile." Raising his hand high, Arth threw the "Relic" onto the floor of the dais, where it shattered into a thousand pieces. He pointed. "That ain't no Diamond, much less one of Sovereign's Relics. Do ya gots any idea the punishment for lyin' to yer King?"

The gnoman leader went completely white in the face.

"*You*," Arth said angrily, "is a fool. You didn't have to make any gift to me at all. Ya din't even have to come here. But instead ya stood here and lied and pretended to sacrifice this wonderful thing, when there's people in attendance who knows there's no such gnoman Relic as this."

The crowd of onlookers watched with wide eyes as this little drama continued to unfold. Pyrsie was smiling.

Shaking his head, Arth went on. "I hereby strip the Burrowcrat of his position and take him into custody, pending investergation into this and other allegations that has been reported to me. Even so," Arth assured the crowd, "I will hold up my end of this new bargain. I *will* protect the gnomen from the ravages of the lugs, as promised."

The Burrowcrat was now quivering with both terror and rage. "Never mind zee bargain!" he blubbered. "Give me back zat paper so I can tear it up now," he ordered the Diplomat. "You no longer have zee authority of me, *King*."

The Diplomat made no move to comply, however, and Arth just shook his head sadly. "You can't tear it up 'cause you ain't ruler no more. I already stripped ya of authority, remember? Try to keep up." He gestured for two of his caped guards to come forward and arrest the fella. "And really, mate. You would deny yer people protection just to save yerself from the fate you deserve? You's just as selfish and corrupt as I thought."

The Burrowcrat began sobbing bitterly as the guards dragged him away.

"Would the Inventor please step forward?" Arth called. Pyrsie promptly pushed through the crowd and popped up before the dais, grinning. "As newly-appointed protector of Gnoburrow," Arth said, "I hereby pardon the Inventor of any past crimes—fully acknowledgin' that such accusations was bogus in the first place—and I order the warrant fer her arrest torn up, blah, blah, blah." He had already done exactly this for Hembrose, and it thrilled him to be able to finally do the same for Pyrsie as well. "Diplomat…"

"I shall prepare the necessary documents at once, O King," the fast-talking shaman agreed. And those weren't the only new legal papers needed, either. By the time Arth was done with the gnomen, he had appointed Pyrsie's friend Pilgrim as interim ruler in the Burrowcrat's place. The fella looked stunned as he melted back into the crowd.

The bestowal of regalia from distant lands resumed, and despite what had just happened to the Burrowcrat, a number of other nilands requested Caymerlot's protection. The crowd whispered more excitedly than ever, gazing upon Arth with awe and approval. And though Arth continued to feel the weight of new responsibilities growing upon his shoulders, the resolution of Pyrsie's conflict with the Burrowcrat left him encouraged. He *wasn't* gonna have the answers for every question that arose during his Kingship. But he knew right from wrong, and when the right of a situation was unclear, he knew how to ask advice.

"Behold, all of ye, behold!" the Archbishop cried when the investiture was over at last. "Arthos Penn the dagman, first King of Caymerlot, friend of Centhule, lawful protector of Gnoburrow, ally of all the little peoples and preeminent among the monarchs of the peoples who love the Sovereign."

"Sovereign protect the King!" the crowd cried in response, their voices deafening. "Sovereign protect the King! Sovereign protect the King!"

When the applause died down, it rapidly became clear that everyone expected a speech from Arth. All of his anxiety immediately returned, almost overpowering despite the waves of peace that always emanated from his Diamond Scepter. As the silence grew uncomfortable, the Sergeant-at-arms whispered from nearby, "I think the people would like to hear about your plan for dealing with the lugmen."

Arth groaned inside. Sarge should know better, since he'd been part of every brainstorming session. Sure, the Squad had discussed their overarching goals for ending the war, but they still had no idea *how* to accomplish those goals.

Squeezing his eyes shut, Arth wished fervently for wisdom and compassion to lead the peoples of Overtwixt, for specific direction on *how* to defeat the lugmen and rescue the people they'd taken captive. He aimed those feelings at the Sovereign's magical Diamond Scepter, almost like a prayer.

And suddenly, the Scepter flared to life, its Diamond shaft and the immense Diamond gemstone in its gold basket glowing brilliantly, emanating a soothing blue light. Moments later, to everyone's complete surprise—Arth's included—all the *other* Relics he held or wore lit up also, even the Diamond Throne he sat upon. That should have been impossible; Sovereign's Relics were only usable by the race for which they were created, and only *one* should be usable at a time anyway. Clearly, Sovereign himself must be sending a message to the crowd if he allowed any one person to tap the power of all these Relics at once.

And Arth knew, in that moment, that this was entirely true. The power of the Sovereign *must* be active; for just like that, Arth knew exactly how to resolve the war.

He began laying out the plan that had just appeared in his head, fully formed. Arth talked for some time, his friends, advisors, and the people of Caymerlot staring, then eventually beginning to nod in understanding. Finally he brought his summation to a close. "So while all our soldiers is fightin' the lugs here, we's gonna send a team of gnoman engineers to Northmount on Hulandia," he said. "But for this to work, I'm gonna need the help of *all* my friends in the Squad—the Inventor and the Wizard most espec'ly." Arth hesitated then, remembering belatedly that he hadn't seen Hembrose in weeks. Standing with some effort under the weight of his regalia, he raised his voice to shout out over the crowd, "Oy, anyone seen the Wizard lately?"

From the back of the assembled dignitaries, a familiar voice spoke up. "I'm right here, Arth."

The crowd parted, and a merman in a shimmering golden mantle appeared. He was holding a wicked-lookin' staff that seemed an awful lot like Arth's Diamond Scepter, except longer and made of twisted driftwood. At the top, instead of a blue-glowing Diamond in a basket of gold, an immense emerald glowed an eerie green between two wing-like growths of petrified wood.

But Arth's eyes were drawn more toward the man himself. The Wizard was still easily recognizable, but this was a version of Hembrose that Arth had never seen before.

"Oy!" Arth exclaimed. "You's *young!*"

· nineteen ·

Hembrose ignored Arth for the moment, though that was difficult; the King was draped with dozens of Diamond Relics, *all* of them glowing blue. That should be impossible, but in this moment, Hembrose was more concerned with bringing about his own third miracle.

He searched the hundreds of faces in the crowd, ignoring their stares as he sought *her*—the Lady of the Lake, the one whose love he had sacrificed so much to earn. At last he saw her, and he rushed to meet her.

"It's you," she whispered, awed by his youthful appearance. Unlike their last encounter, she did not flee screaming before him. Already a huge improvement.

"It's me," he whispered back, heart in his throat.

She raised a tentative hand to touch his cheek, feeling his soft, scraggly peach-fuzz beard. Hembrose was distantly aware of the crowd turning to face the dais as some long-winded cayman gave a final speech to end the ceremony; but Hembrose had eyes only for the Lady, and she for him. They gazed at one another for what seemed hours, until the crowd began breaking up. Then, as if suddenly returning to her senses, the mermaiden jerked her hand back.

"I have been remiss," she told him demurely, polite and proper now. "I never expressed my gratitude for your timely rescue during the battle. Thank you," she said genuinely, as her cheeks turned a beautiful shade of dusky rose. "And I'm sorry, too. It was unfair of me to fear you, after you rendered me such a service. But... when I saw what you did to those lugmen, I was afraid of your magic. Honestly, I still am, a little." She looked away, giving a small shudder. "I'm not the bravest."

"My Lady of the Lake," Hembrose told her magnanimously. "I have ever loved you. You need never apologize nor thank me."

She smiled a little at this, though she seemed conflicted.

"Allow *me* to apologize," he went on. "Despite my love for you, I allowed my studies to come between us and steal the best years of my life. Now I've been given another chance. Come away with me. Let us travel the nilands of Overtwixt together, two youths in love!"

"But the lugman invasion—"

"After we defeat the lugmen, then. Whatever you wish of me, I will do! I care only of pleasing you, seeing you smile."

But the Lady's smile had slipped from her lips. "No, we cannot," she said hoarsely.

"Why not?" he demanded. "I can *see* that you love me again, as you once did."

The mermaiden shook her head silently. She collected her thoughts for a long moment; then when she spoke, it was bluntly, without her usual shyness. "I never loved you. True, I would lay awake at night thinking of you, your strong arms, your piercing green eyes." She gave another little shudder. "I dreamed of your return from the Hidden Chamber, taking up the Diamond Scepter and taking me as your wife—"

"I have returned from the Chamber again!" Hembrose blurted, brandishing the Emerald Caduceus for her to see. "And this is *better* than the Diamond Scepter—"

"But none of that was love," she continued. "Just childish fantasy. How *could* I love a man I never knew?" She sighed. "I remember that childish attraction now, for you *are* a handsome merman again, Hembrose of Hybra-sil. But I'm guessing the man you are inside has not changed. And the man *inside* is the one I want to fall in love with."

"How can you possibly—?"

"Besides, the Guide promised me I would marry the man who frees the Relic-in-the-Rock... and that's Arth."

This obsession with the Relic again? The worst part was the way the Lady's eyes lit up as Arth's name passed her lips.

"*Him?*" Hembrose groaned. "You would marry an ugly, slimy *dagman*? But all those warts and scales and fins—"

"It's the man *inside* that I want to fall in love with," she reminded him dreamily.

Seeing the love in her eyes—which shone with an intensity she'd never shown for Hembrose—the Wizard finally realized he had lost. And his love turned to bitterness.

"Do you have any idea what I've sacrificed for you?!" he demanded. "Do you know what I *lost* when I stepped out of Overtwixt, even for a moment? No, of course not. No one knows!" Even he hadn't known until it was too late.

The Lady's eyes filled with tears at his sudden anger, and she turned, fleeing into the departing crowd.

"Oy, mate!" Arth called, approaching through the crowd. He'd left all of his new Relics back on the Throne, and he looked like his normal self again. But there was concern on his face when he saw the Lady go, and concern for Hembrose too when he turned back to his friend.

Part of Hembrose desperately wanted to hit him, lash out at him, hurt him. How could a *dagman* possibly have a greater claim on the Lady's affections than Hembrose himself? But it wasn't a dagman she was falling for, of course. It was *Arth*. Despite his rough exterior, the unlikely new King had a heart of gold—a pure, selfless good nature that had earned even Hembrose's friendship and trust long ago. So as much as Hembrose wanted to strike Arth, another part of him wanted to pour out his heart, tell him about his *feelings* of all things. It was very confusing.

"How's this possible?" Arth asked, staring at the Wizard's smooth face, dark hair. "Some sorta magic fing?"

Hembrose nodded. "I did it for her, and now..." He groaned, all the anger leaving him, replaced only with exhausted bitterness. "I gave up so much for her."

"Hembrose, mate, yer scarin' me."

Looking into Arth's eyes, Hembrose was amazed by the depth of the compassion he saw there, so very genuine. Arth truly was a better friend than Hembrose deserved.

The Wizard sighed. "I stepped out of Overtwixt, back to the real world for just a moment, and now... now I'm reduced." He swallowed hard, struggling with his bitterness. "Doing that, it washed away all those years I spent in the libraries... but also all of the *power* I amassed in those years. I still have my raw magical talent, of course, and all of the knowledge I obtained here," he assured Arth, tapping his head. "But my skills, reflexes, sheer *strength*—everything I developed in my decades of practice and experimentation and exercise... it's all gone, like those magical muscles were never developed." He sighed heavily, and his breath caught. "Arth, I'm starting almost from scratch again."

Arth's eyes had gone wide. Hembrose could see the empathy was still there, but also a new worry. Of course, this *would* have implications for the war against the lugmen.

"At least I have this." Hembrose hefted his Caduceus. "The crowning achievement of my first life in Overtwixt."

"Aye," Arth agreed. "It's a right wicked-lookin' stick."

Hembrose barked a laugh. "It's a relic, imbued with the physical abilities of... of some of the enemies we've defeated. Enhanced senses, incredible physical strength—and it does magnify magical output to some degree. That's something, at least. But Arth! The power I've lost! With that power *and* this staff, I could have single-handedly defeated the lugman threat forever. And I gave it all up for a woman."

Arth looked at him strangely. "I *did* tell ya it would be best if ya steered clear of the Lady from now on."

Hembrose's temper flared again, and he had to fight to keep it under control. Grinding his teeth, he told Arth, "I think it would be best for our friendship if you and I don't speak of the Lady."

Arth met his eyes, then nodded. "That's fair enuff."

―――――

The rest of the Squad gathered around where the Wizard and the King had been speaking quietly. "Bonjour, Hembrose!" Pyrsie said brightly before turning to Arth. "Zat is quite zee battle plan you have outlined, O King."

"Were you here?" the Knight asked Hembrose. "Did you hear how Arth intends to defeat the lugmen?"

The mermage shook his head. "I arrived late, while Arth was talking." And so Arth and the others began summarizing the plan for his benefit, though without going into great detail. As they all talked, Hembrose found himself calming. He doubted he would ever be free of his bitterness toward the

Lady—or even toward Arth—but throwing himself into work like this would help keep him distracted.

"And so ya see," Arth concluded eventually, "in order to trap the lugs on Lugarth, we also needs a team of gnomen workin' in Northmount to close that avenue of escape. And for them to finish their work in time, we's gonna need one of yer nifty time-slowin' bubbles of magicky awesom'ness." He hesitated. "Ya *can* still make those, right?"

Hembrose frowned and tried to conjure a time bubble for the first time since getting back to Overtwixt. The bubble flickered into existence around just Hembrose himself, barely visible and with very little effect on time. He *pushed* on the magic, trying to expand the bubble while speeding time further, but he simply didn't have the strength. Gritting his teeth, the Wizard tried again, this time funneling his trickle of magic through the Caduceus and finally widening the bubble to encompass the entire Squad. But try as he might, he simply couldn't make the bubble any bigger than that—though he *was* able to compound the dilation several times, until the crowd rushing around outside was moving so slow as to appear almost entirely frozen.

Breathing hard, Hembrose looked at Arth in defeat. "This is the best I can manage. I should be able to maintain it for a while, and speed up time inside by quite a lot, but... clearly a whole crew of gnomen isn't going to fit."

"It weel have to be a crew of only one, then," Pyrsie said boldly. "Just me." Despite her tone, she looked dazed, uncertain. "Zee work will take longer, but... it is in a time bubble, so zat is okay." Hembrose looked away in embarrassment. It was his selfishness that had caused this, his insistence on disappearing to make the Caduceus and then returning to the real world without first discussing the risks with anyone. *He* was the biggest fool of this bunch!

Arth sighed but nodded. "At least this'll make transport easier. Quickest way to Northmount is punchin' through the lugman army and travelin' *across* Lugarth, so the smaller the team the better. Just three people, then? Pyrsie riding Paladin, and Hembrose doing his flyin' monster fing? The rest of us will lead the Caymerlotion army in attacking the lugmen, to make a diversion so you three can slip through."

"I'd rather be part of the attacking force," Paladin said loftily. "Much more glory to be won fighting than running."

Knight and Noble shared a look and a nod. "I can serve as the Inventor's mount if need be," the centman offered.

"Great," Arth said. "So Pyrsie riding *Noble*, and Hembrose still doin' his flying monster fing."

Hembrose cleared his throat uncomfortably. "Only problem... I don't have the strength to transform anymore, at least not to the flying beast. Not even with the Caduceus." It was one of the first things he'd tried after re-entering Overtwixt, in hopes of returning to the Crystal Keep faster.

Paladin was looking at Sidekick, but the kelpie shook his head. "My place is with Arth, whether in battle or beside the hearth."

"Sorry, mate," Arth told the big red eqman. "Looks like it's Pyrsie and you, Hembrose and Noble."

Paladin grumbled something under his breath and stormed off, instantly appearing to freeze in place when he left the compressed time bubble. Sidekick chased after him.

"We best be getting' to it, then," Arth concluded. "The sooner we're ready to launch this offensive, the better."

"And the less chance spies will carry word of our plans back to the Demagogue," the Sergeant-at-arms agreed.

Hembrose dropped the bubble, and the Squad broke apart to their various tasks. The Sergeant left with Altruist and Antagonist to rally the troops and prepare the diversion, while Knight and Noble stopped to speak quietly in a corner with forearms clasped; after all, they were about to be separated, something that seldom happened. Daddie and Bertie formed their usual perimeter for keeping people away from Arth (though without his new Relics and regalia, most people seemed unsure whether he was the King or just another dagman). Paladin and Sidekick were bickering over which of them would be most famous when this war was finally over. That left Hembrose alone with Arth and Pyrsie.

The original three friends in this adventure, not counting poor Morth.

Arth gripped their shoulders, one clawed hand for each of them; Pyrsie followed suit... and after a moment, Hembrose completed the triangle. With tears in his eyes, Arth thanked them for all their loyalty and support, for everything good and bad they'd followed him into. "We's at the last chapter here, or near 'nuff," he said. "This is it, the final campaign to rescue Morth and all them others. I couldn't have done it without ya. You two probably coulda done it without me, but not the other way around."

Pyrsie just rolled her eyes.

Hembrose felt another strange surge of emotion, like his feelings were on a seesaw—and he suddenly realized why. All day today, he'd been dealing with youthful hormones again, for the first time in a lifetime! Even realizing this was the reason, he couldn't stop himself from blurting, "Thanks for being my friend, Arth." He swiped at his eyes and sniffled. "You too, Pyrsie. I haven't had many of them."

The other two youths grinned delightedly. Then they drew Hembrose into a big group hug.

Before long, however, Arth straightened with a sigh. "Alrighty, back to bidness. Is ya both ready to go? Time is already at a platinum, espec'ly fer the two of you."

Pyrsie and Hembrose traded glances. "I am ready," the little gnomaid said with a shrug.

"There's nothing for me here now," the Wizard said with a heavy sigh, making a dramatic gesture to indicate Crystal Keep and Caymerlot in general. Even to him, it came off as *melo*dramatic. Darn hormones. "But I guess this is still a fresh start, a chance to do things differently this time." And maybe this time, he could show bravery from the start.

Arth grinned. "That's the spirit, boyo! Now remember, straight through the middle of the enemy army and across that new Caymerlot-Lugarth bridge. Don't look to the left or the right. Don't get sucked into the fightin'—and don't let Paladin engage neither! Ya ain't got the time or the strength to be distracted." He glanced at Hembrose when he said this. "Yer job is more important, so keep yer eye on the prize."

"Got it," Pyrsie confirmed, and Hembrose nodded. The Wizard felt a sense of relief that he wouldn't need to fight after all.

"Good," Arth said. "You charge straight through the middle of that enemy army, then ride like yer life depends on it!" he reiterated. "'Cause, ya know... it probably will."

· twenty ·

Pyrsie stood with Hembrose, Paladin, and Noble in a big grassy field within the fairgrounds north of Crystal City, just inside the thick glass wall that surrounded the metropolis. From what she understood, this was the very same field where the Circus of Dagmør had camped during their first week in Overtwixt; now, the field was filled with tents belonging to the centmen, humen, and eqmen who had joined the aquatics in their fight against the luggernauts. The center of the grassy area rose into a gentle hill, allowing Pyrsie to look west across the vast blue lagoon where the circus had first raised its big top tent—to where another such tent now stood in its place. This one, however, was striped hot pink and orange with royal blue filigree: the King's new command tent.

At Pyrsie's side, Hembrose shivered at the big tent's color combination, chosen by Arth personally.

There were *countless* tents in sight, for Caymerlot now had many allies. And yet, despite their number, none of the soldiers who had camped in this field remained in the vicinity. Rather, they all waited on the far side of the lagoon, formed up in even ranks with the main Caymerlotion army, just inside the city's northwest gate.

Outside that gate massed the barbarian horde, which outnumbered the good guys two-to-one.

Any minute now, Sarge would open the northwest gate, and Arth's army would stream out to attack the lugmen, going on the offensive for the first time. But even knowing the horrors they would soon face, his army waited courageously, standing or floating with straight backs and heads lifted high. It was an impressive, awe-inspiring sight.

And it was nothing more than a diversion for Pyrsie and the other three squad members who waited here with her.

Paladin stamped a hoof in frustration. "*Much* more glory to be won fighting than running," he muttered again.

Noble placed a calming hand on the eqman's withers. "I would much rather be part of the battle too," he admitted. "I don't like the thought of Karis fighting without me watching her back, even if this *is* just a short skirmish to distract the lugmen."

Paladin tossed his head angrily. "*Today* may only be a diversion, but you know the true Final Battle is just a few more days away. And the four of us are expected to miss it, holed up in a cave on the other side of Lugarth!"

Pyrsie patted her friend's other shoulder. "But what Arth has asked of us, it is important too. You will be protecting zee Wizard and me. And if we cannot block passage through zee Northmount bridge, zee battle here will not matter at all."

Hembrose took a deep breath and nodded, obviously reassured by her words, though he was not their intended audience. He had been so emotional since coming back that he needed constant reminders of his importance in all this.

But Paladin just snorted again. Clearly he didn't believe their mission mattered very much. "That filthy kelpie is gonna get all the glory," he grumbled instead.

At that moment, the gate opened with a creak that was audible even from this distance, but only until it was drowned out by the shouts of Arth's soldiers: "For the King and for Caymerlot! Charge! Charge!" They instantly began streaming through the great double doors, fanning out on the other side to attack the waiting lugmen. King Arth led them, of course, though Pyrsie only recognized his distant figure from the glittering blue shield his Scepter produced, protecting his soldiers as they came through the gate.

Paladin groaned jealously as he watched a detachment of eqmen, galloping in V formation, crash into a mass of enemy giants. Hooves pummeled hairy lugman chests and yellow smoke began to rise from both sides. Arrows arced over their heads, fired from detachments of merman archers kneeling in the shallows just behind the eqmen. Meanwhile, karks and nyms and gnomen intermixed to charge the lugs waiting on the opposite shore, supported by centmen with long bows. Even a few of the normally placid okkies joined the mix, slithering rapidly between lugman legs and climbing up their backs to strangle them from behind. Then Arth and Sidekick were leading a whole group of dagmen mounted on kelpies, wielding tridents and nets as they forged deeper into the waters on the other side of the wall. They looped around and began throwing their nets over the towering lugmen, working together to pull them to their knees, where the tridents proved more effective.

In short, it was an all-out attack, the soldiers of Caymerlot and Centhule and even the small group of volunteers from Gnoburrow fully engaged—ensuring that every battle-hungry lugman on this niland was drawn to the vicinity of the northwest gate.

It was all the diversion Pyrsie could have hoped for.

"Time to go," Noble said. "Mount up!" And he offered Hembrose a hand, pulling the Wizard up onto his back. Despite the mermage's now-limited strength, he had shapeshifted his lower body to give himself dagman legs. So long as he used them only to grip the saddle, he should be able to maintain the partial shapeshift until they reached Northmount.

Pyrsie reached for her own mount, but the big red eqman shied away. "Paladin..." she said warningly.

"This isn't right!" he complained. "I should be *there*, with my people—where the fight is!"

"Paladin!" she cried. "We do not have time for zis! We must go." Already, the few soldiers left behind at the much closer north gate were opening the doors to let Pyrsie's party through.

But the big eqman shook his maned head, turning to look at Pyrsie with anguish. "I'm sorry, my friend. I cannot. This battle calls to me." He spun to leave.

"No, Paladin!" Pyrsie blurted. "I *need* you! How else will I get to Northmount?"

"Ride the centman," he called over his shoulder.

"I cannot carry two," Noble scoffed. "Carrying even one so far will be taxing, galloping so much of the way. You of all people know this, Paladin!"

"Find another mount, then," the eqman yelled without turning. He seemed ashamed, unable to meet their eyes, but also unwilling to turn back. "Any eqman or centman will do!"

"Are you blind, man!?" Noble cried, losing his temper. "There *are* no others left! They're all engaged in this battle already, sacrificing themselves to buy *us* time!"

But Paladin was no longer listening. By now, he was galloping toward the frontlines, dodging between army tents at full speed.

This was a disaster! Without Paladin, Pyrsie couldn't do her part, and this entire attack was pointless. "Hembrose!" Pyrsie cried, "stop him!"

The Wizard twirled his Caduceus, and a sudden beam of emerald light shot between the tents to wrap around the departing Paladin, surrounding him in a green cloud that froze the eqman mid-gallop. "I... can't... hold... this... long," Hembrose gasped almost immediately. "Do... something... quickly."

Pyrsie glanced around hurriedly, looking for something, *anything*, she could use to bring the eqman under control. All she saw were tents in every direction.

Tents held in place by ropes tied to metal ground pegs.

Back on Paladin's home niland a few months ago, Pyrsie and the others had foiled a plot by Lady Karis's own brother to subjugate the eqman people. Pyrsie could still remember the sight of those eqmen with bits in their mouths, attached to reins and halters, as the Prince's men dug spurred boots into their flanks and rode them against their will. The people of Eqland had been miserable.

But they had obeyed.

Clenching her jaw, thinking only of the disaster that would unfold if Paladin got away, Pyrsie drew a tomahawk from her belt. She quickly slashed two ropes, causing a tent to collapse as she muscled the attached tent pegs out of the ground. Clasping the two metal pegs together, she turned to face Hembrose again. "Spot weld!" she ordered.

The Wizard's eyes flashed a painful green as his Caduceus spat a second bolt of blinding emerald light, instantly melting the pegs together. Now Pyrsie held a single piece of thick metal half a span long, with long ropes tied to the eyelet holes on either end. "Hurry," Hembrose begged, clearly at the limits of his strength.

Pyrsie ran toward Paladin, who was straining against the green cloud, slowly but surely fighting his way forward a step at a time. The gnomaid took a running leap and landed in her saddle on his back just as Hembrose gasped and the cloud dissipated. "Ha-ha!" the eqman cried in victory, mouth wide and smiling as he broke free. And in that moment, Pyrsie flung her new contraption over the eqman's head, then jerked back on both ropes—pulling the welded metal bar into Paladin's open mouth.

The eqman instantly reared, screaming in agony as the metal dug painfully into his gums. Pyrsie squeezed her eyes shut and held on for dear life, tears streaming down her cheeks—for she *knew* what a terrible violation this was. Paladin was a person, her *friend*, and she was treating him as an animal. No matter how irresponsible he was being, he didn't deserve this. No person deserved to be controlled by another.

But Pyrsie couldn't afford to let him go, either.

So she held on with all her strength, pulling the bit even tighter against his gums and lips, *knowing* how much it hurt him. Knowing this meant the end of their friendship, hating every moment of it, and doing it anyway. For the greater good.

At last, the eqman settled down, landing on all four hooves again and falling still. Blinking away her tears, Pyrsie met Noble's eyes. The centman was clearly horrified by what she'd done, but he did not argue or interfere. He understood.

"How could you?" Paladin moaned, his voice distorted by the metal bar in his mouth. "How could you do this to me?" He had never seemed so humiliated in all the days she'd known him—not since she first rescued him from lugman slavery during the Battle at Bronze City, that was.

Pyrsie swallowed hard. "I'm sorry," she whispered. "I'm so, so sorry."

"If you're sorry, then let me go. I thought you were my friend."

"I thought you were my friend too," Pyrsie said.

"I *did* give you my friendship!" He was crying now too. "Don't you know how precious that was? You were the first non-eqman I ever trusted with that honor. Now you're spitting on that."

"Because I cannot trust you," she said miserably. "*You're* the one breaking trust—Arth's trust—chasing glory instead of doing what's right." She steeled herself. "Now ride. Through the gate, to Lugarth."

Paladin didn't move.

Squeezing her eyes shut again, more tears spilling down her cheeks, Pyrsie dug her clawed toes into Paladin's flanks, spurring him to leap forward with a yelp. She pulled his head to the right, using her reins to direct him toward the gate.

"I will never forgive you for this," Paladin snarled as he galloped through the gate. "Never, do you understand me?"

"I understand you," she whispered, the words bitter in her mouth. She felt dirty, disgusting, the worst gnoman being to walk the face of the nilands ever—the worst being of *any* kind in Overtwixt. But she did not loosen her tension on the reins, not for an instant. She spurred her mount on to greater and greater speed, wincing with every jab of her claws in his flank.

And so Pyrsie's party left Crystal City behind. They threaded their way along the isthmuses between great lakes as they rode the long way around the bulk of the lugman army, quickly and quietly making their way toward Lugarth.

The Noble and Wizard, following behind, didn't utter another word the entire trek to the bridge; and Paladin certainly didn't. It made for the most painful journey of Pyrsie's life.

Thanks to Arth's distraction, they didn't see a single enemy luggernaut until the Caymerlot-Lugarth bridge finally came within sight, early the next morning. They had ridden hard through the night, Pyrsie filling her Diamond Grail frequently from a canteen, offering it to Noble and a reluctant Paladin to keep them healthy and refreshed.

And as the new day dawned, the Sky Light casting its first glimmer of daylight upon them, Pyrsie found herself grateful to be facing the true enemy again. The entrance to the new bridge was nestled in a thicket of many-trunked trees; the lugs stationed among those trees, guarding the bridge, began to hoot and holler and clash their weapons together as they saw Pyrsie's party approach.

"We charge straight through zee middle of zat enemy force," Pyrsie told her squad mates, breaking silence for the first time in hours as she repeated Arth's words. "Then we ride like our lives depend upon it."

She felt Paladin tense beneath her, unwilling even now simply to run. He was a warrior; he wanted to *fight*. Fresh tears spilled down her cheeks as she spurred him yet again. But she told herself it didn't matter anymore. Even if she turned back now, she had already lost a friend forever.

All that mattered at this point was making that sacrifice worthwhile. Pyrsie Rochelle *would* reach Northmount. She *would* do her part.

"Hup!" she cried, whipping Paladin with the reins. "Ride! Ride!"

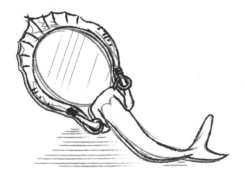

· twenty-one ·

"Refill?" Arth asked gallantly, and Gwen felt a flutter go through her. She nodded eagerly, and the King took up the glistening pitcher, carefully dividing the rest of the seaweed smoothie between her glass and his own. "It's meh Mum's recipe," he told her.

The mermaiden smiled in delight. "It truly is a wonderful concoction." She took another long sip, then sighed contentedly, settling deeper into the warm, bubbling water until only her head was visible above the surface. "You dagmen really know how to relax."

"After the week we's had, I was finkin' *everyone* deserved a chance to relax tonight," Arth agreed. In fact, he had given express orders that his army do exactly that. Spread across the fairgrounds on the northern outskirts of Crystal City, the soldiers of Caymerlot, Centhule, and Gnoburrow were clustered in groups of various sizes, enjoying barbecues or fish fries. Gazing happily from the small pond Gwen shared with the King, she was especially gratified to see how many of those gatherings were made up of mixed groups from multiple races. Lots of those folks were relaxing in pockets of heated water too, thanks to an old dagman recipe of salt and soda that chemically caused water to grow warm—"instant hot tub," Arth had called it, "a great way to loosen up the muscles!" Which, again, *everyone* in Caymerlot needed after this last month.

It had been two weeks since Gwen and her brothers joined the procession to Gatehenge on Merlyn, traveling with the Sergeant-at-arms to officially eject her father from Overtwixt. She still couldn't believe Arth had trusted the Underlord's old armsmen to undertake that task by themselves, without sending his own people to ensure their loyalty. It had been a difficult day for all three of the MerGrand children, parting ways with their father, but Gwen was grateful for the chance to do so without the rest of the Squad watching. Still, the days that followed had been just as hard, for she missed Papá terribly.

And yet Gwen also felt so very free now. She had experienced some guilt over that, considering it only came thanks to her father's departure, though it helped knowing that Papá wasn't gone forever. She would see him again someday when she went home to the real world. But for now, she was finally her own woman.

She had actually explored Crystal City for herself—*really* explored, not like her forays guiding refugees to safety during the First Battle of Caymerlot. She hardly ventured alone, of course, for on these trips she was always joined by guardsmen, *or* her brothers, *or* other members of the Squad, or some combination thereof. But she *was* free, to go where *she* wished to go, simply protected by her companions instead of imprisoned. And oh, what beautiful sights this city had to offer! So inspiring... yet sobering too, for so many of Crystal City's magnificent edifices had been damaged or destroyed in the lugman attacks. And though rebuilding had already begun, it was only amidst the constant threat of further lugman violence.

Now another week had passed since Gwen's friend Pyrsie galloped away with the Wizard, Noble, and Paladin, bypassing the bulk of the lugman army while Arth's forces kept it engaged. That diversionary battle had lasted for hours, far longer than the King intended, as he admitted to Gwen later. He'd barely gotten everyone back inside the gates afterwards, and only then with the help of his Diamond Scepter. Every day since then had seen an even grislier skirmish, as the enraged lugmen attacked with increasing intensity. Still, Arth had delayed committing his troops to a decisive Final Battle for as long as possible, giving Pyrsie the time she needed (or so he hoped) to complete her mission. But the Caymerlotions were losing soldiers every day, and this entire stretch of city wall was nearing collapse. If that happened, Crystal City would become vulnerable again. And even if that *didn't* happen, Arth had confided in Gwen that he needed to go on the offensive soon—for if he lost too many more troops, his army would no longer have the strength to push the invaders back across their strange new bridge to Lugarth.

In short, the inevitable moment had come. The Final Battle between the King's coalition and the Demagogue's barbarian horde would begin tomorrow. And so Arth had insisted on setting aside this time for fun and friendship, on the eve of that conflict. He made a good show of it, too, lounging casually in the steaming water and chatting conversationally; but his eyes told a different story. The burden of responsibility lay heavy upon him, as did worries over his brother, who had been enslaved by the lugmen for months now. Arth was a good man, Gwen decided again. The more she got to know him, the more she wanted to know him even better... which both scared and excited her. After all, he was going into battle tomorrow. *The* battle, the one that would decide everything.

It was time to tell him the truth.

"Sire," Gwen said uncomfortably. "There's something you need to know."

Arth sighed. "My Lady, what have I said about calling me that? I fink all that fancy title baloney is what got yer daddie and so many other rulers into trouble, finking they's all more special than they really is." He hesitated. "Um, no offense meant."

"No offense taken... Arth." As always, when she said his name aloud, it sent a little thrill through her. "Maybe you're right about titles. But that's just it—you're still using *my* title. Everyone is. I know so much about you, but you know so little about me. You don't even know my name or the true role the Guide gave me when I arrived in Overtwixt."

"I'd like to know," he blurted eagerly. "I reckon I'd like to know everyfing there is to know about ya, my Lady." Then he blushed so deeply she could actually see it through his dark dagman skin.

Gwen giggled as he busied himself washing out the empty glass pitcher. "And I'd like to tell you, all of it," she assured him. "I *will* tell you... I just don't want it to put pressure or expectations on our relationship."

Arth was thoughtful for a long moment. Then he just nodded and shrugged.

The mermaiden took a deep breath. "First off, my real name is Gwenverity MerGrand... but you can call me Gwen."

It was Arth's turn to grin delightedly. He took her hand gently in his and kissed the back of it. "It gives me ever so much pleasure to make yer acquaintance... Gwenverity. Oy, but that's a pretty name."

A smile fluttered across her lips. "When I was born, Papá wanted to name me Gwenneth, an upper-class name in my real world that means 'innocence.' But Mamá had her heart set on Verity, which means 'truth.' So they compromised, and I was christened Gwenverity." Gwen hesitated, then added, "And you know what? In all the years since Mamá died, Papá never once called me Gwen, though everyone else did. He always honored Mamá's memory by using my full name."

"Gwenverity," Arth said it again, sounding out each syllable with care. "Innocent but dedicated to truth. Suits you awful nice, it does." He eyed her. "And thanks for sharin' that bit about yer parents. I'm sorry to hear 'bout yer mum. As fer yer daddie, I never thought he was all bad, and this just confirms it."

Gwen smiled brilliantly at him. Then she took another deep breath. "There's still more I need to tell you. On the day I entered Overtwixt, the Guide offered me three roles, same as everyone else. And I made my choice wholeheartedly, but it wasn't the role of Lady that I picked. Calling me the Lady of the Lake was a bit of deception on Papá's part, for my own protection—or so he said."

Arth nodded. "I'd heard sumfing to that effect. So... what *did* the Guide name yeh?"

Gwen swallowed hard. "Queen," she admitted softly. After keeping it a secret for thirteen years, she was barely able to get the word out past the lump in her throat. "I chose to be Queen of Caymerlot."

Arth's eyes widened.

She looked away, unable to keep meeting his stare until she got through the rest of it. "So all these years, with Papá serving as Underlord, he wasn't only meant to be *your* steward... he was also ruling in *my* place, as regent, until I was old enough to act as Queen in my own right. I'm not sure he actually needed to hide my identity, or whether he did it for selfish or selfless purposes... a mix of both, probably. But..." She took a deep breath, let it out again. "There you have it. Just as you've been anointed King of Caymerlot by the Guide, I was anointed *Queen* of Caymerlot. He rubbed warm oil on my head and everything." She smiled fondly as she thought back to that day, when she was only six years old. "I remember how much the oil tickled."

"It did tickle," Arth agreed with a nervous laugh.

"Papá was so stern; he told me to stop giggling. But the Guide just laughed along with me, sharing in my delight."

"That Guide bloke sure is sumfing," Arth said. "I'm still tryin' to figure him out."

The King's voice sounded funny, so Gwen finally turned to look at him.

Arthos Penn, the dagman King, looked as scared as she'd ever seen him. His big eyes were open *extra* big, and he kept licking his lips nervously. When he realized she was waiting to hear his opinion of her revelations, he took a deep breath. "So... if you's the Queen... and I's the King..." His mouth opened and closed a few times, but he was incapable of finishing his sentence.

Somehow, Gwen felt emboldened in the face of this brave man's nervousness. "It means we're destined to be married. Yes." She gazed deep into Arth's eyes, wishing she knew what he was thinking. "The Guide was very clear on this point, Arth. My quest was to win the heart of the man who someday frees the Relic-in-the-Rock."

"But my Lady... *Gwenverity*," he blurted finally. "This is only our first date, and you's already talkin' bout *marriage?*"

This time it was Gwen whose face grew warm amidst a sudden fit of giggles, and Arth couldn't help but burst into laughter too. Gwen ducked down even lower in the water, hiding her hot cheeks so that her eyes only barely cleared the surface.

Arth grew serious again as his laughter subsided. "Calamity! That's quite sumfin', the role and quest the good Guide gave yeh. I get it now, why you was afraid this might put pressure on our relationship and such... but I'm glad you was honest." He thought for a moment as she stared up at him, still mostly submerged. "Well, if that's our destiny," he said at last, "I ain't complaining." He grinned big, showing her more dagman teeth than she'd ever seen in one mouth before. "I can't fink of anyone better to write meh love story than the Guide hisself!"

Gwen let out a breath she didn't even realize she was holding. At least Arth wasn't horrified by the idea.

"But that don't mean we gotta rush anyfing," Arth went on. Holey anemone, *marriage?* I's barely sixteen years old!"

Gwen's blush had barely begun to recede, and now it bloomed hotter than ever. "You're *what?!*" she demanded, lurching back out of the water. "I just turned nineteen!" She buried her face in her hands. "Oh my, oh my. Talk about burglarizing the bassinet." Oh, this was so humiliating.

Arth was silent for a moment. "If it makes ya feel any better," he offered after a moment, "Planet Mersch takes phirteen months to orbit its sun."

"*What?!*" Gwen blurted again. She was already flustered by the turn this conversation had taken, and now he was talking complete nonsense. "What does the astronomy of your real world have to do with—"

Arth was grinning big again. "The years on my real world is longer," he said calmly. "More months in a year, more days in a month," he added. "I know all this fer a fact, having discussed it one time with... a merman friend of mine." He meant the Wizard, obviously, but didn't want to upset her further by saying so.

"So... you're saying... maybe we're actually the same age?" she asked hopefully.

"Or at least not so far apart as yer finkin'!" He shrugged and gave her a wicked grin. "But I don't got no objection to courting a lady who's a *bit* older than me. Always has liked the older women, I has."

Gwen buried her face in her hands once more. "Smoke. Me. Now," she begged him.

"But seriously, my Lady. Gwenverity." His tone was indeed less jovial, so she cautiously peeked out at him between her fingers. "I look forward to what the Guide has planned fer us, but I ain't in no hurry. We's still figurin' out the sort of people we's gonna be in life!" He gently took her hands in his, pulling them away from her face so they could meet each other's eyes unhindered. "If we's to be married, great! But we's got a lifetime to be married. For now, let's just enjoy gettin' to know each other—*and* ourselves—one day at a time. Whaddya say to that?"

Gwen took a deep breath, and when she exhaled, she felt a lot of her embarrassment slide away. Not all, but a lot. She bit her lip. "Besides, you've got a war to win first."

Arth slowly nodded. Just that quickly, she could see the burden of worry and responsibility settle onto him once more. She knew he must be thinking of his brother Morth again, was probably *always* thinking about him. Gwen couldn't imagine how that must tear at Arth from the inside.

"You really think tomorrow's going to be the Final Battle?" she asked, unable to mask her concern for him.

Arth nodded and forced a smile. "I can't afford to wait no more." He gazed out across his troops, many of whom were still laughing and splashing, though other parties had broken up for the hour was growing late. "Tomorrow morn, we's gonna open the gates and ride forth one last time, an all-out battle. We's gonna push the lugs all the way back across to their own niland, then topple that new bridge they made. We's *gotta*... or else get smoked tryin'."

"You won't be smoked," Gwen said, surprisingly confident. "I trust that what the Guide said will come true. You and I *will* be married, and we will rule together for many years as King and Queen. Remember? That prophesied Golden Age?"

Arth grinned.

"Still, maybe carry this with you for luck?" she asked, offering him a handkerchief. It was a dainty cloth square she'd carried for years, with her initial embroidered in one corner: a "G" surrounded by lily pads.

Arth took the cloth reverently, tucking it into one of his pockets and standing up. "This has been right fun," he told her. "I look ferward to spendin' more time with ya when this mess is all cleared up. And I can't wait to introduce ya to meh brother Morth too. Me and a *Queen*, the most beautiful mermaid in all O'ertwixt! Morth'll flip."

Gwen had no more blushes in her. "I can't wait to meet him either," she promised.

"Until then, I best be getting meh sleep. Big day tomorra." Arth took her hand one more time, bending low to kiss the back. A perfect gentleman.

In response, Gwen surprised even herself by reaching up and kissing Arth lightly on one cheek. Before he could express his shock, she turned tail and swam away as fast as her dignity would allow.

· twenty-two ·

Arth tried to keep a silly grin off his face as he watched the Lady—no, Gwenverity, the Queen—swim away rapidly. Her quest was to win *his* heart? *That* amazing woman wanted to be courted by him? Sure, the Guide had set her on this path… but even after getting to know Arth a little, she hadn't fled the other direction? On second thought, that was exactly what she was doing—but only after planting that glorious smackeroo on his cheek!

Arth couldn't help grinning. He was smitten.

When the mermaiden and her guards were finally out of sight amidst the other tents, Arth shook himself and picked up the Diamond Scepter, which he always kept close at hand. Nestling the Relic into the crook of his arm, he turned toward his new command tent… where he saw Daddie and Bertie watching him with huge grins. Arth's father winked, while his uncle waggled his eyebrows. "Oy, none of that now," Arth said good naturedly as he tromped inside, whistling a lively tune.

For a few short moments, it seemed like everything was right in the world—then he immediately felt a horrible, crushing guilt. How dare he feel this happy while Morth was enslaved and suffering? He sighed. This wasn't the first time he'd felt such emotional conflict since meeting Gwen.

Arth's new command tent was an immense, three-peaked construction, much like the tent the circus troupe had originally used on coming to Overtwixt, except done up in proper colors this time: hot pink and orange. It was very different on the inside, however, more like the old Khan's war tent (which Hembrose had told Arth about), subdivided into separate rooms for audiences and planning and resting and the like. With tomorrow's battle set to commence at dawn, Arth made straight for the lavish bedchamber he'd been given. He waved off any of the servants who tried to come with him; they probably wanted to pull back his sheets or help him put on his own pajamas or some other such nonsense, but Arth could do all that stuff faster alone.

"Enjoying yerself, is ya?" a quiet voice asked when Arth stepped into his bedchamber. "Going on dates with pretty girls while the world of bridges falls apart all around ya?"

Arth froze, stunned. It shouldn't be possible for anyone to sneak past Daddie or Bertie or the other guards Sarge had posted around the perimeter of the command tent. But he was even more surprised by *who* was waiting for him in the bedroom.

"*Morth?*" Arth gasped.

"In the slimy dagman flesh," his twin confirmed, giving a flourish and bow of the sort they both used to demonstrate daily in the Circus of Dagmør.

"Morth!" Arth cried, heart leaping for joy as he rushed forward, throwing his arms around his brother. "How'd ya get free?! Calamity, I'm so happy to be seein' yeh again!" He sucked in a huge breath, turning to yell excitedly for his father—

But Morth slapped a hand over Arth's mouth, smothering his happy yell. "Oy, none of that now. I'm just here to talk to *you*, not the rest of that lot."

Arth was still smiling stupidly, overwhelmed with joy and relief as he pulled Morth's hand from his mouth. "Huh? Daddie and Bertie and me's been so worried for ya, you gotta let them see yeh're safe and free now..." He trailed off as he noticed what Morth was holding: an immense iron war hammer with a big ruby set into its hammerhead, a red gemstone that somehow glowed green. Arth gasped. "You got free *and* ya stole the Demagogue's wicked weapon?"

Morth rolled his eyes, but he needn't have. Arth knew as soon as the words left his mouth that they weren't right. He could sense the truth through his Diamond Scepter.

"Nay, it can't be," Arth breathed, almost choking on the truth. "You... *is*... the Demagogue?"

"In the slimy dagman flesh," Morth confirmed again. He raised the Ruby Warhammer and twirled it lightly in one hand, then propped it against his shoulder.

"But how?" Mind spinning, an awful feeling spreading through his chest, Arth thought back to the only other time he'd encountered the Demagogue—on the battlefield when the lugs first attacked Crystal City. "I *saw* you that day, in the city. But I thought you was a lugman!"

"There's more than one man in O'ertwixt as knows how to shapeshift," his twin said smugly. "Deception is an important part of warfare."

"But if you's the one in charge of the lugs, why is we even at war anymore? We can end the fighting! We can do it tonight, before anyone else gets hurt. Make peace with me!"

Morth was shaking his head. "This war ain't ending 'til the oppression of the innocent is corrected."

"But it was the lugs—" Arth began.

"The lugmen did much that was wrong, but they was never the worst perpetrators," Morth declared, with a forcefulness and eloquence that Arth had never heard from his brother before. "That distinction belongs to the rulers of Caymerlot, the mermen and caymen who perpetiated the lie of a false utopia for countless ages. You want to make peace, but I say true peace is impossible so long as inequality exists. *That* is the institution we must tear down—us dagsters and the kelpies and the nags and all the other 'lesser' beings who's been subjugated and humiliated over the ages, on this niland or any other. It is *our* time to rise up!" he concluded fervently, slipping into a sequence of phrases that had the feel of an oft-repeated slogan: "Down with your glass towers! Depose the Diamond-bearers, and exalt the exploited!"

Arth gaped at his brother. Morth's dark distrust for authority had only grown since coming to Overtwixt and seeing that power was abused even here—often by the very individuals who wielded the Diamond Relics of Sovereign, it was true. But the way Morth was talking now went beyond anything he'd demonstrated before his capture. Sure, Caymerlot wasn't perfect, but it was the luggernauts who'd done Morth the most harm, wasn't it?

"What happened to you?" Arth asked his twin quietly, grief crashing over him once more.

"What happened to me?" Morth repeated incredulously. "I grew up. I finally realized that no one else was going to help me, so I would have to help myself." He shook his head bitterly. "Just like all the lugmen's other slaves, I was abandoned by everyone who *should* have come to my rescue—my ruler, my own people, even *you*."

"What?" Arth couldn't believe his ears. "I never abandoned you! I wouldn't!"

"You got any idea the horrors I've endured?" Morth demanded. "Have you ever *seen* a lugman's dirty laundry? And that's hardly the worst of it. Mockery, abuse—"

"I've been fighting my way to yer rescue ever since the day you was taken," Arth insisted.

"And yet here we is, three or four months later, and you's never even set foot on Lugarth."

"I sent Hembrose—"

"Ah yes," Morth said, his lip curling. "Hembrose the Wizard, my old mentor. You're right, *he* found me in the war camps... but even then, he left me behind. Some rescue."

"He *couldn't* have rescued you," Arth tried to explain. "Hembrose didn't have the strength to maintain a drachman shapeshift *and* carry you across the—"

"Don't you dare repeat that lame excuse!" Morth snarled. "I know he could have saved me. I know the true power of magic now. I *know* what the Wizard is capable of, when he really cares about something... because I'm capable now too. He could've found a way to rescue me if he wanted to, but instead he left me behind. And you did too."

"Morth, boyo—"

"*You* coulda rescued me that very week, after defeating the Khan. Deny it. Deny that you turned your back on Lugarth and took the long way returning to Caymerlot, instead of fighting those last few miles to rescue me."

This accusation caught Arth off guard. How did Morth even know about that? But what could Arth say, except to admit the truth? "You's right," he confessed, sudden tears in his eyes. "We was so close to you. But we didn't have the strength or numbers to invade Lugarth, so we turned around and came here. It... it seemed the wise thing to do, fer you *and* fer Caymerlot."

"Sounds to me like you put yourself and Caymerlot before my needs," Morth said darkly.

"No, never! The Guide said I had to trust ya to make yer own choices, that you had some challenges ya needed to face fer yerself."

Morth seemed a little surprised by this, but then he snorted. "Well, I s'pose he was right about that."

"I'm sorry," Arth blurted. "Forgive me, mate, *please*," he begged.

Morth looked away, refusing to answer, refusing to forgive.

And Arth felt his heart break anew. This didn't make sense, any of it. "Morth, please, help me unnerstan. Even if you's upset at me and Caymerlot fer not rescuin' ya, how could ya change sides and join yer *enemy?* It makes no sense." Arth took a step forward, peering intently into Morth's eyes, desperately trying to make sense of this. "What *happened?*" he insisted again.

Morth took a deep breath and straightened his shoulders. "I became a true magicker," he said, "a *dag*magicker, if you will. I moved beyond the silly parlor tricks Hembrose taught me, and I began to wield greater power... but not for myself. For the good of the oppressed."

Arth's brother spoke of doing good in a lofty tone, yet the sense of darkness radiating from him was palpable.

Morth hesitated, then cracked a grim smile. "I guess I *should* still thank the Wizard for my big breakthrough, though it was right accidental on his part. Aye, he abandoned me on Lugarth that day, but still and all, he showed me the path to true power—when he harvested the essences of them lugs who attacked him. And in his haste to save his own skin, he dropped the very thing I needed to start harvesting essences myself." Morth tapped the huge, glowing ruby that was new embedded in the head of his Warhammer.

"I ain't got the foggiest fink what you's talking 'bout," Arth said miserably.

Morth barked a laugh. "No, I s'pose ya don't. It's not the sort of thing ole Hem would ever admit to anyone, much less a goody-goody like you. Basically, our mermage mate discovered a way of using magic to steal the talents and abilities of another person and store them in a gemstone, then draw them out again later, to be used fer his own purposes. How do ya think he became so powerful?"

Arth shuddered, not wanting to believe such an awful thing about his oldest friend... but finding that he *did* believe it. It explained too many things Arth had wondered about.

"Of course, I probably done more harvesting now than Hembrose ever did," Morth went on. "Not the first fella I ever smoked, sadly. That was a lug by the name of Bully, the same bloke who captured me on Centhule and forced me to do his laundry fer the next two months. Boyo, did he have a vicious streak a mile-wide, more deserving than any'un else I ever knew to be enslaved in this ruby fer all eternity." Morth shook his head ruefully. "But naw, him I just smoked, in a desperate panic. All his friends, though, everyone that ever mocked or mistreated me... *them* I harvested, one by one, and *pop-pop-pop*"—Morth snapped his fingers—"just like that, their brawn was mine. Before I knew it, I'd amassed so much raw lugman strength in this here ruby, I could smoke any lug I wanted... *with my bare hands.*"

Arth could only stare in horror. Morth seemed so self-satisfied as he described these terrible things he'd done.

"It was only after I rescued myself that your pal the Guide finally showed up to offer me my three choices," Morth said. "Right after he got done offering *you* the Kingship."

Arth jerked in surprise. "The Guide came to you? On *Lugarth?*"

"Of course he did," Arth's twin snorted. "The Guide comes to Lugarth all the time, turns out. Lugmen are visitors to O'ertwixt just like the rest of us. Who do ya think offers them their three choices if not the Guide?"

Somehow, Arth found this almost as troubling as everything else Morth had told him. "But I thought the Guide was on *my* side," he muttered.

"You *are* still a fool," Morth crowed, "no matter if they call you King now or not. The Guide's not on *anyone*'s side."

Arth looked away.

"Irregardless," Morth went on, "of *my* three options, I chose the role of Demagogue. The Guide told me I could use that role for either good or evil, and I can promise ya this: I've used it only fer the good of the oppressed." Again, Arth could *feel* the darkness emanating from Morth despite his words. "I see the way yer lookin' at me, oh goody-goody Arthos. I'm betting you and the Guide both has a different definition of 'good' than me." Morth snorted. "Well, you's *both* fools if you think there's any good in holding back when you gots the power to make right. I will *always* seize every 'vantage as I reshape this realm the way it should be."

A wicked smile began to spread across Morth's face as he went on. "Once the Guide was gone, I went on a rampage. There's simply no other word for it." The dagman was clearly *very* proud of himself. "I smoked so many lugman slaveowners that I lost count. By the time I was done, the lugs who was left was throwing themselves at my feet. Strength is the only thing their lot respects. But the former slaves, the ones I'd just freed, they wanted to hear what I had to *say*... and the picture I painted them, of a world free from rulers and authorities, it was too good to pass up. They swore to follow along—not following *me*, mind ya, but the ideal. My vision of a *true* utopia, where no person wields power over anyone else... and certainly not 'cause they happen to carry around some silly Diamond knickknack. Depose the Diamond-bearers!"

It made Arth's skin crawl, seeing the glee in Morth's eyes as he told of smoking the lugmen and accepting the devotion of the slaves. Did Arth even know this fella anymore? His own brother? Still, so long as the twins were talking and not fighting, there was hope.

"You's right about one fing," Arth admitted. "Far too many rulers has abused their authority, often pointing at the fact that they carry a Diamond Relic as some sort of evidence that Sovereign favors their rule. But that's not how Sovereign's gifts was meant to be used! They's intended for the greater good; their magic don't even work, except for the pure of heart—though that don't stop fellas like the Underlord and Burrowcrat from hoarding their Relics as status symbols." Arth let out his breath in a rush. "But Morth, boyo, don't ya see? The answer ain't simply to overthrow *all* authority. You really fink it'll work, having no one in charge at all? That won't prevent people from abusin' power; it'll *encourage* it."

"Of course you'd say that," Morth shot back. "You're the King now—the one with the most to fear from a society without rulers. *You're* even toting a Diamond knickknack to convince others that Sovereign's blessing lies upon ya."

The unfairness of these accusations made Arth want to lash out, to say hurtful things in response. Yet even as Morth's words began to rile him up, Arth felt waves of peace emanating from the Diamond Scepter to calm him instead.

Arth took a deep breath. "I can't help but notice you's essentially a ruler now too," he told Morth mildly. "Despite all yer fancy talk about ending that sort of fing."

Morth shrugged. "My people insist on honoring me as the first citizen of our new society. Maybe that makes me the most important, but I'm still just one among many, not a true ruler. I take plenty of input from anyone as wants to give it. There's this one fella especially, one of the other former slaves—a shaman bloke called the Adjunct—who's helped train me in the deeper mysteries of magic and politics."

"You fink true rulers don't take advice?" Arth scoffed. "The *best* rulers take advice and answer to the people for how they use their power." He shook his head sadly. "Morth, you's deceiving yerself if you fink the power you's seized is any different from what a ruler wields."

Morth just waved one webbed hand dismissively, and Arth realized that was *exactly* what his brother was doing: deceiving himself. He had developed this rhetoric to remove others from authority, but he refused to admit it was only to put himself in their place.

"So... now you're here," Arth said quietly.

"That's right," Morth said smugly. "With the Adjunct's help and the support of the other aquatic freedmen, I used my magic to summon a grand new bridge between Lugarth and Caymerlot. And now we're bringing our campaign of liberation to these shores. Down with your glass towers! Exalt the exploited!"

"Exalt the—" Arth repeated in disbelief. "Would ya listen to yerself, boyo? Since you brought the lugs here, there's been hundreds of innocents *slaughtered*, not exalted. Everyday people, dagsters and kelpies included, not rulers nor aristocrats. Can't ya see yer own hypocrisy? You's become the very thing ya hate, but worse—causin' *more* atrocities and pain and sufferin' than the Underlord or Khan ever did."

"Says the bloke who's standing on the old Underlord's shoulders, at the pinnacle of his society. The fella receivin' expensive gifts from other self-important fellas, eating and drinking and livin' a life of luxury in the midst of that same pain and suffering. You ain't innocent neither, *boyo*."

Arth stared. How could Morth possibly convince himself of such a stilted version of the truth? "Is that why ya sent assassins to smoke me?" he asked quietly, hoping to catch Morth off guard by the accusation.

But Morth wasn't put off at all. In fact, he burst into laughter. "Sure enuff."

"You *admit* it?"

Morth shrugged. "When I learned you was callin' yerself King now, I knew it was only a matter of time before ya took a crack at the Relic-in-the-Rock. I was hoping to get there first. See, the Adjunct confirmed what I already 'spected—that there's *nuffing* special about that Relic, nuffin' that lets only a King or Hero wield it. The Diamond Scepter's just a dagman relic, unusable by members of any other race. I coulda pulled it out same as you, just as easy as Daddie or Bertie. The difference is I knew what I wanted and was willing to take it. All for the good of the cause, of course."

"And that justifies everything you's done?" Arth realized he was gripping the Scepter more tightly than usual, grateful to have it with him. "That makes it okay to try killing yer own brother?"

"*Killing* you?!" Morth blurted. "Of course not. Arth, you forget where we is. This is O'ertwixt! Ya can't *be* killed here, only sent back to the real world."

At last, Arth began to understand Morth's perspective. "So this is all just a big game to you. Do whatever ya want, 'cause there's no consequences?"

"Sure, we can call this a game if ya want, with prizes and braggin' rights for the winner," Morth said with a grin, though the expression had a nasty, bitter edge. Maybe he *did* see this as a game, but he obviously wanted revenge for the bad hand he was dealt at the start. "And why not? Don't you get it? Nothing is real here!"

"Some things is real here," Arth disagreed quietly. "The pain you cause is real. The person you become... that's real."

Morth made another rude, dismissive gesture.

Arth felt so sick inside that he feared he might puke, right there on the floor of his beautiful new tent. Taking a deep breath, he forced himself to focus on the soothing thrum of peace emanating from the Diamond Scepter. "So what now?" he asked levelly.

Morth grinned. "I would say sumfing like 'join me or die,' but we just established that ya *can't* die in O'ertwixt. So..." He shrugged, grinned. "Join me or I'll smoke ya."

"No," Arth said simply.

"Ah, well, it was worth a try. In that case, hand over that Diamond trinket—and if ya don't comply, *then* I'll smoke ya. Surely yer oversized conscience can survive that much."

"Just you try takin' it from me," Arth said.

A *very* big smile spread across Morth's pebbly lips at this invitation, and he quickly twirled the immense Ruby Warhammer, sending out a pulse of blinding green-red light.

Arth didn't have to move a muscle. The enemy magic simply dissipated on contact with him, thanks to the Diamond Scepter's protection. "I fink the Scepter is happy where it is. Tell yerself what ya like, you really *wouldn't* be able to wield this thing." Arth's voice cracked. "Yer heart's turned too black and selfish fer that."

With a snarl of anger, Morth shot off several more bolts of destructive green-red energy; as before, they simply dissolved on contact with Arth or his Relic, though a few missed him entirely, burning huge, gaping holes in the walls of the royal command tent. From outside, the first shouts of alarm were raised.

But Arth's attention remained fixed on his brother. "Oy, my turn," he said quietly. "Surrender, and I'll see to it that yer return to the real world is painless."

"Never!" Morth shrieked as he fired off even more bolts, losing control of his temper; but his fireballs missed Arth by a wide margin as often as they came near to hitting him. With a great creak and flutter, the big command tent—which had stood for less than a week—collapsed around them. Morth angrily sent a blast straight up, obliterating the canvas ceiling before it could fall upon them.

And once the tent was down, the Demagogue suddenly saw that he was surrounded. He raised his Ruby Warhammer to blast Arth's guards with magic, but paused when he saw who those guards were: not just unknown karks and nyms in blue capes, but also Daddie and Uncle Bertie, Freddie the Contortionist, the Tumbler and Acrobat, the Walker Brothers and the Danger Sisters and all the other dagman circus performers whom Morth had once worked alongside, what seemed so long ago. They were all gaping at him, astonished... and in Daddie's case, deeply disappointed. Morth flushed with shame, averting his gaze rather than meeting Daddie's eye.

"Guess we'll settle this on the battlefield then," he muttered to Arth.

"Just stop," Arth tried one more time. "*Please*, Morth."

But his twin brother shook his head. The huge ruby pulsed with wicked light, and suddenly there were skeletal wings sprouting from the dagmagicker's back, flapping to bring him quickly aloft. Morth snarled wordlessly, spitting at Arth's feet, then spun and departed with the wind.

Arth sank to his knees, feeling all strength and confidence leave him. His own brother? *Morth* was the true enemy he would face on the morrow?

All this time, he'd known he would need to destroy the new bridge for his plan to work—but also capture or convince the enemy aquatics to abandon their lugman allies, otherwise the bridge could just be rebuilt again. Now Arth recognized that the situation was even more dire, for convincing the aquatics wouldn't be enough. He would also need to convince his own brother...

Or else remove him from Overtwixt altogether.

Part III
The Barbarian Horde

· twenty-three ·

Hembrose and the three squad members with him fought a running battle from the moment they stepped foot on the Lugarth-Caymerlot bridge—and every moment of it was sheer terror for the young-again Wizard. Sure enough, he'd lost most of his confidence and newfound courage at the same time he left behind his experience and strength.

Even so, he almost *welcomed* the danger if it meant avoiding the painful tension that now existed between Pyrsie and Paladin.

The Wizard still rode Noble. With one hand clutching desperately to the centman's braided back hair (in order to keep his seat), he used the Emerald Caduceus to defend against a luggernaut attacking from one side. Flourishing the Caduceus overhead, Hembrose unleashed the most destructive burst of green magic he could manage... then watched in dismay as the fireball lost momentum and splashed to the ground at the lugman's feet. The magic sizzled across the lug's hoofed feet, tripping him up—but that only sent him tumbling *into* the Noble's flank! With a yelp, the mermage clobbered the fellow upside the head with the Caduceus, which was absolutely *not* how his precious magical relic was meant to be used. And yet, because the Caduceus granted him the raw physical might of multiple luggernauts—the ones he'd harvested on Lugarth during his spy mission—*this* barbarian puffed to yellow mist instantly.

How very crude this was, overwhelming the enemy with *brawn* instead of the sophisticated workings of advanced magic! Was this how he'd be remembered? As a brute, rather than the greatest magical practitioner of the age?

Hembrose supposed it didn't really matter, for at the moment, it was simply the best he could do. In addition to physical strength, the Emerald Caduceus also contained the speed, stamina, and enhanced hearing and visual acuity of the four guards he'd harvested in Crystal Keep. All of these were nice bonuses, to be sure, but Hembrose had created the Caduceus largely as an amplifier for his own magical strength—which had returned to its original, undeveloped state. Even with the relic, he was now unable to project his magic very far or with great force, no matter how many impressive techniques he remembered from before. It didn't help that he was required to maintain a pair of *legs* below his waist, constantly tapping his limited magical resources just so he could stay in Noble's saddle. It was a beautiful saddle, at least, an oiled and polished seat and pommel with matching saddle bags, strapped onto the centman's flanks over a richly-embroidered blue-and-white caparison...

The young merman blinked. Why was he staring at his mount's *saddle* of all things? He was so tired, so easily distracted—enough so that he would have fallen to the very next lugman attack if the Noble hadn't parried suddenly, using his own spear to disarm and shove the lug aside.

"Eyes up, Wizard. Head on an axis!" the centman ordered him yet again—even as he tucked the spear under his arm, drew an arrow, and shot it from his longbow, all in one smooth combination of movements. The arrow streaked away ahead of them, drilling an approaching luggernaut between the eyes. In the sudden yellow smoke, the lug's companion darted sideways, only to fall unexpectedly through one of the bridge's many holes. That fellow shrieked in terror as he tumbled from view. "Hah," Noble grunted in understated appreciation. "Two avifauni, one petra." Whatever that meant. "What do you see?"

Rubbing his eyes, Hembrose gazed into the distance, for the Caduceus gave him better eyesight than the centman. "Next clump of lugs is hugging the right side of the bridge, and there's a long crack down the middle. If we hug the left, we should be able to bypass them without violence."

Never slowing from his gallop, the Noble grunted and complied, swerving over to join Pyrsie and Paladin on their side of the bridge. Moments later, a gaping chasm appeared, splitting the Lugarth-Caymerlot bridge into two distinct lanes for half a mile. The next batch of lugs could only stare and stammer as the squad members passed them by, completely out of reach. The Wizard sighed with relief.

The terrain of this new bridge was incredibly treacherous. In one sense, it reminded Hembrose of the giant "natural" staircase that used to join Centhule and Lugarth, a jammed-together series of miniature nilands formed from mismatched chunks of rock. But unlike the Centhule bridge, this new Caymerlot bridge made a single sloping ramp up to the lugman niland—with gaping holes where the puzzle pieces of rock didn't fit together perfectly. There was nothing elegant about it; this bridge had been assembled in haste, for one purpose only... but the good guys had found they *could* take advantage of those dangerous pitfalls.

As they approached more lugs, Paladin leapt gracefully over an empty hole in the bridge, neatly avoiding the enemies clustered on both sides of that gap. This left just one beefy lug on the far side, and Noble—returned now to the other side of the bridge—sent another arrow whistling from his bow to dispatch that one. Pyrsie gave a grateful shout, but she never shifted her focus from the terrain ahead of her. Since the moment they'd left the city, she had ridden Paladin with single-minded focus, knowing he might take the bit in his teeth and then bolt, if she gave him the chance. The little gnomaid had long since run out of throwing knives, and Paladin's metal-shod hooves weren't useful as weapons until they were already face-to-face with the enemy. If not for Noble's longbow—and Hembrose's ability to occasionally recover his squad mate's arrows with magic, as he did now—the four companions would have been in trouble a long time ago. Because this was a very, very, *very* long bridge.

But truly, their biggest advantage was simply speed and surprise. It was an irregular stream of lugs crossing the bridge toward Caymerlot, strung out in clumps of five or six at a time. By the time one group reacted to the squad members' surprising (and surprisingly small) incursion into their territory, Hembrose and the others were usually past them, galloping toward the *next* batch of barbarians. Most lugs had only enough time to react on instinct, swinging clubs or swords in alarm, and the Wizard's team did more dodging than defending, more fleeing than fighting—to Paladin's ever-growing shame.

At long last, the quartet left the treacherous sloping bridge behind, cresting the lip of the niland and galloping onto the red-grassed hills of Lugarth. Mounting the first of those hills, Noble and Paladin both reared, stopping a moment to rest—

And to gape in disbelief at the barbarian horde camped before them, war tents stretching to the horizon. Even the Wizard, who'd seen it before, groaned. Then again, his newly improved visual acuity now let him see *all* of the camps, for miles and miles ahead... so he actually groaned the loudest.

The Noble was first to stir, bending at the waist to run a hand down his own right foreleg, then lifting and inspecting the hoof. Even with the metal hoofshoes Pyrsie had fashioned him long ago, his foot was in bad shape, and he hissed in pain. "Gonna need healing," he grunted.

"I'm dry," Pyrsie said, demonstrating that fact by holding her empty canteen upside down. "Hembrose?"

"On it." The young Wizard was already working his meager magic through the Caduceus, summoning a storm—a very *small* storm, just a single dark raincloud that hovered over their heads, but enough for their purposes. With a curl of his fingers, he spun precipitation into a narrow funnel cloud to deposit the water into Pyrsie's flask; when hers was full, he did the same for Noble's and his own. Last of all, he filled Pyrsie's Diamond Grail, which she then held out for Paladin and Noble both to drink from; the glowing-blue water healed their tired muscles and damaged hooves, restoring them to alertness despite now *two* days without sleep. The squad members did all this with a minimum of talking—none, in Paladin's case—having performed this ritual several times already.

When the Grail was back in her tunic, Pyrsie took out another of her inventions, which looked exactly like a pocket watch as far as Hembrose could tell. Examining the device's needle-like hands closely, Pyrsie looked up and pointed. "Northmount is that way."

"We best get on with it, then," Noble said calmly, gesturing toward the war tents below. By now, the luggernauts there had noticed them, and a dozen of the huge beasts were charging up the hill while their friends in the camp hooted encouragement: "Bah-le-le-le-leeeee-i-oo-uuuu! Bah-le-le-le-leeeee-i-oo-uuuu!"

Before Pyrsie could stop him, Paladin dashed forward to meet them. It took all of the girl's strength, tugging at the bit in his mouth, to redirect the eqman *around* the enemy without engaging in unnecessary battle. Noble and Wizard looped around the enemy fighters on the other side, then joined up again with the Paladin and Inventor right before galloping straight into the middle of the first war camp.

So the running battle continued.

As they'd done on the bridge, the four squad members used the terrain to their advantage. Despite the sheer number of enemy combatants, the presence of tents and cookfires made it impossible for most beasts to even see them coming, much less mob them. Noble and Paladin's maneuverability did the rest, the two men darting gracefully between obstacles and enemies. They never rode in a straight line for long, and that proved especially frustrating for the luggernauts. Just like crocodators back home—vicious predators from Hembrose's real world—lugmen were big, strong, and surprisingly speedy themselves, but they seemed incapable of turning corners very quickly, and they tired out fast. In this way, the good guys sped through one war camp after another, the worst danger and fighting happening in the open spaces *between* camps.

After two more days and nights of this—*four* straight days without sleep, fueled only by the magic of the Diamond Grail—the allies left the last of the war camps behind them, the tents falling out of sight behind a particularly tall red hill. Hembrose tumbled from the saddle, dropping his partial shapeshift. He groaned with relief as his legs knit back together again, into the tail his mam had given him, so to speak. He lay there for several minutes on the ground, resting, but he was the only one. Pyrsie didn't dare leave Paladin's back, and Paladin himself remained stiff and proud. Noble, by contrast, kept a vigilant eye on the hills behind them. "Surely they're still following us," he said.

"They are," Hembrose confirmed, rubbing his tired quadricep muscles with one hand. "I can hear them, but we have time." He shifted his grip on the Caduceus. "And if need be, I can multiply that time—"

"No," Noble said sharply. "Save the rest of your magic until we reach our destination. That's when we truly need it."

"But if it helps lose zee pursuit now…?" Pyrsie began.

"I don't think it will matter," Noble said with a sigh. "By now, even the lugs have to know where we're going."

All too soon, the four squad mates resumed their journey, though at a less-tiring pace this time. They encountered a freshwater pond, and for once were able to refill canteens the old-fashioned way. Hembrose even swam a single quick lap, relishing the feel of water over his entire body, rejuvenating him. Then he formed legs once more and trudged from the water, air-drying himself, and climbed back into the saddle.

Finally, at dawn on the sixth day of travel, the exhausted foursome came within sight of Northmount: the upside-down mountain that stretched up toward Hulandia far above. Turning back the way they'd come, they saw blue and green flashes warring in the sky far behind them, like magical lightning.

The *real* battle had begun.

The Final Battle of Caymerlot.

· twenty-four ·

A pulsing blue flare leapt from the end of Arth's Diamond Scepter at his mental command. Distant shouts acknowledged his signal, followed by the creaking of gates: the north and west entrances to Crystal City, opening at his signal. Next came the quiet thunder of hooves, steadily growing in volume as Caymerlot's eqman and centman allies galloped northwest along the outside of the thick glass city wall.

High above, the King's magical blue pulse finally faded among the Sky Light's brilliant morning rays. Arth dearly hoped he had given Pyrsie and Hembrose enough time, but there was nothing more he could do for them now. He had to fight his own battle.

"Lugs are getting restless," Sarge called down from atop the wall, here at the farthest northwest gate. "They saw the flare and they hear the hoofbeats. They know something's about to happen."

"You gots yer orders," Arth called back calmly. "Stick 'em with some arrows, pref'ably in their squishiest parts."

As intended, this drew some tension-relieving laughter from the soldiers waiting with Arth in rows and columns. Atop the wall, two companies of kark and nym archers loosed volleys of arrows onto the luggernauts massed just outside, eliciting cries of anger and pain.

"Here they come..." warned the Sergeant-at-arms, referring to the Centhulians galloping along the outside of the wall, both south of and north of the King's position.

"Ready yerselves!" Arth shouted to his troops.

Then they all heard a monumental clash from outside, almost like simultaneous rockslides on both sides of them, except with a bunch of *soft* bodies colliding instead of hard rocks. Then more screams sounded, bellows of hate and anger, along with the clashing of weapons.

"Now!" Sarge cried, even as he and his team began turning the cranks to swing the northwest gate open.

"Charge!" Arth shouted, and his personal force of dagmen riding kelpies—including Arth himself on Sidekick—slithered forward at high speed. Closing his eyes, the King of Caymerlot thought about how deeply he cared for the welfare of these allies and friends, and a brilliant blue shield leapt from the Scepter. It formed a broad band of protection in front of the dagsters and kelpies as they sped through the open gate into the battle outside.

Beyond the gate, Arth was gratified to see that the start of the battle was going according to plan. The massed lugs, slow of thought as usual, had spun to face the surprise attacks on their left and right flanks, all of them pushing against each other in hopes of reaching the fighting more quickly. That left their backs turned to Arth's dagman vanguard,* which immediately employed nets and tridents to

---

* The "vanguard" (or sometimes "van" for short) is the leading or front part of an army when marching or attacking.

begin pulling the beasts down. Behind the dagmen came more companies of merman archers and okkie stranglers, repeating their tactics from days before. The merpeople kept mostly to the deep water just outside the gate, some of them attacking lugs from afar while others engaged the traitorous aquatics who so proudly wore those red kerchiefs to identify themselves. Meanwhile, both companies of kark and nym archers filed down from the city wall and exited next. Even a few delphmen charged through the gate, leaping out of the water to ram lugmen with their bottle noses before splashing down again. Of all the aquatics from Crystal City, only the caymen remained entirely behind, unwilling or unable to do actual fighting; and *they* had dedicated themselves to operating the gates, swinging them shut after Arth's army departed.

As with most of Caymerlot, the northwestern reaches of the niland were dominated by a great lake with only a narrow strip of dry ground all along the perimeter. As the last of the lugmen caught in the King's pincer disappeared into yellow mist, Arth's hooved allies reversed direction and began working their way outward along the isthmus. The eqmen pushed the luggernauts back on the left shore of the lake, working clockwise toward the Karks' Fangs land bridges; and the centmen did the same on the right, working counterclockwise toward the rusty truss bridge onto Dagmør.

Considering how much they loved warfare, the lugs refused to retreat; but there was simply nowhere for them to go, since the isthmuses were even narrower than most bridges. The eqmen and centmen were ridden by humen and gnomen wielding swords and spears and bows and slingshots, poking and peppering the lugs with arrows and stones every step of the way. Just as Arth had planned, many of the lugmen were driven into the water alongside their kerchiefed allies—mostly karks and kelpies—where they fought at a disadvantage. Other lugs lost their footing and fell off the other side of the isthmus, tumbling into the empty whiteness below the niland.

That was until the Demagogue—*Morth*—finally got involved. Casting his spells from an unknown location, the dagmagicker summoned an immense, dark-green storm cloud that seemed to cover the entirety of the great lake. Blinding bolts of green lightning zigzagged out of the sky, creating explosions of rock and bodies anywhere they struck the ground. Arth stared in dismay as more and more of the bolts fell, at least fifty at once, for the power Morth wielded was staggering. The Demagogue's problem seemed to be the opposite of the Wizard's, however; for all his incredible strength in the magic, Arth's twin had no control or finesse, and his devastating bolts fell just as often among the lugs as among the Caymerlotions and Centhulians.

Even so, the devastation befalling Arth's forces was bad enough.

"My King?" Lady Karis called. She was riding an eqman in the shallows nearby, fighting from his back, unwilling to stray too far from the Squad. "Arthos, you must do something about that lightning!"

"Aye, the way it hurts us is frightening!" Sidekick agreed as he took out a lug at the knees with his Diamond Aegis. With everything going on, the mohawked kelpie seemed content to finish someone else's rhyme instead of starting his own.

"I'll do what I can," Arth muttered, holding the Scepter before him and filling himself with urgent thoughts of concern for the people being blasted all across this watery landscape. One after another, tiny shields of blue began popping into existence, in exactly the right place to catch a lightning strike and disappear again as soon as their job was done. It was impossible for Arth to predict where a bolt would land before it even appeared, but somehow Sovereign's magic knew and positioned itself where needed.

"Oy, it's workin'!" Daddie blurted in relief. In his moment of distraction, he nearly lost his head to a notched lugman blade, except Uncle Bertie blocked the blow with his own huge luggernaut club.

"Hold on, now," Antagonist cried from where he reloaded his Diamond Harpoon in the shallows nearby. "You're protecting the lugs as well as our own people!" he accused Arth.

And sure enough, Arth noticed that the Diamond Scepter was blocking *all* the lightning strikes, including those falling among the enemy. Frowning in concentration, Arth tried to exclude the lugmen from the feelings of goodwill emanating from the Scepter—and for the first time since he drew the Relic out of the Rock, its magic faltered and failed. A chorus of screams sounded from nearby as the next bolt sent a dozen centmen over the edge of the niland.

"No!" Arth cried, his eyes filling with frustrated tears, and he willed Sovereign's magic to prevent any more such pain. As before, the little shields of blue began blinking into existence across the landscape, even over the lugs. "Calamity," he gasped. "Sovereign's magic, it gots a mind of its own, and it don't like takin' sides." The blue magic really was the opposite of the green, he was starting to realize. Where the green was happy to destroy *everyone* given the opportunity, the blue wanted to *protect* everyone.

Yet Arth was sure Sovereign's magic could be used as a weapon sometimes, as in the case of Sidekick's Aegis. On reflection, the reason for that was obvious, and exactly as he'd always been told: whether used for correction or protection, Sovereign's magic only worked if wielded by the pure of heart and *for the greater good.*

The King's eyes fell upon the Antagonist as he fired his Diamond Harpoon, teeth gritted in hatred, sending a bolt shooting through the back of a fleeing lug. No glow of blue accompanied this violence, for there was nothing but spite in the merman's heart—and it was aimed at an enemy who wasn't even a threat. His brother Altruist, by contrast, glowed brilliantly in the chainmail of his Diamond Hauberk, which protected him from enemy fire as he focused his own bow-and-arrow attacks on the lugmen who were currently attacking his allies. Even Sidekick, for all his joking about gleefully slaughtering the enemy, seemed to use his Aegis as a weapon only when needed, and it glowed brightly too.

Morth's lightning bombardment ceased abruptly, as the Demagogue finally realized how much strength he was expending to no purpose. Just as suddenly, his voice filled the air, jarring and eerie:

"Freedom fighters!" he cried, "Believers in the cause—fall back to the thicket!" The very surface of the great lake's water rippled in time with his words, circles within circles, as if he was distorting the water itself to amplify his voice. "Fall back to the trees, then turn and fight again!"

· twenty-five ·

Pyrsie heaved a sigh of relief. After almost a week of frantic running battle, her team of squad mates had arrived. They had no time to spare, since Arth's Final Battle had clearly begun, but at least she'd accomplished the first part of her mission: reaching Northmount.

Which meant Pyrsie could finally release Paladin.

She offered the Grail to her former friend one last time. Despite his smoldering fury, Paladin lapped up every drop, desperate for relief. Yet the water's blue glow was feeble, and he groaned after swallowing, not fully healed. Though Pyrsie didn't understand it, she could no longer deny the Grail's diminishing returns. The longer she had pushed Paladin, the less power the Relic seemed to have to heal any of them. Was its magic running out? Or was something else wrong? *

---

* This is tricky. Pyrsie's heart may have been in the right place to accomplish something important, and maybe Paladin really was being selfish and wrong. But did that give Pyrsie the right to *force* him to do the right thing against his will? Do the ends ever justify the means, even when there's so much at stake? I don't know... —*N*

Pyrsie sighed. As far as Paladin was concerned, it no longer mattered. She had required enough of the big red eqman. With a groan of her own, the gnomaid slipped from his back for the first time in a week—for the last time ever—then moved around front and gently pulled the bit from his mouth. The eqman was frothing, his eyes wild. "I am so sorry it had to be zis way," she started to say, patting his muzzle.

Paladin had barely spoken since Caymerlot, and he didn't speak now. Instead, with a wordless scream of rage, the stallion bit her hand—hard!—and dashed away.

Noble looked between the two former friends, trying to think of something to say. Then he shrugged sadly, at a loss. Hembrose averted his eyes, embarrassed.

Crying from the pain (and not just the throbbing of her crippled hand), Pyrsie tucked the Diamond Grail into the crook of her injured arm then slopped in some water from her canteen, one-handed. She drank greedily, groaning as her mangled fingers straightened and healed, far too slowly.

Stopping at a distance safely out of her reach, Paladin called back to Pyrsie in anger and disgust. "I will never forget this, Inventor of Gnoburrow." He spat her name as if it were a curse. "Every positive sentiment I ever felt for you has turned to hate. And I shall make sure my children hate you, and my children's children, and the child of any other eqman who enters Overtwixt. Before I am done, no one will remember the crimes of the Prince's human raiders, or even the atrocities of the luggernauts themselves, though my people suffered terribly under both regimes." His voice rose to a fever pitch of self-righteous fury, but for all his pomposity, the Paladin was clearly speaking from his heart. "Instead, what the eqmen will ever recall is the betrayal of their so-called friend—the gnoman who pretended to be the most steadfast of companions, but in the end proved herself the most cowardly of turncoats."

Pyrsie hung her head in shame—all the more so, since she knew she would make the same choices again, given another chance.

Paladin stomped one hoof, demanding Pyrsie return her attention to him. "If I have my way, no friendship will ever again exist between eqmen and gnomen, from now until the end of time," the heroic eqman concluded, voice thick with emotion. "*That* is what this betrayal has cost you."

Pyrsie was sobbing as Paladin turned and galloped away. Lowering herself to the ground, burying her face in her hands, she allowed herself a well-earned pity party.

But all too soon, Noble was shifting his feet, and Hembrose was clearing his throat uncomfortably—as well they should, knowing it was only a matter of time before the pursuing lugmen caught up with them. So Pyrsie sniffled and wiped her eyes, straightening once more. Rather than meet her friends' gaze, she looked up at the bulk of Northmount, looming over them like an upside-down mountain hanging from the niland of Hulandia far above. The hollow tip of the massive stalactite hovered about two stories over Pyrsie's head, connected the rest of the way to Lugarth with several loops of spiral staircase. Even that staircase seemed foreboding, each of its metal steps wide enough for four lugs to climb side by side.

"I guess we go on foot from here," Pyrsie said hoarsely.

Hembrose slipped silently from Noble's polished saddle and followed as Pyrsie began to climb. The centman, bringing up the rear, had to duck to avoid banging his head on the underside of the steps above.

Both the staircase and Northmount itself had clearly seen better days. Small rockfalls showered from above almost constantly, the pebbles striking their heads painfully, and the metal stairsteps were rusty and unreliable. The three friends had to take care where they placed their feet, because some steps bowed alarmingly under their weight, creaking dangerously. At one point, they had to jump over a gap where two steps were missing entirely; and the tall railing that ringed the outside of the spiral was no help, for rust had turned the welds to dust in many places, causing the handrail to swing free.

If the magic that held a bridge together was indeed a representation of the friendship between the peoples of its linked nilands, it was clear that relations between humen and lugmen had been neglected entirely. Well, no surprise there.

Before long, the three squad mates reached the top of the metal staircase and entered the hollow mouth of a great cavern that opened up over their heads. Hembrose summoned a green ball of light and set it to hover high above so they could see the interior of the cave. Many more steps had been carved out of the walls of rock, continuing the path of the spiral staircase in a twisting corkscrew through the inside of the stone funnel. The path widened steadily from here—but the cave mouth itself was just as narrow as the metal staircase, too small to allow more than a few lugmen through at the same time.

In other words, the entrance was a literal bottleneck, making for an excellent defensive position.

Noble looked at all the open space above them, then back down at the opening, and he nodded with shoulders sagging. "If I make my stand here, I should be able to hold this pass indefinitely. Like those alleys between the Branch Library huts, no matter how many lugs they send against me, there's only room for a couple of them to fight me at once." He gave Pyrsie and Hembrose a grim smile. "I will buy you some time, Inventor—time that the Wizard can multiply."

Pyrsie nodded, not trusting herself to speak.

The centman placed a hand on her shoulder, even that small curve of his lips straightening to complete seriousness.

"Much has been sacrificed to make this possible," he said quietly. "Make it count for something."

Pyrsie blinked away tears, nodding more firmly. "Thank you," she told him raggedly, then seized one of his legs in a hug. Somehow she knew she would never see the Noble again either, but she was determined to part on better terms than she had with the Paladin. "Thank you for everyzing, my friend."

The centman lifted her easily to his height and gripped her tiny body in a crushing, heartfelt hug. "And I thank *you*, my friend. Go with the Sovereign."

Then he turned to face the cave opening, readying his weapons. And Pyrsie and the mermage resumed their climb into the bowels of Northmount, looking for the right place to begin her work.

· twenty-six ·

The King's forces reached the northernmost point of Caymerlot the following evening. It was there that all three of his coalition's armies reunited, with the eqmen galloping up along the western rim of the niland and the centmen doing the same along the northern shore, meeting the aquatics at a thicket of kanban trees—for Arth had led Caymerlot's own blue-caped soldiers in swimming straight across the middle of that great lake. For the last day and a half, the three armies had harried the Demagogue's retreating forces with barely a pause in the fighting. Now, though, as the lugmen and their kerchiefed allies reached that dense copse of kanbans, they turned and faced their pursuers again.

Karis Priamos, the Knight of Overtwixt, could hear a voice echoing among the woods, issuing orders, though she couldn't make out the specifics. How very like Arthos that voice sounded, but with a harsh, bitter edge she had never heard from her friend—for it was the King's brother, the Demagogue, who led the invaders now.

Oh, how she lamented *that* terrible revelation. For Karis knew what it was like to face your own loved one in battle, having confronted—and banished from Overtwixt—her own brother Bias mere months ago on Eqland. It was a trauma she did not wish on anyone, and certainly not her dear young friend Arthos Penn.

In the distance to Karis's right, the King of Caymerlot raised one hand high, calling on his soldiers to wait before resuming hostilities. She followed his gaze as he examined the kanbans. They were a strange type of multi-trunked tree that many peoples considered exotic, though Karis had learned they were commonplace on Dagmør, being native to the dagman real world. It did not surprise Karis to find a growth of such trees here, for they were now close to Dagmør itself; in fact, the army of Centhule must have passed that niland's rusty truss bridge on the way here. The thicket made for a distinct change in terrain from Caymerlot's usual lagoons and isthmuses, but the Knight wasn't so foolish as to think it any less treacherous for her and the other outlanders. Like the dagman portland itself, this new battlefield spreading before her was undoubtedly marshy.

Karis shook her head. She would follow Arthos to the very end, but even she tired of all the constant moist and damp in this part of Overtwixt. Bad enough to simply travel through the muck before her; but she despaired of further fighting while ankle-deep mire sucked at her every footstep.

Beyond the kanban thicket, the Demagogue's ugly new bridge sloped up and away, toward the red niland of Lugarth just visible in the far distance. "I see dry land ahead," she said in a joking tone, for the benefit of the other groundwalkers in her vicinity. "Aye, the fight between here and there won't be pleasant, but at least we have something to look forward to."

Her allies—mostly gnomen and other humen riding eqmen—all laughed, appreciating the momentary levity.

Unfortunately, it wouldn't be that simple. As she thought about it, Karis realized the tide of this conflict had now fully turned. Whereas the Demagogue had been throwing his forces against the thick glass walls of Crystal City for weeks now, this thicket represented *his* most defensible fallback position. Most of the aquatics, enemy and ally alike, would be comfortable in the marsh; but of the groundwalkers, the lugmen enjoyed a significant advantage because of their size—as always, it seemed. The shallow mud simply didn't hinder them as much as it would a centman or human, much less one of the little people. More to the point, the thicket protected the entire narrow entrance to the Demagogue's new bridge, packed not only with trees but also the Demagogue's so-called freedom fighters.

Karis feared that the King's forward momentum would stall here. For all her joking, the Knight's allies seemed unlikely to penetrate the thicket and reach the bridge anytime soon, unless the enemy simply gave up.

Even so, when the King gave the signal, the forces of Caymerlot and Centhule raised their heads high and marched into the outskirts of the small marsh. "Attack!" the Sergeant-at-arms relayed his ruler's orders, barely discernible at this distance despite the way he bellowed. "Repel these invaders from our shores!"

This time, the blue-caped karks and okkies surged up the middle, engaging the towering lugs in the muddy marshwaters. The two lines of fighters met with a terrible clash—and the lugs didn't even budge. Instead, the Demagogue's front line began to curl around on both sides, coming back out from the protection of the trees in an attempt to enclose the Caymerlotion vanguard. "Archers, loose!" Sarge cried next, and the companies of nym and merman archers began to fire volleys into the exposed enemies. "Fire at will!" The commander's next words washed over Karis at full volume, magically enhanced by the power of Arthos's Scepter, for this time she was among his intended audience. "Eqmen and centmen, advance!"

"Ready, Prancer?" Karis asked as she drew her twin curved swords.

"Ready, Lady Knight," cried the young eqman who had volunteered to be Karis's mount for the Final Battle.

And so the eqmen and their riders crashed into the exposed enemy forces on the King's left flank, even as the Centhulians did the same on his right. And until the moment Karis's blades struck the first luggernaut, arrows continued falling among the enemy forces, the bombardment only ceasing when it posed a risk to Karis's detachment.

The battle quickly resumed its former intensity, as the good guys strove to push deeper into the kanban marsh. The King's forces were soon completely engaged, the majority of his army moving in among the outlying trees—though most of the mermen fell back with the delphmen, finding the marsh's muddy pools too shallow to swim. That didn't stop the stalwart Altruist or Antagonist, however, both of whom continued to fight at close quarters with limited mobility despite the increased danger. Nor were they the only ones. All across the crowded battlefield, other members of the Squad were setting an example of bravery, inspiring the rest of the King's coalition to acts of daring.

Karis smiled grimly, never more proud to be part of the Squad than she was right now. She only wished Gerald were here to fight with her. Instead, she made do with the eqmen, humen, and gnomen who'd been placed under her command. "On me!" she cried, steering Prancer into battle with her knees, knowing the other eqmen would follow in his wake—even as *their* riders lashed out with blade, bo, bow, or bolo every step of the way.

Time and again, the Knight led her people in sorties against the enemy battle formation. And as night fell once more, her brilliant blue armor acted as a beacon for them to follow as they strafed the lugs—slashing recklessly as they galloped along the front line, then curving around to repeat the process. It was a dangerous tactic, riding at such speed through the mud, especially in a wooded area. As the fight stretched on and visibility worsened, more than one of her riders was clotheslined by low-hanging branches, then set upon by kerchiefed karks or kelpies. In frustration at their inability to fight back effectively, the lugmen finally began stepping out of ranks to extend their clubs just above the ground, tripping the eqmen as they passed. But each time they did, one of Karis's mount-and-rider pairs would plunge into the gap the lug had left in his line. In this way, her force finally began to push the enemy back—but oh, how slowly!

Meanwhile, the Sergeant-at-arms was leading a force of kark loyalists to support the centmen on the King's right flank. Mimicking Karis's tactics, the centmen distracted the towering lugs with slashing attacks at their faces—for the centmen, of all the coalition peoples, were the only ones tall enough to reach that high. This left Sarge's karks free to attack from below, bringing down one luggernaut after another with blows to the knees, after which they would slither atop downed foes to pummel chest and head. Sarge made even more progress than Karis for a time, until the Demagogue shored up that line with more of his own karks.

Most karkmen, ally and enemy alike, wielded multiple weapons: two or even four of their tentacles brandishing flails or swords and shields while they slithered nimbly on their other four. But Sarge himself was a marvel, flourishing his distinctive ceremonial maces in *all eight* tentacles. Pausing between sorties to remove her helmet and sip from her canteen, the Knight watched the other veteran's fighting style with a critical eye.

Somehow, the Sergeant-at-arms was able to stand on just two tentacles at a time, but it was seldom the same two tentacles for long. He moved among the enemy karks in a blur, whirling and spinning and battering with his blunt weapons until his foes were reduced to yellow smoke. Each mace was unique, some with dangerous edges, others with spikes, some heavy and clublike, but none merely ornamental. And as Sarge fought, *one* of those maces glowed with a flickering blue light—the Diamond Truncheon of Truth, which he had shown to Karis before the battle, finally admitting that he too bore one of Sovereign's Relics. Tonight, it was that weapon's faint blue streaks that drew the Knight's gaze, illuminating the man's efforts despite the gloom of the marsh. The Sergeant spun his Truncheon in elaborate attacks, often juggling it and his other maces from one tentacle to the other in order to bring the most effective weapon to bear on his enemy.

Even as Karis watched, Sarge overwhelmed one young enemy karkman, batting the last of the man's weapons from his grip. He raised his Truncheon high, but the other kark cried, "I surrender!" The Sergeant-at-arms hesitated, the blue light of his Diamond Relic seeming to throb more powerfully as the lad ripped the red kerchiefs from his arms.

Sarge turned, obviously looking for Arthos and finding him instantly despite the deepening darkness—for the King's Relic glowed more brightly than any other. Arthos nodded, and Sarge lowered his weapon. He growled something, and the grateful youth fled the battle, slithering away with head down. Another foe soon took his place, and Sarge resumed the fight, though his Truncheon now glowed brighter than before.

Arthos himself was not doing much fighting, which Karis thought was wholly appropriate. He wasn't just the leader of one small Squad anymore, but of an entire nation—and at the moment, he was acting general of a coalition of three full armies. He *needed* to stay out of the worst fighting so he could see where to send reinforcements, or where to apply the incomparable protective power of his Scepter. Just as importantly, he needed to stay fresh for the moment when he was the only one who could fight.

When the time came to confront his brother the Demagogue, personally.

And yet Karis sometimes forgot that Arthos was still just a boy. He had only limited experience as a warrior and leader, and he owed most of his success—in both war and leadership—to his huge heart and surprising humility. He still made mistakes, however.

And he was making one now.

"Arthos!" Karis bellowed, pointing. "The van! You must support the vanguard!" The King shifted his focus at her encouragement, then immediately charged into the thick of it himself. "Oh, Arthos," she muttered, in fond exasperation. So much for keeping himself fresh.

"Should we ride to his aid?" Prancer asked eagerly, sidestepping several times in an overabundance of youthful energy.

"No," Karis replied, though she wished for nothing more. "We have our own responsibilities." Then: "On me!" she cried yet again, launching her own force into yet another sortie against the left flank.

· twenty-seven ·

While Arth had been distracted, the karks and okkies that made up his own vanguard had begun losing ground to a combined force of lugs and kerchiefed kelpies. At the Knight's warning, Arth and Sidekick surged forward to support his people, leading the rest of his own force of dagsters and kelpies.

The King of Caymerlot no longer carried traditional weapons, only the Diamond Scepter, which was more than sufficient on its own. Wielding that Relic like a quarterstaff—a kind of long, blunt weapon the Lady Karis had taught him to use in the early days of the Squad—Arth jabbed one lugman hard in the gut. The fella doubled over, making a much easier target for Uncle Bertie as the Bodyguard rode up on his own kelpie. Arth himself was already spinning in Sidekick's saddle, swinging the Scepter to clothesline a luggernaut rushing past on his other side. A pulse of blue magic augmented his strength, and he effortlessly laid the lug out flat on the ground—easy pickings for one of the other dagmen.

As he fought, Arth tried to empty himself of ill will toward the lugmen personally, reminding himself of his goal. His intent wasn't necessarily to smoke his enemies, but simply to push them back onto their niland. And in this mindset, Arth felt the welcome influence of the Diamond Relic once more, guiding him not only with throbs of compassion and mercy but also wise *insight*. When to parry, when to press the attack. When to nudge Sidekick in this direction or that. And yes, even when to smoke an enemy fighter, but also when to stay his hand.

Nearby, Daddie fought with bullwhip and short baton—the traditional tools of the kugar-tamer, which had been his role in the real world circus as a young man, long before rising to Ringmaster. Unfurling his whip, he cracked it expertly in midair, causing a nearby luggernaut to falter in his charge towards Arth. As the big fella blinked at Daddie, the Ringmaster flicked his wrist once more, and the long whip wrapped around the enemy's ankles, lightning fast. Daddie and his kelpie *heaved* backwards, toppling the fella like a fallen tree. Arth's father cracked the lug across the temple with his baton as he went down, knocking him out cold, then spun to scan for more threats against his son.

He never saw the next attack coming. Moving even faster than his bullwhip, a crossbow bolt shot through the battle to pierce the chest of Daddie's kelpie mount. In an instant, the kelpman puffed away into yellow, and Pythagoras Penn collapsed face-first in the marshwaters.

Arth sucked in a breath to order Sidekick that direction, but his friend was already moving. By the time they arrived, Daddie had pushed himself onto hands and knees, gasping, but a huge luggernaut was bending over to slap him down again—the same huge lug who'd fired the crossbow bolt.

"Ransacker!" Arth cried, feeling like he'd been in this exact situation once before... because he had. During the

Battle for the Branch Library, Arth had screamed this same lugman's name in a desperate attempt to distract him from smoking someone *else* he cared about, Lady Karis the Knight.

"Squawk Leader!" the Ransacker growled with obvious pleasure. "Us meet again!"

"The man you face is Squadleader no more," Sidekick shot back. "Now he's the new King with soldiers galore! And try though you might, you'll fall in this fight. For Arthos the dagman will soon end your war!"

Ransacker threw back his head and howled in delight. "Yes! You brave, more fun for me." He cocked his head. "Need me tie hand behind back? Give you chance, like last time? Ransacker like challenge!"

"You's the one who insisted on no magic last time," Arth responded. This banter in the middle of a battle felt silly to him, but he joined in anyway; maybe it would distract the Ransacker long enough for Daddie to crawl away. "*We* was the ones fightin' handicapped before," Arth pointed out. "Maybe you need us to take it easy on *you*?"

Ransacker smirked, clearly enjoying this immensely.

"Surely you know we've smoked lugs by the dozen," Sidekick declared, full of bravado. "Or didn't you just see what we did to your cousin?" He hooked two tentacles back over his shoulder, gesturing toward the lugmen they'd taken down on their way here.

"Good! Use magic!" Ransacker declared. "Then no one question me bigger baddie when I smoke you anyway." It may have been the longest complete sentence Arth had ever heard from a lugman, but Ransacker didn't pause for breath when he finished speaking. Raising his crossbow quick as a flash, he shot the next bolt at Sidekick's face from point blank range. There was no time for the smack-talking kelpie to get his Diamond Aegis off his chest to protect his head.

But with the Diamond Scepter in his grip, Arth felt the next moments stretch long, giving him more than enough time to react—which he did by thought alone. A blue shield winked into existence, catching the crossbow bolt and shattering it. The shards of that metal arrowhead rebounded, peppering Ransacker's hand and causing him to yelp in pain, dropping the crossbow. But the luggernaut was already swinging the long-handled battle axe he carried in his other hand.

Arth brought up the Scepter to catch the attack smoothly. Even so, the sheer force of the blow, backed by the immense weight of the lugman behind it, should have broken Arth's arm or at least driven him out of Sidekick's saddle. His arm didn't even buckle. Instead, the Diamond Relic flared a blinding blue, slicing neatly through Ransacker's battle axe—separating the blade from its long handle. Wide-eyed, the luggernaut was suddenly off-balance, putting one foot down on the Ringmaster's back before tripping and stumbling to the ground beside him.

"Oy, get off meh daddie!" Arth shouted.

It was entirely the wrong thing to say. "*This* your daddy?" Ransacker asked, taking an interest in Pythagoras Penn for the first time since Arth appeared. "Special bounty, this one. Big boss promise, great reward." And he seized Daddie by the neck.

Copying something he saw Pyrsie do once, Arth leapt from Sidekick's back and clambered onto the big fella's shoulders, which were conveniently accessible at the moment. Even so, he obviously moved faster than the Ransacker thought possible, for the fella cried out in surprise at the sudden weight. Arth didn't hesitate, swinging his Scepter around to clasp tightly over the lug's throat—but not tightly enough to choke him. For even in this moment of fear for his father's life, Arth recognized a distinct sensation from the Scepter, like there was a wiser path unfolding.

"Let meh Daddie go!" Arth ordered the luggernaut.

Ransacker slowly released his grip, and the Ringmaster splashed to the ground, coughing. Meanwhile, the lug rose once more to his full height, giving Arth an impressive view through the trees across the darkened battlefield.

"So ya chose to foller my brother the Demagogue, did ya?" Arth asked, trying to keep Ransacker talking while he thought furiously.

Another delighted grin split the lugman's bluff features. "I number two big boss," he confirmed.

"You was already number two when the Khan was here, wasn't ya? Don't ya wanna be number *one* big boss?" Arth asked. In the back of his mind, he was wondering if there was any way to create a rift in Morth's forces, maybe by turning the Ransacker against him.

But for all his brutish tendencies, the Ransacker wasn't stupid. "Nice try," he hooted. "But follow Demagogue, me get lots of fight. He scrawny guy, but not wimpy—best fighter ever."

"Yet you's the one out here fighting on the front lines, while he's hiding somewhere in the back."

Ransacker shrugged, effortlessly raising Arth's entire body where he still crouched on the lug's shoulders. "More fight for me."

"You don't mind all the changes the Demagogue made on Lugarth? All them lugs he slew, all them slaves he freed?"

Ransacker's face clouded. "Never liked we take them slaves. No honor, that."

Arth ground his teeth in frustration. The Ransacker was proving to be a better person all around than he'd realized, and yet that was only making Arth's job harder under the circumstances. "All these weeks, I was so afraid *you* was the one leading the lugs now. Oy, how I wish you was," Arth said miserably. He tried a different tack. "So Morth—the Demagogue—he's leading from the rear. That means *you's* prackickly in charge here on the front lines."

Ransacker shrugged again. "Number two big boss—"

"Order yer men to lay down their weapons."

The luggernaut looked scandalized. Yeah, Arth hadn't really expected that to work, but he was getting desperate. The Scepter had guided him up onto the Ransacker's shoulders for this nice little chit-chat, but it wouldn't last forever, and Arth still failed to see what it was supposed to accomplish.

"Order them, else I'll smoke ya!" the King demanded, squeezing harder with his Scepter. "Lay down yer weapons!" he shouted, but it did no good.

"Never... stop... fight," the Ransacker gasped defiantly.

So much for *that* plan. All around Arth, the battle lines had blurred, lugs and kerchiefed kelpies intermixed with his own karks, okkies, kelpies, dagsters, and nyms, though a strong force of luggernauts still held a firm line north of them to prevent the Caymerlotions from pushing through. Taking an enemy commander hostage should have been worth something to Arth, but it seemed to make no difference. The surrounding lugs could clearly see the Ransacker's situation, but not one of them had come to the big man's aid. Nothing seemed to stifle their killer instinct as they continued battering Arth's forces.

By contrast, the lugs' kerchiefed kelpie allies showed no such killer instinct whenever they met their own kind in battle—nor did Arth's own kelpmen. Many of the kelpies on both sides knew each other; they were fighting brothers and friends, he realized. And just that suddenly, with another flash of insight from his Relic, Arth knew how to alter the outcome of this battle... simply by saying something he had wanted to say all along.

Using the Scepter's magic to amplify his voice across the thicket, Arth proclaimed, "Caymerlotions and luggernauts likewise, gimme yer ears!" The fighting continued, of course, but its intensity seemed to abate as he got everyone's attention. "I, Arthos Penn the dagman, new King of Caymerlot, offer clemency to any of the Demagogue's peeps who would throw down yer weapons and quit this fightin'."

The Ransacker began to laugh deep within, his whole body shaking with it—and causing Arth to shake as well—but he wasn't the one who responded.

An eerie green mist began to spread through the kanban trees, and with its appearance a hush fell on the many fighters. Then came the voice of the Demagogue.

· twenty-eight ·

Morthos Penn was no longer a Clown, and he certainly wasn't a victimized Captive. He was the Demagogue now, a victorious commander with the power to bring down Caymerlot's elitist glass towers using nothing but the right words spoken in the ears of his willing followers. And when words weren't enough, there was always magic, which he channeled through his peerless Ruby Warhammer. Between his eloquence and his enchantments, Morth was now the most powerful, most important man in all of Overtwixt—and if these fools fighting against him couldn't see that, they would be *made* to see that.

Now his naïve brother Arth thought he could turn the hearts of *Morth*'s people, using the very weapons that *Morth* had proven himself the master of?

Until this moment, the Demagogue had been keeping out of sight with several of his commanders, getting regular reports from messengers and scouts, directing the battle from afar. He and his tables and maps had been stationed here at the entrance to his new bridge ever since a small team of Arth's people barreled through a week earlier. It worried Morth, wondering what they were up to on Lugarth, and he'd been furious with the lugs who let them pass while he himself was distracted by that skirmish at the city gates. But so long as no more of Arth's Squad got through, it should be fine. Unfortunately, Morth couldn't trust anyone else to do what needed doing, so he'd been forced to remain here personally ever since.

Now, at the sound of Arth's magically-enhanced voice, Morth couldn't help but respond in kind. Grinning wickedly, he waved his free hand in a circular motion over the immense ruby set into his weapon, drawing out wisps of green that he pushed into the trees. Not too much, mind you. He kept the green tendrils of mist thin and high so as not to freeze the movement of his own followers; his goal was simply to carry his voice into every corner of this thicket. And then Morth spoke, demonstrating for Arth the true power of words:

"Of course the so-called *King* wants you to give up," he told his followers, knowing they would recognize their master's voice. "Of course he's willing to offer you *mercy*." He kept his tone calm, unworried, but allowed it to drip with the condescension he now felt for his brother. "My people, if we give up now, things go back to the way they were before."

"That's not true!" Arth's amplified voice replied. "Caymerlot is already changing. The Underlord hisself has been held to account—and banished from Overtwixt for his actions while ruler of Crystal City."

Morth scowled at hearing this. His disenfranchised aquatic followers despised the old merman ruler, and Morth himself had played upon their bitterness to justify this invasion of Caymerlot. If the Underlord was indeed gone, that could prove problematic for the cause. "Lies!" he cried, leaping into the air as great wings sprouted from his back. He needed a better view of the battlefield.

"I speak no lie," Arth called. "The Underlord was escorted back to Merlyn and from there to his real world, weeks ago now. It was done all fair and legal-like!"

A tendril of doubt wormed its way into Morth's gut, and he scoured the battlefield for inspiration. Off to the left, one of those eight-legged freak karkmen was making a spectacle of himself with a weapon in every tentacle—one of them clearly a Diamond weapon—and seemed to be single-handedly carving his way through the lugmen there. On the right, the eye was drawn instantly to an even brighter Diamond display: that blasted huwoman friend of Arth's, the Knight, was leading one charge after another along Morth's lines. Meanwhile in the center, even Arth's kelpie pal wielded a Diamond Relic, as did two mermen nearby. But for a moment, Morth's attention was arrested by the unexpected sight of Arth himself perched on Ransacker's shoulders, holding the luggernaut hostage with his Diamond Scepter.

How had *that* happened?

Of all the lugmen who'd adopted Morth as their new alpha, the Ransacker was probably his favorite. The fella was surprisingly intelligent and well-spoken for a mere lug, and he'd told the new Demagogue all about his encounters with the Squad on Eqland and Hulandia. Morth *knew* the Ransacker had been toying with Arth and Sidekick during their "duel" in the Branch Library courtyard. After Arth's mediocre performance on Hulandia, how had he now managed to disarm the most accomplished fighter in Morth's army?

With that Scepter, of course. It had to be. There was no way Arth himself was capable of such deeds otherwise.

The King was still prattling on about truth and justice and reunification, but Morth wasn't listening. His eyes returned to Arth's two merman armsmen—the Diamond-bearers he'd seen earlier—and he smiled, throwing his faith once more behind his own oratory skills.

"Lies, I say!" he interrupted victoriously. "You claim the Underlord has been put in his place, yet the man's own children—his accomplices in corruption—stand there at your side, O King! Or do you pretend that is not the Altruist who wears the Diamond Hauberk? Or the Antagonist who wields the Diamond Harpoon?" Alone among all the Relics on the battlefield, the Harpoon barely flickered, but its glow was just powerful enough to remove any doubt from Morth's mind. The Adjunct had described each of Sovereign's Relics in detail, so Morth would be sure to recognize the enemy's greatest weapons on sight. "Any punishment the Underlord deserves, his sons deserve as well," he continued. "And if you had truly smoked the Underlord, his sons would never follow you now. I call you liar twice over!"

"I speak no lie," Arth repeated, slowly and clearly. "No man is answerable for another man's crimes, even their own father. And the Altruist and Antagonist prove their decency by fighting at meh side, despite their daddie's fate."

"So the King admits it!" the Demagogue crowed. "Those *are* the Underlord's sons. No doubt the Underlord rules still, pulling strings from the shadows. This King is nothing but a puppet!" Morth grinned, pleased with how he'd handled that. He could still use the Underlord's crimes as justification for this invasion after all. "Depose the Diamond-bearers! Exalt the exploited!"

"The Underlord ain't with us no more," the King repeated. "He literally stabbed me in the back, so believe me, I was betrayed by our old ruler too—the same fella who shoulda been our fiercest protector. All you exploited people of Caymerlot, ya gots cause fer complaint! Caymerlot's been a breedin' ground of injustice longer than any of us was here. But I *will* change that, you has my word. I've already started!"

"Mark *my* words," Morth rejoined, "the puppet King will only continue the injustices of the past, preserving the class system and the oppression of the lesser aquatics. Don't listen to his lies—"

"Ya keep callin' me a liar," Arth shouted, his temper finally slipping. "I reckon I don't mind you attackin' me personally. But speaking lies of yer own and callin' them truth is sumfing I won't stand fer. By the power of the Sovereign hisself, I declare there will be no more lies spoken in these woods tonight!"

The Diamond Scepter pulsed suddenly, its light exploding outward in all directions—completely obliterating Morth's green mist. In a sudden panic, Morth raised his own voice again. "You's the liar, Arthos Penn! Who are you to call yerself King? You're nothing but a Fool, a... a..." He trailed off as he belatedly realized no one could hear him. The green magic no longer projected his voice.

Oh no.

"True enuff, Caymerlot was *not* a utopia," Arth agreed, his words still crashing over every set of ears in the marsh. "But change *is* coming. Not that you peoples gots any reason to trust me personally; I unnerstand, truly I do. But if ya can't trust me, you can sure and certain trust the Sovereign and his prophecy."

The blue light pulsed again, that throb moving throughout the entire thicket—and at the sound of the Sovereign's name, everyone seemed to hesitate in their fighting, which somehow had continued even 'til now.

The King removed his Relic from the throat of the Ransacker, lifting it high for all to see. "Yeh *know* that the one who wields this Scepter—this Relic-in-the-Rock—is prophesied to usher in the true Golden Age of O'ertwixt. It is *his* job to right wrongs."

Some of Morth's aquatics began to stir, taking a step back from the fighting. No, no, *no*. Arth would *not* turn the tide of this battle with words alone. Words were the province of the Demagogue, not this upstart King! Snarling, Morth spun his Ruby Warhammer, sending little jolts of green to shock any of his minions he saw slacking off from fighting. Eyes wide, they quickly resumed hostilities.

"I don't mean any of ya harm," Arth continued, and for a wonder, there was kindness in his voice. "Not even you lugs, ugly and stinky though ya may be. So I tell ya again now," Arth said, with sudden steel in his voice. "Throw down yer weapons. Any lug who flees back to Lugarth will be spared, and any aquatic who rips off the red kerchief will be welcomed back to Caymerlot—the new-and-improved Caymerlot—with open arms."

Heart thumping in his chest, Morth stared down at the battlefield below him, full of dread. For a long moment, nothing happened. Then a war cry sounded from one of his karks on the front lines, and the battle restarted in earnest. The Demagogue heaved a sigh of relief.

Then a great clatter sounded as a bunch of Morth's kelpies cast their weapons to the ground, ripping red bandanas from their arms. "No!" Morth screeched, swooping low towards the center of the battlefield. "Smoke those traitors! Make it hurt!"

Riled by his words and enraged by the betrayal of their one-time allies, the luggernauts turned on the kelpies in their midst. Those kelpies were already fleeing toward the safety of Arth's army, however. Lugmen, never being the greatest tactical thinkers, broke ranks to pursue them.

"*No!*" Morth shrieked again. "You fools, not like that!"

Just that fast, there were suddenly several gaping holes in Morth's defenses. Only a fraction of his aquatics had switched sides, he saw now—mostly just the kelpies in Arth's vicinity—but with those holes in the Demagogue's lines, the tide of battle might shift again at any moment.

And then it did.

"Eqmen!" shouted the Diamond-armored huwoman. "With me! With me!" And she led her force straight at the nearest gap, plunging deep into the marshlands, strafing luggernauts on both sides.

Arth brought the butt of his Scepter crashing down on the Ransacker's head, knocking him unconscious. Pivoting in midair, Morth swooped towards them, intent on rescuing his fallen ally—not for the Ransacker's own sake, of course. Sure, Morth liked the bloke, but more than that, he *needed* him to keep the less considerate lugs in line.

But before Morth could get there, another one of those maddening blue domes sprang up around Arth. Morth struck the dome at full speed and bounced backwards, his momentum reversing in an instant without losing any of its power. It shot him way out over the thicket again; and by the time he righted himself, Morth could only stare in dismay at what had become of his army.

Arth was back in his kelpie's saddle, leading the other dagsters and kelpies in flooding through the gap the Knight had widened. "Drive hard!" Arth was calling, still amplified. "Make for the bridge!" Meanwhile, the Knight and her force of eqmen was peeling off to the west again, cutting a swath through the barbarian horde. Disaster! If Morth didn't act soon, she was going to carve off an entire chunk of his army, isolating them. But with Arth's blasted blue magic filling the thicket, what could Morth do? He was powerless to make his own orders heard.

The forest went dark suddenly, and Morth reacted without thinking. "Fall back again!" he snarled, carrying his words on waves of green to every corner of the barbarian horde. "All *true* believers fall back to the bridge."

As soon as the orders left his mouth, Morth realized his mistake. The Knight's tactic was nothing but a bluff; the last thing Arth's people wanted was to be trapped between two forces of lugmen. On the contrary, what Arth needed more than anything was to get all lugmen off this niland... and Morth had just been tricked into ordering exactly that.

"No, belay that!" the Demagogue shrieked. "Stand your ground!" But it was no use. Blue light was flooding the thicket once more, smothering the green magic before it could amplify his voice. Morth swooped to deliver his orders personally, willing to shout in the ear of each and every lugman commander one at a time if need be, but it was too late. Even as he watched, the last of his horde broke and ran. Arth's coalition surged northward once more, all three of the King's armies joining together and pushing forward as one.

A Diamond Harpoon hurtled through the air, glowing much brighter than before and only narrowly missing Morth. With a shriek of mingled terror and fury, the Demagogue tucked his wings and fled back toward his new bridge with everyone else.

So he'd lost his beachhead on Caymerlot. So what? The Demagogue would lead his forces back to Lugarth and resume this fight there, on their home turf—the very seat of Morth's power.

And if Arth followed Morth all the way back, he was still a fool indeed. The King would come to regret entering the Demagogue's lair.

· twenty-nine ·

Hembrose trailed after Pyrsie as she climbed into the bowels of Northmount—up the corkscrew steps to a ledge at the top of the huge cavern, then into the first of several narrow passages beyond. He kept his magical green orb of light floating above their heads, so it illuminated the path ahead without blinding them. Then the two old friends walked *those* corridors for a while without speaking, until Hembrose wondered if Pyrsie would ever ask him to engage his time magic. Though his body remained strong, a spring in the step of his dagman legs, the mermage was mentally and magically exhausted. He had already taxed his now-meager abilities to their limit, just getting this far.

Eventually they reached a natural intersection, a wider opening in the rock with corridors branching in two other directions. Pyrsie explored each path a short distance, then came back smiling. "Zis is where I will begin my work," she said confidently.

"And what exactly is that work?" Hembrose asked. No one had fully explained this part of the plan to him. Arth only said that Pyrsie would be doing something to prevent the lugs from escaping Lugarth via Northmount—and that the Wizard's magic was required to give her enough time to complete that task. "Will you be creating traps and pitfalls, like in the Burrowcrat's Treasury?" he guessed.

Pyrsie shook her head distractedly, eyes already tracing veins in the rock. "Could you improve zee light, please?"

Hembrose obliged, concentrating in order to steady the orb's flickering, trying to project brighter, whiter light. "Simple demolition, then? Are you bringing down the entire mountain, destroying the bridge outright?" As if on cue, a rumbling tremor ran through the ground as more dust and small rocks settled from the ceiling. "Because that hardly seems necessary. Between the lugs kidnapping humen, and now the humen openly fighting back as part of Arth's army, I'd say lugman-human relations are at an all-time low. This place is pulling itself apart as it is!"

But Pyrsie was shaking her head again. "No, there will be no demolition either. Arth would not allow zee lugs to be cut off completely." She gave Hembrose an impish smile. "What I do here will not be destructive. It will last through zee eons, greater than zee Treasury, which I myself immediately defeated and plundered. *Zis* masterpiece, my crowning achievement, will confound and confuse, but it will never harm a soul."

"And it is...?" Hembrose prompted patiently.

"A *maze*," she said, eyes glittering. "Zee greatest, biggest, most convoluted maze in history, either in zis world or any other. I will make it impossible for zee lugs or anyone else to leave Lugarth without a map, and zee only map will be entrusted to zee keeping of zee King of Caymerlot."

Hembrose thought it through, then slowly nodded. "I guess we'd best begin, then." He gestured at the intersection around them. "And you say *this* is where you'll start?" She nodded, so he seated himself against one wall and released his partial shapeshift, allowing the dagman legs to knit back into a merman tail. That allowed Hembrose to funnel most of his remaining magical strength through the Emerald Caduceus, dilating time by half, then experimentally compounding the dilation as he'd done in Arth's grand throne room.

When he'd conjured four nested time bubbles, Hembrose decided that was as much as he could maintain for long. "There," he said, a little shakily. "You now have about a quarter hour within this bubble for every minute that passes on the outside." He ran the numbers in his head. "That's a full day in here for every hour and a half the battle rages out there."

The gnomaid eyed the almost-visible bubble worriedly, and Hembrose knew what she was thinking. It still wasn't a lot of time, and it wasn't a very large enclosed space—not for whatever advanced engineering she planned to do, at least.

"I will move with you as you work," he promised. It was, after all, the best he could do.

"It will be enough," she decided. "It has to be." Then she drew a chisel and a small mallet from loops on her tool belt. Placing the tip of the chisel at a very specific place along the vein she'd identified, she gave two exploratory taps, then pounded once very hard. With a resounding *crack*, a huge rift appeared in the wall, gaping open several feet.

Pyrsie grinned.

The work actually went quickly from there, faster than Hembrose ever would have guessed. Gnomen really were masters at working stone, and Pyrsyfal Rochelle was the *Inventor*, the greatest gnoman craftswoman alive today.

They fell into a new routine as Pyrsie moved slowly through the upside-down mountain, tapping here, drilling there, hammering and chiseling and constantly making notations on the huge roll of map she was creating. Every step the gnomaid took, Hembrose dutifully dragged his merman body after her, ensuring she always stayed at the middle of the time bubble he maintained through the Caduceus. They would work until one of them felt fatigued, then they would drink from the Diamond Grail and continue on. Even here, there was no time for sleep.

By the end of the second day (roughly three hours in the outside world), Pyrsie had opened up a dozen new twisting paths. She had an uncanny knack for knowing where the rock was weakest, and in which direction fissures already existed, which she expanded into tunnels. The two squad mates also discovered several deep crevasses, down which they dumped all the rubble she steadily produced. Hembrose had never realized how many cracks and pockets of open space existed in "solid rock," but an undertaking like this would have been impossible if such gaps weren't so prevalent. In her own words, Pyrsie was simply "taming" those natural openings, tying them together into a single convoluted network of pathways. And she was truly a master at working with rock, a skill she said she'd developed during the early days of creating the Burrowcrat's Treasury.

For now, Pyrsie focused on the broad strokes of her maze, opening up rough-hewn passages just large enough for a lugman to move through. Later, if there was time, she would polish off the jagged edges and explore some of her ideas for making the tangle of tunnels *truly* confusing. Hembrose thought it was already plenty confusing as it was. The finished maze would have multiple levels, of course, for the whole purpose was to travel between two nilands that floated at different altitudes. But few of Pyrsie's maze levels would be entirely flat. Some had corridors with subtle inclines, so that you changed levels without realizing as you walked along. Pyrsie also carved more than a few twisting staircases at weird and irregular intervals that encouraged you to think you had climbed much farther than you actually had. She seemed to take a fiendish joy in every disorienting detail as she chip-chip-chipped away with her tools.

It didn't take long before Hembrose, at least, was hopelessly lost in the burgeoning maze, but he also recognized it still wasn't good enough. As confusing as these passages already were, it wouldn't be sufficient to stop a well-coordinated group of people—even lugmen—if they invested the time and effort to thoroughly map every corridor. There were still many more passages for Pyrsie to carve and refine, and Hembrose began to worry that she wasn't moving fast enough. As their fourth day in Northmount came to a close (marking six hours outside), he wondered how long a single Final Battle could possibly last, no matter how decisive. To give Pyrsie the time she required, he needed to compound his dilation even further, but he simply didn't have the strength to do so.

Hembrose was still reeling from the implications of that realization when the surprise attack came.

It was a band of lugs, of course, but they didn't come from the direction of Lugarth below (where Noble had stayed behind to prevent exactly this danger). No, these marauders came from *above*, on Hulandia, where the lugmen had left a small garrison after retreating from their defeat at the Branch Library. They hadn't even know about Pyrsie and Hembrose when they embarked on their journey home, but they were quite confused by the new maze. And their bewilderment turned steadily to anger as they followed the echoes of rapid chisel-tapping to their source.

When they came around the corner and saw Pyrsie chiseling, with Hembrose propped against one wall like an invalid, they went berserk. Fortunately, from inside the time bubble, the lugs seemed to charge in *very* slow motion, which gave the good guys plenty of time to plan their defense.

*Un*fortunately, the two squad mates were at the dead end of a new branch Pyrsie was chiseling through the rock, so there was nowhere to run. They *had* to stand and fight.

"You ready?" Hembrose murmured through tight lips, and Pyrsie nodded, brandishing her tools. The Wizard dropped one of the bubbles, and the approaching lugs sprang forward at twice the speed of their previous slow motion. The mermage redirected that extra power to form legs for himself, stood up, then dropped the rest of his bubbles and rushed forward with a wordless war cry. "Aaaaahhhhhh!"

With the physical strength of a half dozen lugs himself, Hembrose swept his Caduceus through the attackers' legs, knocking them off their feet. Then he began pummeling them with the staff. He *hated* using it this way, but he needed to be holding the relic to access the harvested attributes that were stored within—and, well, it was a two-handed staff. It occurred to Hembrose suddenly that a necklace would make a more practical relic, that way he could *wear* his emerald and still fight with fists or other weapons. Alas, it was far too late for that now.

One of the luggernauts staggered to his feet and came at the Wizard from behind, grabbing him in a bearfish hug. A second lug raised a sword to the mermage's throat, but Pyrsie flung her mallet into his eye, causing him to stumble away. Hembrose placed both feet firmly against one wall and *pushed*, propelling himself—and the lug who held him—into the opposite wall with jarring force. The lugman puffed into yellow, and a resounding *crack* echoed down the hall as yet another rockfall began.

"Hembrose..." Pyrsie said warningly.

But the Wizard was still fighting for his life. Now surrounded on all sides by angry barbarians, he jabbed his staff desperately in every direction, just trying to keep them back. He landed a couple lucky blows, but he'd never been trained as a fighter. He was a *magicker*. Screaming, he raised his staff high and rushed one of the luggernauts, swinging blindly with all his enhanced strength. The lug dodged, and the Caduceus struck bare rock wall.

With another terrible crack, the wall split wide from floor to ceiling. Big chunks of rock began falling in earnest, as a harsh grinding sounded from above.

"Hembrose!" Pyrsie shrieked, and he turned to see the girl was already up to her knees in loose rock. Horrified, the mermage dropped his Caduceus and dove, knocking Pyrsie out of the way as the ceiling came crashing down. Wrapping his larger body around hers, he tucked and rolled, then pushed them both against the back wall of the dead end.

The cave-in seemed to last forever. When the last of the rock finally settled, a subtle blue light appeared in the darkness as Pyrsie produced her Diamond Grail. And what that glow revealed made Hembrose want to cry. There were no lugmen visible, at least... but that was because the corridor behind them had filled completely with fallen stone.

Claustrophobia closed in on Hembrose. "We're trapped," he gasped, beating his open hands against one wall. "Get us out of here!"

"I can't!" Pyrsie said helplessly. "I threw all my tools at zee lugmen, trying to distract zem from you! *You* get us out of here. Use zat fancy staff of yours."

"I lost it in the cave-in! And without it, I can't handle *any* significant amount of magic." As if to prove his point, Hembrose's legs buckled at that very moment, and he flopped onto the ground with his tail restored once more. "This is bad," he whined. "This is very bad."

Pyrsie began to weep softly. "We've failed him. We've failed Arth. He is trusting us to build zis maze to trap zee lugs on Lugarth, and we've *failed*. Without your magic or my tools, we can never complete our mission now!"

Hembrose stared at the little gnomaid in the faint blue light, incredulous. "Forget about the mission!" he spat. "Think about *us* for half a second!"

"Us? What about us?"

"Don't you get it? We're gonna die here!"

· thirty ·

The King of Caymerlot rode up the steep slope of the Demagogue's ugly new bridge, perched atop his trusty Sidekick. The Knight and her eqmen galloped to his left, Sarge and the karks and centmen to his right, with Dad and Bertie and the rest of the amphibious Caymerlotions bringing up the rear. Meanwhile, volley after volley of arrows arced over their heads to land among the retreating lugmen, courtesy of the merman archers lined up along the northernmost shore of Caymerlot far behind. Thanks to the relatively narrow confines of the bridge, the lugmen were so tightly packed that missing them was practically impossible. Every volley resulted in dozens of puffs of yellow.

Sidekick gave a shout of satisfaction at the sight. "Like shooting fish in a barrel!"

The Knight's brow wrinkled. "I cannot say I'm familiar with that expression," she called back to the kelpie.

Despite the seriousness of the situation, Arth clapped his free hand over his face. "Oy, mate," he told Karis, "you walked right into that one. How often has you known Sidekick not to rhyme, 'less he's up to sumfing?"

The mohawked kelpie, now grinning ear to ear, had obviously been hoping someone would ask. "In my real world, the fish are all feral," he explained. "If you leave them unchecked, it's truly a peril. But they love to eat cheese—They swarm it like fleas!—So just leave a lid off, then shoot them in the barrel!"

Arth frowned. "Wait, ya store yer cheese in a barrel? *Underwater?*"

Sidekick shrugged. "Don't you?"

Karis, at least, seemed to understand. "So if something is easy, you say it's like shooting fish in a barrel?" She shrugged and aimed a grin at their kelpie squad mate. "I like it! I think I'll take that expression home to my real world too... even if no one there will ever understand what it's supposed to mean either."

The last of the barbarian horde soon moved out of range of the archers. Looking back, Arth saw Altruist and Antagonist shouting orders at their fellow mermen, fists lifted high to stop further volleys from endangering Arth himself. Good. "Charge!" he ordered his vanguard. "Press the 'vantage!" And so they did, picking up speed and crashing into the back line of lugmen just as the brutes began turning to fight. Just that quickly, Arth's people started disappearing in yellow smoke again too.

The King frowned in grim determination. "Knight, Sergeant! I wanna try sumfing." He hurriedly explained his new tactic, giving Daddie and Uncle Bertie instructions as well. Then Karis donned her helmet once more, and the squad members hurried past the front line of aquatic fighters to take the brunt of lugman aggression upon themselves.

Arth rode up the center projecting a wedge-shaped bulwark of magic from the Scepter, preventing any of the lugs from attacking in the middle. Those who wanted to turn and fight were forced to either side. On the left, Lady Karis wove among those monsters, spinning and slashing and stabbing, forcing almost as many lugs off the edge of the bridge as she smoked outright. Her footwork and sword forms were exquisitely deadly, as usual, but in such tight confines—and swinging only two swords—it was inevitable that some enemy attacks got through her defense. Even so, lugman weapons bounced right off her Diamond Armor, rebuffed by the magic of Sovereign's Relics. Meanwhile, on Arth's right, Sarge's exotic style of fighting with so many weapons at once had a similar effect on the lugmen there—except *nothing* got through his maelstrom of maces to harm him personally. Pythagoras and Roberthoras watched their backs, defending all three squad mates from any lugman stragglers who survived the brunt, and also calling out warnings anytime Arth or the rest approached a hole or hazard in the malformed bridge.

The tactic had a devastating effect on the lugman rearguard, and Arth feared at any moment, the magical blue bulwark would sputter out due to how much pain it was causing. But pain was not Arth's intent, and intentions *did* seem to matter to the Relic. And the truth was, only the most bloodthirsty lugs were affected—those who refused to abandon their dreams of conquest. Arth despaired as he watched so many lugs fall, but he *needed* to drive them back to Lugarth and destroy this bridge. So the Scepter's light stayed solid, even as Arth steeled himself to keep doing what was needed.

Then dark green storm clouds gathered suddenly, and lightning strikes fell once more. Now that Arth's army was out from the canopy of the kanbans, there was nothing to protect them from above except Arth's own Scepter. The King pulled Sidekick to a halt and angled his bulwark upwards to catch the bolts, protecting the Squad, but other fighters fell on both sides of the conflict—lugs farther up the bridge as well as coalition soldiers farther back. Enemy and ally alike were sent tumbling into the abyss before Arth could create smaller shields to catch bolts as he'd done before.

"Demagogue!" Arth cried angrily, projecting his voice magically for all to hear. "Stop hidin' like a coward. Come out and face me in person so we can settle this like men!"

Thunder roared as Morth unleashed a sudden barrage, catching Arth by surprise. More than a hundred green lightning bolts zagged through the sky all at once, making it inevitable that some would get through. Dozens of bolts struck the bridge with concussive force, sending people catapulting over the side. Anyone who survived shied back in panic, triggering a stampede that pushed still *more* folk over the edge. Arth quickly called upon the Scepter to preserve his falling soldiers, catching them in an embrace of magic, then lifting them up and over the lip to deposit on the bridge far behind him. He felt no strain at all, even as he did this for a dozen or more allies at once. Then, before he knew it, he was doing the same for a cluster of *lugmen* who'd been knocked off, catapulting them forward to land gracelessly on the distant shores of Lugarth. Next Arth rescued a handful of kerchiefed traitors—except he wasn't sure what to do with *them*. Meanwhile, the fighting resumed in earnest, stalling Arth's advance.

"Can't you lot see the truth yet?" Arth boomed at the traitors, who he brought to hover in the air right before him. "Yer own ruler, this Demagogue, throws yer lives away. But it's me, the one you's fighting, who's tryin' to *save* yer sorry skins." The rescued aquatics, two karks and a kelpie, looked terrified—probably because of how high above the ground they were floating. "Please, take me up on my offer from afore: I'll grant clemency if ya just throw down yer weapons and quit this fighting. I offer peace and freedom."

As before, Arth's offer of mercy finally goaded Morth into speaking. "Don't listen to the King's lies," his brother's voice boomed back. "Depose the Diamond-bearers! There's no freedom in being ruled over by another man."

"Ain't *you* ruling over yer people, Demagogue?" Arth asked pointedly, lowering the traitors to the ground. "Ain't *you* been oppressin' them? How many lugs did you slaughter on yer way to the top? How many dissenting voices has you silenced since then, doin' whatever you like by the power of *your* ruby knickknack?"

"Lies!" Morth's voice spat in return.

"I'm not talkin' lies *nor* truths now," Arth replied. "I'm simply asking questions you refuse to answer."

"I don't *rule*," Morth insisted. "I am merely the first citizen, chief among equals. Exalt the exploited! Down with your glass towers, you elitist snob!"

Some of the enemy aquatics took up the cry, though not all of them. And the lugs didn't care one way or the other.

"I'm all for deposing anyone as abuses the power he's been granted," Arth said evenly. "But from where I's standing, I only see *one* person holdin' power in Lugarth, O Demagogue… and you sure ain't using it to nurture the people in yer care."

"Any power I've taken up, I use *only* for the good of my people!" Morth claimed loudly. "I will gladly lay my power down when this struggle is ended."

Feeling a pulse of insight from the Scepter, Arth took a huge risk—and seized the opportunity. "Oy, well, I'm willin' to lay down my power right now." And he leapt from Sidekick's saddle, walked forward, then laid his Diamond Scepter at the feet of the closest stunned lugman.

"Arth, no!" Daddie cried.

The battle came to a ragged stop as *everyone* turned to stare at Arth with goggle-eyed disbelief.

"See, being King ain't about *me*," Arth said. Even though his voice sounded normal now, he could see that everyone else on the bridge still heard him. "I may be the ruler of Caymerlot, but the secret of true rulership is behavin' like a servant. Giving up what's best fer you and doing what's best fer the people you lead. Well, there ya have it. I've laid down all my magicky power and I'm pretty much defenseless now. I'm willing to risk mehself if it means a chance to end this awful war.

"What about you, *Demagogue?*" he asked, turning the question on his twin. "Is you willing to do the same?" Silence had fallen over the war-torn bridge, aside from the sound of Arth's voice. "Join me here, now, brother," he pressed. "We can throw our relics into the abyss together. Then we can shake hands, make peace, and go our sep'rate ways—nuffin' more than mortal men with no special power to subjugate *anyone*. You can *see* I got no desire to oppress others with my power, so you know Caymerlot is finally on its way to being that true utopia of prophecy. But what about Lugarth under *yer* rule, Demagogue?"

Silence stretched for another moment, then at last Morth appeared from the sky. He circled once warily, then swooped in on those skeletal wings, dropping to the ground a foot away from the Diamond Scepter. He was smirking. "You really is a fool," he said softly, for only Arth to hear. "You think I would ever give up my power? Now you've handed me your power too. With the Ruby Warhammer *and* the Diamond Scepter, I'll be unstoppable—with absolute power over Lugarth *and* Caymerlot *and* any other niland I choose to conquer." He grinned exultantly. "You's given me everything I ever wanted, Arth." And he bent to pick up the Scepter.

But the Scepter wouldn't budge, no matter how Morth heaved. It behaved exactly as it had for ages before, when it was trapped in that rock in the Crystal Keep's courtyard. "Ya ain't worthy, son," Daddie told Morth quietly. "Ya gots nuffin' but evil and selfishness in yer heart, and that fancy Diamond Relic only responds to the pure-hearted."

Morth snarled in frustration, heaving all the more.

"What's worse, you's still the Clown," Uncle Bertie put in. "It don't matter how quiet-like you was talkin' just now... that Scepter's magic still made yer little speech loud enough for every'un to hear. And now ya's gone and showed yer true colors." The Bodyguard glanced toward Arth, more than a little awe in his expression. "How come you's so good at gettin' people to reveal their real selves like that? First the Underlord, now Morthos?"

"I don't fink it's me so much as the Diamond Scepter," Arth said quietly. "Like the Sovereign who made it, the Scepter esteems honesty. By its power, the truth will always come out."

And now that the truth was out, the aquatics of Morth's army saw how badly they'd been misled. All across the jagged terrain of the land bridge, karks and kelpies were throwing down their weapons and tearing the kerchiefs from their arms, abandoning the Demagogue's false cause in droves. But not the lugmen, of course. Even as Arth watched, the lugs once again turned on their old allies before they could rush to the safety of Arth's front line.

"Forward!" cried the Sergeant-at-arms, and the Scepter carried *his* voice to every ear too. "Rescue our long-lost brethren! Come to their aid as we should have done so long ago, when the lugmen first took them captive!" And with cheers of joy at their pending reunion, the army of Caymerlot crashed forward, pushing the lugs back yet again and enveloping the pockets of karks and kelpies who had been wearing enemy colors until this moment.

The barrage of lightning resumed with a vengeance as Morth realized his mistake, and Arth dove for the Scepter, raising it high. But this time, instead of producing little blue shields, the Scepter acted as a lightning rod—drawing *all* the lightning to itself, its glow building to a radiance that half-blinded both armies. Meanwhile, Morth took to the air and disappeared into the storm clouds.

The lightning abruptly ceased again. Perhaps Morth had realized the pointlessness of such a display, or perhaps such an incredible outlay of magic had exhausted the dagmagicker. Or maybe he only used the lightning as a distraction to escape? Whatever the reason, Arth was grateful that using the Scepter for defense and preservation never seemed to exhaust *him*.

Then he blinked in realization. If Arth himself could wield so much power without growing weary...

"Hold here!" he shouted to his forces. "Hold the line!"

· thirty-one ·

Pyrsie sat hugging herself in the tiny enclosed space, trying not to cry. It was just her, Hembrose, and the Diamond Grail, which shed barely enough blue light to show how cramped their surroundings really were. It had now been hours—*real* hours, same as in the outside world—since the cave-in.

Hours since the mermage declared they would die here.

Of course they wouldn't actually die. At worst, they'd eventually be ejected from Overtwixt, and Pyrsie wasn't even sure of that. They hadn't been hurt, simply trapped, and she doubted they'd be expelled even if they went months without food (though *that* thought horrified her). Overtwixt was a realm of magic, after all, not a real physical place.

None of this changed the fact that she'd failed her mission. Even if Arth won the Final Battle, the surviving lugs could still escape via Northmount. With Pyrsie's work incomplete, they would undoubtedly find a way through the partial new maze given enough time.

The awful thing was the familiarity of this situation, for she'd been buried in rock before. This had been her fate back when the Burrowcrat betrayed her, leaving her locked in the Treasury she herself had designed and booby-trapped. At least that time she'd had resources and freedom of movement, allowing her to make a daring escape through the lava tubes deep underground. Here and now, she had none of that. Just herself, a much-reduced Hembrose, and the Diamond Grail in a tiny pocket of air within the rock.

A small smile tugged at her lip, even so. The Diamond Grail of Goodwill, one of Sovereign's Relics. It was pretty humbling to think that she—little Pyrsyfal Rochelle, the troublemaker from the orphanage—had wielded one of Sovereign's unique artifacts for a time. And that had only happened *because* of the Burrowcrat's betrayal, which had allowed her to plunder the very treasure trove she was trapped within.

Then again, the Guide had charged Pyrsie with recovering the Grail when she first arrived in Overtwixt, almost like he'd known from the beginning what challenges she would face. The Diamond Grail had been the first part of the Inventor's quest, which she would need to fulfill the *second* half of her quest: helping her friends defeat the lugmen. And to be sure, the Squad never would have made it this far without the Grail. On this mission alone, the Relic's magic had sustained Pyrsie and Hembrose without food or sleep for ten days, making it at least *possible* to finish the new Northmount maze in time.

But in the end, none of it had mattered. Even with the Grail's help, she had failed anyway, and now all was lost. Too bad the Guide hadn't foreseen *this* impossible situation.

Or had he?

"When you come to zee end of your quest..." Pyrsie whispered, suddenly remembering, if barely. "When you..." She strained, trying to recall the words. "When you think all is lost... you only need to ask for help." Yes, that was it.

Hembrose roused himself from his own misery. "What's that?" he muttered, face haggard in the dim light. He was so young now, so smooth-skinned, but there was a hundred years of exhaustion in his eyes. "What did you say?"

"Something zee Guide told me when I first arrived. He said my quest was to make friends—obviously he meant you and Arth and zee Squad—and together we would defeat a great threat." She felt cautious excitement growing within. "And he said when I feared all waz lost, to just ask for help."

Hembrose shrugged. "Well, obviously *this* friend can't help, because I'm here in the pit of despair with you. And I doubt Arth will hear no matter how loud you holler!"

Pyrsie shook her head emphatically. "I don't think zat is who I am supposed to ask. Tell me, what quest did zee Guide give *you*?"

"To become the greatest mortal magicker in history," the Wizard recited, in an almost-bored tone of voice. "To uncover some lost absolute truths, overcome evil, and discover true greatness. To... to preserve my innocence and avoid envy, or else I'd make myself miserable." His mouth twisted as he remembered this last part. "I suppose the Guide's words were prophetic on that point," he muttered.

"Did zee Guide ever tell *you* zat you could ask for help?" Pyrsie pressed excitedly.

"Are you kidding?" Hembrose retorted. "That fellow tries so hard to be helpful, I had to beat him off with a stick. Um, not literally, mind you."

"See?" Pyrsie blurted. "I think *he* is zee one we're supposed to ask."

Hembrose barked a laugh. "Be my guest."

Pyrsie cleared her throat uncertainly, then forced herself to call out loudly: "O Guide? He who welcomed me to Overtwixt on my first day here? I humbly ask your assistance in my most desperate hour of need, when I fear all is lost. Help me, help *us*, I beg of you, for we are trapped."

The Wizard's chest was shaking with silent, bitter laughter. "Shout all you want. There's no one in earshot, except maybe the lugger…"

Hembrose trailed off, interrupted by the sound of muffled but obviously excited voices. Next came a whole sequence of rapid tapping, as if a half dozen chisels were chipping away at the other side of the solid rock wall behind them. Then a hole appeared in the wall, rapidly widening until a gnoman head popped through.

It was Alexandre Léandre, the Bailiff, whom Pyrsie had known since her youth in the orphanage.

Pyrsie gaped, unable to believe what she was seeing. Incredible enough that someone had found them, but someone she knew? This young man she'd known all her life? Pyrsie was obviously hallucinating.

Eyes wide, Alexandre squealed, "She is here! Zee Inventor is here!" The hole widened further, and more faces appeared, including those of the Architect, Conservationist, Stonemason, Excavator, and other gnomen Pyrsie had met before and after coming to Overtwixt. And standing back behind all of them, a big grin on his face, was a familiar centman.

Pyrsie wasn't hallucinating. This was the help she had finally been willing to ask for. They were rescued!

She pushed her way through the crowd of gnomen, sputtering her thanks to each of them, but not stopping until she reached the Guide. By the time she got there, he had folded all four of his legs to kneel at her level. She threw her arms around his neck and sobbed with gratitude. "Thank you, thank you, thank you!"

When she looked back, she saw Hembrose still hadn't moved; he was just staring through that new hole. "You... actually heard her cry for help?" the Wizard asked.

Alexandre the tiny Bailiff bobbed his head excitedly. "We were passing down zis tunnel when we heard someone calling for help. Fortunately, we have plenty of tools wiz us." He gestured. Among the dozen gnomen in the group were several wheeled carts laden with food, tools, lumber, and uncut amber glowstone.

"But why are you all even here?" Pyrsie blurted, wiping tears from her eyes.

"Well, you see," the Guide spoke up conversationally, "I mentioned to the Poet—you remember him, human fellow?—what you were going to be doing up here. He was quite impressed! But I voiced concern that you might not finish the job in time, all by yourself, and he suggested hiring more gnomen. The Poet even offered to pay the extra workers from the Branch Library coffers, as an enticement to get as big a crew as possible to travel up here from Gnoburrow. Apparently the Poet wants to ensure that no lugman raiding party *ever* pillages his Branch Library again."

Pyrsie was smiling delightedly, yet she was still thoroughly flummoxed. "But *how?* It makes no sense. For you to arrive here now, in zee nick of time, with zis big crew... the travel time alone, from Hulandia to Gnoburrow and back again... Why, your conversation with zee Poet must have happened before Arth even came up with zis plan in zee first place!" she concluded jokingly.

The centman just smiled back at her, a twinkle in his eye. "And?"

"But zat is imposseeble!"

The Guide threw back his head and laughed, the sound deep and warm and contagious, drawing chuckles from some of the other gnomen as well.

Hembrose wasn't laughing or even smiling, however. "Please don't misunderstand," he hurried to say when the Bailiff asked why. "I *am* grateful not to be trapped anymore. But this rescue comes too late to complete our mission. By now, the battle must be nearly over."

The Guide nodded. "Indeed. As we speak, the King takes his final steps toward Lugarth, where he will face the Demagogue in single combat."

"And my Caduceus was buried, probably destroyed, in the cave-in," Hembrose said, gesturing over his shoulder at the mound of rubble. "Even with it, and even with all these workers, there's just not enough time remaining to multiply. We sat too long in the dark awaiting rescue. We've *lost*."

The Guide raised an eyebrow. "You and I both know there's an alternative method of multiplying time."

· thirty-two ·

Concentrating fervently, Arth focused on the terrain of the bridge climbing away from him toward Lugarth, picturing what he wanted to accomplish. At the same time, he filled himself with goodwill toward the lugmen as well as his own people—the sort of love all men and women deserved from their ruler. The power of the Sovereign surged within him, and Arth pushed it out through the magnifying lens of his Diamond Scepter.

Glowing blue guardrails winked into existence along both sides of the bridge, all the way from Arth's position to Lugarth, and half a mile in either direction along the outer shores of the lugman niland. Glowing blue patches suddenly filled the treacherous gaps in the bridge as well, and a glowing blue wall appeared between the two armies.

Then that wall began to move, steadily pushing, pushing, pushing the lugmen back towards their niland. It moved far too slowly to cause any harm, but its progress was inexorable, unstoppable. Many of the lugs banged weapons against the barrier, hollering in disbelief, but inevitably they turned away. They had no other choice. Before long, the lugmen were retreating once more toward their niland.

Arth sighed gratefully, not the least bit taxed by using the Scepter's magic in this manner. He could do this all day.

As the Squad neared Lugarth at last, Arth realized their mission was almost complete. With all those traitors back on Caymerlot's side, the only aquatic still fighting for the enemy was Morth himself. And all the lugmen were home on their own niland now. The Squad just needed to prevent them from escaping again—by locking down the passage through Northmount (assuming Pyrsie hadn't already done so) and destroying this bridge on which the Squad stood... a bridge that, at this point, was held in place by nothing more than Morth's own status as ruler of the lugmen.

If only Arth could change Morth's mind. Then the twins could walk back to Caymerlot together and let the land bridge simply dissolve behind them. But Arth was increasingly certain there was only one possible solution to this situation: using force to remove his brother from Overtwixt.

And so dread grew inside him with each new step toward the lugman niland.

The Squad stopped just shy of cresting the lip onto Lugarth, and Arth began issuing orders, all while keeping his focus on the magic barriers he continued projecting. "Sarge, take the army back to Caymerlot. This bridge ain't gonna last much longer, and when it falls, I want our people safe."

"As you command, Arth." The Sergeant-at-arms gave a sharp salute, touching the Diamond Truncheon to his own brow, then turned and issued orders of his own.

"Daddie, Uncle Bertie—" Arth began.

"We's with ya to the end, boyo."

But Arth shook his head. "Not this time. Ya don't wanna see what happens next."

"But Arth—"

"Please don't argue," he begged them, voice cracking. "This is gonna be hard enough without worrying 'bout you lot too. You swore yerselves to obey me, now honor that oath."

There were tears in the elder dagmen's eyes, but they nodded. By now, Arth was back in Sidekick's saddle, and Pythagoras placed one hand on his son's knee. "I'm right proud of yeh, lad. And I trust ya to do what's right. Just... try not to hurt that wayward brother of yers any more than ya absolute must."

Arth could only nod. Then his father and uncle turned away, riding after the army on their own kelpie mounts.

"I've got something to say before you try ordering *me* away," Sidekick said gruffly. "You may be royal, but I'm loyal, so you'd best be letting me stay."

"He's right," Karis agreed softly. She had climbed down from Prancer, who was already galloping back with the army. "This will come down to a duel between you and your brother. And you'll need to fight mounted if the Demagogue takes lugman form again, to offset his height advantage." She removed her helmet and shook out her braided auburn hair, then proceeded to roll her neck and stretch her arms.

Arth smiled sadly, eyes wet as he looked upon the older woman who'd become such a dear friend. "I reckon there's some reason you fink *you* should get to come along with us too?" By now, the three squad members were alone on the edge of the lugman niland.

"Quite so," Karis replied lightly, smiling easily. "If you two are focused on the Demagogue, you'll need someone to keep the rest of the luggernauts off your back."

Arth shook his head, growing even more emotional. "This may be meh last hour in O'ertwixt. I can't ask you lot to sacrifice yerselves too."

"You don't have to ask," Karis told him with a wink, then pulled the helmet over her head and stuffed her braids back inside. "And besides, you don't have to worry about the outcome of this fight. The prophecy guarantees that you will rule Caymerlot for the Golden Age to come."

"The Knight speaks true, as true as she's blue," Sidekick chortled, holding up a tentacle to shield his eyes from the brilliant glow of her Diamond Plate-Armor. And with that, the three friends stepped over the threshold into Lugarth.

Arth swallowed. They were right: as the prophesied King, he *was* pretty much guaranteed to survive this battle.

But the two of them had no such guarantee.

As the three squad mates crested the lip of the ridge that ringed the niland, the King sealed off the entrance to the bridge with another blue wall behind them. Meanwhile, he continued to use the first wall to push the lugmen back in a broad arc, forming an open circle for his inevitable confrontation with Morth. As if on cue, his brother reappeared in the sky above them.

Dropping out of a storm cloud, the dagmagicker crackled with visible green energy, little bolts of lightning crawling up and down his arms and along the shaft of his Ruby Warhammer. Morth flapped his skeletal wings just twice on the way down, slowing his descent only marginally before slamming into the ground at the exact middle of the clearing. He spun his Warhammer in one hand and the wings disappeared in a swirl of green. Then, as the immense ruby pulsed with eerie light, Morth's muscles began to bulge, his stature growing until he towered over Arth at the full height of a luggernaut—while somehow remaining dagman. "You say you want to settle this?" he snarled gutturally, his eyes now glowing the same colors as his ruby.

Arth was overwhelmed with sadness at the bitter hatred in those red-and-green orbs. "It ain't too late to—" he began.

But Morth bellowed and sprang to the attack. Sidekick leapt forward beneath Arth, and Arth brought the Diamond Scepter up to catch the first blow from Morth's Warhammer. It struck with all the weight of a mountain collapsing. Sovereign's Relic was sufficient to the task of defending him from the attack, but as Arth focused on this duel with his brother, he felt himself dropping most of the magical walls and guardrails and patches he'd projected until that moment. The only shield he forced himself to maintain was the one blocking access to the bridge behind him.

"What's ya gonna do," Morth crooned, "keep conjurin' that wall forever?" He pressed his Warhammer even harder upon Arth's Scepter until their faces were barely a span apart, the space between them filled with green and blue sparks from the clashing relics. "Ya ain't got that kind of power, no matter how many Diamond Relics you possess. Besides, this bridge ain't the only way off of Lugarth!" he declared with a patronizing laugh.

"That's where yer wrong," Arth said calmly.

Morth's eyes narrowed in suspicion, then widened in realization. "No. No!"

"That's right," Arth said confidently. "The bridge behind me will soon fall. And assuming it ain't already, the bridge 'tween Lugarth and Hulandia will be closed to ya too."

"That team as broke through our lines?" Morth asked in horror. "But it was only four people! No way they could make a difference on their own."

Arth pushed hard with his Scepter, sending the much taller Morth stumbling backwards. "Guess it depends who them people is, don't it?" Then he leapt to the counterattack.

So began the final confrontation between brothers who had once been the closest of friends. Arth couldn't worry any further about Northmount. He could only hope his confidence in Pyrsie and Hembrose was not misplaced.

· thirty-three ·

The Wizard of Merlyn, who knew more about magic than any other mortal in all of Overtwixt, stared at the Guide skeptically. "You're suggesting I use the blue magic to manipulate time?"

"Not to manipulate so much as *preserve*," the centman corrected him lightly. "Sovereign's magic is for preservation and protection, after all. I would go so far as to suggest that the blue is even better suited to this use than the green."

"Well..." Hembrose hesitated.

"Yet you always reach for the green first."

Pyrsie glanced back and forth between the two men, obviously not understanding. "I do not care what color zee magic is. If there is still a way..."

Hembrose looked away. "It doesn't matter," he said, voice cracking—curse these teenage hormones! "Blue or green, I don't have the strength for either anymore. Not at the level of output we still need."

"You have learned so very much, my dear Wizard," the Guide said. "Truly you did become the greatest mortal practitioner of magic in the world of bridges." He smiled gently. "So how is it that you fail to recognize one of the most basic truths of magic in Overtwixt?"

Everyone turned to stare at the Guide, Hembrose in skeptical disbelief. "And what is that?"

"The power of the green magic comes from within—from your own strength, or worse, the strength you steal from others. But the power of the blue always comes from outside yourself... from the Sovereign. And that means it is *unlimited*."

"I can't believe that," Hembrose said flatly. "The greatest strength I ever wielded was at the height of my powers, when I held the Emerald Caduceus in my hand for the very first time. For that brief moment, before I threw it all away, I was practically unstoppable..." He was overcome with bittersweet nostalgia at the memory, but he forced it down ruthlessly. "I never experienced anything like that kind of power with the blue. And you say the blue is unlimited?" he scoffed. "Ridiculous."

"Your access to Sovereign's magic was only ever limited by your own inclinations," the Guide said. "You're right—you couldn't wield the blue to do anything great, but only because you refused to give up the green for long enough."

"And why should *that* matter?" Hembrose demanded. "What difference does it make if I wield the green also?"

"Because the green is evil," the centman said simply. "As you well know."

Hembrose snorted. "I know nothing of the sort. Certainly no one ever told me that, not even you. And I don't believe it," he repeated. "The green... it's simply a different path from the blue. Neither one is good or bad."

"I don't need to argue with you about it," the Guide said mildly. "You *do* already know the truth. You yourself know that you've done evil wielding the green, evil both great and small. You have stolen what is precious from others, causing them immense pain in the process, a terrible perversion of what is good and pure. But you've also used the green to cut corners, to accomplish admirable goals in less than admirable ways, choosing the green specifically because you knew the blue would not work in the way you wished." The Guide shook his head, expression solemn. "You certainly didn't need anyone to *tell* you the green was evil. That form of magic is only suitable for destruction and deception, and that's exactly how you used it. Free yourself of this fiction that you acted in ignorance."

There was a long, awkward silence. "Very well," Hembrose muttered, the admission surprising even him. "Some part of me knew what I was doing." He spoke defiantly, to hide the shame he was sure everyone could see.

Even so, the Guide seemed pleased. "I'm glad to hear you say that. Acknowledging the truth is the first step."

Hembrose looked away. Truth again? If there was one thing his quest had taught him, it was this: everyone had different ideas about truth.

"The next step is this," the Guide went on. "You must make a decision. That tainted form of magic has all but abandoned you in your weakness, but you may continue clinging to it if you wish. Or you can embrace the Sovereign's strength wholeheartedly. You cannot choose both, however, for a person cannot simply dabble in evil. So long as you rely on the green to even the smallest degree, it will always find a way to consume your heart, leaving you selfish and alone. But the blue will set you free, uninhibited, capable of accomplishing *any* great task so long as it's for the greater good, in accordance with the Sovereign's wishes."

"And this is truly what the Sovereign wants?" Hembrose asked uncertainly. "This mission to create a maze, trapping the luggernauts on their niland forever?"

"This maze will protect the other peoples of Overtwixt, but without isolating the lugmen forever," the Guide said. "A way to reach them will always remain. And so there will always be hope that someday, they can return to healthy fellowship with the outside world."

"Fine," Hembrose grumped, meeting the Guide's eyes again. "I'll give the blue another shot, to see if it won't help us complete this mission. Not because I agree with everything you've said," he added sullenly. "Though... I do trust Arth and Pyrsie, and they seem to trust you." The mermage shrugged. "Mostly because I've got nothing left to lose."

The Guide—the Guide himself!—rolled his eyes.

Hembrose pretended not to see it. Instead, he squeezed his own eyes shut, reaching out with one hand to grasp something intangible. "Unlimited, my right tail fin..." he began, but then something happened that washed his petulance away. Without warning, strength had flooded his body, so much more than ever before, so overwhelming that he couldn't deny its source was outside of himself. "The power!" he gasped. "Oh, the *power*... I never knew!" Feeling suddenly alive in a way he'd never experienced, he dropped his hand, opening his eyes to goggle at the Guide. "You... you were right," he said in wonder, voice cracking again—though this time, he didn't care.

"That power you are wielding right now," the centman said, "is similar to what you might experience if you held one of Sovereign's Relics in your hand. As you know, a relic acts as a vessel to focus magical power."

Hembrose raised both hands. "But I hold no relic."

"In this case, *I* am your vessel," the Guide said simply.

The mermage continued to stare at the centman in wide-eyed confusion, but the Guide did not explain further. At last, Hembrose shook himself and closed his eyes once more. He began the arduous task of restoring the necessary time dilation—and found it not arduous in the least. He couldn't stop himself from smiling with genuine delight and relief. "There. Our time has been multiplied... now at *many* orders of magnitude more than before."

Pyrsie glanced around. "So... where is it? Zis wonderful new time bubble? I see nothing."

Also smiling, the Guide looked up and to the left, off into the distance beyond the rock walls. "Truly, Mistress Inventor, your friend is *still* the greatest magical practitioner of the age. Now that he wields the power of the Sovereign for the greater good, the Wizard has accomplished what no other mortal could: he has enveloped the entire mountain in a bubble of preserved time."

Pyrsie gaped, as did the Bailiff and the other gnomen, all of them regarding Hembrose with wonder.

But instead of pride in his abilities, Hembrose felt... shy, unworthy. This power had not come from him. "You now have as much time as you could possibly want," he told Pyrsie quickly. "No need to rush anymore."

"So do the job right, and make sure it really will last," the Guide told her. "Make your plans, direct your workers, dig and shore up every tunnel properly. Implement every one of those mischievous tricks you're so eager to try," he added with wink. "Make this new Mazemount a marvel that will stand the test of time—not as a testament to yourself, but to the power of the Sovereign and the value of selfless teamwork."

Pyrsie shared a look with Hembrose, and he saw her eyes were glistening. His were too. Then she turned to the other gnomen and unrolled her map across one of the carts.

· thirty-four ·

Morth hammered at his brother again and again, throwing all of his considerable strength into every blow of his Ruby Warhammer. The green magic roared through his veins, engorging his muscles, until Morth's arms bulged more impressively than any dagman that had ever lived—certainly more than that puny Strongman he had once called uncle. And yet, despite his obvious physical enhancements, Morth was still a dagman.

An improved super dagman.

"Give up now," he gloated. "Yeh obviously can't stand against me fer long. Just look at me."

Arth did so, his expression twisting with dismay. "Oh, Morth, what's become of ya... it breaks my heart. This ain't the way, boyo."

Morth blinked, unprepared for *pity* from his brother. What Morth had become was magnificent! Dangerous and frenzied and absolutely one of a kind.

Hembrose once said that the bodies he shapeshifted into always represented some race that actually existed. Whether or not the Wizard had ever seen such a creature himself, magic guided him into a form that was "true" on some niland or real world. That's why his entire body changed when he needed to fly, instead of just manifesting wings on his own merman body. And even when Hembrose morphed just *half* of his body, his new overall form still existed somewhere—for everyone knew that each race in Overtwixt was a half-and-half hybrid of two others. There were countless possible combinations, but even so, Hembrose was prevented from becoming *anything* he desired.

Morth experienced no such limitation. He suspected the difference was that Hembrose *let* himself be held back... by the blue magic. Even though the Wizard preferred the green and used it so much more than the blue, he obviously wanted to preserve the option of using blue on the rare occasions when it had something to offer. His commitment to either form of magic was half-hearted.

But Morth had no interest in playing by the blue magic's strict rules. He refused to be limited by how someone else viewed truth, and so he'd dedicated himself wholly to the green. And with the Adjunct's guidance, he found he *could* become anything he wanted. Entirely lugman when that suited him. Or better yet, entirely himself, his body augmented with the specific traits he desired from some other race—like tusks or fur or wings.

Or the immense size and strength of the luggernauts.

So Morth's muscles bulged with the raw physical brawn of dozens of lugmen, all the monsters he'd harvested in his rise to power as Demagogue. And so too did he now stand at twice his normal height, all the better to crush this pest that Arth had become.

Yet Arth refused to be crushed. Partly that was because he fought from the saddle of his pet kelpie, which helped offset his height disadvantage. More than that, however, a little blue shield popped into view every time Morth brought his Ruby Warhammer crashing down, protecting the King's slender body.

The Demagogue refused to let that stop him, however. He was relentless in his attacks, coming at Arth time and again with his glorious Warhammer. He fought without any finesse, of course, refusing to be embarrassed by his own lack of training. Instead, Morth just battered Arth over and over, hammering heavy overhanded blows upon his brother.

And Arth weathered each blow. Calmly.

Through it all, the Diamond Scepter *throbbed* with cool blue light, its pulse regular, rhythmic... reassuring? The glowing wall behind Arth—the one preventing Morth from returning to Caymerlot—pulsed in time, as did each little shield that appeared long enough to rebuff his attacks.

It was maddening. And yet, now that Morth knew he couldn't wield the Scepter himself, he wanted it all the more.

"Just give it to me!" he snarled in frustration, knowing how senseless his words were even as he shouted them. "Quit now and give me that muddy Scepter. I want it!"

Arth shook his head sadly, so secure in his moral superiority.

Morth screamed in wordless fury, even as another of his hammer blows bounced harmlessly off a blue shield that hadn't existed moments earlier. Stepping back, the Demagogue tried something different, swinging his Warhammer around in an underhanded blow meant to catch Arth's kelpie in the ribs. But the filthy creature caught the strike on his Diamond Aegis, which *also* pulsed—emitting a distinctive strobe of blue light, accompanied by a sound like chimes.

The Warhammer rebounded wildly, and Morth had to wrestle to get the weapon back under control. Then he ground his teeth, feeling them lengthen into wicked fangs.

His muscles bulged once more, sparking and sizzling with renewed electrical activity, and he gouged a deep furrow in the ground at his feet. A massive shower of rock sprayed out at Arth and his kelpie, intermixed with clods of clay that still had tufts of red grass attached.

"This fellow won't rest," the kelpman complained, holding out his Aegis to block the flying debris. "My patience he does test."

"Oy, that was weak," Arth said, leaning lower in his saddle and adding the power of his Scepter to shield the two of them better. "If ya gotta talk backwards just to make yer rhyme work, it ain't nearly as satisfyin'."

"I'm a little busy right now," the kelpie shot back with a snort. "*You* try rhyming in the middle of a fight! Um, wow."

Morth gaped. These two simpletons were joking with each other? In the middle of combat? How *dare* they scoff at the danger Morth posed to them. With an angry growl, he sent an immense green fireball streaking out of his ruby towards Arth's head.

The King deflected it with an almost casual gesture of his Scepter, which he then leveled at Morth. "These days the Demagogue finks he's quite sumfing," he said. "But as a wee dagling, he had leaky plumbing." Arth frowned thoughtfully, choosing his words with care. "His diaper would fill, and soon over-spill, and then he'd wail loudly 'til Mum came a-running."

The kelpie burst into laughter. "I stand corrected. You're better at rhyming than I expected!"

Morth's huge dagman eyeballs nearly popped out of his skull at this affront. The kelpie laughing at him; Arth smirking. Knowing his twin as well as he did, Morth understood that Arth was intentionally riling him, trying to distract him like he used to do when Morth was first learning to juggle. But it worked anyway. Flushing with humiliation, the Demagogue glanced around quickly to see the reaction of his lugman underlings.

To Morth's shock, they weren't even looking at him. During these past several minutes that he'd dueled his brother, Morth had assumed he was the center of attention, the object of focus for every luggernaut in his horde. But he saw now that their eyes were locked on the huwoman Knight—for she, in her spectacular Diamond Armor, was single-handedly holding her own against seven or more of Morth's top lieutenants.

With an enraged howl, Morth turned back to his smarmy-mouthed brother. He resumed beating at the ground with his Warhammer, sending more showers of rock in his direction. Predictably, Arth and the kelpie hunkered down to weather the barrage. So the Demagogue thrust his Warhammer into the air, willing his green magic to electrify the storm clouds that swirled above. In response, a bolt of lightning forked from the sky and exploded into the ground just behind Arth, catching him by surprise. It sent him and his mount tumbling toward Morth, landing hard and rolling on the ground. Morth leapt forward to stomp on Arth's head with one huge foot, but the King thrust his Scepter between the Demagogue's legs to trip him up.

Suddenly *Morth* was on the ground, that filthy kelpie slithering atop his chest to press the Aegis to Morth's throat. The buffoon probably thought he could force a surrender—as if it would be so easy! The dagmagicker dealt the kelpie a powerful backhand, sending Arth's little friend flying through the air. Then Arth and Morth were on their feet again, facing each other one-on-one with weapons out.

Except Morth was still the size of a lugman, while Arth now stood on his own two feet. The dagmagicker began raining blows like before, but with even greater force thanks to his relative height, every hammerfall like a tonne of bricks that the King had to catch directly on his Scepter in a sizzle of green and blue sparks.

"I'm... so sick... of you... getting all... the glory," Morth raged between attacks. "Just... go home... already... and let *me*... be the King..."

"That ain't the way, boyo," Arth said, enduring the onslaught with Scepter held over his head in both hands.

But Morth was crazy with anger and embarrassment and a fervent desire to *punish* his brother for... for... he couldn't even remember anymore. He wailed on the smaller dagman with all his impossible strength, until his vision had gone completely red and green, like lava and wabasi mustard intermixed and burning in his streaming eyes.

Abruptly he came to his senses, arms aching and chest heaving, realizing he was now deflecting attacks from Arth instead of the other way around. With surprise, he noted that his beautiful Warhammer had become damaged, misshapen.

Yet Arth and his Scepter remained intact.

What's worse, the King was mounted on his kelpie once more, delivering each flurry of blows with a calm discipline that belied their ferocity. Stunned, the Demagogue began to give ground, desperately trying to regain his rhythm and the initiative. But Arth's Scepter-strikes kept coming, Morth's Warhammer warping even worse beneath each impact.

Without warning, Morth's back was against the wall. Wall? What wall? He didn't have time to wonder, however, for a sensation was flooding through him: a taste of *freedom* like he had never imagined, which everything in his being tried—and failed—to reject. He was defenseless against this power, and yet he fought it all the same, his belly filling with nausea at his inability to escape.

And then, to his horror, Morth began to shrink.

· thirty-five ·

Pyrsie immediately put the Excavator to work digging the next tunnel she had planned, assigning three other men to help him. The Conservationist and his assistants were tasked with following behind them, building timber scaffolding with the lumber they had brought, spaced at even intervals along each tunnel to minimize the risk of further cave-ins. Last came the Stonemason with his belt full of finishing tools, smoothing each wall to make it a thing of functional beauty. Meanwhile, the Architect pored over the growing map with Pyrsie, discussing enhancements or alternative approaches. Each of the older gnomen was deferential, acknowledging the Inventor as the master craftswoman in charge of this project; but Pyrsie quickly realized that their experience would help her achieve a far more extensive, effective, and enduring maze than she could have managed on her own.

All of this freed Pyrsie herself to start work on her "mischievous tricks," as the Guide had called them—the special features she had wanted to apply to the maze all along, to make the tangle of tunnels *truly* confusing.

First, she did a quiet walkthrough of the existing maze, ignoring the twists and turns and paying attention to the walls and floor instead. She documented the landmarks that already existed at each intersection—a narrow shelf in the rock here, a small pool of water there, a distinctive gouge left by a chisel... basically anything that might help a traveler recognize places he'd been before. Then, instead of removing those features, Pyrsie *duplicated* each one in multiple other junctions throughout the maze. That way, travelers would constantly feel as if they'd been in a particular place before, reinforcing the sensation of walking in circles even when they were not. Meanwhile, she kept an eye out for places where additional corridors might be cut to sow even greater confusion.

As she continued to expand the maze on her map, drawing new passages for the Excavator to open up, Pyrsie played with strange angles of intersection. While she crossed some passages at obvious right angles, she caused other corridors to branch in unexpected ways—sometimes hiding the junction in deep shadow so it could only be seen from one direction, looking closely. This made it almost impossible for travelers to retrace their steps, visually guiding them along a different route entirely whenever they turned around. Pyrsie and her companions also widened the openings to certain tunnels that curved back toward Lugarth no matter which direction they were entered, so that all the obvious "main roads" would lead lugman explorers back home again.

Despite all the mischief she worked, however, the Inventor created no dangers, no traps or pitfalls to cause harm or distress. Conversing daily with the Guide, and continuing to drink regularly from the Diamond Grail (which behaved like its old self again), the gnomaid found she didn't even *want* to hurt the residents of Lugarth. More and more, she came to think of her enemies as misguided, the luggernauts as well as the aquatics who'd fought at their side. They were dangerous to be sure, deserving of some harsh discipline, but they weren't evil in and of themselves. She felt this truth stronger than ever when she found out she knew one of the bad guys personally.

"Morth?" she blurted in response to the Guide's casual revelation. "You're telling me zat Arth's brother—*that* Morth—is zee one leading the invasion of Caymerlot?" She blinked. "Arth is fighting his own twin brother?"

"Morthos Penn," Hembrose repeated, making sure he hadn't misheard. "That goofy lad who used to play the Clown at all our circus performances? *He's* the Demagogue?" The Wizard frowned. "Now that I think of it, the Demagogue's rhetoric always did sound familiar. Oh my," he added. "I suddenly wish I'd never introduced him to magic..."

The Guide just nodded.

"But how can zis be?" Pyrsie wanted to know.

"Obviously Morth freed himself without our help," Hembrose said. "But... to then *join* his captors in hurting other people? I don't understand it."

"Do you remember meeting Lady Karis's brother Bias?" the Guide asked.

Pyrsie blinked. "Zat human who enslaved the eqmen?" She tried not to think of her similar treatment of Paladin. The situations were vastly different.

Hembrose nodded. "The Prince, he called himself."

The Guide continued. "Do you recall Karis saying how Bias was bullied in his youth, by older brothers that were bigger and stronger? She asked why he would ever treat others the same way, when he knew what it felt like."

"He said... he never wanted to feel powerless again," Pyrsie whispered, remembering. "So instead, he put others under his power, which made him feel power*ful*."

"Something like that." The Guide looked at her with profound sadness. "It's not easy, healing from trauma. It takes work, and patient guidance from someone who has your best interests at heart. But young Morthos suffered much, and he blames others, wants them to feel that same pain: the Underlord, Arthos, even me. He rejected my attempts to help him, choosing the counsel of another instead—someone with his own self-serving agenda." The centman's eyes flashed. "And so he repeated the Prince's mistake... and will now share the Prince's fate. Refusing to turn away from his self-destructive path, Morthos now forces someone who loves him into an equally unfair position."

Pyrsie swallowed, eyes misty as she thought of how Karis had been forced to fight her own brother, ultimately ejecting him from Overtwixt for the good of others. Now Arth, at this very moment, was fighting *his* brother to prevent *him* from hurting anyone else. "Why does the Sovereign even allow people to get hurt in Overtwixt?" she demanded. "Doesn't he care?"

"Of course he cares," the Guide said. "So much so that he offers every visitor to Overtwixt one of the greatest gifts of all: choice. The choice of roles, the choice to do evil or fight evil, and a thousand smaller choices in between. He certainly could protect everyone by removing their ability to choose evil, but..."

"That would be slavery," Pyrsie realized. Of the sort Morth and the eqmen had experienced. Of the sort she herself had forced upon Paladin for a time. "But... but..."

"But that doesn't make these truths any easier to accept," the Guide agreed softly. "Each person must wrestle with the implications on his or her own." And Pyrsie knew he would say no more on the subject unless she asked.

In the days that followed that terrible revelation about Morth, Pyrsie established work shifts for her craftsmen, as well as a quitting time each day, after which they ate, talked, and even slept. Following weeks without rest, it took the gnomaid some time to recover. The Grail was still sufficient to refresh her, of course—and everyone else too, whenever they felt tired—but men and women were never meant to go without sleep. Now, though, she enjoyed an abundance of time under Hembrose's new time dilation, waking enthusiastically with each new day. And she continually marveled at the strange magic of Overtwixt, how mere moments passed for Arth and Morth for every day she spent in this maze.

Just as marvelous was the transformation of Hembrose, who was now a joy to be around. He contributed plenty to the project simply by maintaining the time bubble, but that didn't seem to tax him anymore. The mermage was frequently seen moving throughout the maze (they *all* had copies of the map to get around, updated nightly) offering help and running errands. Of course, he was effectively a fish out of water these days. He could no longer form legs, since shapeshifting was different under the blue magic; it didn't allow making that kind of fundamental change to yourself unless you were in imminent danger. Instead, the Wizard sped deftly through the corridors in a wheeled chair Pyrsie had pieced together one night from cart parts.

And the Guide himself prepared their daily food—breakfast, lunch, and dinner. The craftsmen had wisely included plenty of meal ingredients in their carts full of supplies; even so, the centman made the provisions last so long that Pyrsie wondered if he was multiplying the food using magic, as Hembrose was doing with time. For that matter, Pyrsie was amazed that a man of the Guide's importance would stoop to perform such a humble duty as cooking. But when she asked, he just smiled and said he was happy to be of service.

Last but not least of their team, Alexandre the Bailiff had no specialized fabrication skills—he worked in law enforcement, after all—so he followed the Wizard's and Guide's example, helping where he could and offering moral support. Being a gnoman, he *was* still good with his hands, so Pyrsie eventually honored him with a special task. Alexandre would be the one to mount glowstone at intervals along each tunnel to light the way, with larger fixtures at each intersection to act as street signs of a sort. It was a common practice in the tunnels on their niland of Gnoburrow, but with one distinction here. Within the maze, these directional signs had to be *coded*. Pyrsie entrusted the little Bailiff with devising an original sequence of symbols to chisel into these larger glowplates, which would make sense only in conjunction with the master map. By now, the maze was so convoluted that even possession of the map alone did not guarantee escape. Alexandre's coded symbols ensured that approved travelers would still be able to get through.

Weeks turned to months, and before Pyrsie knew it, months turned to years. Yet in all that time, they never saw another lugman; so she *knew* Arth's duel must still be raging outside, slowed down to nearly a standstill. Either that, or Arth had lost and the Lugarth-Caymerlot bridge still stood, Crystal City overrun with invaders. But somehow Pyrsie knew that wasn't the case. Maybe it was the constant, calm presence of the Guide, reassuring by his proximity.

When the project was complete, down to the very last trifling detail she or the Architect had ever dreamed, the team gathered for one last evening meal together. In celebration, the Guide had prepared an elaborate feast of steamed slugs, perfectly-aged cheese, and sauteed mushrooms on a bed of other fungi, along with foaming mugs of fresh-brewed root ale. Even Hembrose tucked in excitedly, claiming it was little different from the shellfish and seaweed his own people enjoyed. Pyrsie just shook her head in wonder at the Guide. He *had* to be using magic to accomplish something like this.

The next morning, everyone said their goodbyes, which were surprisingly tearful. Then the Guide and the workers traveled up through the maze tunnels toward Hulandia, returning the way they'd come so long before. The gnomen had already destroyed their copies of the map, but the Guide was confident he could, well, *guide* them out of the mountain by memory. When they were gone, it was just Pyrsie and Hembrose once more, the thick roll of the master map tucked protectively under the Inventor's arm.

It was so quiet, suddenly.

"Well, here we are," Pyrsie said, as much to fill the silence as anything. "Standing in zee midst of my greatest professional triumph." She gazed upon the walls of the maze with pride. It was truly a thing of beauty. "But I could not have done zis alone, obviously."

Hembrose grinned from his chair. "This is probably *my* greatest accomplishment too. Preserving time within an *entire mountain*... but I couldn't have done that alone either."

Pyrsie took a deep breath and let it out contentedly. "Are you ready?"

The Wizard nodded, concentrated for a moment, then sagged. "The bubble is released. We're back at normal speed again," he gasped, suddenly feeble. "The power... I held it for so long, and now to release it..." His eyelids fluttered closed, and he began to breathe more evenly. Pyrsie helped him drink from the Diamond Grail before he fell at last into a very deep sleep.

Then she locked the wheels on his chair and left him there to rest, tucked in a dark corner just inside the first turn of the maze. And with mingled feelings of excitement and dread, she descended to the cavern below to see what had become of their squad mate Gerald, the Noble.

· thirty-six ·

Arthos Penn was by no means the most accomplished fighter in the Squad; in fact, he ranked himself and Pyrsie near the bottom. But by now he *had* gained plenty of experience battling lugmen and even karks and kelpies. And to be fair, compared with all the enemies he'd faced in battle so far (aside from the Ransacker), he *was* the one still walking the nilands of Overtwixt. He had learned a lot from his squad mates, and compared with anyone outside the Squad, Arth was a decently skilled fighter. Certainly he was much better trained than his brother Morth.

And yet Morth fought with a ferocity unlike anything Arth had seen before.

For the first several minutes of their duel, the towering Demagogue pounded away at the King without pause or rest. He wielded that dodgy Warhammer with about as much technique as a child with a stick, but it little mattered. Every fall of that hammer was backed by the entirety of Morth's magically-enhanced weight and strength.

Arth endured each blow the best he could, breathing deeply and staying calm as he drew on the magic of the

Diamond Scepter to maintain his defenses: the blue wall to keep the Demagogue and the barbarian horde off the bridge, and of course his own personal blue shield against the dagmagicker's attacks.

When Morth switched tactics, using his Warhammer to gouge furrows out of the red hillside—showering the King and his Sidekick with sharp rocky shrapnel—the two friends hunkered down behind their shields. For the first time, Arth could safely turn his attention away from Morth for a moment, to see how Lady Karis was faring.

The Knight was badly outnumbered, of course, drawing the attention of the entire lugman horde onto herself so that Arth could focus on Morth alone. Constantly moving, she danced along the crest of the next red hill, singing a battle hymn from her real world. She did not fight to smoke her enemies, merely to injure them, slow them down. Karis had always been quick to show mercy, but Arth knew this was a sound defensive ploy too. Whenever she defeated a foe entirely, he puffed from existence, making room for the next; but an injured lugman took up space, making it difficult for others to attack her. And indeed, this was working to her advantage so far, considering her surroundings were crowded with moaning luggernauts on their knees. But if the ones still on their feet ever managed to trap the Knight in close quarters, boxing her in from all sides, she'd be in serious trouble.

A bolt of lightning forked from the sky and exploded into the ground just behind Arth, catching him by surprise. He tumbled from Sidekick's saddle, rolling over just in time to see Morth's oversized boot descending. He reacted instinctively, tripping the bigger dagman with his Scepter, then scrambling to his feet while the Demagogue was distracted by Sidekick. The poor kelpie went flying, and just that fast, Arth was facing Morth alone.

And Morth was still twice his size.

"I'm... so sick... of you... getting all... the glory," Morth snarled between falls of his Warhammer, which Arth caught on his Scepter in an explosion of green and blue sparks. Unlike before, Arth was now holding the Diamond Relic in arms locked overhead; its magic protected him, but he still felt like a nail being driven into the ground. "Just... go home... already..." Morth growled, his eyes blazing like unholy red-and-green orbs. "Let *me*... be the King..."

"That ain't the way, boyo," Arth said through gritted teeth, persevering as best he could.

The effort of hammering at the King over and over had to be exhausting, but the Demagogue seemed fueled by hate—or perhaps the green magic. Was there any difference? Arth didn't know much about magic. He'd watched Hembrose wield it this last year, using its blue and green forms interchangeably, though Arth never understood the distinction between the two. Now, though, watching what Morth did with the green—and what the green did to *him*—Arth didn't need an explanation.

By contrast, Sovereign's blue magic continued to stream through Arth from the Diamond Scepter, promoting peace within his broken heart. To see his brother turned into this monster, worse than any lugman brute he'd faced before, would otherwise be unbearable. Arth was glad he'd forced their father to stay behind, for there was no longer any doubt in his mind. His only option was to banish Morth from Overtwixt forever.

As much as he wished for the alternative, as much as it was in the nature of Sovereign's magic to grant second chances (not to mention thirteenth and seventy-seventh), Arth now knew Morth would never turn from this path he had chosen.

And the King had a responsibility to protect the peoples of Overtwixt from this Demagogue's villainy.

As Arth's resolve grew, the Diamond Scepter grew more resolute as well. His brother's Warhammer began to warp and deform with each heavy-handed blow, while the Scepter only glowed the brighter.

Then Sidekick was back, diving between Arth's legs from behind and lifting him into the saddle again. Together, they went on the offensive, pressing the attack. By now, the brothers had circled several times, and Arth was pointing back the way he'd come. Directing his mount with his knees, the King forced his much-taller brother to retreat, one step at a time—all the way to the entrance of the bridge, which was still blocked by the magical blue barricade. Before he knew how much ground he'd given up, Morth retreated right into the wall. His muscles spasmed, and the Warhammer dropped from nerveless fingers. An expression of horror crossed his face, and yet Arth knew the contact with the blue wall caused no physical pain. Sovereign's magic was love, after all.

But Sovereign's magic was also truth.

The touch of that magic immediately freed Morth from the web of lies he'd wrapped around himself. Before Arth's very eyes, the Demagogue began to shrink—his unnatural muscles deflating, his impossible height decreasing—until only the true version of Morth remained. The green magic that had crackled up and down his body hissed away to nothing, and Morth's eyes even lost their green-and-red glow... though not their hateful expression.

Arth leapt from his saddle and placed the basket of the Scepter against Morth's chest. "Stay down," he warned his brother, though it was obvious Morth was still dazed. Arth glanced around quickly, worried for his friend Karis.

What he saw made his heart sink. His worst fears had come to pass, for the Knight was close to being overrun.

The air she breathed was thick with the yellow smoke of her foes, but the lugs who remained were overwhelming her with sheer numbers, crowding so tightly that she no longer had room to swing her swords. Even as Arth watched, one of the brutes kicked her legs out from under her, then the rest began piling on top.

"Go!" Arth told Sidekick with an anguished cry. "Help her if ya can!"

"If I can," the kelpie muttered, "me against the whole lugman van..." He slithered off rapidly, Diamond Aegis gleaming before him like a battering ram.

Arth forced himself to focus on Morth, knowing that Karis was suffering this abuse for *him*, to give him this opportunity. The thousand-faceted Diamond sphere within the Scepter's basket seemed to explode with even greater light than before, pressing Morth against the blue wall so the Demagogue could barely move. Arth was so angry, so hurt and betrayed, that he wanted to lash out with his words and put Morth in his place. Instead, something totally unexpected came out of his mouth: "I love you, boyo."

Morth gawped at him.

"You's defeated," Arth said fervently. "Please, give it up. Surrender finally."

Face filling with rage yet again, Morth snarled, "What, so ya can drag me to Dagmør in chains, then kick me back across the bridge home anyway?"

"Aye," Arth said honestly. "I'd rather not have to smoke meh own brother. But I will if I gots to."

"I don't fink yeh've got it in ya," Morth sneered back. "Besides, if ya smoke me, this bridge goes too, leaving ya stranded here—in the middle of the barbarian horde. You'd be sealin' yer own fate." He tried to dive for his Warhammer, but Arth slammed him against the wall again.

Obviously Morth thought the plan was to destroy Northmount entirely, and Arth didn't bother correcting him. He couldn't be sure Pyrsie had completed her mission, after all; and even if she had, Arth and Sidekick still needed to get from here to there. But whether the King had an escape route or not, he was determined to do the right thing regardless of the cost.

"Don't make me smoke ya," he begged his brother sincerely.

Morth smiled, catching sight of something over Arth's shoulder. "Oh, don't worry. I don't fink yeh'll have to."

"Arth!" Sidekick cried as he hurried up again. "Arth, they've got the Knight!"

Glancing back again, Arth almost cried out in dismay. The barbarian horde was closing in around him, led by two giant luggernauts with matching grins. But that wasn't what filled his heart with despair. Rather, it was the sight of the figure they were dragging along between them:

Lady Karis, her body limp and unmoving within that resplendent Diamond Armor.

· thirty-seven ·

Karis's head was spinning, and it was all she could do not to be sick. Even in her dazed state, she could remember doing that inside her helmet once before—in her early years as Knight of Overtwixt—and she'd never made that mistake again. Judging by the vice-like grip on her arms, she was no longer in control of her own fate. But she could, at least, maintain her dignity.

She shook her head, and her vision swam into partial focus. She was being dragged toward two figures... two dagmen. She blinked. The King and the Demagogue. That's right, she'd been fighting to give Arthos time, the time he needed to end the threat posed by his very own brother. Oh, poor Arthos. Karis knew exactly how he was feeling in this situation.

Her lugman captors stopped abruptly, throwing her to the ground. Before Karis could even take a breath, they began stomping on her, driving her body into the stony red earth. She coughed and groaned, her body spasming under the abuse. Even though her Diamond Armor was completely enclosed, magically locked so that no one but Karis herself could take it off, it only protected her from broken bones and the most serious damage. Clearly, the lugs were still capable of causing her pain as they continued to kick and stomp gleefully.

"Stop!" an angry voice commanded, magnified to such a volume that Karis could *feel* the lugmen stagger back from her. That would be her friend Arthos, coming to her rescue. Dear, sweet Arthos. Alas, the lugs soon resumed their abuse of her bruised body, laughing with every blow they rained upon her.

"Stop it, I say!" Arthos bellowed desperately.

"Release me," replied a second voice, this one a dark mirror of the King's. The Demagogue—the villain the Squad had come here to defeat. "Let me go, and they'll stop hurting yer friend."

Resolve swelled within Karis. "No, Arthos!" she cried with all the strength left in her. "Do what... do what we came here to do."

A vicious kick took Karis in the ribs, and she doubled up, wrapping her arms around her knees in a vain attempt to protect herself. The air filled with the horde's hooting laughter as the lugs pummeled her all the more, though it must have hurt them too, striking her Armor with bare hands and hooves. They didn't care. They lived for violence.

"Please!" Arthos cried. "Enough, alright! I'll let him free. Just stop it, ya cheeky monsters!"

The abuse ceased instantly. With a groan, Karis forced herself to roll over, levering onto her elbows so she could see what was happening. Arthos had stepped back from his brother, lowering his Scepter so it no longer pressed the other dagman into the glowing blue wall.

"Arthos, please," she rasped. "You have... to do... what we came here... to do," she repeated between coughs.

"But Lady Karis—"

"We all... have to make... sacrifices," she told him, suddenly overcome with emotion.

Karis had always seen the world differently from her fellow squad members, even Gerald. For them, Overtwixt represented adventure, excitement, maybe even a vacation from reality. But for her, this place was so much more. Being the Knight gave her purpose and meaning, the power to help others—none of which she'd known in the real world, where culture placed severe limits on who and what she was allowed to be. Since the day she arrived in the world of bridges, Karis had dreaded ever returning to reality.

And yet, if she'd learned anything in Overtwixt, it was this: She had immense worth, whether or not anyone else acknowledged it. And she *did* have the power to do good, even if she remained powerless in the world's eyes.

"We all... have to... make... sacrifices," she repeated, her throat thick. "I make mine... willingly. Thank you, Arthos. Thank you... for being... my friend." And before she could second-guess herself, she reached up and twisted her helmet, unlocking and lifting it from her shoulders. Her thick braids tumbled across her glowing breastplate as she felt the tender kiss of fresh air on her sweaty face. She heaved a sigh of surrender.

For the longest moment, everyone stared at her in surprise. Had she really just removed part of her magic Diamond Armor? The only thing that kept her from being smoked outright? No one could believe it.

It gave Karis time to offer Arthos one last smile. A reassuring smile, dimples and all, so he would know this wasn't his fault. She was willing to sacrifice the remainder of her time in Overtwixt rather than be used as a hostage— whether or not anyone else understood what a sacrifice it really was. She did this not only for her friend, her King, but for everyone else the Demagogue's tyranny might someday threaten.

Then one of the lugs raised a club high overhead.

"No!" shrieked Arthos *and* his brother at the same moment. But it was too late.

The club crashed down on her skull. And in an instant, Karis Priamos—*Hippea tis Tetraodías*—was transported back to the catacombs beneath the burnt-out husk of a temple in lost Troia, from whence she'd first arrived so many years before.

· thirty-eight ·

The Knight herself disappeared first, replaced by a vibrant cloud of yellow that oozed from every joint of her hateful Diamond Armor. The Armor remained a moment longer, then *it* pulsed an even brighter blue than normal and winked out of sight too.

"No, you fools!" Morth screamed. "That woman was my leverage!"

But Arth was wailing too, distracted by the loss of his friend. Morth seized the opportunity, shoving away from that terrible blue wall and diving for his Ruby Warhammer. He came up out of his roll with the weapon in both hands, a sickly sweet relief flooding him.

The King turned to face him, such animosity on his face that Morth hesitated. He'd never seen this version of Arth before, teeth clenched, eyes burning with an instinctual thirst for vengeance. The Diamond Scepter's brilliant glow suddenly dimmed, but Arth didn't seem to notice. His knuckles popped audibly as he squeezed the Relic in a death grip, preparing to unleash its power on Morth.

But Morth was faster. Leaping forward, he swung the Warhammer with all his might—and to Arth's obvious shock, knocked the Scepter completely out of his hands. Morth was equally surprised, however. Having swung his huge weapon so wildly, he overbalanced, spinning all the way around and stumbling toward the blue wall once more. Awful as that wall was, the touch of Sovereign's magic trying to convince Morth of things he didn't want to believe, he was suddenly glad for it. It had stopped him from falling off the side of the niland before, and it was about to do so again.

Except Arth was no longer holding the Scepter.

The glowing blue wall disappeared. Morth tripped, dropping his Warhammer as he tried to catch himself on something—a rock, a tuft of grass, *anything*—then tumbled over the edge.

He struck solid ground only moments later, causing the breath to go out of him in a painful but relieved woosh. Of course. The magical rocky bridge that Morth himself had created still stood between Lugarth and Caymerlot; its angle of descent was just so steep that he hadn't been able to see it from above.

Oh no. It was *very* steep.

Morth's momentum barely slowed with the impact. Tumbling still, he went head-over-heels backwards, screaming the whole way. Somewhere distant, Arth was yelling too. Morth struck the rocky ground again, and again, then slipped sideways, falling painfully through a jagged crack in the uneven surface. Eyes wide, he scrambled once more for purchase, and this time caught the lip with one hand—barely.

Chest heaving rapidly, Morth tried to solidify his grip. He was in a crevasse in the middle of his bridge, one of the imperfections he'd never cared enough to fill—and now he really was dangling over empty white nothing. Straining with all his might, he reached up carefully with his other hand, groping for a second grip. But every possible handhold crumbled beneath his touch, dropping away like loose dirt instead of rock. His bridge was falling apart around him!

"Hold on, Morth, I'm comin'!" Arth cried, and Morth looked up to see him skidding recklessly down the incline after him. Apparently the sight of Morth in mortal danger had driven all anger and vengeance from his mind, for Arth's face held nothing but worry as he slid to Morth's rescue.

Morth hated him all the more for it.

By now, the air was filled with the sounds of avalanche as great chunks of Morth's bridge fell into the abyss, all up and down its miles-long span. Its collapse had probably started minutes earlier, when he'd lost control of his Warhammer the first time. Left untended, the green magic always sought destruction.

Determined that his story would not end this way, the Demagogue summoned every last ounce of power from within himself. Green magic crackled up and down his arms and he heaved with all his strength, both physical and magical. And in his moment of greatest need, the green magic finally betrayed him. One last charge ran up Morth's arms and *zapped* him, right on the tips of the fingers he was hanging from. In shocked reflex, he let go, just moments before Arth could reach him.

And Morthos Penn, the Demagogue from Dagmør, tumbled into the abyss.

Falling backwards in utter disbelief, he stared up at his brother's horrified face as it grew rapidly distant. The last thing he ever saw in Overtwixt, before the infinite whiteness closed in around him, was the remainder of his precious bridge collapsing into the abyss after him.

But even as he plummeted amidst the detritus of his dreams, Morth took some small comfort. For he knew that Arth, now stranded with all those bloodthirsty lugmen, would soon be joining him in the real world.

· thirty-nine ·

"Morth, boyo," Arth whispered. His own brother, his closest mate for as long as he'd lived. He wasn't dead, of course, but he might as well be—from Arth's perspective—if Arth was expected to rule in Overtwixt for the entire Golden Age to come. Losing his twin was bad enough, but the terms on which they'd parted ways tore at his very soul.

And even if he *could* hope to see Morth again, someday far in the future, the same could not be said of dear Karis.

Arth felt a desperate sense of loss. If not for Sidekick pulling him urgently back toward the niland lip, he probably would have fallen into the abyss too, when what remained of Morth's dodgy bridge finally collapsed entirely.

But even once he climbed back onto Lugarth, the King wasn't given time to mourn. "I know this moment is solemn," the kelpie said awkwardly, releasing Arth from his grip, "but we've got a problem."

Oh right. The luggernauts.

Slowly, Arth turned to see that the mass of lugs was already converging on them. With Morth and Karis gone, it was now just Arth and Sidekick surrounded by the barbarian horde.

Although he felt like giving up, Arth put one foot in front of the other until he reached the Diamond Scepter. Bending, he picked it up... and the lugmen hesitated a moment before resuming their slow approach. Then Arth walked over to the misshapen Ruby Warhammer. Bending again, he picked it up also. Despite its immense weight, it seemed that Arth was capable of lifting it just as easily as Morth had. Was that the blue magic of Sovereign giving him strength once again? For a minute there, when Arth had been consumed by grief at the loss of Karis, he had wanted nothing more than to punish his brother... and the blue had retreated from him. Had it returned? Or was this a different form of magic that strengthened him now?

For half a heartbeat, Arth was tempted to use the Warhammer to conquer these monsters who had threatened Overtwixt—not only to defeat and confine them to Lugarth, but to utterly and painfully *destroy* them. The Warhammer would let him do that, for it was a relic of the green magic. It *wanted* to be used in this way, in a way the blue magic of Sovereign's Relic would never allow.

But Arth took a deep breath and resisted that temptation. Immediately, the green glow of the Warhammer fizzled to nothing as the Scepter burst into brilliant blue radiance once more.

And the luggernauts began to shrink back from him.

· forty ·

Hembrose woke slowly, yawning as he stretched his arms and tail luxuriously. Then he sagged back into his wheeled chair and smiled. He had actually gotten good rest throughout these last couple years of compressed time, but even when he slept, he had constantly been maintaining the magic of the time bubble. Now, his mission accomplished, he'd finally been able to rest completely. There was a certain satisfaction that came only from a job well and truly *done*.

Looking around and not seeing Pyrsie, he quickly guessed where she must be. Releasing his chair's brake lock, he wheeled himself out of the maze and down the corridor leading toward Lugarth.

He realized he was *whistling*. Truly, he felt on top of the world after what he had accomplished with the help of the Guide and the Sovereign's magic. Nor was he left with any aches or nausea in the aftermath. In fact, never had Hembrose felt so healthy, so clean, so free of guilt or unease or suspicion toward others. The blue truly was liberating, as the Guide had said. If not for his lingering worries about Arth and the outcome of the larger battle (which he'd never been able to completely ignore while in the bubble), everything would have been right in Hembrose's world.

"Are ye proud of me now, Mam?" he asked the open air as he wheeled himself along. He did this sometimes, imagining conversations with the mother he had left behind in his real world.

"What do you think, me wee son?" she turned the question back on him.

Hembrose grinned, sure of that answer for the first time ever. "I think ye are," he said, happily slipping into the diction of his youth. "I finally gave up me dreams of power and fame, and I focused entirely on people. I been putting their needs above me own for a few years now. And not just me friends! People I don't know and will never meet."

He imagined Mam holding his gaze with quiet intensity. "And are ye happy?"

His grin widened. "I am. For maybe the first time in me life—either of me lives, haha—I actually am. Living for others is so much more rewarding than living only for meself."

The fiery-haired Moira O'Hildirun smiled brilliantly, and from that expression (imagined though it was) Hembrose could tell that she was happy *for* him. "And who's to say?" she noted. "With all ye've accomplished, maybe fame will find ye anyway."

Now there was an interesting thought. In the grip of the blue for so long, he'd been concerned about other people, yet barely gave a thought to their opinions of him. He'd been secure in who he was and what he was doing. Now, though, with what he'd accomplished, he realized he probably *would* be thought of as a great hero in the years and centuries to come. Along with the rest of the Squad, of course. It was humbling... but also exciting.

"But oh, me wee boy," Mam said, "I am *so* proud that ye finally have your priorities straight."

Hembrose closed his eyes, cherishing the rare sensation of his mother's approval.

"And your beard is looking quite dashing."

Hembrose laughed, running one hand through the full dark scruff on his cheeks and chin. After these years of time dilation, he was finally old enough (again) to grow proper facial hair.

"So, now that ye've completed your quest... Do this mean ye'll finally be coming home to see your dear old Mam?" she asked hopefully.

That brought Hembrose up short. He certainly had accomplished great things. But he hadn't actually completed his quest yet, had he? "I guess ye'll find out the same time I do." And he continued on his way, wheeling his chair along the subterranean corridor.

Breathing deeply, he detected his first whiff of fresh air when he rolled out onto the platform he thought of as the mezzanine—the broad ledge overlooking the cavern at the bottom of the upside down mountain. Then he caught sight of the long, twisting path of steps that led the rest of the way down, and he realized the obvious: his wheeled chair wouldn't work here. He could drag himself down on hands and tail, but Hembrose knew he would just have to climb back up again once he found Pyrsie; and what a pain all *that* would be. In the past, he would've fashioned legs for himself, thinking nothing of venturing where other mermen were incapable of treading... but that required the green magic, which he'd successfully avoided for two years now. Besides, he didn't have the strength to shapeshift without a vessel or relic anyway.

Except he *did* have the strength, he realized suddenly. After two years of continuous exercise with the blue, he had developed his magical muscles to an astounding degree—far faster than he'd managed during the first two years of his original visit to the Hidden Chamber, when he'd worked entirely with the green. Why, he was already well on his way towards regaining the power he'd thrown away for the Lady of the Lake. He *could* now flex the required muscles to perform a shapeshift, without assistance.

Still, he hesitated. That was the *green*. It had taken a while, but Hembrose had eventually come to believe that the Guide was right; he was better off without the green magic and its complications. He didn't like the way it made him feel, the way it twisted his outlook or opinions of others.

But he really did need to climb down and find Pyrsie, and his intentions were innocent, after all. It wouldn't do any harm if he used it briefly, just this once. Right?

A small groan passed his lips as he seized the green magic, splitting his tail down the middle to form dagman legs. He stood from the chair and took an experimental step. Good enough, though not very satisfying. He waved his hand and shifted into full human form, pleased to feel his dark beard grow out longer and flop onto his chest. That was better. There was a bit of a sour aftertaste, but he smiled anyway, pleased with himself that he could still handle that form of magic. He wouldn't allow himself to do anything more with it, of course. Just a few simple spells for expediency and old times' sake.

Ignoring the faint but distinct sensation of loss in the back of his mind, Hembrose hurried down the steps.

He found Pyrsie just past the mouth of the cavern, sitting on the top step of the spiral staircase and hugging something to her chest. Behind her, dozens of swords and clubs were strewn about the entrance, mute testament to the number of lugmen the Noble had fought back in his mission to defend Inventor and Wizard. The centman's polished saddle and saddle bags had been placed to the side in a tidy pile. It was his beautiful blue-and-white caparison that Pyrsie clutched to her chest as she wept softly. The Noble had indeed completed his mission, but at the cost of any future adventures he might have enjoyed in Overtwixt.

Hembrose patted Pyrsie consolingly on the shoulder, and she stood, seizing him in a tearful hug. Then the two friends descended the rest of the way to Lugarth together.

The staircase itself had somehow shrunk—magically, of course—and was now just wide enough to climb single-file. It was no longer rickety, and it didn't show even a spot of rust. Above them, the upside-down mountain of Northmount disappeared into whiteness above, tall and slender, no longer raining constant small rockfalls upon them. Hembrose knew this was a magical side effect also, the result of being enveloped in the Sovereign's magic for so long, constantly preserved and renewed.

"Northmount is stable again," he said in satisfaction.

"What?" Pyrsie asked distractedly, sniffling. "Oh. No, not Northmount anymore." She swiped at her eyes and forced a grin. "Zee Guide was right. From now on, it weel be known as... Mazemount."

But Hembrose was barely listening anymore. He had just noticed a small group of people coming over the horizon from the direction of the war camps: a dagman carrying an immense Warhammer, accompanied by half a dozen lugmen. The mermage swallowed convulsively. "It's Morth," he hissed, grabbing Pyrsie's arm and pulling her back up the steps toward the maze. "Did he win the battle after all?"

Pyrsie pulled free, squinting into the distance and shaking her head. "No, zat is Arth. See, it is Sidekick he is riding." Hembrose hadn't even noticed the dagman's mount. "And look at zee way those lugs hang their heads in shame. They *are* defeated."

The Wizard was forced to admit the gnomaid was right. Even so, it made him nervous when she grabbed *his* arm and stepped away from the staircase to ensure the approaching party saw them. The distant dagman gave a shout of joy and leapt from his saddle, covering the rest of the distance at a sprint—leaving no doubt that it was Arth and not his twin. Throwing the Ruby Warhammer to the ground (but holding onto the Diamond Scepter that he also carried), he enveloped both Hembrose and Pyrsie in a fierce hug. "Oy, it's a blessin' to see you lot alive and well!"

Overcome with emotion, he quickly shared the details of the Final Battle, and his duel with the Demagogue. They already knew the lugman leader was none other than Morth, but not how twisted and cruel their old friend's heart had grown before the end. Hembrose felt sick by the time he heard of Morth's ultimate fate. Sidekick arrived during the retelling, his bearing uncharacteristically solemn, and he laid comforting tentacles on all their shoulders. For once, the Wizard didn't feel a shiver of revulsion at being touched by a filthy kelpie.

Entirely aside from the loss of his twin brother, Arth was heartbroken to hear of Noble's sacrifice, as were Hembrose and Pyrsie to learn about Karis. After a long moment of shared silence, Arth sent two of the lugs up the spiral staircase to collect the centman's caparison and saddle gear. Seeing Hembrose's look of confusion, Arth shrugged. "You know the lugs," he explained. "They's only impressed by one fing—strength. Fer the moment, they's followin' me around and doin' what I say 'cause I carry the Warhammer." He waggled his eyebrows suggestively, and the Wizard understood. The Warhammer was too heavy for mortal lugmen to carry, and Arth only managed because the *Scepter* gave him strength. But he could hardly tell the lugs that. "They respect me, see?" Arth concluded. "But they *really* respect the Knight. While I was fightin' the Demagogue, one-on-one, she took out *loads* of lugs all by herself."

"Best fighter I ever know," one of the lugmen rumbled.

"We going tell stories 'bout Knight," another agreed. "Be big legend someday, you see."

The dagman King's lips quirked up in a small smile. "They was already building an extra special war tent for Morth usin' some of the fake animal skins and bones from those ancient monster exhibits they plundered on Hulandia. But now that Morth don't need the tent, they wanna turn it into a shrine to Karis instead—to honor her bravery and sacrifice and such. They already gots one of her swords. I fink the gear she and Noble used in their long partnership would round out the collection nicely."

"What about her armor?" Pyrsie wanted to know.

"The Diamond Plate-Armor?" Arth asked, then shook his head. "Disappeared right after she were smoked."

"Sovereign's Relics always return to their place of origin when their bearer falls," Hembrose explained absently. "Unless the person makes a point of transferring stewardship beforehand. Remember the Baron and the Diamond Crown?"

Arth nodded at the memory, but Pyrsie just shrugged.

"So that's it?" Hembrose asked. "The luggernauts' reign of terror is ended?" He continued to eye the big fellows nervously, though for the moment they seemed placid.

"O'ertwixt is safe from the lugs," Arth confirmed, "assumin' you lot completed yer part of the mission?" Hembrose and Pyrsie assured him that they had. There would be time to share all the details later. "Then I guess all that's left now is to fulfill the rest of the prophecy and usher in a Golden Age of O'ertwixt." Arth said the words lightly, but Hembrose could see that the new King felt an immense burden of responsibility. "All I gotta do is rule Caymerlot better than anyone else before, balancin' the needs of all my people while treating all *other* peoples fair-like, so no one ever feels the need to revolt or attack or even complain." The dagman took a deep breath. "Yeah, one story is ended... but I reckon we gots a much bigger story just startin' now."

"I think you are up to zee challenge," Pyrsie said, beaming. "And I imagine zat a certain special someone is eagerly awaiting you in Crystal City, ready to face zat challenge at your side."

Arth brightened at this, but Hembrose had to turn away, teeth clenched.

The two lugs returned with the Knight and Noble's gear, and Arth sent the whole group of them on their way back east. Then he shouldered Morth's Ruby Warhammer once more, still cradling his own Scepter in the crook of his other arm. It all looked rather silly, but Arth wasn't willing to leave the powerful green-magic relic behind. Following after Pyrsie, he began to tromp up the narrow spiral staircase toward Mazemount and Hulandia beyond.

Licking his lips, Hembrose stared jealously at the Warhammer as he brought up the rear.

Part IV
The Golden Age

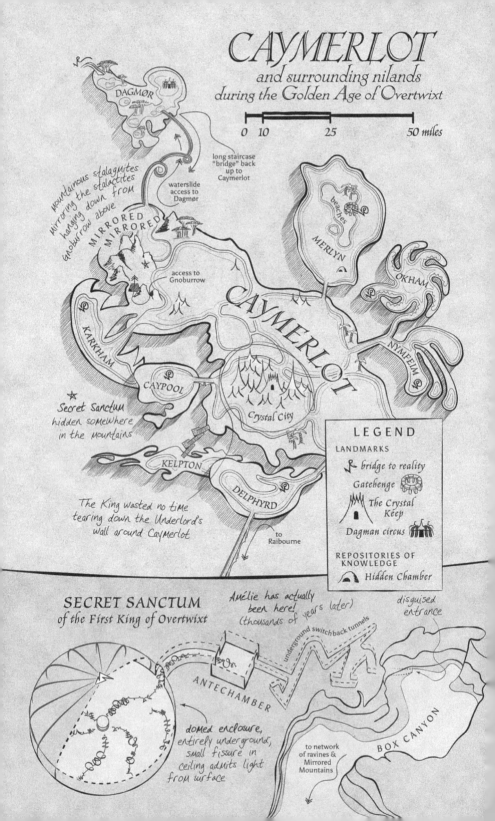

· aftermath ·

Pyrsie took time to show Arth the various features of the maze as they passed through (while Sidekick and Wizard bickered over whose contribution to the Final Battle was greater); but soon enough the four friends arrived at the level of Hulandia far above. They should have been huffing and puffing from the climb up so many levels, but everyone had sipped frequently from Pyrsie's Grail, so no one was winded.

At last the tunnels began to brighten from the rays of the local Sky Light, and they all hurried forward. They emerged from one of the many caves that dotted the slopes of Mazemount, pausing to enjoy the fresh air. Then Arth led them down the path and right to the very edge of the niland, where he leaned far enough over the abyss that it made Pyrsie nervous.

"Fallin' into all this whiteness 'tween nilands," he mused, "it's good as gettin' smoked. I hope it was less traumatter-like for Morth, but…" He sighed. "One way or the other, if you get tossed into that void, yer time in O'ertwixt is through."

Pyrsie and the others nodded sadly. There really wasn't anything else to say.

The King took a deep breath and then spoke firmly. "Well, if it works fer people, I reckon it works fer magicky trinkets too." And without further hesitation, he cast the Demagogue's mangled Ruby Warhammer into the abyss after its owner. It happened so suddenly that Hembrose cried out in surprise, but it was already too late to change Arth's mind. The King just shrugged, gave an innocent smile, and started trudging up the path toward the Branch Library.

Pop! Pop-pop-pop! A barrage of staccato sounds suddenly filled the air. *Pop-pop-pop-pop-pop*.

Suddenly there were dozens of lugmen milling around, having appeared out of thin air. Pyrsie and Sidekick gaped at the unexpected sight, even as Arth whirled and gave a similar reaction. Only Hembrose seemed to understand, his expression turning to horrified comprehension.

"It's all the lugmen Morth harvested," the mermage whispered. "On his rampage. The ones whose strength and skills he stored in that ruby... which Arth just destroyed."

"Well isn't that unprecedented," Sidekick finally said. "Why do they seem so disoriented?"

"I don't know," Hembrose admitted. For sure enough, some of the lugmen wandered aimlessly, confused, while others clutched their heads or bent over, getting sick. Uncharacteristically, not a single towering luggernaut showed any signs of aggression.

As his three friends continued to stare, Arth began moving among the lugs, patting shoulders and speaking quiet reassurance. Then he took one man by the hand and led them all back toward Mazemount. Heart in her throat, Pyrsie hurried to catch up, knowing they would need her guidance to find the correct way to Lugarth.

By the time all those freed luggernauts were back on their own niland again, and the squad mates had returned to Hulandia once more, hours had passed. The Sky Light had turned to night.

Pyrsie and her friends took lodging that evening at the Branch Library—where she found that the Bailiff, Excavator, and other gnomen had also been staying since leaving the maze. The last time Pyrsie had been at the Branch Library, it was with all seven members of the original Squad. Now, glancing sidelong at Arth, Hembrose, and Sidekick as the Poet led them on a tour of his newest exhibits, she tried not to think about the faces that were missing: the Knight, the Noble, and even the Paladin, who probably hadn't survived the battle either.

The following afternoon, the Library staff hosted a sumptuous feast for the remaining members of the Squad—and the gnomen too—grateful that they would never again suffer a lugman raid. The bushy-bearded Poet was pained to hear of the Knight's sacrifice, having known Karis since her childhood in the human real world, but he wasn't especially surprised. "I always knew that one would accomplish great things in Overtwixt, even at the cost of her own future here."

"Aye, she was the best of us," Arth concurred.

"That said," the Poet added, moving on quickly. "I want to hear all the specifics of this artful new maze you've constructed." And so Pyrsie began relaying the story, shyly at first, but with increasing gusto as the head librarian proved himself genuinely interested. "This is the stuff legends are made of!" he said more than once, eventually declaring that he would commit the story (or something like it) to verse the next time he returned to his real world. "Huge half-man, half-bull creatures attacking innocents all across the countryside, ultimately defeated not by force of arms but by *ingenuity!*" he crooned. "My dear Inventor, you can be sure I will incorporate you and your maze, your... *labyrinth*, shall we call it... into this latest epic I am crafting. Mark my words, men and women will sing of your deeds for many ages to come, or my name's not Orfeo."

Pyrsie tried to point out the valor of her other squad mates—that Arth's battle against Morth was more dramatic, and that the brave sacrifices of the Knight and Noble were more heroic—but the Poet would hear nothing of it. "Tales of kings and heroes and sword fights are so cliché. Trust me, I will give Princess Karis of Troia her due. But what you accomplished with your wits is entirely original." And he proceeded to question Pyrsie about her previous escapades also, until she'd related every last detail of her escape from the Treasury on wax wings as well.

The day after that feast, the four squad members traveled with the gnomen to Centhule, where they informed the local government of the Noble's and Knight's fate. The centwoman Captienne introduced them to Centhule's brand-new Baron, who was *human*—the first to ever hold that position. Even though he was new in Overtwixt, having come straight to the Hillfort Castle after his interview with the Guide, he immediately announced a weeklong observance to celebrate the life and sacrifice of the Squad's centman and human members.

The Wizard and Sidekick were eager to return to Caymerlot, and Pyrsie could tell that Arth yearned to spend more time with Gwen. Even so, Arth and Pyrsie agreed that they should all stay to honor their fallen comrades. For Pyrsie, they'd been more than just allies. Noble had sacrificed himself in combat to protect her. And the Knight... Karis had been a personal hero, a mentor, a big sister to the gnomaid. Pyrsie needed to take this opportunity to grieve them both in a healthy way, rather than pretending their loss meant nothing to her. Yet even in her grief, she found comfort—for she knew this was not the end. Both of her friends lived on, having returned to the greater reality.

When the weeklong celebration ended, the Squad traveled yet again to Centwick, then down its elevator shaft to Gnoburrow. There they checked up on the Pilgrim—Alain d'Creux—and the new gnoman government he was forming. It was quickly apparent that the old adventurer really was a capable administrator. He'd already taken steps toward eliminating corruption, and the citizens of Denali showed more civic pride than Pyrsie remembered from when she lived here (her first year in Overtwixt). As protector of Gnoburrow, Arth had originally named the Pilgrim as interim ruler only, but now he made the appointment permanent—leading to cheers in the streets. And the citizens were even happier when they heard the luggernaut threat was now contained. The Pilgrim arranged yet another banquet, to honor the King certainly, but even more so to celebrate the contribution of the gnomen who constructed the maze.

Most of those craftsmen remained behind when the Squad departed later that week, but of course Pyrsie did not. True, with the Burrowcrat overthrown, she was once again welcome on her home niland, and she certainly had friends there. But the Squad was her family, and that made Caymerlot her real home.

So the Inventor traveled onward with the Wizard, Sidekick, and King, more eager than ever to see what the future would hold.

· absolute truth ·

Now just the four of them again, the last remaining members of the original Squad reminisced extensively on the road home. They told stories and laughed, and they shed tears over their lost loved ones. On passing through Raibourne, they ran into the Guide welcoming new arrivals from the raiman real world, and he joined them on the final leg of their journey to Caymerlot.

By this point, the Guide felt like an unofficial member of the Squad, so Hembrose was happy to have him along... until the centman looked the Wizard up and down and raised one eyebrow. That's when Hembrose remembered he was still wearing the shapeshifted body of a human, weeks after leaving Mazemount—despite promising himself he wouldn't use the green magic for much or for long. Unfortunately, he'd left his wheeled chair in that same mountain, so he didn't have any other option at this point.

"... and I said, 'You tell 'em, hoss! Show them lugs who's boss!" Sidekick concluded yet another story with a laugh.

"Paladin never did show much fear of them lugmen, did he?" Arth recollected fondly.

"No, zat he did not," Pyrsie said with sadness. "For good or ill, he was fearless."

"Well, *I* for one was almost always afraid," Hembrose found himself saying with a nervous chuckle. "I've never admitted this to anyone, but... did you know I actually hid in the Backwater for the first twenty minutes of the Battle at Bronze City?" Surprisingly, it felt good to say this out loud.

"Weren't many who didn't," Arth assured him.

To the Wizard's surprise, not even the Sidekick mocked him. "You weren't unwise to hide," the kelpie said. "Anyone who did otherwise was crazy, bona fide!"

"Zee luggernauts truly were terrifying," Pyrsie agreed. "And there were so many of zem! Is it just me, or are there more lugmen in Overtwixt than any other race?"

"It sure do seem so," Arth said.

"Do you ever wonder..." the girl began tentatively. "How is it zat such a small Squad of Heroes proved so effective against zat huge barbarian horde?" She bit her lip before continuing. "Especially in zee beginning, at Bronze City, when we were so unprepared. Or later at zee Branch Library, when we were even more outnumbered. We should have been crushed!"

Sidekick clearly took offense at the question. "Because we're heroes, not a bunch of weirdos! Armed with bravery and magic, we stopped those beasts from doing more that was tragic."

"I think sheer pluck and bravery probably *was* part of it," Hembrose agreed, thoughtfully stroking his long black beard.

"Don't forget loyalty to each other, and the fact that our cause was just," Arth pointed out. "We was defendin' the innocent, we was. There's power in that."

"Indeed there is," the Guide said, nodding. "A kind of power that Sovereign's Relics were designed to multiply. Still, there were other magical truths at play as well."

"There were?" Hembrose blurted, surprised. He met the Guide's eye and immediately looked away again.

"Indeed. Tell me, O Wizard, how goes your quest to uncover the absolute truths lost to history?"

During the journey home, Hembrose had resumed wearing a magnificent mantle that he conjured magically, much as he had done in the days before his unfortunate return to the real world robbed him of so much power. Unlike that mantle, which was gold, this new one was the color of the sea—neither green nor blue, but something in between. At the Guide's question, the Wizard reached into one of the mantle's voluminous pockets and pulled out a leather notebook. "I uncovered many lost truths in the libraries of the realm, but those truths are sometimes at odds with one another."

"Truth is never at odds with truth," the Guide said mildly. "Have you uncovered any truths about the balance of power in Overtwixt?"

Hembrose barked a short laugh. "I've discovered that every race thinks itself greater or wiser or more important than the other races. Obviously they can't all be right."

"Are *any* of them right?" the centman asked coyly. "If you had to guess, which race would you say stands preeminent in Overtwixt?"

The Wizard shrugged. "Honestly, it's probably true that *no* one race is greater than any other."

The Guide's eyes sparkled. "Congratulations. You have deduced the Second Fundamental Law of Overtwixt, one of the long-lost truths I asked you to uncover."

Hembrose gaped at him. "I have?"

"And that particular absolute truth also provides the answer to Pyrsyfal's question," the Guide went on. "When Sovereign created Overtwixt, he allocated every race an equal amount of power here. There were many reasons for this, for the Sovereign's purposes are always manifold. But one reason is this: it prevents any race of people from conquering another race simply through strength of numbers."

Arth abruptly stopped walking. "Oy, you mean to say..." He thought about it for a moment. "Ya mean if you double the number of lugs in O'ertwixt, each one is half as powerful as he was before their population increased?"

The Guide nodded.

"Even *my* race held equal power wiz their race?" Pyrsie asked incredulously. "You're saying zat even I, a gnomaid, was powerful enough to face a lugman, one-on-one."

"On the contrary," the Guide corrected her. "Seeing as there were roughly five times more lugmen than gnomen in Overtwixt at the start of this conflict, you could have faced down *five* lugmen all at once."

Pyrsie covered her mouth in shock.

"And that's not even counting our Relics and their extra power," Sidekick put in, pretending like he had understood this shocking truth all along, which obviously he had not. "That's why the lugmen we did scour!"

"Oy. Oy!" Arth repeated. "Sure and certain, this woulda been nice to know *before* the campaign!"

The Guide's eyes remained steady on Hembrose. "I agree," he said levelly. "That is why I tasked the Wizard with uncovering these truths, to aid you all in your fight."

"But if zis is true," Pyrsie pressed, "how did zee luggernauts cause so much destruction? If they were so weak, how did they conquer and enslave so many people?"

"Fear," Hembrose mumbled, as he finally began to understand. "Because the lugs were big and violent and there were so many of them, everyone else was paralyzed with fear—and *that* granted the luggernauts the power to do what they wanted."

"All except for the Squad, who refused to be intimidated," Pyrsie said, comprehension spreading across her face now too. "We were afraid—except Paladin, maybe—but we stood up to zee lugs anyway. We negated their power when we fought back."

"You mean when the *King* inspired us to fight back," Sidekick pointed out. "Something he managed because of his leadership knack."

"So, considerin' how this Second Fundamental Law of yers works," Arth said to the Guide, his brow furrowing. "Suddenly the terms of that blasted Treaty don't seem so favorful no more." At Pyrsie's questioning look, he explained. "By signed Treaty with one of the previous Underlords, us dagsters is always required to have 'zactly two hunnerd and eleven of ourselfs in O'ertwixt at all times.* I used to fink that was an honor, havin' so many more dagmen in O'ertwixt than the mermen allow of their own people. We was told it was 'cause Caymerlot treasures the entertainment we provide. Now I realize it was meant to keep us down, keep us weak. I guess Morth was a little right after all." He shook his head ruefully. "Still and all, I don't get why?"

---

* The terms of that Treaty required the dagmen to maintain eleven "brigades" in Overtwixt: three circuses, four carnivals, and four drama troupes. With nineteen members in each, plus the Portmistress and her assistant, there were 211 dagmen in Overtwixt at all times. A *lot* more people than any other race except the lugmen.

By the by, don't ask me why we never hear about these other dagman brigades. Maybe they traveled outside this realm during the conflict with the lugmen. —*N*

"You already know the answer to that," the Guide said.

"Because one of the old Underlords knew, or at least suspected, that the King was meant to be a dagman," Hembrose said promptly. "And he thought he could prevent it from happening with this Treaty, same as he and his successors intentionally corrupted the prophecy, making us think it was about a mere Hero instead of a true King."

"We see how well zat worked out!" Pyrsie chortled.

"Even so," Arth sighed, "them Underlords bodged up a whole lot which I gotta now fix." But he wasn't complaining. In fact, there was an excited light in his eye now. "Abolishin' this silly Treaty seems a good enuff place to start as any!"

The friends traveled the rest of the way to Delphyrd and then to Caymerlot with growing excitement, for Arth was eager to right more wrongs. If there'd ever been any doubt in Hembrose's mind, it had long since disappeared. Arth truly was the right man for this job. He was faithful, he was humble—rare in any person, much less a ruler!—and he yearned for justice.

That didn't mean Hembrose wasn't still jealous, a little.

As the Squad came within sight of the southwest gate into Crystal City, the watchman on duty there spotted them and raised an excited cry. Soon, countless other voices joined in his jubilation. The gate was already open—why shouldn't it be, when there was nothing left to be feared?—and Hembrose could see into the city. There, hundreds of people already gathered at the water's edge to greet their King.

And waiting at the forefront was their Queen, tears of relief and joy streaming down her cheeks.

Something inside Hembrose clenched painfully.

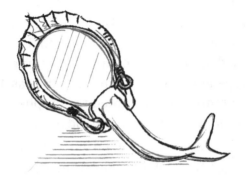

· happy ever after ·

In the months following the Final Battle, Caymerlot finally began to heal—not only from the physical destruction caused by the luggernauts, but also from the ragged gouges left in the fabric of society. The Demagogue had exposed and widened those gashes, to be sure, but he wasn't the root cause. Quiet prejudice had always existed among the aquatic races, giving the Underlords of old ample opportunity to perpetuate injustice with their Treaty. Now that the King was in charge, seeking the advice of the Guide and following the wisdom of Sovereign's Diamond Scepter every day, society's wounds finally began to stitch back together again—even as the Inventor worked with teams of craftsmen to rebuild Caymerlot's demolished buildings. In fact, even *her* efforts helped heal old animosities, for she carefully blended the work crews of many different races, proving to everyone that everyone else had something valuable to offer society too.

Gwen had some healing to do too, now that her father was gone. For even the best parents fail their children in numerous ways, leaving wounds that might fester if left untreated—and Gwen's father was far from the best parent. But over the course of many conversations with the Guide, Gwen was able to remember her father's love and good qualities with gratitude, while forgiving him his many failures. She even helped her brothers Alber and Ander do the same, though she worried for Ander, given his sour disposition. The Antagonist would have to make a concerted effort to keep forgiving in the years to come, or else bitterness would eventually overtake him.

And then there was Arthos Penn, the new King.

Not surprisingly, Arth knew how easy it is to be injured by those you love the most. If anything, he understood even better than Gwen, for he'd been actively betrayed by his brother. Nevertheless, the young King was eager to forgive. Gwen enjoyed many more conversations with Arth as they reflected on the good times they'd enjoyed with Papá and Morth respectively, and to some degree, they healed together. It helped knowing that they would see Papá and Morth again someday, though not anytime soon. After all, this was destined to be an entire Golden *Age* during which they ruled Caymerlot together.

Gwen and Arth went on many dates, enjoying every moment of their courtship, not rushing these precious early days in which they grew acquainted. They learned everything there was to know about each other (or so they thought), the good and the bad: their motivations, preferences, pet peeves, and secrets, as well as both the similarities and differences between them. At last they were married in one of the grandest ceremonies Overtwixt had ever seen—after which they were surprised to discover they were *still* getting to know each other. They fell more in love with each passing year, as marriage was meant to be, and they knew great joy. And through all of that time, they ruled Caymerlot together with peace and justice, as King and Queen.

Arth's father, the great Ringmaster Pythagoras Penn, stayed in Overtwixt long enough to celebrate the wedding, by which time even Gwen had started thinking of him as "Daddie." Then he finally made arrangements to return home to his wife and other two children in Lundunium. As he put it, Arth had things well in hand, but Morth—long back in the dagman real world by now—was gonna need some tough love. "Don't worry, that lad'll be grounded when I get home, if I gots anyfing to say about it!"

By contrast, Daddie's brother Roberthoras chose to remain in Caymerlot. Being unmarried himself, and serving in the role of Bodyguard (not just Arth's but Gwen's now too), he felt his place was still at the King and Queen's side. But considering his year in Overtwixt had long since ended, he eventually ran afoul of the Portmistress, who was committed to upholding the Treaty so long as it remained in effect. She tried repeatedly (and with great creativity) to arrest and return Uncle Bertie to the real world, until Arth finally and officially abolished the Treaty and its unfair restrictions. Then the tables turned, and it was Bertie who began chasing the Portmistress, claiming, "Oy, Fair Paloma, it's *you* who's gone and stole *meh* heart." To everyone's surprise, after a great deal of patient wooing on Bertie's part, the formidable woman soon returned his affections. After that, there was never any question of the two remaining in Overtwixt long into their olden years.

Once the Treaty was no more, *any* person of any aquatic race was finally free to come and go as he or she wished, and more dagmen flooded into Overtwixt than ever before. Though it was impossible for Morth to visit, having already squandered the one life he'd been granted here, Pythagoras eventually returned with Arth's mum Ythyl and little sister Ethlynn (who had grown considerably from the dagling child Arth remembered). Despite having heard Daddie's tales of the Squad's exploits, the two dagwomen were astounded to see for themselves the power that Arth wielded here—and beamed with pride at how deftly (and humbly) he did so. More than that, they were overwhelmed with joy to finally meet Arth's beloved Gwen. Together with Alber and Ander, as well as Pyrsie (who would always be Arth and Gwen's sister), the extended family enjoyed a lengthy private vacation at a spa in Nymfeim. The four women got along especially well, pairing off for various activities and forming beautiful memories that would endure long after Pythagoras, Ythyl, and Ethlynn returned to Lundunium for the last time. Gwen and Pyrsie actually cried when they waved goodbye.

With all the extra traffic across the old Dagmør truss bridge, the rickety metal finally began to give way. Arth's gnoman allies disassembled it before anyone could be harmed; and in its place, they constructed the longest, most elaborate twisty-turny water slide ever created. The new "bridge" was based on a design envisioned by Arth himself, but made practical by Pyrsie. Overnight, Dagmør became one of the hottest destinations in Overtwixt, simply because so many people of all races enjoyed the thrill of racing down that terrifying chute (which only *seemed* dangerous due to the proximity of empty nothingness on both sides, but was quite safe thanks to advanced gnoman engineering). And on reaching the bottom, travelers had no choice but to take rooms or meals at one of the new inns opening up on Dagmør, to regain their equilibrium before starting the long hike up the twisty-turny stairway back to Caymerlot.

Ruling a utopia wasn't all fun and games, however. In the early days after the Final Battle, even before reconstruction could begin, Gwen and Arth were shocked to learn that the luggernauts had *not* been cast from Caymerlot entirely. Instead of being smoked or pushed back to Lugarth, more than a few lugs had been knocked unconscious during the fighting, only awakening after Morth's bridge toppled. Fortunately, there weren't enough displaced lugmen to cause real danger, but Arth was eager to resolve the situation before new misunderstandings could occur. When given the option, most of the lugs chose exile on their own niland. They were eventually escorted to Hulandia and down through the maze to Lugarth—blindfolded all the way—by a mixed-species detachment of soldiers led by Alexandre the Bailiff.

The diminutive Bailiff was an ideal choice for this mission. Having been the one to engrave the signpost glowplates at each confusing intersection throughout the maze, he still had the safe path memorized. There was no need to send a map on this first expedition back to Lugarth, and thus no risk of said map falling into the hands of the lugmen. They would remain safely isolated.

At that point, it had been almost a year since the Demagogue's defeat. On reaching Lugarth, the Bailiff was surprised to encounter Paladin still alive and kicking. Having been trapped on the lugman niland just as effectively as the lugmen themselves, the big red eqman had long since gone native; for he loved the thrill of combat just as much as his old enemies. The Bailiff later reported that when he first laid eyes on Paladin, the eqman was shoulder-deep in one of the skirmishes the lugmen constantly waged amongst themselves, fighting for no better reason than the fun of it. Even so, he joyfully accepted the Bailiff's offer of escape. Yet his mood turned foul on passing through the elaborate maze for the first time, and he was overheard muttering curses against the gnomen every step of the way.

When they stepped out onto Hulandia, Paladin galloped away without a word of thanks, and no member of the Squad ever saw him again. In fact, the entire race of eqmen became increasingly isolationist in the years that followed, showing no interest in diplomatic relations with

Caymerlot so long as it retained Gnoburrow as a protectorate. The last anyone heard, Paladin had dedicated his remaining time in Overtwixt to finding the Horn of Destiny. Though he acknowledged Arth as King, he had come to believe that the prophesied Hero was someone else still to be revealed—probably himself, once he found the Diamond Horn.

Gwen had never gotten to know Paladin, but she saw how his distance pained both Arth and Pyrsie, so it pained her too. Terribly.

Surprisingly, the Ransacker—whom Arth had knocked out personally during the Final Battle—was not one of the lugmen who returned to Lugarth. He chose to remain behind in Caymerlot. Over the course of many interactions through the years, Arth actually came to think of him as a trusted friend, though the big man always made Gwen slightly uncomfortable. He became one of Arth's favorite partners for sparring, during which the two would trade witty but lighthearted gibes. The King never let the lugman forget how he'd fallen for the Squad's Troian mool deception; to which Ransacker would always retort that Arth needed help from a buddy just to fight a "one-on-one" duel. And the truth was, Arth *did* usually invite Sidekick to their sparring sessions, because his skills really were no match for the lugman's. Not unless he "cheated" and used the Scepter.

One day Ransacker confessed that the role he'd originally chosen from the Guide was that of Researcher. Of course, this surprised almost everyone in the Squad, for who could have guessed there were lugmen who cared about knowledge and learning? Nevertheless, the Researcher had decided to return to his first calling; and from that point on, he also acted as a sort of ambassador between Lugarth and Caymerlot, occasionally carrying messages back and forth between the two societies. Still, Arth's trust in the

Researcher didn't extend to sharing the map of the maze, and so the lugman was always accompanied by the Bailiff.

In fact, even by the time Arth was old, the lugmen as a whole had failed to change their warlike ways—not enough to be allowed back into the outside world, at least. Arth did, however, ask Pyrsie to make duplicates of her original map, which he then distributed to several of the libraries in the realm. Even doing that much was a risk, but he didn't want to risk the alternative either. After all, if the only copy of the map was destroyed someday (accidentally or otherwise!), the lugmen would be *forever* isolated without hope of escape. It might be many more ages, but he knew the time *would* someday come when the lugman people could be granted a second chance at interacting with the rest of Overtwixt.

As the King's diplomacy continued to strengthen relations with other peoples and nilands (aside from Eqland), the geography of Caymerlot the niland grew as well. Soon there were more thickets in the west, and of different types of trees native to other real worlds. Then hills swelled beneath those thickets, and eventually true mountains began thrusting high into the sky. Even after the King's official protection of Gnoburrow ended, the aquatics and gnomen enjoyed close diplomatic ties, and their nilands drew *physically* nearer as a result. The tallest of the new Caymerlotion mountains began growing up to meet the longest of the upside-down spires that hung from Gnoburrow's underside, like stalagmites and stalactites on a monumental scale. They formed what ultimately became known as the Mirrored Mountains—until one day, a mountain and spire actually joined to create a single, solid column. In the years that followed *that* miraculous marriage, Pyrsie the Inventor was instrumental in building a second great elevator within that column (like the one that already existed between Gnoburrow and Centwick), to directly link Gnoburrow with Caymerlot.

Even as the world of bridges continued to change throughout the Golden Age of Overtwixt, the Squad of Heroes went on many more adventures together—though none *quite* so exciting as the one that brought them together in the first place. Although Gwen seldom left Crystal City, she was unanimously accepted as an honorary member. She was sure her marriage to Arth played a small part in this, but she liked to think it had more to do with her wise counsel. (After all, she still carried the Diamond Looking Glass at all times, allowing her to examine her own motives before rendering her opinion on important questions.) For that matter, Arth himself might as well have been an honorary squad member, since affairs of state prevented him from participating in adventures as much as before. He eventually named the Sergeant-at-arms his official second-in-command, since the Squad had already *unofficially* been relying on Sarge for everyday leadership.

Other members of the Squad came and went, of course. Gwen's brother Ander eventually left seeking bluer waters, and a nym woman called the Jouster was his natural replacement. The little Bailiff soon joined at Arth's invitation, in some ways filling the void left by the Knight. And after that came Freddie the Contortionist—whom the Guide gave the choice of changing role to Raconteur.

To Gwen's constant amusement, the Sidekick remained with Arth to the end of his days, though he talked constantly (in rhyme, of course) about retiring to the Backwater on Centhule once more. But Arth took it hard anytime one of the others left the Squad. Not that he felt betrayed or any such thing; rather, he hated saying goodbye. Still, he got through each departure with Gwen's help, for he knew that change was unavoidable, and often a healthy part of life.

Anytime the Squad's membership dropped below ten, they began actively recruiting new heroes to join their ranks. Personally, Arth preferred it when they numbered exactly thirteen: a good, round dagman number. But no matter how the makeup of the Squad changed, they continued to meet regularly for meals or meetings around the unique and exotic Round Table that Pyrsie had fashioned so long ago.

Through everything, the Squad stayed true to its original purpose: helping those who couldn't help themselves. And the Squad's members, old and new, also fulfilled the charge Arth had given them that first time they gathered around the Round Table: to treat the King as a normal man, so that he never grew proud or self-important.

All in all, it was a Golden Age indeed, not only for the common people, but for their leaders. And Gwen and Arth and the Squad lived happy ever after.

Until at long last, one of Arth's two closest friends in Overtwixt finally broke ties.

· first and last quest ·

Arth's relationship with Hembrose grew increasingly strained as the decades passed. Part of it was the hurt Hembrose continued to feel, forced to watch Arth fall more and more in love with the woman of Hembrose's own dreams—but only part. No matter how hard he tried, the Wizard could never resist the lure of the green magic for long.

As newer and younger squad members joined over the years, some of them with Diamond Relics of their own, Hembrose was increasingly surrounded by people he resented. One day, he gathered the Squad and excitedly showed them the so-called "Diamond Amulet" he had just recovered, one of Sovereign's Relics he could finally call his own. Everyone was suspicious, of course. Never mind that all four of the merman Relics were already known. Though his new necklace talisman exhibited *some* of the properties of a Diamond Relic, it was only a pale imitation of Sovereign's craftsmanship. The King himself quickly discerned (through the wisdom of his own true Diamond Scepter) that the

Wizard's Amulet was fashioned of *Quartz*, not Diamond—a relic of the green magic.

By now, of course, Arth understood the true nature of the green magic. He pointed out that Hembrose was being foolish, "dabbling" in the evil of the green once again and expecting that somehow this time—unlike all the other times—he wouldn't succumb to it completely: "Honestly, mate. How could you of all people ferget? The green magic deceives completely, then it destroys completely."

Hembrose had exploded in anger. "It's you that's still the Fool, Arthos Penn! You think everything is blue or green, good or bad, with nothing in between? That's simplistic and narrow minded."

"You's the one as explained that to me, boyo! Blue is the Sovereign's magic and green is his Adversary's magic."

"Well, now there's a third kind," Hembrose declared with satisfaction. "The *teal* magic, the best of both worlds— the *Wizard's* magic."

Arth was taken aback by his old friend's hubris. Sure, he was powerful for a mortal... but to think he by himself was on the level of Sovereign's Adversary, much less the Sovereign himself? "Oy, mate, you's deceivin' yerself."

What Hembrose could not admit, but which was patently obvious to Arth, was that this "teal" was no different from the green in any meaningful way. After all, it was Hembrose himself who had once told Arth that the blue and the green were diametrically opposed. It was simply impossible to blend or use them simultaneously.

Still, despite the words that were spoken that day, the two men somehow remained on speaking terms—but only because Arth held his tongue from that point on.

When both men had grown old and stooped, and their skin was mottled (with gray hair sprouting from Arth's ears in tufts), the King learned that the Wizard had locked himself away in the Hidden Chamber of Merlyn once more. He knew what this heralded. So with heavy heart, he dispatched Sarge and the Queen's brother Altruist to bring the Wizard back. The squad members were too late, however, only catching up to Hembrose outside Gatehenge.

Hembrose O'Hildirun had made another brief return to his real world, and was now embarked on his *third* incarnation in the world of bridges. Yet again, he had made himself young in hopes that *this* time, all his dreams would finally come true.

There was nothing wrong with coming and going from Overtwixt, of course, being a citizen of two worlds. But Hembrose continued to abuse that privilege, using it in a way never intended—to play at living multiple mortal lifetimes, as if the single life granted each man or woman was not enough.

This was exactly the sort of magical abuse Arth, as King, was tasked with preventing. Until now, he had turned a blind eye to the Wizard's misconduct, which in turn created tension between the King and the Guide. No more. He ordered the young-again Wizard brought to a private audience with the King, the Queen, and the Guide.

But *not* in the throne room. Rather, in Gwen's favorite reading alcove.

It was now Arth's fifth decade in Overtwixt, which made it Gwen's *sixth* decade (she was still fastidious about tracking time in her diaries). But despite all the years that had passed, the alcove appeared much the same as it had in Gwen's youth: stacks of scrolls on shelves with a podium at the center of the small room, lit directly by the Sky Light itself as it shone down through the vaulted ceiling above.

"You's chasin' all the wrong things," Arth told his oldest friend quietly. "Lookin' for happiness where none can be found."

Hembrose sneered, the expression twisting the now-smooth skin of his face in an ugly way. "Says you." He glanced around the alcove with hurt and anger. "Why did you bring me *here*, of all places?"

"Because this is a place of truth," Gwen said simply.

Hembrose met her eye only briefly before turning away. For all the Wizard's many faults, Arth admired this about him: his love for the Queen remained undiminished despite her advanced age, even though the Wizard himself was now young again.

Arth cleared his throat. "We don't bring ya here to hurt you, but to help you. As the Guide hisself likes to say, yeh'll find no greater satisfaction in life than when yer being who you was meant to be, doing what you was meant to do."

The Guide nodded agreement but didn't speak. Arth was amazed he could even stay in this underwater room for so long. Unlike any other centman Arth had known, the Guide was capable of speaking and holding his breath for hours underwater, same as an aquatic.

The King turned back to the Wizard and peered deeply into his young friend's eyes. "Hembrose, mate. We's here to help ya fulfill yer quest at last. You's already found one of them absolute truths which been lost to history: the Second Fundamental Law, right? Now we gotta find the other four."

Scowling, Hembrose turned to the Guide. "The whole point of that quest was to help in 'overcoming the evil soon to come.' I remember your words exactly. But the lugman threat has already been overcome, as has the Demagogue. This quest is now pointless."

The Guide finally spoke. "Finding truth is never pointless. And those were not the only evils soon to come. A much greater evil looms on the horizon."

The Wizard took a moment to digest that information, then turned and eyed the Queen briefly. "Why here? What makes this alcove a place of truth?"

The Guide fielded this question too. "You of all people know there's a lot of information out there. Enough to drown in. Much of it is valuable, but much of it is also contradictory, even flat-out wrong." The centman glanced around at the bookshelves fondly. "Only the truest, most important, most *accurate* ancient accounts are kept in this small room. Copies of all these tomes exist in the Hidden Chamber as well, of course, along with every other word ever penned by a merman. But this alcove was set aside ages ago for a special purpose, as an altar to wisdom and not merely knowledge."

"That way," Gwen spoke up, "the Underlords would always have easy access to truth." She looked sad. "But none of them ever made use of it. In the days of my father's rule, only I ever came here. These days, Arth does too... and we're inviting you to join us."

Hembrose's face softened. He fingered the Quartz Amulet at his neck, obviously conflicted, but then he nodded. "Very well, let us complete my quest." Arth would have preferred the Wizard remove the Amulet completely, freeing himself from its influence, but he'd take what he could get. That had to be the man's own choice, after all.

And so Arth and Gwen and the Guide helped Hembrose complete his original quest. Really, it was Gwen who did most of the work, for she knew the contents of the alcove like no one else—not just where to find which volume, but how their contents were organized. More than a few of the books were translations of tomes from the *First* Age of Overtwixt, beautifully illuminated and inscribed with direct quotations from Sovereign himself in purple ink. These, the friends focused on almost exclusively.

And slowly but surely, they puzzled out the absolute truths of the world of bridges: the Five Fundamental Laws of Overtwixt.

Each time they went astray, the Guide would calmly redirect their efforts. And each time they began circling in on a new truth, he would encourage them to continue. Sometimes, the Guide would leave the room for a time to fulfill his other duties, and Gwen would look to her Diamond Looking Glass for clarity. Amazingly, for all the misinformation and misunderstandings about truth out in the world, the Guide and this artifact of Sovereign never contradicted each other.

The Guide could have just *given* the friends the information they were looking for, of course. It would have taken mere moments. But he seemed to think the search for truth was as important as finding the truth. By steadfastly questing after truth for themselves, instead of having it handed to them, the seekers proved it really was truth they desired.

Days passed, but it felt like mere hours. And in the end, Hembrose inscribed the Five Fundamental Laws on a fresh leaf of plapyr in his flowing handwriting. Then he stepped back and examined them with a critical eye.

None of the five axioms were new to the Wizard, of course. He had found all of them in other libraries before, mixed in with all the rest of the maxims, tenets, and teachings. But now, for the first time, he'd allowed someone else to help sift the absolute from the conditional and the truth from the falsehoods. "My quest is finally complete," he whispered.

"And how do ya feel?" Arth asked earnestly.

A smile flickered at the corners of Hembrose's mouth, but at the same time, he fingered his Quartz Amulet again. Still he seemed conflicted.

Reverently, Gwen raised the sheet of plapyr and placed it against the wall, as if she would mount it there. Then she stopped, laughing at herself. "What am I doing? These truths are not only for our benefit. We need to publish these far and wide, disseminating this information throughout all of Overtwixt, so that absolute truth can never be lost again."

Arth nodded eagerly. "This were the Wizard's quest, but it was fer the benefit of all people. Oy, if ya fink about it, findin' and applying these truths is sumfing *everyone* needs to do. Living as if every life is unique and precious..."

"Realizing no person or race is greater than any other," Gwen agreed.

"Learnin' from the past and workin' toward a better future," Arth went on, tracing his finger across the third law.

"Choosing a worthy master," the Guide intoned.

"The Sovereign, of course!" Gwen grinned. "Then recognizing that we only have one life to live, so we must live it well..."

The Five Fundamental Laws of Overtwixt

Every Life is Unique and Precious

No one Race is Greater than any other

Time marches Forward independent of constraint

All must Choose one Master

Once only may any man Live, and after, to know Reality

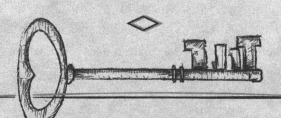

Arth spoke solemnly. "These truths, collectively, represent the first and last quest of our entire life."

But Hembrose, now clutching his Amulet like a lifeline, shook his head. "No, no, I can't accept that. I *won't*."

"Boyo, you gotta," Arth insisted. "You was here with us this whole time. Our scholarship was impleccable, you saw to that. These are the fundamental truths of the Sovereign, as he laid down in the First Age!"

"Then the Sovereign is a liar."

All the water in the small room seemed to turn to ice in an instant.

"Look, Arth," Hembrose said, stabbing his finger at the plapyr. "I myself have defied *two* of these so-called laws—the third *and* the fifth."

"Only if you's extra-creative in yer interpretation," Arth shot back angrily. He was about to say more, but the Guide interjected himself into the dispute with calm words.

"My dear Hembrose," he said with tears in his eyes. "For as many times as you have 'reset' your age, you've never truly rewound time. You merely continue the same meager thread of existence." He shook his head. "And while I admit that the Fifth Fundamental Law *is* a mystery—even to me, to some degree—I can assure you that your mortal actions have never invalidated it. Only one person can abolish that Law, and that's the Sovereign himself."

"You three can believe that if you wish," Hembrose said rigidly. "But I reject these laws, *all* of them. I choose to believe my own version of the truth."

"Hembrose," Arth pleaded. "You can't reject these truths. They's *absolute*. That means they's true for everyone."

"Well, I don't believe in absolutes. Not anymore."

Something died within Arth. "Then I mourn fer you. That's a scary way to live."

And those were the last words the two friends ever spoke to one another. Turning, the Wizard swam from the room, and neither King nor Queen ever saw him again.

But Arth thought of him often in the years that followed, for what remained of his own time in Overtwixt. And Arth *did* mourn: the loss of the man Hembrose had once been, but even more, the great man he might have become. Not just the greatest mortal magicker Overtwixt had ever known. He could have become one of the greatest *people* to ever walk the nilands as well, a true hero.

If only Hembrose had chosen differently.

The Roster of the Squad of Heroes
in the Golden Age of Overtwixt

Role	Real Name	Race	Relic(s)*
			listed in order of recruitment (aside from Queen)
The King	Arthos Penn	dagman	Scepter of Sovereignty (dag), Throne of Judgment (mer), Crown of Compassion (hu), et. al.
The Queen *Honorary Member of Squad*	Gwen MerGrand	merwoman	Looking Glass of Clarity
~~L.7. The Wizard~~	~~Hembrose O'Halloran~~	~~noman~~	~~Quartz Amulet~~ ~~Emerald Enhancers (lost)~~
The Inventor	Pyrsyfal Rochelle	gnowoman	Grail of Goodwill
~~fell The Noble~~	~~Geniff Valorian~~	~~entman~~	~~none~~
~~L.7. The Paladin~~	~~Koelan Mathias~~	~~ogman~~	~~none~~
The Sidekick	Limerick van Gimmick	kefman	Aegis of Warding

fell	~~The Knight~~	~~Karis Priamos~~	~~huwoman~~ ~~Plate-Armor of Assurance~~
	The Bodyguard	Roberthoras Penn	dagman none
↙	~~The Ringmaster~~	~~Pythagoras Penn~~	~~bugman~~ ~~none~~
	The Altruist	Alber MerGrand	merman Hauberk of Exoneration
L.F.	~~The Antagonist~~	~~Amber MerGrand~~	~~merman~~ ~~Harpoon of Enforcement~~
	The Sergeant-at-arms	Drust Cornfeldt	karkman Truncheon of Truth
	The Bailiff	Alexandre Léandre	gnoman Lance of Sanction
	The Jouster	"Sharps" McGhee	nywoman Stirrups of Stability
	The Raconteur	Ælfred Bartolomew	dagman none
	The Researcher	Belaklav Krasnootin	bugman none
	The Charmer	Ilsa vander Spliink	okkwoman Wand of Asylum

fell = "smoked" in battle / L.F. = Left Fellowship / ↙ = embraced Reality (went home of own volition)

* Unless otherwise noted, all listed relics are Diamond Relics of Sovereign.

· end of the age ·

Ultimately, Arth's reign drew to a close—and with it, the Golden Age of Overtwixt. One day, when almost all of Arth's old friends had long since departed (and even Gwen had passed peacefully into yellow smoke from old age), the Guide arrived in the grand throne room of the Crystal Keep. "It is time," he said simply, taking Arth by the hand. And Arth rose to follow, Scepter clutched in his other hand as always.

Pyrsie was awaiting them in the hall, and the now-stately gnowoman embraced Arth warmly. "Zee time, it has come," she agreed. Unlike with Hembrose, Pyrsie and Arth had remained close over the years. He still thought of her as a sister, and she'd always been an encouragement to him, especially after Gwen passed out of this world. Just as it was now their turn to do.

Arth smiled in response. It *was* time. He was ready.

To his surprise, the Guide—who hadn't aged a day during Arth's entire sojourn in Overtwixt—pulled Arth and Pyrsie up onto his back to ride, for they had many miles ahead of them. Then the three of them cantered out of the Crystal

Keep and along the network of isthmus sidewalks through Crystal City, leaving the metropolis via the fairgrounds (where the northwest gate used to stand, though the walls around Crystal City had been torn down long ago). From there, they trekked into the Mirrored Mountains in the western reaches of Caymerlot, the new mountain range that continued to grow with each passing year.

Arth and Pyrsie talked as they traveled, dear friends reminiscing and re-telling old jokes, often finishing each other's sentences. But when the Guide entered a network of narrow ravines, Arth felt a kind of hush fall over his soul; he dismounted, helping Pyrsie down as well. The King peered around in keen interest as the centman led them down one turn after another, until they came to the dead end of a long box canyon. Then, to Arth's shock, the Guide disappeared through the side wall of the ravine.

Pyrsie just grinned and pulled Arth along after the centman, down a narrow corridor whose entrance was cleverly hidden. Yet again, they turned one corner after another, ultimately reaching a small room—all of it impossible to find unless you knew to look. "Zis is my final gift to you, Arth," Pyrsie said impishly, clearly excited to be revealing a secret. "Sorry, *our* final gift," she corrected herself with a glance at the Guide. "We have been working on zis place in secret for many years now."

The Guide gestured, and long lines of writing began to glow from where they'd been chiseled into the walls in unbroken lines of cursive. By now, Arth knew this script, for Hembrose had taught him to read and write Epitopian long ago. Fingers tracing the blue-glowing letters, Arth read the words aloud: "Every Life is Unique and Precious." The same phrase repeated over and over again as he followed the engraving down another hall, through an arch, and into the room beyond: "Every Life is Unique and Precious. Every Life is Unique and Precious." The First Fundamental Law, which he, Gwen, Hembrose, and the Guide had rediscovered.

Entering the room beyond, Arth gawped in awe, for it was covered floor-to-ceiling in blue mosaic tiles that glowed as well. The unbroken line of engraved text flowed along the walls and floor, turning to gold as it cut through the tiles, until it met four other lines of text—the other four Fundamental Laws—in a sort of sunburst pattern at the center of the room. Standing there was an empty pedestal.

"Do you like it?" Pyrsie asked. "We call it zee Secret Sanctum." She pointed around the perimeter of the room, indicating small alcoves that held keepsakes from Arth's time in Overtwixt: the quarterstaff Karis had first trained him to wield; the woven saddle he and Sidekick always used when riding; the intentionally misleading map of Crystal City, which Hembrose had drawn for Arth and Morth on the day they first tried seeing the Relic-in-the-Rock. In one place was a single glass table leg, left over from when Pyrsie reforged the Underlord's feast table into the Squad's round table. Another alcove held nothing but Gwen's braided wedding band, to which Arth now added his own ring, knowing he wouldn't be able to take it back to his real world.

There was even a long shelf that held the three hats Arth had worn during his adventures in Overtwixt: the Fool's cap with bells sewn at the ends of its floppy tails; the armored helmet he'd donned as Squadleader; and even the crested crown that sat atop his brow during his early days as King.

Pyrsie grinned as Arth circled the room, overcome with nostalgia. Both of them had tears in their eyes.

"It is time," the Guide repeated once more, placing a hand on the pedestal at the middle of the room. "Time to lay down the burden you have born these many years."

Knowing exactly what the Guide meant, Arth stepped forward and held out the Diamond Scepter... but then he hesitated. Ruling Caymerlot *had* been a burden, made bearable only by the peace and wisdom that this Relic provided. He would not miss the responsibility, but he *would* miss this feeling of tangible connection with the Sovereign.

"Trust me," the Guide said softly, and Arth let go, releasing the Scepter to rest upon its new pedestal.

The room suddenly thrummed, the blue glow pulsing all around him with even greater vibrancy than before. And more importantly, Arth felt the power of the blue magic pulse within him as well—the power to be humble and wise, to protect and defend those in need without fear for his own wellbeing. "The peace of the Sovereign will be with you always," the Guide promised him, putting into words what Arth already realized was true.

The old dagman felt the breath rush out of him in relief.

Then the Guide waved one hand casually, and liquid gold appeared from nowhere, climbing up the length of the Diamond shaft—muting its brilliant blue glow. Within moments, the entire smooth length was encased in an ornate golden scabbard, matching the pure-gold basket that already encased the Diamond sphere at its head.

"What's that all about?" Arth asked.

"As you know, only the prophesied King may wield the Diamond Scepter of Sovereignty," the Guide explained. Indeed, Arth still recalled vividly the thrill that went through him when he and he alone proved capable of pulling free the Relic-in-the-Rock. "But rather than immobilize his Great Relic in solid stone once more, the Sovereign foresees a day when certain chosen ones might carry his glory without unlocking it completely. Hence this scabbard."

"Until zat day comes," Pyrsie put in, "there is no safer place to hide zee Scepter than zis chamber. Only we three know of zis place, and two of us will soon be leaving."

The Guide nodded. "The other Relics you received at your coronation were fine to leave in the Committee's keeping, as you so wisely did. But the Scepter is too powerful, too easily misused—even as a mere symbol, with its true power locked away. Here it will remain until your successor's arrival at last draws near."

"Oy, what's this?" Arth blurted, his eyebrows raising. "My successor?"

The Guide grinned. "Don't you realize by now? While you are certainly *a* King, and this is certainly *a* Golden Age—in fulfillment of prophecy—you are not *the* King, and this is not *the* Golden Age, which will never end once it finally begins. You, my friend, are but a foreshadowing of what will come."

Arth felt strangely encouraged to hear that. For while Caymerlot had done very well for itself under his rule, coming much closer to true utopia than any society in history, his Golden Age had still not been perfect. How could it, when he himself was far from perfect? But now he realized that something greater—and some*one* greater—was still to come.

A warm feeling suffused Arth as he followed the Guide and Pyrsie out of the Secret Sanctum they had created to honor his legacy. He followed them in silence back out of the box canyon, through the network of ravines, and all the way to the nearby column that housed the elevator between Caymerlot and Gnoburrow. There, he and Pyrsie hugged fiercely and said their goodbyes as tears flowed freely.

Then Pyrsyfal Rochelle, the Inventor of Gnoburrow, began the ascent towards the Conduit: the bridge to her real world.

And Arth, alone now but for the Guide, continued the rest of the way to Dagmør. Upon reaching the top of the famous water slide he'd commissioned, Arth and the Guide *both* rode to the bottom, whooping all the way—even though many would have said this was beneath the dignity of two such prominent men. But Arth had never cared overmuch about dignity, and his respect for the Guide grew every time he saw that the centman didn't either.

Before long, the two men stood at the far end of Dagmør before the entrance to Bridge Port. Arth remembered suddenly that this was the very same place he had first laid eyes on the Guide, after sneaking into Overtwixt a lifetime ago. As before, only half of the ancient stone bridge was visible, disappearing into whiteness somewhere near the peak of its arch; but Arth knew it was anchored securely in Lundunium in the real world on the other side.

Throat suddenly thick with emotion again, Arth asked, "You's capable of enterin' Gwen's real world, ain't ya?"

The Guide gave Arth a patient look. "We've had this conversation before, my friend. You cannot travel to a parallel world any more than someone from that world can travel to yours. That is why Overtwixt exists, so you can meet in the middle."

Arth smirked despite himself. "I weren't askin' if *I* could do it. I was askin' whether *you* could."

The Guide slowly smiled back. He had, of course, known what Arth was asking all along.

Arth grew serious. "Remind her of meh love for her. Unless..." His eyes widened in realization. "When she went back, did she turn young again, like when she first entered? Like Hembrose does every time he comes and goes?"

"No," the Guide reassured him. "Young*er*, yes, but some time passed in her real world while she was gone. She returned home as an adult, in the prime of her life."

Arth's wrinkly brow wrinkled further, in confusion. Wasn't Gwen's real world the same as Hembrose's? But then... Never mind. "Just tell my wife I love her, would ya?"

"She needs no reminding, and yet I know she longs to hear it nonetheless," the Guide said with a nod.

"And come visit me sometimes too?"

The Guide lifted an eyebrow. "So that you can continue to pass messages with your beloved, like schoolchildren?"

"Oy, not *only* fer that reason," Arth laughed, though his smile faded again quickly. "I's known the fellership of many dear friends in this place. But truly, there's been no greater friend to me—within O'ertwixt and without—as you, my Guide. I'm only sorry it took me so long to realize, and now that I has, I don't wanna lose you too."

To Arth's surprise, the Guide blinked rapidly, overcome with emotion himself. "If that is your desire," he agreed softly, "then our fellowship will only deepen in Reality."

Arth bowed his aged head gratefully.

"But there's no reason why your fellowship with Gwen and the others cannot resume as well, in time," the Guide added casually.

Arth jerked his head up in surprise. "But ya just got done sayin'... But *how?* How is such a fing possible?"

The Guide shrugged. "It's not."

Arth waited for an explanation that never came. "You's not gonna tell me, is ya?"

"What is there to tell?" the Guide asked, his eyes glittering with mischief now. "It truly *is* impossible. But then, nothing is impossible for the Sovereign. It's a mystery."

"Okey dokey, then," Arth said with an answering grin. "I guess you's proven I can trust yeh, even if ya don't always make a lick of sense to us normal folk." He clasped hands with the Guide one last time, then turned to go.

And with this sudden new glimmer of possibility bright in his mind, the thought that some great adventure might yet reunite Arth and his dearest friends, the King crossed back over the bridge... and knew Reality.

· epilogue ·
two millennia later

Geoff raised a hand to block the sudden bright light as he reappeared in his human real world. Blinking rapidly, he looked up at the blue sky high above, filled with puffy white clouds and an actual yellow sun. Ah, how he had missed the real world sky.

He turned slowly to get his bearings, examining the immense stone blocks that encircled him. Oh, good! He'd returned to the same portal he used for departure several years earlier. This was one of many henges in the cosmos, sharing the same design as the Gatehenge between Merlyn niland and the merman real world. The human-folk in these parts had no idea there were others like it in other worlds, serving as portals to Overtwixt. So far as they knew, it was simply "Stonehenge," the one and only.

Geoff frowned, seeing that another of the big standing stones had fallen while he was away. That was unfortunate. If Stonehenge deteriorated any further, it would probably cease to work as a bridge to Overtwixt. But since many of these stones weighed twenty tonnes or more, there was little he could do about it. He heaved a sigh and began the last leg of his journey home.

"Home" was Monmouth, just over the border from England into Wales. That was only a hundred miles away, meaning Geoff should be back in his cell at the monastery within four or five days... assuming he didn't fall victim to highwaymen along the way. But there was little he could do about that either, except hope that his clergyman's robes protected him. A dubious hope at best.

Still, he began to smile and then whistle as he walked, for his worries couldn't drag him down for long. The story he'd unearthed in Overtwixt was too exciting.

Geoff was a cleric by profession (actually, he had been *the* Cleric these last few years), but his greatest passion was storytelling. And so far as he was concerned, it didn't much matter whether the specific events of a story were "true" so long as the story conveyed an important message. A good story could be moved to a new setting, or have some of its characters substituted for others, in order to speak to an entirely new audience—and then prove all the more powerful as a result. In fact, that was the whole reason Geoff had journeyed to Overtwixt in the first place, to seek such stories.

See, this island on which he walked was at a turning point in its history. Until now, it had floated on the outskirts of an empire, unimportant except to the barbarian armies that had fought to control it ever since the Romans gave up and left. So long as the peoples of this island continued squabbling, they would never rise to greatness. If instead they could set aside their differences, as the Caymerlotions and Romans did before them, there was no telling what these residents of Britain, these... Britons... might accomplish. Why, maybe *they* could leave a legacy that spanned continents and centuries as well!

That was Geoff's dream, at least. And the easiest way to start his people along that path was through story—for *story* had the power to wiggle past a reader's defenses to influence his opinions. But it had to be a powerful story if it stood a chance of uniting the disparate peoples of this island, a shared mythology to inspire patriotism and national identity. Still, history showed that this approach had worked to some degree with the Greeks, then even better with the Romans who followed. And in both those cases, that unifying mythology had evolved from stories originating in Overtwixt.

Now Geoff had identified another unknown tale from antiquity, one he could use for the new mythology he was crafting. The *British* mythology, but a different kind from the mythologies that came before. Unlike the old Greeks and Romans (or even the Norse), Geoff didn't plan to get bogged down in details about gods and monsters. He wanted this to be a human tale, of human success and failure, for humans were entirely capable of achieving both extreme heroism and terrible villainy—and Geoff hoped both to inspire and caution his all-human audience.

Who better to accomplish that than human versions of the ancient dagman twins, Arthos and Morthos? Geoff would have to work on those absurd names, of course, along with all the other details. He would incorporate the Trojan woman into the tale too, somehow; yes, the ancient Trojans would be *very* important to the beginning of this yarn. As would the shapeshifting wizard from Merlyn... except maybe Geoff would make that fellow's *name* Merlyn? The possibilities were endless, for it little mattered how closely his final product resembled true history. So long as Geoff's story served its purpose.

But first, Geoff needed a title. His source material came from a book called *The Story of the King of Overtwixt*, which he'd found in the Grand Library of Hulandia. (The volume had been penned by a lugman, of all things, some old fellow called the Researcher.) Well, something like that would work here... maybe *The History of the Kings of Britain?* No, it should be in Latin—the whole thing written in the language of the Romans—to give it a more authentic ring: *Historia Regum Britanniae*, then. Yes, Geoff *really* liked the sound of that.

Just ninety-nine more miles to go. Barely enough time for Geoff to get his thoughts in order before dipping quill in ink. For as soon as he got back to the monastery, he would begin inscribing his revision of ancient history. No doubt it would become the most famous of his works, an epic tale of heroism and chivalry, culminating in the greatest legend of them all...

King Arth and his Heroes of the Round Table.

glossary
of persons, places & things
(with pronunciation clues in **bold gray**)

Note: *[Dg.]* indicates a "dagmanism," unique pronunciation or slang used by dagmen that sounds unfamiliar to American human ears (though their speech sometimes bears resemblance to the Cockney dialect used in London in our real world).

Adjunct, *shaman* – former assistant to the Baron who offers advice to Morth during their shared captivity

Adversary, *unknown race* – mysterious enemy of the Sovereign

Ælfred (AL-fred) or **Freddie,** *dagman* – 25-year-old performer in dagman circus troupe; see Contortionist

age (AYJ) – see epoch

Alain d'Creux (AL-awn duh-CROO), *gnoman* – gentleman adventurer who took Pyrsyfal and Alexandre from the orphanage and brought them to Overtwixt; see Pilgrim

Albernorm or **Alber,** *merman* – 26-year-old son of the Underlord, brother of Anderbrich and Gwenverity MerGrand; see Altruist

Alexandre, *gnoman* – former orphan and childhood acquaintance of Pyrsyfal; see Bailiff

Altruist, *merman* – someone devoted to helping others; armsman of Underlord who sometimes guards the Relic-in-the-Rock; see Albernorm

Amerlon (AM-ur-lawn), *real world place* – capital city of Hybra-sil in the merman real world

Amphitheater (AM-fuh-thee-uh-tur) – meeting hall of the Committee and Assembly, an open-air pool capable of "seating" more than a thousand people; in legendary times, it served as the courtyard of the Crystal Keep

Anderbrich (ANN-der-brick) or **Ander**, *merman* – 23-year-old son of Underlord, brother of Albernorm and Gwenverity MerGrand; see Antagonist

Antagonist, *merman* – someone who sets himself in opposition to another; armsman of Underlord who sometimes guards Relic-in-the-Rock; see Anderbrich

anyfing *[Dg.]* – anything

aquatics – general term referring to the cay-, dag-, delph-, kark-, kelp-, mer-, ny-, and okkman races

Arthos (ARR-thohss) or **Arth**, *dagman* – 16-year-old boy, twin of Morthos; see Fool, Squadleader, and King

Backwater – large community of aquatic immigrants living in Bronze City on Centhule; refers to both the people and their underwater neighborhood within the large lake at the foot of the Hillfort

Bailiff, *gnoman* – a law enforcement official; see Alexandre

Baron – traditional ruler of the humen and centmen

Bertie – see Roberthoras

bloke *[Dg.]* – a man of any race

Bodyguard, *dagman* – new role offered to Roberthoras Penn by the Guide, quested with protecting the King

Bridagnon (brih-DAG-nuhn), *real world place* – homeland of Arthos and Morthos in the dagman real world; parallel of Britain in the human real world

Bridge Port, *real world bridge* – arched slab-stone bridge between the dagman real world and Overtwixt

Bronze City – major metropolitan area on Centhule

Burrowcrat, *gnoman* – leader of Gnoburrow who betrayed the Inventor after she designed his new Treasury

caparison (kuh-PAR-uh-sun) – an elegant ornamental covering for an eqman or centman, like clothing

Captain, *centman* – leader of the guards sworn to protect the Baron (and later the Empress in modern times)

Captienne, *centwoman* – see Captain; variant title used sometimes when the leader of the guards is female

Captive, *dagman* – someone taken hostage or prisoner in war; role forced upon Morthos Penn by the lugmen following the Battle at Bronze City

Castle – see Hillfort Castle; known simply as the Castle in modern times

caymen, *race* – see Nachton's Reference Book

Caymerdelphia (cay-mur-DELF-ee-uh) – modern name for Caymerlot

Caymerlot (CAY-mur-laht), *niland* – hubland joining Caypool, Merlyn, Delphyrd, Karkham, Nymfeim, Okham, Dagmør, and Kelpton in legendary times

Caymerlotion (cay-mur-LOW-shun) – anything or anyone from Caymerlot; see aquatics

Caypool, *niland* – portland of the caymen

Centhule (sin-THOOL), *niland* – hubland joining Hulandia and Centwick in legendary times

Centhulian (sin-THOOL-ee-uhn) – anything or anyone from Centhule; see centmen and humen

centmen (SINT-min), *race* – see Nachton's Reference Book

Centwick (SINT-wik), *niland* – portland of the centmen

Clown, *dagman* – a comic performer in a circus troupe; role "chosen" by Morthos Penn upon entrance to Overtwixt

Committee – lawmaking body of Caymerlot, which acts as intermediary between its ruler and citizenry

Conduit, *real world bridge* – underground passage between the gnoman real world and Overtwixt

Contortionist, *dagman* – a circus performer who bends his body into painful-looking poses; role chosen by Freddie upon entrance to Overtwixt

Crystal City – major metropolitan area on Caymerlot

Crystal Keep – glass fortress at the center of Crystal City, from which the Underlord ruled in legendary times

dagling – a very young dagman or dagwoman

dagmen, *race* – see Nachton's Reference Book

Dagmør (DAG-moor), *niland* – portland of the dagmen

dagsters *[Dg.]* – see dagmen

delphmen (DELF-min), *race* – see Nachton's Reference Book

Delphyrd (DELF-urd), *niland* – portland of the delphmen

Demagogue (DIM-uh-gawg) – someone who comes to popularity and power by playing on people's emotions and prejudices; mysterious new leader of the lugmen

den – gnoman equivalent of a town or village

Denali – capital den and largest settlement in Gnoburrow

Deputy, *shaman* – chief advisor to the Burrowcrat

enuff *[Dg.]* – enough

eon (EE-on) – see epoch

Epitopia (ep-ih-TOH-pee-uh), *unknown place* – apparently the very first society in the First Epoch of Overtwixt, about which little knowledge survives

Epitopian or **High Epitopian,** *written language* – see Intro to Ancient Languages of Overtwixt on page 417

epoch (EP-uhk *or* **EE-pok)** – any period of time during which a race inhabited Overtwixt, marked before and after by periods of non-habitation; also known as ages, eons, or eras by some races

Eqhustan (EK-yoo-stan), *niland* – hubland joining Eqland and Centhule in legendary times; no modern equivalent

Eqland (EK-luhnd), *niland* – portland of the eqmen

eqmen (EK-min), *race* – see Nachton's Reference Book

era (AIR-uh *or* EER-uh) – see epoch

everyfing *[Dg.]* – everything

faemen (FAY-min) or **fae** (FAY), *race* – see Nachton's Reference Book

faery (FAIR-ee) – slang for any faeman or faewoman

fella *[Dg.]* – fellow, a man of any race

fing or **fink** *[Dg.]* – thing or think

Fool, *dagman* – a jester who makes a fool of himself; role "chosen" by Arthos Penn upon entrance to Overtwixt

Freddie – see **Ælfred**

Gatehenge, *real world bridge* – mystical ring of monolithic standing stones that provides a magical portal between the merman real world and Overtwixt

Gerald (JAIR-uhld), *centman* – long-time companion and fellow adventurer of Karis; see Noble

glowstone – stone mined by gnomen that gives off a natural amber (yellow-orange) light; used to provide illumination and act as signposts

Gnoburrow (NO-bur-oh), *niland* – portland of the gnomen; its occupants travel and live within tunnels and dens carved out of the interior of the niland

gnomen (NO-min), *race* – see Nachton's Reference Book

Guide, *centman* – the first person to greet every new visitor to Overtwixt; responsible for presenting newcomers with three paths to choose from; otherwise provides assistance and guidance as requested by the visitor

Gwenverity (gwin-VAIR-ih-tee) or **Gwen**, *merwoman* – 19-year-old daughter of the Underlord, sister of Albernorm and Anderbrich MerGrand, whose true role is unknown; see Lady, Underlady, or Siren

Hembrose, *merman* – greatest mortal magicker in history, who repeatedly left Overtwixt to re-enter as a 19-year-old boy once again; see mermage and Wizard

Hidden Chamber – the secret merman repository of knowledge on the sea floor in Merlyn

Hillfort Castle – seat of the Baron's rule on Centhule

hippea (hip-PAY-uh) – female version of the ancient Greek word for an armored cavalry defender; see Knight

hisself *[Dg.]* – himself

hubland – a hub niland, any new niland created by the inhabitants of Overtwixt when two or more peoples desire to come together for mutual benefit

Hucentia (hyoo-SINCH-yuh), *niland* – modern name for Centhule

Hulandia (hyoo-LAND-ee-uh), *niland* – portland of the humen

humen, *race* – see Nachton's Reference Book

hunnerd *[Dg.]* – hundred

Hybra-sil (HEE-bruh SIL), *real world place* – homeland of Hembrose in the merman real world; parallel of Ireland in the human real world

Inventor, *gnowoman* – role chosen by Pyrsyfal Rochelle upon entrance to Overtwixt; member of the Squad

kanban – type of tree native to the dagman real world, similar to a banyan

Karis Priamos (KAIR-iss pree-AHM-ohss), *huwoman* – close friend and role model to Arthos and Pyrsyfal, and long-time companion of Gerald; see Knight

Kark's Fangs – the double bridges connecting Karkham to Caymerlot, one a land bridge, the other a deep canal

Karkham, *niland* – portland of the karkmen

karkmen, *race* – see Nachton's Reference Book

kelpie – slang for any kelpman or kelpwoman

kelpmen, *race* – see Nachton's Reference Book

Kelpton, *niland* – portland of the kelpmen

Khan, *lugman* – tribal leader who united all the luggernaut clans into a single barbarian horde; defeated at the Battle for the Branch Library by the Inventor and Knight, who ejected him from Overtwixt

King, *dagman* – prophesied future ruler of Caymerlot, ultimately revealed to be Arthos Penn after he chose the role from (and was anointed by) the Guide

Knight, *human/woman* – champion who defends the honor of his or her ruler, enforcing justice and carrying out punishments; role chosen by Ewan Ollivaros in modern times and Karis Priamos in legendary times

lad – a boy or young man of any race

Lady of the Lake, *merwoman* – see Gwenverity

lass – a girl or young woman of any race

Library System – the human and centman repository of knowledge, consisting of Main Library and Branches in legendary times, later becoming the Grand Library of Huland after many epochs of growth and expansion

Loremaster, *human* – chief advisor to the Empress in modern times; role chosen by Nachton Ollivaros upon entrance to Overtwixt

Lugarth (LOO-garth), *niland* – portland of the lugmen

luggernauts (LUG-ur-nahts) – informal name for the lugmen in legendary times, when they undertook a campaign of terror against the other nilands

lugmen, *race* – see Nachton's Reference Book

Lundunium (luhn-DOON-ee-uhm), *real world place* – capital city of Bridagnon in the dagman real world

mage (MAYJ) – general term for someone skilled in magic

magicker – general term for someone skilled in magic

maiden or **maid** – a girl or young woman of any race

Matron Bex, *real world place* – the merman real world, whose name means "Mother Beach"

Merlyn, *niland* – portland of the mermen in legendary times

mermage (MUR-mayj) *[Dg.]* – a merman mage

mermen, *race* – see Nachton's Reference Book

Merpool – modern name for Merlyn

Mersch, *real world place* – the dagman real world, whose name means "Marsh"

Moira (MOY-ruh), *merwoman* – mother of Hembrose

mool – type of domesticated animal native to the dagman real world, similar to a donkey or mule

Morthos (MOR-thohss) or **Morth**, *dagman* – 16-year-old boy, twin of Arthos; see Clown and Captive

Mother Earth, *real world place* – the human real world, whose name means "Dirt" or "Land"

niland (NY-luhnd) – an island landmass floating in nothingness

Noble (NO-bull), *centman* – highest-ranking official in Centhule following the Baron; member of the Squad who typically acts as steed for the Knight; see Gerald

Northmount – the strange mountain at the north end of Hulandia, which included a large hanging stalactite beneath; its carved out passages connected Hulandia to Lugarth as a sort of bridge

nuffing *[Dg.]* – nothing

nym – slang for any nyman or nywoman

nymen (NIM-min), *race* – see Nachton's Reference Book

Nymfeim (NIM-fighm), *niland* – portland of the nymen

Okham, *niland* – portland of the okkmen

okkies *[Dg.]* – see okkmen

okkmen, *race* – see Nachton's Reference Book

Orfeo (or-FAY-oh), *human* – a composer of epic narrative poetry hailing originally from Thraki (Thrace) in the ancient human real world; see Poet

O'ertwixt (OR-twixt) *[Dg.]* – see Overtwixt

Overtwixt – the world of bridges, where all parallel universes (or alternate dimensions) intersect

Paladin (PAL-uh-din), *eqman* – a legendary adventurer often known for his chivalry and gallantry; member of the Squad who typically acts as steed for the Inventor

Père Pierre (PAIR PYAIR), *real world place* – the gnoman real world, whose name means "Father Stone"

phirteen *[Dg.]* – thirteen

Pi Gate, *real world bridge* – jet bridge between the Atlanta airport in the human real world and Overtwixt, in modern times

Pilgrim – someone who undertakes a journey to a special place as part of tradition; role chosen by Alain d'Creux

Planet Mersch – see Mersch

plapyr (PLAY-purr) – a papyrus-like material mermen use for books and scrolls (in both the real world and Overtwixt) due to its water-resistant qualities

Poet, *human* – someone who writes metered literature (poetry) that might be put to music; see Orfeo

portland – a port niland, any landmass that exists where a real world intersects with (bridges into) Overtwixt

Portmistress, *dagwoman* – government official responsible for enforcing dagman compliance with the Treaty

Prince, *human* – traditional ruler of the eqmen, typically an eqman; role taken forcefully by Bias Priamos when he enslaved Eqland, before he was defeated in battle and ejected from Overtwixt by his sister Karis, the Knight

prolly *[Dg.]* – probably

Pyrsyfal (PUR-sif-uhl) or **Pyrsie (PUR-see),** *gnowoman* – 16-year-old girl, former orphan, diminutive even among gnomen; see Inventor

Pythagoras (pith-AGG-or-uhs), *dagman* – father of the Penn twins, Arthos and Morthos, and a renowned showman in the dagman real world; see Ringmaster

Raibourne (RAY-burn), *niland* – portland of the raimen

Raignokia (ray-NO-kee-yuh), *niland* – hubland joining Raibourne and Gnoburrow

raimen (RAY-min), *race* – see Nachton's Reference Book

Ransacker, *lugman* – someone who is fierce and uncivilized; a highly intelligent subcommander of the luggernauts who dueled the Squadleader and Sidekick at the Battle for the Branch Library; carries a crossbow into combat

relic – any magical artifact

Relic-in-the-Rock – one of Sovereign's Relics, currently sunk to the hilt in a small island of stone in the Amphitheater; according to legend, can only be withdrawn and wielded by a Hero or King

Ringmaster, *dagman* – a leader of a circus troupe, and the one who announces each act; role chosen by Pythagoras Penn upon entrance to Overtwixt

Roberthoras (row-BURTH-ur-uhs) or **Bertie,** *dagman* – uncle of the Penn twins, Arthos and Morthos, and brother of Pythagoras; see Bodyguard, Strongman, or Bertie

Sarge – see Sergeant-at-arms

Sergeant-at-arms (SAR-jint-at-arms), *karkman* – ceremonial officer in the government of Caymerlot, and leader of Crystal City's army and guards

Sidekick, *kelpman* – a companion or protégé of a more important person; member of the Squad who typically acts as steed for the King

Siren, *merwoman* – see Gwenverity

Sky Light – one of countless celestial artifacts put in place by the Sovereign to provide illumination to the nilands of Overtwixt; bright like a sun one side and dim like a moon on the other, it rotates on its axis to simulate daytime and nighttime

Squad of Heroes – a diverse band of adventurers who joined forces for the purpose of rescuing their friends and other innocents from lugman captivity

Squadleader, *dagman* – temporary role filled by Arthos Penn when he first assumed leadership of the Squad of Heroes

smoke, *verb* – to hurt a person badly enough to eject him or her from Overtwixt; example: "That fella got smoked"; see yellow smoke

soarpalm – type of tree native to both the merman and nyman real worlds, similar to a royal palm

Sovereign (SAWV-rin), *unknown race* – distant supreme ruler of all the infinite dimensions of the cosmos

Sovereign's Great Relic – see Relic-in-the-Rock

Sovereign's Relics – special magical artifacts of enormous power that can only be used by the pure of heart for the greater good; legend states that four were gifted to each and every race when Overtwixt came into being

Strongman, *dagman* – a circus performer who lifts heavy weights; role originally chosen by Roberthoras Penn

sumfing *[Dg.]* – something

teensy *[Dg.]* – tiny or small

Tetraodías (tet-ruh-OH-dee-ahss) – ancient human name for Overtwixt, literally meaning "crossroads" in Greek

tonne (TUHN) – ton, a very heavy weight

Treasury – the Burrowcrat's treasure room in Gnoburrow, designed by Inventor and protected by elaborate traps

Treaty – agreement signed into law between a past Underlord and all the aquatic peoples of Caymerlot, setting forth restrictions for how many members of each race are allowed to enter Overtwixt at any given time

Troia (TROY-uh), *real world place* – ancient city located in modern-day Turkey (known in modern times as Troy), with Greek language and customs

Troian mool – elaborate trick played on the lugmen by the Squad, inspired by the Trojan horse deception that resulted in the destruction of Karis's home city

twenny *[Dg.]* – twenty

Underlady, *merwoman* – see Gwenverity

Underlord, *merman* – traditional ruler of the aquatics who reigns from Crystal Keep, though legend states he is only intended to be custodian for the coming King; father of the Altruist, Antagonist, and Lady of the Lake

Undersecretary, *cayman* – primary administrator of Crystal City, who handles many of the Underlord's custodial responsibilities (while the Underlord plays at being an actual ruler in the King's absence)

Unterstygian (un-tur-STIJ-ee-uhn), *written language* – see Intro to Ancient Languages of Overtwixt on page 417

war camp – one of many semi-permanent tent settlements on Lugarth

Wizard, *merman* – role chosen by Hembrose O'Hildirun upon entrance to Overtwixt; member of the Squad

yellow smoke – the emission that appears when a person is hurt badly enough to be ejected from Overtwixt

introduction to the
ancient languages of Overtwixt

(condensed from a primer
by the Ancient Wizard of Merlyn)

Observant visitors to Overtwixt (in any age or epoch) will soon notice that they can easily understand the speech of other races, even though each people speaks one or more languages unique to its own dimension. This is one of the passive magical functions of Overtwixt, to facilitate communication and understanding.

The written word is translated automatically in much the same way. Any book a person reads (in one of the many libraries or elsewhere) will appear to be inscribed in the reader's own language.

With just two exceptions.

The oldest treatises are written in one of the two ancient languages that originated within Overtwixt itself. The first is **High Epitopian**, a graceful script that was used during the First Age in Epitopia, the earliest society in the world of bridges. The Epitopian language relies on simple, easy to remember rules of grammar and spelling, and the words for many concepts are spelled symmetrically. However, these many rules are rigid and unyielding, such as the requirement that Epitopian always be inscribed from right to left. It also has a limited lexicon, and many concepts simply cannot be expressed in Epitopian.

Example *(right-to-left):*

!rule (of (Human race, *lit. The Stubborn Ones*)) Doom [is] *[FUT]* ←

The other ancient language is **Unterstygian**, which was developed in the ages after the Schism as a proposed improvement on Epitopian. It employs a boxier, utilitarian script, and is much more flexible in its use. Unlike Epitopian, Unterstygian can be inscribed in any direction: right-to-left or left-to-right, top-to-bottom or bottom-to-top, or even some combination of the above, with lines of text changing direction as needed. Unterstygian's only unbreakable rule is that words are *never* spelled symmetrically.

Example *(left-to-right):*

→ *[FUT]* [is] Destiny (of (Human race, *lit. The Proud Ones*)) rulership!

Interestingly, vocabulary and pronunciation are both highly similar between these two languages, since again, Unterstygian evolved from Epitopian. However, varying connotations and subtle gradations of meaning between the two can result in significantly different interpretations.

As one might expect, many of the oldest tomes written on the subject of Sovereign or the blue magic are inscribed in High Epitopian, while the morally flexible green magic is typically documented only using Unterstygian.

OVERTWIXT Reference Book

Your Guide to Overtwixt

See, it's the Guide (get it?)

Prepared by Nachton Ollivaros, 782nd Human Epoch

and updated 784 H.E.

INDEX

Introduction ... 2
About Nilands ... 2
About Flora and Fauna ... 3
About the Peoples of Overtwixt ... 3
About the Ollivarian System of Classification ... 4

The Peoples of Overtwixt

— Human/Equine Race
- Humen ... 6
- Centmen ... 8
- Eqmen ... 10
- Lugmen ... 12

— Little Peoples
- Gnomen ... 14
- Nagmen ... 16
- Raimen ... 18
- Shamen ... 20

Aquatic Species
- Caymen ... 22
- Dagmen ... 24
- Delphmen ... 26
- Karkmen ... A-2
- Kelpmen ... A-4
- Mermen ... 28
- Nymen ... B-2
- Okkmen ... B-4

— Shadow Creatures
- Drachmen ... 30
- Impmen ... 32
- Phomen ... 34
- Spookmen ... 36

— Insectoids — 38ff

Appendix: HEMBROSE: 44

Warning ~ This document deals with topics that are perhaps less interesting to younger readers.

Introduction ~ Having been in this place called Overtwixt for a few weeks now, I will to document my observations. Overtwi "world" or "planet" as we would normally things. It is a conceptual realm wher worlds intersect, and where the people worlds can interact. Even though it's N place, our minds still visualize it that w the physical world is most familiar to why we find ourselves walking on land (through water, in the case of the aquatic think that our non-physical link to this accounts for the irregular and relative pas time, much as we experience when dreami

SKYLIGHTs rota on their own axis switching between day and night side

About Nilands ~ Overtwixt has no core structure, and it only obeys the laws of physics when it feels like it. It appears to consist of unending white nothingness, with an infinite number of "nilands" floating inside. (Just as an "island" is land floating in water, a "niland" is land floating in nil, or nothing.)

Portlands - For each real world that intersects Overtwixt, a single port niland—or "portland"—occurs naturally. (Huland, for example, is the portland linking Overtwixt to the human real world.) Portlands are then linked to each other by bridges of all sorts.

Hublands - New nilands can be created by the inhabitants of Overtwixt if two or more peoples want to come together for mutual benefit. These hublands must be "planted," at the intersection of two or more bridges, by bringing together <u>soil from</u>

Nilands have no gravitic relationship with skylights. They do not rotate, revolve, or orbit. They just... drift.

or sand? water? coral? How was Caymerlot first formed?

each of the linked portlands. The new niland is then "cultivated" through inhabitation. The more people come to live on the burgeoning niland, the greater the landmass (or body of water) will become as it grows to accommodate its population.

About Flora and Fauna ~
As a conceptual realm, Overtwixt has no naturally occurring species of animal life. Each niland DOES feature plant life reminiscent of its linked real world(s), but these plants are not truly alive. They are simply mental constructs created by the niland's inhabitants—the mind's way of surrounding itself with the familiar.

About the Peoples of Overtwixt ~
Since no true flora or fauna exist, the only real life in Overtwixt is INTELLIGENT life. That's why Overtwixt exists, after all—to bring together every people from every dimension of reality, for a "meeting of the minds."

Each race represented in Overtwixt (as far as I know) has both males and females, and they are referred to as men and women (or boys and girls), just like in OUR real world. It isn't two arms and two legs which makes someone a man or woman. Instead, it is the state of personhood—the existence of a personality and a soul. It's taken some getting used to, but I've come to recognize (for example) that a merman is just as much a "man" as I am.

(or lads & lasses / maids, as some peoples prefer)

The rest of this notebook represents my initial attempts to study and document just ~~sixteen~~ twenty-one(!!) now of the infinite races present in Overtwixt—the peoples of this realm ~~who have been trapped by the Vizier.~~

Realm **Caelux-2A42...**

This realm is only a miniscule fraction of the whole!

I always knew Overtwixt was "infinite," but I'm only now beginning to realize just how big it really is, in size as well as history.

About the Ollivarian system of classification ~

The longer you study the peoples of Overtwixt, the more clearly a pattern emerges: every race is essentially a hybrid of two other races (and each of THOSE races is a hybrid of the first and yet another, and so on and so forth).

And dagmen think of centmen as a cross between themselves and "mools," their world's amphibious-mule beast of burden:

As I've noted, this methodology of describing all races as hybrids of each other is simplistic. But it's not far from the truth. For my system of classification, I think of the contributing "halves" in terms of dominant and secondary, as follows:

- DOMINANT ~ upper body features, including circulatory, respiratory, and (usually) integumentary systems (body covering like skin, fur, hair, scales, feathers, etc.)
- SECONDARY ~ lower body appendages and overall stature

Notation – All peoples, therefore, can be classified as having one dominant half and one secondary half. For example, using the races discussed above:

- Humen – Hu>hu
- Centmen – Hu>eq
- Lugmen – Eq>hu
- Eqmen – Eq>eq

– see page 44-45

Base races – The "halves" used in this notation (whether dominant or secondary) always reference what I call "base races." Base races are those races I've identified as being physically identical to organisms from Earth. (I acknowledge this is a very hu-centric way of thinking. No offense toward non-humen is intended by this.) Base races include:

- Hu – humen
- Eq – eqmen – horses
- Del – delphmen – dolphins
- Spu – spookmen – bats
- ... an~~d~~ ~~...~~

~~This system~~ ~~without its~~
~~flaws and ex~~ ~~all hybrids~~
~~with dominа~~ ~~e aquatic,~~
~~therefore th~~ ~~ust come from~~
~~their seco~~

Corr~~ect~~ ...men (like dolphins) are m~~ammals~~, ... are aquatic, they must surface to breathe air, which they process through lungs. The pattern holds—and the Ollivarian system of classification works.

Same for Dagmen, despite their fishy appearance

(sticky note:)
- Oct — okkmen
  - octopuses
- Seg. – segmen
  - insects
- ?
- Many others

The illusive #

Humen

Ollivarian classification: Hu>hu

Traditional liege lord: Baron of Hucen ~~(historically)~~

Nilands occupied: Huland, Hucen

Anatomy: Your garden variety human be— originating from Planet Earth; two arms, forth and so on

Ancient Knight 394 H.E.

782 H.E. (modern)

Middle: Vizier, Baron
Bottom: Empress, Knight, Princes.

★ *I now believe Epoch 394 spanned several hundred years in our real world*

Culture: As best I can tell, there has seldom existed any great population of human in Overtwixt; at many times in history, Overtwixt has gone a long time without any human at all, hence our method of recording human history within Overtwixt as occurring during human epochs. (My own visit to Overtwixt marks the 782nd Human Epoch—the 782nd time humans have come here.) From what I have read, ~~the only epoch~~ [one of several epochs] that lasted long enough to establish a true human society was (Epoch 394★), when travel between Overtwixt and Ancient Greece was almost commonplace. Not surprisingly, much of Classical Greek mythology was influenced by events taking place here during that time... Perhaps MORE surprisingly, that era of Overtwixt's history bled back into our real world AGAIN much later, in the form of legends regarding King Arthur and Camelot. I fully intend to study/document more about the ancient human Knight and ~~his~~ involvement with the utopian niland kingdom of Caymerlot as soon as I get the chance.

right: ~~the Most Illustrious~~ Schiller → humble Loremaster

Centmen

Ollivarian classification: Hu>eq

Mythological cognate: Centaurs

Traditional liege lord: Baron of [...]
~~(historically a human)~~

Nilands occupied: Centwick, Hucentia,* Gnocentia

Culture: Centmen prize loyalty and wisdom above all other character qualities, and are famous for demonstrating those same qualities themselves. A person cannot ask for a better bodyguard or advisor than a centman, or so most people believe. In the absence of a ruling baron, the centmen in Overtwixt are led by a Council of four elders (two men and two women) identified as the wisest among their people.

Anatomy: The upper body of a human attached at the waist to the four-legged lower body of a horse, covered in its entirety by a pattern of skin and hair; the hair grows especially long along the back of the human upper body (much like a horse's mane) and in thick tufts along the spine/back haunches, forming patterns similar to tiger stripes. The females of the species, which are generally more slender, grow an even shaggier pelt below the shoulders to protect their modesty, while the males are known to braid their hair down their backs.

> *a.k.a. **Centhule** in legendary times ... back when centmen were in charge, NOT the humen!*

Eqmen

Ollivarian classification:	Eq>eq
Base Race cognate:	Horses (male)
Mythological cognate:	Unicorns (female)
Traditional liege lord:	Prince of Eqland (historically an eqman)
Nilands occupied:	Eqland and don't forget Eqhustan

Anatomy: Identical to the Arabian stallions of Earth; the males of the species exhibit the same variety of coat colors normal on Earth (browns, blacks); females tend to be markedly smaller and display more whimsical colors (including white, pink, and red coats, with even more vibrant and varied manes and tails); the eqwoman's forehead horn is undoubtedly what gave rise to the human legends of unicorns.

I know now about their singing!

Culture: Eqmen are sometimes considered primitive by the other races, partly because they lack fingers or opposable thumbs (even though they've developed their own forms of technology which seem magical by comparison with our own), but also because of their overwhelming interest in simple pursuits: running, eating, and talking. *and singing!!* Nevertheless, eqmen are renowned deep thinkers, and their Archives (essentially a library of philosophical audio recordings) rivals that of many other races.

Eqmen are also very adventurous. At times in the past, they established trade with other races, ~~both for the construction of their settlements and~~ for the acquisition of the seashells they use at the Archives.

An eqwoman's horn is like a work of art.

Lugmen

Ollivarian classification: Eq>hu

Mythological cognate: the Minotaur

Traditional liege lord: ~~none~~ varies

Nilands occupied: Lugard

Culture: *(Lugmen have little culture to speak of, at least not in the traditional sense. They are isolationist with respect to other races and warlike amongst themselves, constantly fighting with little need for provocation. They fight most viciously with close friends and family members, though they always stop short of doing serious harm.)* Family reunions and other gatherings typically consist of a feast followed by a free-for-all with blunted weapons.

Anatomy: Bipedal thanks to secondary human traits, but immense, with a horsey head and face; males and females both feature a single thick horn sprouting from the end of the muzzle; despite this similarity in appearance to a rhinoceros (or the fact that lugman facial features are equine, not bovine), I am convinced the lugman is the inspiration for our human myth of the Minotaur. Lugmen of both genders grow great shaggy pelts over the upper chest, similar to a buffalo; their upper arms end in hooves like a horse, but articulated into three fingers and an opposable thumb. Most lugmen wear trousers or kilts but otherwise hate clothing. *or LOINCLOTHS ...ugh*

Gnomen

Ollivarian classification: Hu>spu

Mythological cognate: Gnomes

Traditional liege lord: Mystic of Shanagrailia

Nilands occupied: Gnobury, Gnocentia, Shanagrailia

Ha! Gnoburrow actually IS what they called Gnobury in ancient times.

Culture: The gnomen are a people most comfortable underground. As such, their portland looks like nothing more than an un-navigable chunk of stone from the outside. On the INSIDE, Gnobury is riddled with warrens and tunnels, hence its name (equivalent to <u>Gno-burrow</u>). Gnomen are incredibly crafty, very creative, and quick with their hands, and this area of Overtwixt knows no better stone masons or sculptors.

young gnomen of both genders typically grow thick, peach-fuzzy beards, but the hair falls out by the time they become teenagers

14

Anatomy: Short of stature, like all races with secondary spookman attributes (those races generally called "little peoples"); at a glance, gnomen are easily confused for small humen, or young humen not yet fully grown, primarily because of their dominant human traits and their propensity for wearing clothes; on closer inspection, gnomen prove to be extremely bowlegged, with the same padded and clawed feet as bats; young gnomen of both typi— " grow
—y
hair
time
s

Nagmen

Ollivarian classification:	Eq>spu
Mythological cognate:	none
Traditional liege lord:	Mystic of Shanagrailia
Nilands occupied:	**Nagland**, Shanagrailia

Culture: Nagmen are cliff dwellers, but there is nothing primitive about their habitats, which they carve meticulously from sheer cliffs in geometrically-precise shapes. Known as peacemakers and lovers of harmony, nagmen have been compared favorably to the hippies of Earth's 1960s. Nagmen play a wide variety of musical instruments unique to their real world (many of which they have recreated in Overtwixt) and are famous for producing more talented musicians per capita than almost any other race.

Styles and tastes and instrumentation may vary across peoples and cultures but music itself is universal.

Anatomy: One of the so-called "little peoples" (short-statured, thanks to secondary spookman attributes), nagmen are capable of walking naturally on all fours or on back legs only, as humen do; reminiscent of nothing so much as Earth's Shetland ponies, though much smaller; like lugmen, their front hooves have articulated "fingers" (three, plus an opposable thumb); nagman hair grows uniformly across the entire body, thick and shaggy, though a recent fad among younger nagmen involves shaving that coat in places in order to wear gnoman clothing.

Raimen

Ollivarian classification: Delzea
Mythological cognate: none
Traditional liege lord: Mystic of Shanagrailia
Nilands occupied: Raibourne, Shanagrailia

Culture: Raimen enjoy a strange reputation among the other peoples. Known as wise and insightful, they are also mocked for their tendency to speak in riddles (and for their physical appearance too, of course!). Many a pilgrim has sought answers to some great question in the (Alabaster City of Shanagrailia), only to turn away confused at the end. This has given rise to the saying, "A raiman would set you straight, if only you could get a straight answer." The raimen lost significant political clout when the current Mystic (a raiman) was forced to abdicate as a result of the Baron's campaign of unification (which led to the Vizier's eventual seizure of power). The raiman portland of Raibourne is one of the most isolated nilands in this part of Overtwixt.

Or in ancient times, the Monastery of Mysteries on Raibourne

(Having now met the Mystic, I can confirm: he's clearly a smart dude, but I've got NO CLUE what he's saying 2/3 of the time!)

Anatomy: The same hybrid mix as a cayman, but in reverse—the head of a dolphin affixed to the body of a miniature horse—the entire body covered with smooth gray skin; raimen tend to be rotund, with stubby little legs barely long enough to keep their bellies from scraping the ground; raiman heads feature a unique growth of cartilage running like a fringe from just above the eyes to the back of the head, and this ridge contains olfactory and secondary breathing apparatus (operating much like a human nose or dolphin blowhole).

Shamen

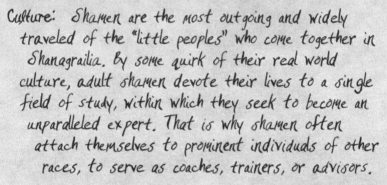

Ollivarian classification: Del>s pu
Mythological cognate: none
Traditional liege lord: Mystic of Shanagrailia
Nilands occupied: Shaland, Shanagrailia

Culture: Shamen are the most outgoing and widely traveled of the "little peoples" who come together in Shanagrailia. By some quirk of their real world culture, adult shamen devote their lives to a single field of study, within which they seek to become an unparalleled expert. That is why shamen often attach themselves to prominent individuals of other races, to serve as coaches, trainers, or advisors.

Anatomy: The upper body of a dolphin attached at the waist to the lower body of a bat, including upper appendages that seem a cross between the dolphin's fins and the bat's winged arms; the shaman's arms are broad and flat, ending in extremely dexterous articulated fingers; vestigial webbing grows from the armpit to the elbow, but does not grant the ability to fly; shamen have sharp, carnivorous teeth; they often wear pants and shoes, and sometimes bowler-style hats with ponchos (especially for the shawomen), but their underarm webbing makes it impossible for them to wear actual shirts or tunics.

Caymen

*a.k.a. **Caymerlot** in legendary times*

Ollivarian classification: Eq>del

Mythological cognate: Hippocamps

Traditional liege lord: Underlord of Caymerdelphia*

Nilands occupied: Caypod, Caymerdelphia*

Culture: Caymen are essentially the eqmen of the sea, though more sedate and individualistic. They have the same propensity for lengthy philosophical discourse, and are favored speakers at the Amphitheater in Caymerdelphia. More so than any of the other aquatic peoples, caymen prefer to remain in their underwater environs, ignoring groundwalkers and surfacing only for air—or to debate their aquatic brethren about some topic or another.

Anatomy: A cross between a horse and a dolphin, they look more like a mix of sea horse and manatee; they are physically ponderous, even if they ARE known to be quick-witted.

Nothing but toadies of the Mermen in ancient times ??

UNDERSECRETARY was a cayman. When was that role abolished? Or was it ever official ?

Probably very effective as administrators in ancient Caymerlot, but the "red tape" they generated was undoubtedly endless

Dagmen

Ollivarian classification: Del>hu
Mythological cognate: various
Traditional liege lord: none
Nilands occupied: Dagmoor,[†] Caymerdelphia *

[†] port niland known as **Dagmör** in legendary times

Culture: Dagmen are renowned pranksters and thrill-seekers. One of Overtwixt's most versatile species, dagmen are comfortable on land or in water (though they must rehydrate their skin at regular intervals while out of the water). Dagmen are nomadic, sometimes banding together with like-minded associates rather than members of their birth families. Outside of Dagmoor and Caymerdelphia, roving bands of dagmen have historically provided entertainment for the other races, by putting on carnivals or building amusement parks. Circuses too!

Fins flex to radiate heat, or lie down entirely beneath clothing

Anatomy: Think "Creature of the Black Lagoon" and you're most of the way there; dagmen (like both dolphins and humans) breathe air through the mouth and process it with lungs; dagmen otherwise are fishlike in appearance (ribbed and pointy), with rigid fins atop the head, behind the ears, and on the back, and also collapsible fins on the reverse of every joint; hands and feet have the same skeletal structure as human hands and feet, complete with fingers and toes, but webbed for underwater propulsion; despite the fish-likeness of some of these features, dagmen skin is pebbled instead of scaly.

As a wise old man?

That looks ridiculous.

Delphmen

Ollivarian classification: Del>del
Base Race cognate: Dolphins
Traditional liege lord: Underlord of Caymerdelphia ✱
Nilands occupied: Delphyrd, Caymerdelphia ✱

Culture: Delphmen are widely considered the friendliest and most welcoming people in this area of Overtwixt. They are known as care-free and fun-loving, but their play has less of an edge than the dagman pranksters. By their lifestyle, delphmen illustrate their belief that responsibility must be taken seriously, and that life contains many serious moments—but that life should never be taken TOO seriously.

INSERT "A"

Anatomy: Identical to the bottlenose dolphins of the human real world, with smooth gray skin covering a thin layer of blubber

Males — have a broad, dark gray band from nose to tail along the back

Females — distinguished by thinner, lighter gray stripes running in wavy lines along their sides

Like eqwomen, delphwomen also have a small horn just above the eyes, but very short and stumpy, barely breaking the surface of the skin.

A-1

Karkmen

Ollivarian classification: **Del>oct**

Mythological cognate: **Lusca**

Traditional liege lord: Underlord of Caymerlot *

Nilands occupied: **Karkham**, Caymerlot *

Culture: Karkman society is highly competitive and highly disciplined, but that doesn't necessarily make them evil or even ruthless.

Young karks are trained to a particular line of work from a very young age, and they pursue their goals with single-minded determination and unwavering commitment. From what I've read, you'll never find a more loyal friend than a karkman, assuming you can gain his trust in the first place. Karkmen make fine soldiers, businesspeople, and really anything else they set their mind to.

In terms of personality, karkmen are essentially the polar opposite of dagmen.

A-2

Anatomy: Per the Ollivarian classification system, karkmen would be a cross between dolphins (dominant/upper body/"skin") and octopuses (lower body/tentacles), despite the fact that their multiple rows of wicked teeth (and overall disposition) make them seem more shark-like than dolphin-like. Of course, having the same respiratory system as a dolphin (delphman) would mean karkmen must be mammals... but that makes sense, considering that (so far as I've encountered) all peoples in Overtwixt are indeed mammalian.

Below is my best guess of what they might look like, as I have never met one. They seem to have inspired legends of luscas (half-shark, half-octopus) in our real world Caribbean Sea.

A-3

KelpMen (kelpies)

Olivarian classification: **Eq>oct**

Mythological cognate: **Kelpies**

Traditional liege lord: **Underlord of Caymerlot ✱**

Nilands occupied: **Kelpton, Caymerlot✱**

Culture: My studies suggest that kelpies are largely misunderstood. As a result of their poor personal hygiene ~~and propensity for mischief,~~ they are often looked down upon by the other races. However, careful research has uncovered numerous unsung kelpman heroes in the annals of Overtwixt.

~~They have little culture of their own, and kelpies seldom band together once reaching adulthood. Instead, they~~ Members often go their own way or (within Overtwixt) attach themselves to a member of some other race as an assistant or follower.

At this point, I don't know WHAT I don't know about Kelpie culture!

I'm not sure now where I read all this... (aside from the Sidekick!)

A-4

Anatomy:

During my time in Caymerdeck (in the last days of that niland), I was fortunate to see a single kelpie fleeing the destruction of Crystal Bay, and will never forget my fascination with its anatomy. To say its top half is equine (like a horse) and its bottom half is octopoid (like an octopus) barely scratches the surface. The kelpie already has a complete skeletal system (unlike an octopus), right down to the bones of its tentacles.

Like an egman, the kelpman only has shoulders and hips for four limbs, but behind the elbow each leg splits into two tentacles. Amazingly, those tentacles CAN be made rigid to support the creature on dry land, or of course they can undulate along numerous joints for underwater propulsion. The kelpie will never be as swift as an egman on land or an okkman underwater, but what it lacks in speed, it makes up for in versatility.

Above the elbows, the kelpie more closely resembles a donkey than a horse, squat and stolid instead of tall and graceful. Its entire body (tentacles included) is covered with long hair in black, brown, or gray, which grows easily tangled and matted unless routinely cleaned.

or unless they shave it like this weirdo

A-5

Mermen

Ollivarian classification: Hu>del
Mythological cognates: Mermen/mermaids
Traditional liege lord: Underlord of Caymerdelphia *
Nilands occupied: Merpod, Caymerdelphia *

Culture: The merpeople hold beauty in high esteem, and are sometimes considered vain and self-important as a result. But they care as much for inner beauty as outer, and much of their culture revolves around the creation of artistic masterpieces. They are famed for the masterful glassblowing they perform on their hot sandy beaches, which results in small works of art as well as delicate underwater towers.

Anatomy: The upper body of a human attached to the lower body of a dolphin; for the females of the species, the transition occurs just below the shoulders, while the males transition at the waist, exposing a muscular human torso; in both cases, the lower body is covered in the blubbery gray skin of a dolphin; only the females have a dorsal fin. Both the men and the women wear their hair long, either loose or in dreadlocks.

Nymen (nyms)

Ollivarian classification: Hu>Oct

Mythological cognate: Nymphs, Cecaelia

Traditional liege lord: Underlord of Caymerlot★

Nilands occupied: Nymfeim, Caymerlot★

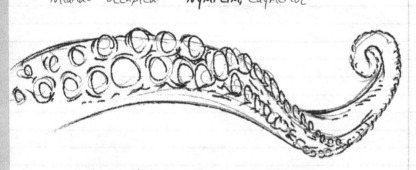

Culture: Nymen society is matriarchal, which means nywomen are the traditional nym leaders in family and politics. Even so, both the females and the males are known for devoting themselves to causes and crusades. From what I understand, the nyms were very outspoken in the Committee of old Caymerlot with respect to social injustices they identified as needing attention; the changes the ancient nyms brought about over time were part of what led to Caymerlot's reputation as a utopia.

Nymen and nywomen both are invariably beautiful by the standards of other Hu-dominant races (like humen), but I suppose they probably have their own standards. More importantly, nyms are known to have huge personalities. They are fans of wordplay and riddles, though without the mischievous edge displayed by dagmen and kelpies. ρ

B-2

Anatomy: Nyms seem a strange cross between humen and okkmen (octopuses), except with four larger tentacles below the human waist, and four slimmer tentacles hanging from the human head, sorta like hair. Everything in between is very human-seeming, with human face, arms, hands, and torso, all covered with human skin. That said, nyms are typically more slender and slightly shorter on average than humen.

Like kelpies, nymen are equally comfortable stiffening their leg-tentacles for use on dry ground as for use swimming, but they much prefer to remain in the water. Their head tentacles also serve a practical use, more than mere "hair." Nymen are known to use them for gesturing when arguing a point, in much the same way humen employ facial expressions. When swimming, they also provide a means of steering and offsetting any spin introduced by their powerful leg tentacles, kinda like the way a tail rotor works on a helicopter.

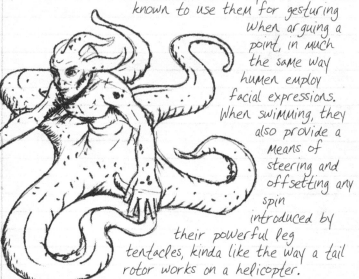

Obviously, not all nyms are female (despite the myths that endure in our human real world about nymphs). Perhaps their matriarchal society caused this confusion. Or maybe their long cranial tentacles and fine-boned facial features contributed to some misconception among early human visitors to Overtwixt.

Okkmen (okkies)

Ollivarian classification: **Oct > oct**

Base Race cognate: **Octopuses**

Traditional liege lord: Underlord of Caymerlot★

Nilands occupied: **Okkpod**, Caymerlot ★

Culture: Quiet and introspective, okkmen are famously neutral. Except in the most dire of circumstances, they are quite happy to drift wherever the currents take them—both metaphorically and literally.

Anatomy: Exactly like an octopus from our human real world. Back home, I always found their strange anatomy fantastical; but here, it seems almost boring in comparison with all the other variety Overtwixt has to offer.

B-4

Missing Okk Races?

The Ollivarian system demands the existence of other ancient peoples I can currently find no mention of. Because of the fact that each race could be described as a hybrid of two other races, the existence of okkmen means there must be numerous other races joining okkmen attributes with those of the other peoples I have come to know in this place.

Namely:

- Oct > hu
  — like a Mon Cal?

- Oct > spu

- Spu > oct
  - fangs and batwings attached with eight writhing tentacles beneath? Sounds scary

- Oct > eq - I can't even picture this

- Oct > del

TODO!!

29

Drachmen

Ollivarian classification: Spu>del

Mythological cognate: Dragons

Traditional liege lord: Kaiser of the Shadowlands (historically a drachman)

Nilands occupied: Drachölm

Culture: Bombastic and always the largest ~~person~~ people in a room, drachmen are used to being the center of attention. In a social setting, that makes them the life of the party; in a political or military setting, they have a thirst for command. The Kaiser of the Shadowlands was always a drachman, ever since the days when the first Kaiser conquered Impstead and Spookwood, making its inhabitants his minions. It is no coincidence that all three races now serve the Vizier, led by a drachman Warlord.

Anatomy: The largest of the races I've observed in Overtwixt, drachmen are best described as huge bats, their muscular bodies long, slender, and sinuous from shoulders to tail, covered entirely in thick black hair; drachmen have two sets of shoulders, the lower equipped with meaty forearms and (prehensile) hands, the upper with immense wings that fold along the back; the drachman's ears are huge and side-facing, and its long body ends in two pairs of crossed, dolphin-like fins that give it the appearance of having a barbed tail.

"prehensile" means being able to grab or hold things, like tools... or throats

Impmen

Ollivarian classification: Spu>hu

Mythological cognate: Gargoyles

Traditional liege lord: Kaiser of the Shadowlands (historically a drachman)

Nilands occupied: Impstead

Culture: Impmen have strong clan ties and typically flock in large groups. Much like the ducks and geese of Earth, they are fond of <u>long flights during which they sing in five-part harmony</u> while flying in rotating formations. Impmen do not have strong leadership tendencies, and historically have been quick to accept outside authority. Some few impmen break the mold, forming small companies and hiring themselves out as mercenaries that fight or offer airlift services.

Think sea shanties, sung loud and dissonant, but kinda fun

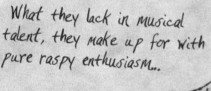

What they lack in musical talent, they make up for with pure raspy enthusiasm...

Anatomy: Closely resembling the body of a human, with a well-muscled torso, but the head of a bat; the bat-like wings attach directly from the creature's back to its strong human arms (as opposed to being mounted on the back, as with the gargoyles from human stories); impmen have very human hands, but with sharply taloned fingers; most impmen wear nothing more than patterned trousers in bright colors, with ripped cuffs, while impwomen add colorful strips of cloth to protect their modesty; most prefer to go without footwear, except when flying into battle.

Phomen

Ollivarian classification: Spurea

Mythological cognate: various

Traditional liege lord: none

Nilands occupied: Pholand

Culture: Phomen are the most bizarre and frightening of Overtwixt's peoples. It isn't only their physical appearance but also their strange ability to hear one another speak across vast distances, as if standing side-by-side. Perhaps their apparent eccentricity is accentuated by the fact that only two exist in all of Overtwixt at this time, twin brothers who serve the Vizier... but it is difficult to imagine these creatures as anything other than villains.

Anatomy: The body of a horse, so gaunt that every bone shows beneath the hairy black skin; while equine in shape, phoman heads retain bat-like features (oversized ears, upturned nose, exposed fangs); phomen have two sets of wings: vestigial webbing beneath the forelegs and a larger set folding behind the back when not used for flying; phoman tails are hairless like a rat's; size-wise, phomen are comparable to horses and theoretically could be ridden; as such, I imagine they are the inspiration for Pegasus from myth... though how these monsters ever inspired such a beautiful creature, I'll never know.

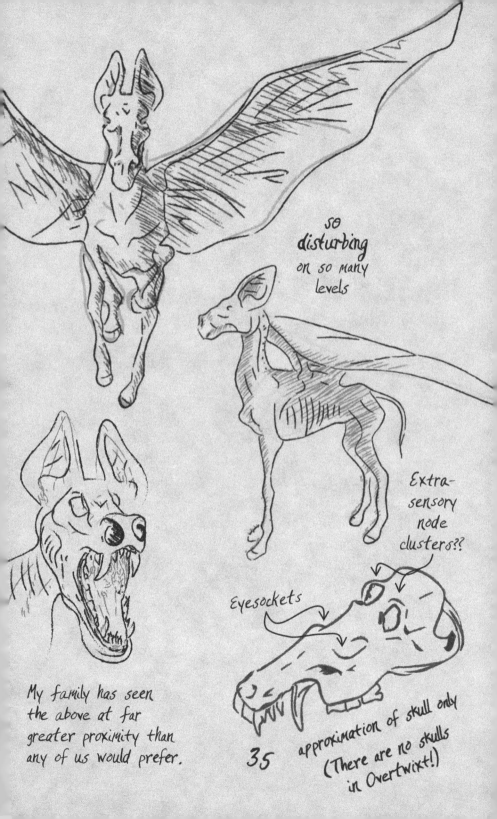

Spookmen

Ollivarian classification: Spu>spu

Base Race cognate: Bats

Traditional liege lord: Kaiser of the Shadowlands (historically a drachman)

Nilands occupied: Spookwood

Culture: Much like humen, great variety exists in spookman social patterns; some prefer to live in large groups (called "legions") while a significant minority have loner tendencies. Incredibly crafty and dexterous, with prehensile hands and feet both, spookmen have a well-deserved reputation for being thieves and con-artists. They are not to be trusted.

Anatomy: Most similar to the vampire bat of Earth, roosting upside down (in caves, but more preferably from the upper reaches of forest trees), spookmen are also capable of walking/running on all fours and of course flying; spookmen or "spooks" are the smallest of all the races I've observed in Overtwixt, ranging in size from that of a rat to that of a small lapdog.

RACE: **Faemen**

Cognate: **Faerie, fairy**

( ) Base Race   (X) Mythological

Traditional Liege Lord: _____

Race: _____

Nilands occupied: **Faevon**

Ollivarian classification: **Hu>seg**

ANATOMY:

At first glance, the fae appear quite similar to humen, with the exception of an extra pair of arms. I believe those additional limbs are a result of their secondary insectoid traits (since insects always have six limbs). A careful inspection of the faerie's back reveals two sets of shoulders visible beneath the skin, to accommodate the extra arms.

An immense pair of butterfly-like wings is mounted on the faeman's pronounced spinal ridge. When not in use, these wings fold back almost flat against the back; however, much like a butterfly, they often twitch and flex subconsciously, sometimes revealing their owner's mood.

Despite stories about fairies in our real world (actual "fairy tales"), real faeries are tall and muscular, big-boned, not petite.

CULTURE:

I've been unable to learn very much about fae culture, aside from what my sister Amelie heard from her friend (see misc. note below). The fae portland of **Faevon** was once joined to Hucentia, but that bridge apparently decayed when relations between our peoples lapsed. The fae have a library called the **Thenaeum**, rivaling even our human Grand Library, except that theirs is devoted almost entirely to knowledge about the Sovereign's magic. Apparently, once visiting faemen are trained in that magic (over a course of years!), they are sent out into the rest of Overtwixt to act as traveling do-gooders.

MISCELLANEOUS:

My sister claims to have met a faerie during her perilous flight from Caymerdelphia, during our first visit to Overtwixt. That faewoman was an accomplished purveyor of magic who had disguised herself to escape the Vizier's notice..

RACE: **Segmen**

Cognate: <u>insects, specifically dragonfly</u>

(X) Base Race   ( ) Mythological

Traditional Liege Lord: _____

Race: _____

Nilands occupied: **?**

Ollivarian class: **Seg>seg**
ANATOMY:

Other than their size —
3 feet long from head to
tail, with a wing span of
4-5 feet! — they appear
comparable to dragonflies
from our human real world.
Except they're also people who
think, and talk, and plot.

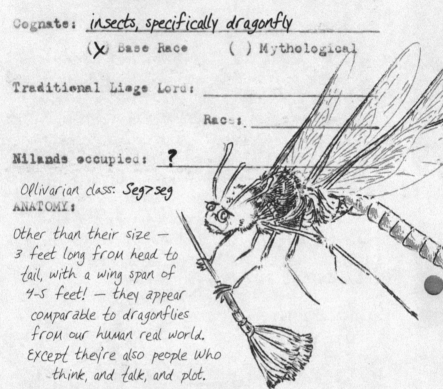

I can find little mention of them outside of writings from
H.E. 394, during which members of the race were
apparently enslaved by the lugmen. They were prevented
from fleeing through use of interlocking "clips"
which kept the segmen's wings locked in
a furled position at all times.

still
mammals?

Pykkmen ~~culture~~ a.k.a. PYXIES

Myth cognate: pixies

Ollivarian classification: spu>seg

~~Miscellaneous~~ Pyxies' spook-like traits are obvious, from their fur to their big-eared acute hearing to their short stature (barely a foot tall!).

Their segman (segmented insectoid) traits seem limited to their waspish wings.

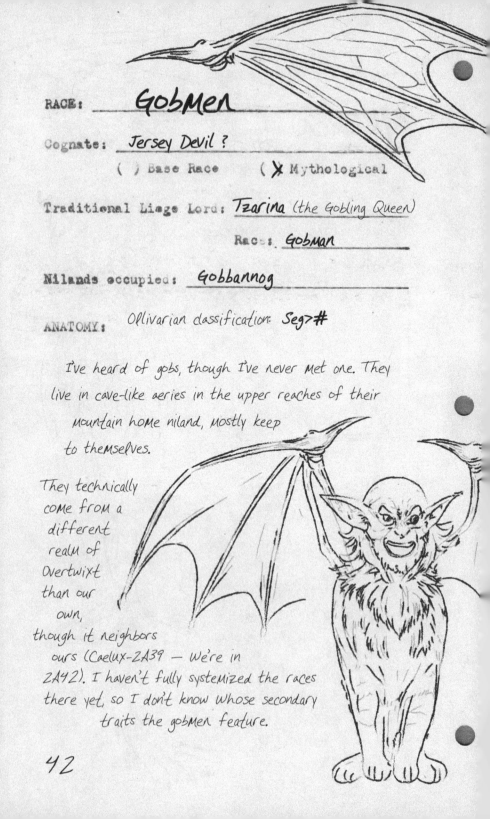

RACE: Gobmen

Cognate: Jersey Devil?

( ) Base Race (X) Mythological

Traditional Liege Lord: Tzarina (the Gobling Queen)

Race: Gobman

Nilands occupied: Gobbannog

ANATOMY: Ollivarian classification: Seg>#

I've heard of gobs, though I've never met one. They live in cave-like aeries in the upper reaches of their mountain home niland, mostly keep to themselves.

They technically come from a different realm of Overtwixt than our own, though it neighbors ours (Caelux-ZA39 — We're in ZA42). I haven't fully systemized the races there yet, so I don't know whose secondary traits the gobmen feature.

42

I wonder if Tolkien ever visited Overtwixt? Or Peter Jackson?

ORQMEN of Orqland

~~CULTURE:~~

Mythological Cognate:
actual goblins from human stories

Ollivarian class: #>?
Also pay tribute to the Gobling Queen

These are the same orqs whose Relics were apparently stolen by some human child, starting a ~~MONKEYPOX~~ war (long after Caymerlot, long before now). A child named Jaques... who crossed a beanstalk bridge.

I kid you not. Amélie told me the story.

Note: Orqs are obviously NOT insectoid. I've grouped them here (for now) for lack of a better place, since they share that currently-unknown # trait with the gobmen

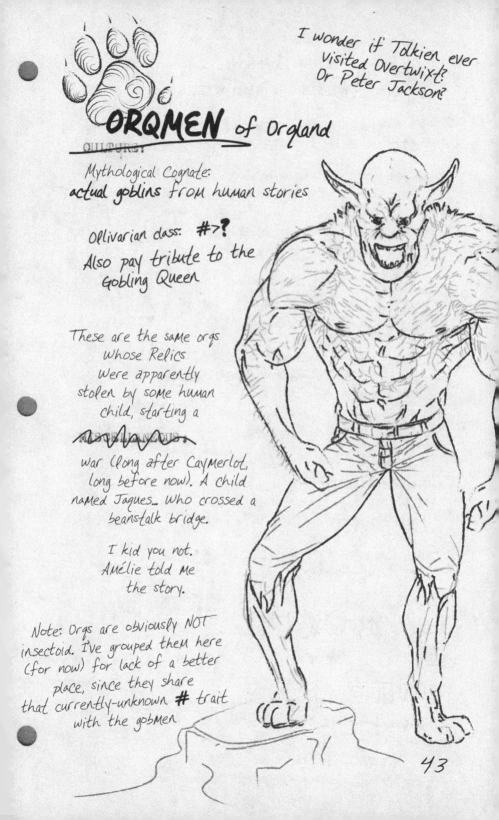

Special Appendix:
HEMBROSE THE WIZARD

This reference book was meant primarily to document the infinite peoples of Overtwixt, with one page/spread per race.

Hembrose O'Hildirun, the Wizard of Merlyn, is a special exception deserving of individual study, due to his ability to shapeshift between races using the deceptive power of green magic.

Hembrose was born in the Merman real world of Matron Bex. He entered Overtwixt as a young man, but aged rapidly (as seen from objective "outside" time) when he spent his entire first year in Merlyn's Hidden Chamber library.

"WHELP" haha

WIZARD

It was there that he fashioned the **distinctive golden mantle** he would wear the rest of his days in Overtwixt... and first began experimenting with **shapeshifting**.

mantle embroidered with blue Epitopian script on one side and green Unterstygian on the other

Epitopian reads right-to-left

From what I've been able to piece together, I believe the embroidered phrases were:

[AXIOM] I...

. beloved / and / one-of-a-kind / everybody [AXIOM]

or:

"Every life is precious."
(the First Fundamental Law)

valuable/beloved   above   people   other.
or perhaps

"Greater than others all I"
(a perversion of First and Second Laws)

Unterstygian goes any-which-w[ay]

44

HEMBROSE: continued

Anyway, back to **SHAPESHIFTING.**

Hembrose learned that the longer he held a transformation, the more tiring it was. He could shapeshift his friends also, but that only multiplied his exhaustion.

There were other limitations to this power. His facial features always remained vaguely recognizable. And he could NOT morph into a younger version of himself.

Plus, "All that gray hair has to go somewhere"

WISEMAN

WHIRLER

WINDOW-DRESSER

WADDLER

WINGMAN

All of these restrictions are apparently governed by the magic of Overtwixt. Odd that there is NO restriction enforcing the conservation of mass

WYVERN

WARMONGER

acknowledgments

Due to time constraints and publication deadlines, fewer folks were available to assist with, edit, or proofread *King of Caymerlot* than on the Overtwixt volumes that came before (not to mention the fact that, being longer than previous volumes, it required more of a time commitment in the first place!). Therefore, I am correspondingly more grateful than usual to those individuals who made this the best book it could be in a relatively short period of time.

Thank you to Sarah Akers (Countess, but yes, also my Queen as the dedication suggests), Monica Robinson (Defender), Ruth Akers (Lounge Pianist—Billy Joel's got nothing on you!), Les Akers (Salesman), Beth Paul (Minstrel), and Lois Bartelme (Crone).

Thank you also to Charlotte Bauman (Artisan *and* Overtwixt's newest illustrator) for a beautiful original front cover design and numerous other fun sketches throughout the pages of this book, depicting new characters and relics.

And though he was unavailable to provide any new artwork to this volume, thank you one more time to Jesse Lewis for all the sketches he previously contributed to the Overtwixt universe (which, obviously, I continue to reuse!).

Jesus Christ, my Lord and Savior, I thank you first and last and most, for all that is good in my life, family, and career. I pray this series honors you with its rendering of truth.

about the fonts

The text of this novel was set in 11-point Asul Regular, a baroque humanist typeface designed by Mariela Monsalve. With its subtle semi-serifs, Asul is perfectly suited (in the author's opinion) for younger readers.

Since Asul lacks an italic variant, italicized text was set in Amerigo BT Std Italic, a typeface designed by Gerard Unger in 1987, which complements Asul nicely.

Various incarnations of "Nachton Hand" were designed by the author using quill-and-ink or ballpoint pen, then digitized into a font with multiple variants per character to make it feel more natural.

Hembrose's annotations were rendered in Seaweed Script, which the author finds appropriately evocative of the sea. It was designed by Stuart Sandler and David Cohen and published by Neapolitan.

Section headers, illustration text, and many place names on the maps were set in Mercator Regular, designed by Arthur Baker in 1995. Mercator's calligraphic strokes give it a hand-scribed feel that's ideal for this application.

Finally, all hublands on the maps were beautifully identified using ITC Locarno Italic (in all caps), designed by Alan Meeks in 1922.

about the author

R.L. Akers loves stories. He loves hearing them, loves telling them, loves embellishing them, and loves forging them from raw materials. He is convinced that every person who ever lived has an interesting story, and he's only met one person in his life who came close to proving otherwise.

Holder of an undergraduate degree in computer science and a master's degree in business administration, Akers has worked in software development as well as non-profit fundraising and publicity. His love for children has led him in the past to be a foster parent and a coordinator of the K-5 ministry at his church. His interests include graphic design, orchestral movie soundtracks, and anything remotely creative. Within the pages of these *Overtwixt* stories, he has even begun learning to sketch (simple illustrations only!).

Akers lives in West Virginia with his wife Sarah and the four children he loves most in this world. Visit him online at RLAkers.com.

about the illustrator

Jesse Lewis is an award-winning published illustrator and graphic artist, who specializes in breathing life into worlds beyond our own and the characters that reside within them. After studying for and attaining his bachelor's degree in fine arts at Savannah College of Art & Design, Jesse went on to expand his skills through numerous book-, video game-, and animation projects both within the U.S. and around the world.

While always pursuing continued development of his own skillset, Jesse has also kindled a passion for sharing his knowledge and experiences by educating new generations of aspiring artists.

Instagram: jnoah.art
Facebook: jesselewisdesign

about the illustrator

Charlotte Bauman is an emerging artist hailing from Brighton, Michigan. She graduated with concentrations in oil painting and graphic design from Spring Arbor University. She is constantly looking to broaden her horizons in all things creative.

For more information, visit
www.charlottebauman.com